Tony Hillerman

Also by James McGrath Morris

The Ambulance Drivers: Hemingway, Dos Passos, and a Friendship Made and Lost in War

Eye on the Struggle: Ethel Payne, the First Lady of the Black Press

Pulitzer: A Life in Politics, Print, and Power

The Rose Man of Sing Sing: A True Tale of Life, Murder, and Redemption in the Age of Yellow Journalism

Jailhouse Journalism: The Fourth Estate Behind Bars

Tony Hillerman

A LIFE

James McGrath Morris

UNIVERSITY OF OKLAHOMA PRESS : NORMAN

Publication of this book is made possible through the generosity of Edith Kinney Gaylord.

Quotations from the works, letters, and notes of Tony Hillerman are used by permission of the Hillerman estate, Anne Hillerman, literary executor. All rights reserved.

Library of Congress Cataloging-in-Publication Data

Names: Morris, James McGrath, author.
Title: Tony Hillerman : a life / James McGrath Morris.
Description: Norman : University of Oklahoma Press, [2021] | Includes bibliographical references. | Summary: "Full-length biography of mystery writer, Tony Hillerman (1925–2008), whose Leaphorn/Chee novels introduced non-Native Americans to the mysteries of Navajo culture"—Provided by publisher.
Identifiers: LCCN 2021012589 | ISBN 978-0-8061-7598-0 (hardcover)
Subjects: LCSH: Hillerman, Tony. | Novelists, American—20th century—Biography. | Detective and mystery stories, American—History and criticism. | Navajo Indians in literature. | BISAC: BIOGRAPHY & AUTOBIOGRAPHY / Literary Figures | SOCIAL SCIENCE / Ethnic Studies / American / Native American Studies
Classification: LCC PS3558.I45 Z78 2021 | DDC 813/.54 [B]—dc23
LC record available at https://lccn.loc.gov/2021012589

The paper in this book meets the guidelines for permanence and durability of the Committee on Production Guidelines for Book Longevity of the Council on Library Resources, Inc. ∞

1 2 3 4 5 6 7 8 9 10

This book is dedicated to
Patty Morris
Going on forty years, my partner in crime

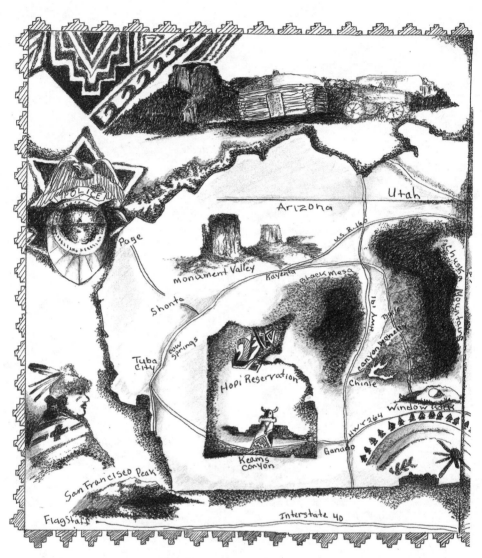

Map of the Navajo Nation by Henry Kinlicheene Jr.

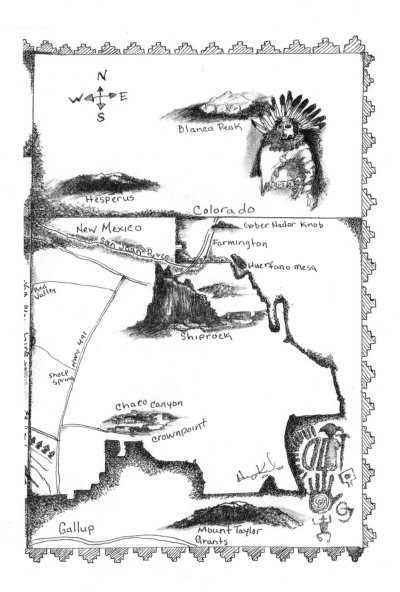

◆ Contents ◆

Everything is connected. Cause and effect is the universal rule. Nothing happens without motive or without effect. The wing of the corn beetle affects the direction of the wind, the way the sand drifts, the way the light reflects into the eye of man beholding his reality. All is part of totality, and in this totality man finds his hózhó, his way of walking in harmony, with beauty all around him.

Tony Hillerman, *The Ghostway*

The spelling of Navajo words in this book have been updated and made consistent with the orthography in Leon Wall and William Morgan, *Navajo-English Dictionary* (New York: Hippocrene Books, 1994).

◈ Prologue ◈

In late August 1945, two trucks stirred up plumes of dust on a dirt road in western New Mexico as they neared the delivery point for the oil-drilling equipment they carried. It had been a long trip from their starting point in Oklahoma City to this barren spot on the edge of the Navajo Nation. For one of the two drivers, still nursing wounds from combat in the war that had just ended, the long trek had been particularly arduous. The vision in his left eye was limited, the land-mine damage to his left leg still gave him a pronounced limp, and haunting memories of war remained fresh in his mind. On this late afternoon, as he drove the last miles of the journey, a group of Navajos dressed in ceremonial clothes emerged on horseback from the side of the road in front of him, crossed over, and disappeared among the piñons and junipers.

A few miles later, upon reaching the delivery site, he asked the white rancher what the Navajos he saw had been doing, especially dressed in that manner. The riders, said the man, were headed to an Enemy Way, a Navajo ceremony to cleanse two returning marines of the evil to which they been exposed while fighting in the Pacific. Would they let him attend? the driver asked. Yes, said the man, they would likely permit it if he didn't disturb the ceremony with drink or rude behavior.

That night, twenty-year-old Tony Hillerman parked his truck and limped over to the campfires where the Navajos were gathered. "I still remember," he wrote years later, "the bonfires lining that packed-earth dance ground, the dust raised by shuffling feet, the flickering yellow firelight, the perfume of the burning piñon and juniper, the sparks blown by the night breeze, the four drummers, the smell

1

of roasted mutton, and two marines—exhausted but happy to be cured of war and home again—surrounded by their friendly people."[1]

Years would pass before Hillerman returned. When he did, however, he would be the one to create unforgettable memories for millions of readers around the globe with novels that captured Navajo culture and the people's spiritual devotion to achieving *hózhó*, a harmonious existence with one's surroundings and place in life. In doing so, Hillerman would travel a path of healing that began that night in the summer of 1945. He, like the two marines, would find in the Navajo world a salve for the horrors of combat. He would come, as the Navajos might say, to walk in beauty.

CHAPTER 1

◈ Sacred Heart ◈

A s they did every week, the few dozen members of Sacred Heart's hilltop church gathered for mass on June 7, 1925. Breezes usually caressed the crest of the 1,060-foot-high Church Hill, making the spot one of the few places in central Oklahoma where relief could be found from the summer's heat.

On this particular Sunday morning, August "Gus" and Lucy Hillerman came to present their eleven-day-old son to the parish. Standing by the baptismal font, Father William Ospital, a Basque monk, held the child in his arms with family members by his side. The parishioners watched from the wooden pews in the luminescent church with white tin-clad walls and ceilings on which, on most days, danced specks of colored light from the stained-glass windows.

Father Ospital anointed the baby with oil, asked those who had gathered to instruct the infant in the practices of the Catholic faith, and poured holy water over his head. Afterwards, Father Ospital recorded in a leather-bound book that Anthony Grove Hillerman, born May 27, 1925, had received his baptism. His first name was a family namesake. August's brother Henry Anthony Hillerman had died thirteen years earlier, at age forty. The baby's middle name was the surname of his mother's family.[1]

His passage to heaven safeguarded, little "Antnee" and his parents made their way home on the wagon-wheel dirt roads that bisected the small hamlet. Stretching out before them as far as they could see was the Northern Cross Timbers region, a pastiche of dense oak woods and grasslands.[2]

For centuries the strip of land before them, running from central Texas to Kansas, marked the boundary between the eastern forestlands and the Great Plains to the west. As many as seven thousand years ago indigenous people fished, hunted, and scavenged food here. But latecomers, such as the Spaniards in the 1700s, found the thick forest impossible to cross. A century later, the Louisiana Purchase brought droves of white settlers who turned the southern portions of the Cross Timbers into farmland. But the land around Sacred Heart, as in the rest of Indian Territory, as it was then called, remained reserved for Native American tribes being removed from their eastern homelands.[3]

Among them were Potawatomi Indians whom the US Army had marched in 1838 from their homes by the Great Lakes to a spot along the Osage River in Kansas. Called Mission Band Potawatomi for the members' widespread adherence to the Catholic Church, a legacy of early French missionaries, the band feared the encroachment of white settlers would trigger another forced relocation. So, in 1870 they accepted a plan to sell their Kansas land and move to a vast tract of land they acquired in this portion of Indian Territory. To further ensure their future, members of the Mission Band took US citizenship and were renamed Citizen Potawatomi.[4]

The Potawatomis gave Father Isidore Robot, a French Benedictine priest, permission to establish a monastery in 1877, in exchange for opening a school for their children. Land was cleared on the western side of Bald Hill, which was renamed Church Hill, and soon St. Benedict Industrial School was established for the Potawatomi boys and St. Mary's Academy was opened for the girls. Within two decades Sacred Heart Mission, mostly built by Potawatomi carpenters and stonemasons, grew into a well-kept compound containing a church; a three-story, fifty-room monastery; a convent; the two schools; a bakery that produced hundreds of loaves of French bread and sweet buns daily; a tool house; a carpentry shop; orchards; gardens; and a small cemetery. Monks ordained at the monastery fanned out across the state, establishing more than forty Catholic parishes to serve the influx of German, Polish, Italian, and Irish immigrants. The devout came to think of Sacred Heart Abbey as the "Cradle of Catholicism" in Oklahoma, and the town growing up around it took the same name.[5]

In 1901, a fire destroyed the monastery and other buildings, fortunately without any fatalities. The monks and nuns reconstructed the abbey and school buildings but not the mission church. Instead, parishioners constructed a concrete—thus fireproof, they hoped–church above the mission. The sturdy white church, topped with a red tile roof, opened in 1915. Even in its diminished post-fire reconstruction, what remained of Father Robot's mission was the most visible landmark and dominant characteristic of the tiny central Oklahoma town. As steel was to Pittsburgh, Catholicism was to Sacred Heart.[6]

A few hundred yards below the Sacred Heart church, Tony Hillerman's father, Gus, could be found on most days behind the counter of his general store. Gus was well liked by the townspeople. He was generous with credit and respected by the Citizen Potawatomi. His store was one of two serving Sacred Heart. The closest town was five miles away, so townspeople frequented the local stores for the occasional canned goods or sundry items. The Hillerman store carried groceries, shoes, pig feed, kerosene, and bib overalls, the garb of choice in Sacred Heart. But the inventory was modest in comparison with the store's competitor across the road, owned by the Zoellers. A large, prosperous family of German immigrants, the Zoellers also operated a loan company and the town's only cotton gin. The family lived in a two-story brick house unlike the log cabins and wood-frame structures that housed the remainder of the town's population. They were the closest Sacred Heart had to an upper-class family.[7]

Like the Zoellers, the Hillerman family had migrated to Sacred Heart because the Potawatomi citizenship stratagem had not protected the land from white settlers. In 1887, the Dawes Act forced the Potawatomi to open up hundreds of square miles of the reservation to settlers. Gus, his wife Josephine, and his Prussian-born parents arrived in 1899. They had been living in Texas, where Gus had worked as a cowboy, farrier, farmer, and schoolteacher after completing one year of college.[8]

Gus and Josephine arrived in Sacred Heart with one daughter, Mary Celesta, and soon thereafter a second daughter, Gertrude, was born. Josephine, however, died at age forty-three on December 10, 1918, a victim of the Spanish flu, which had reached Oklahoma a few months earlier. Josephine's mother moved into the house to help with the teenage children.[9]

But that was only a temporary solution. Like most rural widowers, Gus Hillerman needed a new wife. He won over the daughter of a Sacred Heart farming family, Lucy Mary Grove, a tall and slender woman ten years younger than he.

The Grove family had arrived from Nebraska in covered wagons in 1894. Lucy's father, Christopher, was English and had worked in the Canadian lumber industry before coming to the United States to farm, first in Iowa and then in Nebraska before making the arduous trek to Oklahoma. Lucy's mother had died giving birth to her. For several years Lucy was raised by a German family and was said to have returned to her father speaking only German.[10]

The Groves discovered farming in Sacred Heart was a challenge. "Coming from the bare prairies of Nebraska, as I did," said Lucy's brother Christopher, "all these great oak trees looked wonderful to me when I first saw them. When I had to chop and deaden them with an ax, then guide a plow around the stumps and roots, they were not so wonderful."[11]

Lucy and Christopher, six years her senior, were undaunted by their circumstances. In 1900, Lucy, still only a teenager, and her brother moved 360 miles away from their parents to take advantage of the Homestead Act. This law allowed a person to apply to take possession of 160 acres of land. A homesteader who improved the land and remained on it for five years received ownership of it. The two siblings built a house from cut sod, carried water from a distant stream, and stayed warm by burning dried buffalo dung. After they were given title to the land, Lucy and Christopher sold it and returned to Sacred Heart. Lucy used her share of the money to buy forty acres of farmland just south of town.[12]

When the Great War broke out, Lucy attended St. Anthony Nursing School in Oklahoma City. She hoped she might be shipped overseas, but she got only as far as Camp Travis, near San Antonio, Texas, where she tended wounded veterans and victims of the Spanish flu. When the war ended, she returned to Oklahoma and took a nursing job there. The marriage proposal from Gus brought her home to Sacred Heart. The wedding took place in Oklahoma City's St. Joseph Cathedral on November 23, 1920. In quick succession, Lucy gave birth to three children: Margaret Mary in 1922, Bernard in 1923, and Anthony, whom everyone called Tony, in 1925.[13]

To house the growing family, which still included the mother of Gus's late wife and his two adult daughters, Gus obtained two "shotgun houses." These small, narrow wood-frame shacks were usually used to house workers near manufacturers or oilfields. Gus adapted the two shacks into a family home by connecting them perpendicularly. Across the front, he built a porch suitable as a place to sleep on hot summer nights when the wet towels hung across the windows didn't sufficiently cool the air.[14]

The house had neither electricity nor plumbing. Baths were taken in a zinc tub with water heated on the wood-fired kitchen stove. While the roof sufficed to keep water out, winter cold seeped through the warped floorboards. In warm weather, the openings in the floor became passageways for the fleas residing on the dogs sleeping in the crawl space under the house. "Thus," said Tony, "we three warm-blooded Hillerman kids learned not to linger over the cracks between the warped boards of our bedroom floor during the summer."[15]

The parents slept in the portion of the house closer to the road. Their bedroom doubled as the family den, where on many nights the family gathered around the radio for broadcasts of *Little Orphan Annie, Jack Armstrong—The All-American Boy, Amos 'n' Andy, Bring 'Em Back Alive*, and *Charlie Chan*.[16]

With few toys beyond marbles or Margaret Mary's doll, the children learned early how to entertain themselves. The mail delivered one solution. The Hillermans, like most American households, received copies of the Montgomery Ward and Sears, Roebuck & Company mail-order catalogs. The three- to four-pound catalogs were paper versions of the multistory department stores filled with sewing machines, kitchen appliances, musical instruments, firearms, bicycles, clothes, jewelry, clothes, and toys. Almost anything one could think of was for sale. In fact, Sears, Roebuck & Company even sold houses, some assembly required. But as the Hillermans could rarely afford anything in the catalogs, Margaret Mary devised a new use for them. She and her brothers would cut out the drawings of sofas, chairs, tables, and appliances and make dioramas that they populated with figures cut out from the pages featuring clothing.[17]

Reading was also a dependable source of amusement, much encouraged by their mother. Being the eldest of the three children, Margaret Mary often read to her brothers when they were toddlers. Tony's favorite was Hans Christian Andersen's *The Ugly Duckling*. The taunting of the ugly duckling made Tony cry, only to cheer up when the duck turned into a swan.[18]

All of the play and reading took place under the watchful eyes of Lucy, who spent her days tending to the household. The two cows had to be milked; water had to be brought up from the well or the rain barrel; beets, beans, corn, and fruit from the garden had to be canned; slaughtered hogs smoked; and the root cellar stocked by fall. On most nights Gus would come home after nine o'clock, but the children frequently waited up for him. "Especially on a Friday night," recalled Margaret Mary, "He always brought home a bag of candy and fruit stuff from the store. So, when he came home from work on those nights it was wonderful."[19]

When Tony reached the age to join Margaret Mary and Bernard at school, his mother dressed him in a set of blue coveralls purchased from a Sears, Roebuck & Company catalog. Unfortunately, the dress of choice among Sacred Heart boys was denim bib overalls with straps like those their father farmers wore. "Thus, I became the swan among the ducklings, an object of scorn and derision," said Tony. "But a little bit of serious sobbing into Mama's apron solved that problem and got me back into my own overalls."[20]

Lucy was the loving mainstay of her children's lives. "Mama could create a tale of magic for her kids while bandaging a skinned knee, canning beets, or turning the hand-cranked clothes wringer beside the washtub," recalled Tony. She filled the house with music, either with song—her favorite being a homesteader's tune—or with 78 rpm records on a hand-cranked Victrola. She read fairy tales and offered life lessons from her storehouse of aphorisms, many of which served as reminders of biblical lessons. "Much was expected of us," Tony said. "Bumps, bruises, and winter colds were not to be complained about; whining and self-pity were not allowed."[21]

There was a one-room public school in Sacred Heart, but Lucy sent her children to St. Mary's Academy, the mission school for Potawatomi girls run by the Sisters of Mercy. Tony and Barney (like his little brother, Bernard shortened his formal name) were allowed to go because the sisters admitted a sprinkling of boys whose parents wanted their children in the more academically oriented classes. The school was housed in a two-story wood building lined with porches, built to replace the one lost in the 1901 fire. The Sisters of Mercy, founded in Dublin in 1831 by Catherine McAuley, believed in a compassionate expression of Catholicism that called for living in a contemplative community and providing service to the disadvantaged. In addition to taking vows of poverty, chastity, and obedience, the sisters took a fourth vow of service to the poor and needy. This veneration of service took early root in the Hillerman children.[22]

Attending school with Indian children provided Tony a rare opportunity for that era when US schools were resolutely segregated. The nuns discouraged the girls from speaking their native language and sought to inculcate white Catholic virtues along with their lessons. But they also treated the Potawatomi children with respect, believing they were equally entitled to an education. They were, in the Sisters of Mercy's view, God's children. "So, I grew up knowing that we're all the same species," said Tony. "They're just like we are, in other words. That's a hard thing for people to learn. I grew up knowing it as a child."[23]

By the time Tony attended St. Mary's Academy it was about the only active part of the original mission. The monastery now stood empty, having moved to Shawnee, thirty miles to the north. One could no longer catch the aroma of fresh bread in the ovens of the bakery, the barns held almost no livestock, and the gardens so lovingly tended by the monks were overgrown. Yet at noon and six every day, the bells of Sacred Heart Catholic Church still tolled.[24]

Motivated by her devotion, Lucy made certain that Catholicism played a persistent and important role in her children's lives. Each evening the family gathered for prayers, kneeling on the linoleum floor of the kitchen under a print of the Crucifixion. On Sundays, she took them to mass, while Gus usually tended the store. In the afternoon, the children returned for catechism classes.[25]

In June of 1935, Tony was confirmed and selected for his confirmation name that of Saint Jerome, known for his fifth-century Latin translation of the Bible, an edition of which was still in use. While First Communion usually precedes Confirmation, Hillerman received his First Communion two years later, at age twelve, and began to serve regularly as an altar boy. "I breathed the perfume of Sunday's incense, old wood, candle smoke, and a sense of God's presence," recalled Hillerman.[26]

One Sunday, when he was twelve or thirteen, Hillerman came across stacks of boxes in a room adjoining the church's sanctuary after completing his duties as altar boy. The boxes contained books that had been left behind when the monks moved to Shawnee. The Latin, German, and French texts were of no interest. "But others—worn, torn, and hard-used castoffs though they were—were treasures to a kid who loved to read and had never been inside a real library," said Hillerman. He sought out Father Bernard Mazurowski, the new pastor. Could he, Hillerman asked, be granted permission to sort out the literary treasure and compile a list?[27]

The project took months because Hillerman decided he needed to read portions of each book before entering the cataloging information in his Big Chief brand notebook. The stops on this literary journey through the boxes included, among others, *Plutarch's Lives of the Noble Greeks and Romans*, Charles Darwin's *The Origin of Species*, and William H. Prescott's *The Conquest of Peru* and *The Conquest of Mexico*. He found it difficult to accept the accounts of Aztec human sacrifice. The parents of the Potawatomi children he knew retained "grandmother memories" different from what he learned in school. "I grew up skeptical of Indian atrocities," he said.[28]

Reading about the saints in the multivolume *Lives of the Saints* by Alban Butler particularly drew his attention. "I picked those who attained sainthood not by praying but by dying," said Hillerman, "their martyrdom inspiring vivid descriptions of tongue extractions, beheadings, boilings in oil, burnings at stake, flayings, and impalements." Stories bound to entrance a sixth-grade boy.

Darwin's book prompted discussions with Father Bernard. The young, newly ordained priest from Chicago counseled his young would-be librarian that Darwin's theories were not in conflict with the church's teachings. Rather they were a way of understanding "the dazzling complexity of God's creation." In these discussions, Father Bernard also provided a long-lasting Gospel lesson to his acolyte. "Christ tried to teach us that happiness lay in helping others, selfishness was the road to damnation," Hillerman remembered Father Bernard telling him. "His bottom line always boiled down to God loves us. He gave us free will, permission to go to hell if we wanted, rules to follow if we preferred both a happy life and heaven, and a conscience to advise us along the way."

Hillerman broadened his literary repast beyond the ecclesiastical offerings when his dad took him and Barney to Shawnee. The two boys, with pocket change earned from picking blackberries, selected magazines from the rack at Owl Drug Store on Main Street. "Barney reading the *Flying Aces* and *Model Airplane News*," said Tony, "and me the lurid-covered pulp fiction."[29]

Lucy provided a more significant source of reading material. She learned that her family could obtain books from the Oklahoma State Library. In the 1920s, librarians at the state facility had begun shipping boxes of books on loan to organizations in rural areas. The program was later expanded to include individuals and soon books were on their way by mail, or in some cases by Model T Ford, to every county in the state. "Sending out the books was like pouring water on parched soil," according to one report.[30]

The contents of the boxes, however, were often a surprise. The librarians substituted books when the titles the Hillermans selected from the list were unavailable. "We would have requested something like *Little Women* and *Anne of Green Gables* for Margaret Mary, and stuff like *Captain Blood, Death on Horseback, Tom Swift and His Electric Runabout*, and *Red Badge of Courage* for Barney and me," said Hillerman. "The package would contain such volumes as *History of the Masonic Order in Oklahoma, The Bobbsey Twins on Blueberry Island, The Decline and Fall of the Roman Empire, Tom Brown's School Days, Post-Bellum Cotton Economy on the Mississippi Delta*, and *Pollyanna and Her Puppy*." As one observer put it, "title substitution became a fine art." In any case, whatever books arrived were read.[31]

The Great Depression did not initially affect the Hillerman children. "We heard about it," said Margaret Mary. "But we really were not deprived of anything." There was no lack of food. Hams and sides of bacon hung in the smokehouses, onions, potatoes, and Mason jars of vegetables and fruit lined the root cellars, chickens clucked in the yards, and cows waited to be milked in barns each morning. "A well-fed boy in bib overalls is not likely to be concerned about money, when none is in circulation among his peers," said Tony. "We were safe in our innocence from the ruinous knowledge that a richer world existed, and safe in our youth from concern about tomorrow."[32]

For Tony, Barney, and their friends, Sacred Heart was a playground. The Zoellers' cotton gin and pond was a destination of choice for the boys. One Christmas Barney received a BB gun and it inspired new games. Tony and Barney took the potato bugs they removed from their garden and placed them in a tin can. When they had a sufficient number, they floated the can out onto the gin pond, then shot holes in the can until it sank with its load of insect passengers. Another time the boys loaded matches in the gun, and when Tony took a turn, his shot ignited some bales of cotton. The boys managed to extinguish the flames.[33]

For small infractions, Lucy Hillerman would scold her children in private. More serious transgressions however, required more. In such cases, she promised to tell their father what had happened when he got home. "That sounds mild," said Hillerman, "but it produced awful hours of waiting for sundown, for the sight of Papa trudging homeward down the dirt path along the section line, for sitting on the porch trying to overhear Mama's infraction report, and finally for the summons into the kitchen for the hearing, the judgment, and the sentence."[34]

Due to his long hours at the store, Gus remained mostly uninvolved in his children's lives aside from such moments. After he interrogated his son, Gus told him to go out to the yard and bring back a switch. Hillerman selected a branch from the peach tree—"neither painfully large nor ridiculously small." He gave the branch to his father, who asked if Tony could remember family rules without a whipping. Tony replied that he did think he could remember the stricture, and his father dismissed him without a swat, telling him to see if his mother needed help.[35]

When not shooting at cans or bales of cotton, the boys took up war games, inspired by reports of the brewing conflicts in Europe and Asia in their father's copies of the Sunday *Kansas City Star* or the *Life* magazines in the dentist's office. They turned the cotton gin and its mountains of residue into battlefields. They would dig trenches in the cotton hull pile and form two armies, with the Hillermans on one side and Potawatomi boys on the other. (When they reenacted battles between the cavalry and Indians, the Potawatomi boys insisted on playing the role of the cavalry, having seen who won in the movies playing down in nearby Konawa.) "Life in Sacred Heart," said Hillerman, "was a good deal for boys." The war brewing overseas remained only an inspiration for play.[36]

On some sweltering summer days, Hillerman would walk up into town to seek out the cooler breezes at the top of Church Hill, bringing a book as a companion. "When I sat in the shade of its trees to think boyhood thoughts I could (by Pottawatomie County standards) see forever," he said. "And in every direction stretched the great blue dry-weather sky of Dust Bowl drought, and the towering clouds that waited for winter before delivering rain."[37]

To the east lay the cemetery where white and Potawatomi Catholics found repose together. Excluded were Protestants, who were buried at the south end of the field, and non-Catholic Potawatomi who were placed in a small plot across the road by the Zoellers' pear orchard. Faith rather than skin color separated or united Sacred Heart residents in death as in life. To the west were the remaining buildings of the once-thriving mission that had spread Catholicism to the farthest points of Oklahoma. But the buildings were mostly empty now that the monks had departed. Still operating was St. Mary's Academy, where for eight years the Sisters of Mercy had instructed Hillerman in math, English, history, Latin, and the eleemosynary demands of God.

The once-elegant grounds surrounding the two-story school showed increasing signs of neglect. Only the white church on the crown of the hill stood in pristine condition, lovingly maintained by the congregants, many of whom had helped build it. If the hill was the epicenter of Sacred Heart, then the church at the top was its spiritual heart. "Even though neither I, nor anyone else, ever considered me a pious kid," said Hillerman years later, "that graceful old place was important to me in ways I had to grow old before I began to understand."

CHAPTER 2

◈ The World Beyond ◈

The already anemic recovery from the Great Depression stalled, then collapsed. To many Oklahomans, the economy in 1937 and 1938 was like the turbulent weather that created the Dust Bowl and turned day into night west of Sacred Heart. There was nothing to do but adapt. "The trouble wasn't food," said Tony Hillerman. "It was lack of money to pay property taxes and to buy things you couldn't grow in Pott County—such as sugar, salt, flour, the other kitchen staples, barbed wire for fences, medicine, parts to keep the old auto running, etc."[1]

The poor economy and bad health forced Gus Hillerman to close his general store. Approaching sixty-three, he tired easily and was short of breath. The family gave up the shotgun house in town and built a house on the forty acres of land that Lucy had bought with her homestead sale. They paid for the construction using mineral rights Gus had acquired as collateral on an unrepaid loan he made to a Potawatomi family. The two-story house had two bedrooms with dormers upstairs and another bedroom adjacent to the living room and kitchen. Best of all, there was running water in the kitchen and bathroom. It was delivered by means of a pump powered by electricity, which had come to Sacred Heart thanks to President Franklin D. Roosevelt's Rural Electrification Commission.[2]

The Hillermans' new home lay two miles south of Sacred Heart. "I quit being a village kid and became a farm boy," said Tony. The chores had been simple in the old house—keeping the yard and chicken house tidy—but grew in number on the farm. Tony and Barney were expected to build fences, seed pastures, and fight off invasions of Johnson grass, a noxious weed that could sicken livestock. But the added tasks gave Tony a sense of doing adult work. "For me," said Tony, "this gain in prestige was balanced by a sense of loss. We were no longer in easy walking distance of the Sacred Heart Church."[3]

At the end of the summer in 1938, thirteen-year-old Tony joined Barney in riding the bus to Konawa High School, five miles to the east. With its paved streets, stores, and railroad station, Konawa was the closest thing to a city for miles around. Thanks to new oil wells, its three thousand residents were spared from the worst of the Depression in comparison to many other Oklahoma communities. The ten-year-old brick, one-story Konawa High School was a source of civic pride. Several additions and new buildings had just been completed using Works Project Administration funds. But like other isolated Oklahoma towns, Konawa shared a sense of apartness from the world. "The gnashing of titanic forces on the world scene were far beyond the purview of our common consent and understanding in Konawa," said Arthur Ward Kennedy, who graduated from Konawa High School as Tony entered.[4]

Hillerman joined a student body very different than what he was used to at St. Mary's Academy. "The town boys got their hair cut in barber shops, knew how to shoot pool, didn't carry their lunch in sacks, wore belt pants and low-cuts instead of overalls and work shoes, had spending money, knew about calling people on telephones, and were otherwise urbane and sophisticated," said Hillerman. This fed his growing suspicion that there were two kinds of people in the world: "Them and us—the town boys and the country boys."[5]

Hillerman's academic career at Konawa High School was not stellar. He maintained a B average, earning C's in English, American literature, and shop. His only A's came in American history, general science, and geometry. Evidently, he liked geography, earning a first place in an interscholastic meet. The instructor for algebra and geometry was the coach of the Konawa Tigers football and basketball teams. "Since the coach didn't understand either subject very well, and since no one seemed to sign up for them except members of the team," said Hillerman, "we'd spend a lot of our time going over single wing football plays, pass patterns, and so forth."[6]

Hillerman played substitute right field on the baseball team and second-string guard on the football team. One day the Tigers football team traveled north to take on the Bowlegs High School Bison team. The unusually named town had no stadium, so fans watched from backs of pickup trucks circled around a playing field. The coach put Hillerman in the game with instructions to clear the way for the ball-carrying halfback. But Hillerman failed to reach the spot on time. The linebacker, whom Hillerman was supposed to block, tackled the Konawa player and forced a fumble. "Hillerman," yelled the coach, "you run like a broke-dick dog!" It was a simile never forgotten.[7]

Despite not being the best student in English class, Hillerman remained an avid reader. He read two dozen books for outside reading in English, from Alexandre Dumas's *The Count of Monte Cristo* in his freshman year to Rudyard Kipling's *Captains Courageous* in his senior year. Other books on his list included both classics such as *Strange Case of Dr. Jekyll and Mr. Hyde* by Robert Louis Stevenson, *The Last of the Mohicans* by James Fenimore Cooper, and *Don Quixote* by Miguel de Cervantes, as well as books popular with boys, such as *Captain Blood* and *Captain Blood Returns* by Rafael Sabatini, *The Virginian* by Owen Wister, and *Stepsons of France: True Tales of the Foreign Legion* by Percival Christopher Wren. The future mystery writer also read Edgar Allan Poe's *The Murders in the Rue Morgue*, a short story that is widely considered to be the first modern detective tale. In the story, a double murder that baffles the police is solved by the deductive powers of an eccentric whose work is chronicled by his companion in the style that Arthur Conan Doyle would adopt for his Sherlock Holmes stories decades later.[8]

The only contemporary fiction on Hillerman's extensive reading list was Herbert Clyde Lewis's *Spring Offensive*, a little-reviewed World War II novel. In the story, over the objections of his mother, twenty-three-year-old Peter Winston joins the British Expeditionary Force in order to fight in the war while the United States still remained out of it. On the battlefield, Winston is wounded and takes cover in a crater. A German soldier spots him and stabs him with a bayonet.

The book would have been heady reading for the teenaged Tony. His brother was now of draft age, and he would soon be as well. The war was no longer an abstraction nor an inspiration for games in the cotton gin. Americans of his age were already dying on distant battlefields. *Spring Offensive*'s detailed depiction of the protagonist's sense of futility added to the uncertainty of life ahead as Hillerman approached graduation.

As Gus grew weaker, Barney took over many of his chores. One autumn day, Tony sat with his father under a tree on the farm. A priest was coming over from Sacred Heart church for a visit, and Gus said he was not keen on it. "You know," he said, "you never should let the church get in the way of God." Neither Tony's father nor his mother were ever short on advice. Lucy told her children never to be afraid. Later, Tony summed up the specifics: "Not of spiders (avoid the black widow, and she avoids you), not of lightning (avoid standing under trees during storms), not of storm clouds (see the beauty in them, the majesty; but if you see tornado funnels, we'll have a little picnic in the root cellar). Not of drowning (God loves you but He expects you to use common sense)."[9]

In 1941, Tony's sister Margaret Mary came home for Christmas, a holiday Americans were uncertain how to celebrate only weeks after Pearl Harbor and the US entry into World War II. Seeing her father now through the eyes of a nursing student, Margaret Mary knew what was happening. Certainly Lucy, an experienced registered nurse, also knew. Gus Hillerman's frequent shortness of breath, continuous fatigue, and edema were signs of a failing heart. He was dying. Sixteen-year-old Tony was clueless. "I was no more aware of this economic crisis in American history than I was that Papa's heart was wearing out."[10]

On Christmas morning, Gus's heart ceased beating while he sat on the sofa surrounded by his family. Neither Barney nor Tony had driver's licenses, so Margaret Mary took the car to the church to fetch the priest. He rushed through Christmas mass to come to the house. "After that it fell to Mother to keep the family together and going," said Margaret Mary.[11]

Five months later, on May 10, 1942, forty-seven Konawa High School students took their places in the auditorium for graduation ceremonies. Three different religious leaders offered prayers, a benediction, and a reading from scripture. The Sunday ceremony came at the end of a week filled with discouraging news of the war. Ten thousand US and Filipino troops had surrendered in Corregidor and the Japanese occupation of the Philippines was complete. On the other side of the world, Churchill was trying to reassure his people on his second anniversary as prime minister that the tide of war would eventually turn in their favor.[12]

For his senior yearbook photo, Hillerman selected a photograph of himself unlike any his classmates chose. On a page with more than three dozen closely cropped headshots of his classmates, Hillerman appears alongside a tree, wearing a loosely knotted tie, his mouth wide open in laughter.[13]

Hillerman, chosen as class reporter, penned a spritely senior history for the yearbook. It was his first published work. He reviewed the attrition of their class, down from the seventy-one who enrolled in 1938, and extolled his classmates' performances in *Don't Darken My Door*, a one-act play by Harry Wright Githens, and *Everybody's Getting Married*, a three-act comedy by William Russell Moore. He also recounted the travails of raising money for the junior-senior banquet: "We used every means short of dark glasses and tin cups." But the money was found and the banquet was a success. "It was a Hawaiian affair," wrote Hillerman, "complete with grass skirts, artistically filled, and pineapple center pieces which were not, as we discovered later, to be eaten." The banquet was followed by a senior prom, Konawa's first. "To sum it up," concluded Hillerman, "we've been a pretty 'classie' class. Anyway, we've had fun."[14]

Finished with school, Tony joined Barney on the farm. They worked to lessen erosion, create pastureland for grazing, and turn bottomland into a productive field. Their efforts failed. Their time together, however, was sweet. "It was an ideal situation for two brothers pulled a bit apart by adolescence to get reacquainted." One day as the two worked together, Tony waxed enthusiastically about a Nash roadster he had seen parked in front of the Zoellers' store after mass on Sunday. Someday, Tony proclaimed, he would have the money to buy a sports car like that. Barney thought it a bad idea. Instead, the older brother advised that money was only of value if it gave you freedom. To acquire items beyond the necessities might require one to slave away at a job one did not like. "Don't find a way to make money," Tony recalled his brother advising him. "Find a way to make a living doing what you like to do anyway. Otherwise you're just raising funds to buy yourself out of slavery."[15]

That year the cotton crop was destroyed by armyworms, so named because they move about like armies, destroying everything in their path. Only the fruits the Hillermans grew and the sale of cattle brought in any cash. Their father's plan turned out to be a failure. The Hillermans could not make it as farmers. Barney took a job at a meatpacking plant in Oklahoma City. Margaret Mary had almost completed her training as a nurse and her employment was certain. Only Tony was without work. Lucy decided that one of her sons should go to college and it should be Tony. "It was a revolutionary idea those days when colleges were for the children of the affluent," recalled Hillerman, "but we decided to try it." Barney, now twenty years old, chose to remain with their mother, at least until he was drafted.[16]

In September 1942, Lucy and Barney drove Tony to Stillwater, ninety miles north of Sacred Heart, to enroll him at Oklahoma Agricultural and Mechanical College. With ten thousand residents, Stillwater was about four times the size of

Konawa. The red brick neo-Georgian buildings of Oklahoma A&M, the state's land grant college, stood on several hundred acres of land at the edge of the township. The war had made it a busy place. By the time Tony arrived, thousands of military servicemen and servicewomen were being trained on campus.

Lucy provided her son with enough money to pay for fall semester tuition, books, and $15 for one month's rent for one-half of a double bed on the second floor of a boardinghouse. To cover his expenses, Tony took a six-day-a-week job as a busboy and dishwasher, a weekend job cleaning a dentist's office, and occasional work on irrigation ditches.[17]

A goodbye hug from his mother, handshake from his brother, and Tony stood watching the family car drive away. On his own for the first time, he was struck by fear, loneliness, exultation, and excitement. "Suddenly I was a formally recognized adult," Hillerman said. "Free at last from boyhood, a career at which I had not felt myself successful." Academics proved also not to be successful for Hillerman. He earned Cs in English, chemistry, and military science; received a D in trigonometry, and failed to complete his course in algebra.[18]

The poor science and math grades were understandable, especially considering the less-than-adequate instruction he had received in those subjects at Konawa High School. But for a consummate reader who already displayed advanced writing skills, Hillerman's poor performance in English Composition is a puzzle. The most likely culprit was working three jobs, not to mention fleeting attempts at a social life. When the semester ended, Hillerman returned home to his mother with a miserable report card. "By then," he said, "It was clear that college was not for me."[19]

The semester, however, had provided important lifelong lessons. Hillerman became acquainted with a wealthy student who had enrolled at Oklahoma A&M and was staying in the rooming house after his parents cut off his allowance for his poor performance at the family's preferred college. From this friendship, Hillerman said, "I learned about a social class system that I had no idea existed outside the Victorian-era novels I'd read."[20]

Other aspects of college life were equally eye-opening. "At seventeen," he said, "I had only an abstract notion of social structure and at the campus the ignorance that had been my shield was swept away." His classmates had cash and families who paid tuition, room, and board. Some even had cars. One night, coming home from his dishwashing job, Hillerman passed by a fraternity house. Outside, convertibles surrounded the building; inside, coeds in dresses and men in tuxedos partied. "My first look at the unequal distribution of wealth," said Hillerman. "I recall no sense of the resentment we have-nots are supposed to suffer when we first see the haves. It was more a sense of surprise." But he confessed to a touch of envy.[21]

Back home after his failed attempt at college, Tony celebrated Christmas with Barney, Margaret Mary, and their mother. It had been a year since their father had died and the war was drawing closer. Barney was called up, and Tony and Lucy drove him north to the town of Maud to catch the bus to his military induction. On the way home, Tony pulled over at the Sacred Heart church when his mother suggested they stop in and say a prayer for Barney. "We knelt for a while in the back pew and I think it was then I first realized the reality of war," said Tony. "That Barney might not come back."[22]

It now fell to Tony to take up Barney's farm work. "Along with obtaining custody of the car keys," said Tony, "I had more or less, at least in my mind, become farm manager—for which I had no more competence than I had for trigonometry." The subject of the farm's future came up one evening at the supper table, Barney's chair unoccupied. Lucy decided to auction off the farm's livestock and equipment and join Margaret Mary in Oklahoma City. As an experienced nurse Lucy was certain she would easily find work. Tony, who would turn eighteen in May, made it clear he wanted to follow Barney into the military.[23]

"She must have known she would never return to her home here," said Hillerman, looking back on the evening. "Having seen what war does to mothers' sons in her nursing of World War I wounded, she could have had no illusions about that either." But unlike Peter Winston's mother in the novel *Spring Offensive* that Hillerman had read, Lucy consented to her son's enlistment.[24]

CHAPTER 3

◈ Inductee ◈

Livestock were finally coming out of the shade under trees in the fields alongside the dusty road that took Tony Hillerman from Sacred Heart to Maud, Oklahoma. Thermometers that had reached the 110-degree mark the day before now registered in the sixties. It was August 16, 1943, and the summer's infernal, record-breaking heat had finally broken, at least for this day.[1]

Hillerman had made the same ten-mile drive north on May 27, his eighteenth birthday, to appear before Draft Board No. 2 of Pottawatomie County after Congress lowered the draft age to eighteen. Under the provisions of the law, Hillerman could avoid military service by virtue of his widowed mother's dependency on him to operate the farm. But she said she would not stand in his way, even though her only other son was in the armed forces overseas. The boyish-faced, jug-eared, six-foot, 150-pound farmer's son presented himself before the draft board. His scrawny physique was no barrier to service. On average, recruits raised in the years of the Great Depression weighed 144 pounds.[2]

Now, three months later, Hillerman was returning to Maud to catch an inductee bus. In the twenty-one months since the United States had entered World War II, the nation had assembled a military of more than nine million men. There was a growing sense of optimism. German and Italian forces had been routed in Africa and the American Seventh Army was taking Sicily. On the Monday when Hillerman waited for his bus, postal carriers placed that week's issue of *Time* in mailboxes. The magazine's editors proclaimed their confidence about the war, writing, "Somewhere in Valhalla an unseen hand struck a mighty cymbal note, and the sound of doom was heard across Germany."[3]

Along with other young recruits, a nervous yet excited Hillerman climbed into the bus. The driver put the engine in gear and headed west. During the ride, Hillerman acquired a new friend, an equally scrawny eighteen-year-old named Robert M. Huckins. He had grown up in Sasakwa, no more than twenty miles from Sacred Heart, and his father, like Hillerman's late dad, was also a small-town merchant. Several hours later, the bus pulled through the gates of Fort Sill, near Lawton, Oklahoma. Almost soon as they arrived. Hillerman and Huckins were handed train tickets and dispatched with four other Oklahomans to the Army Infantry School at Fort Benning, Georgia.[4]

As the train crossed the Mississippi, Hillerman entered the eastern half of the United States for the first time. In the sweltering summer Georgia heat, Hillerman endured the army's infamous basic training that consumed every waking breath. Just when he might have felt battle ready, the army announced it had other plans for him. Hillerman, Huckins, and a few other Oklahomans were selected for the Army Specialized Training Program (ASTP), which sent academically promising recruits to college. The idea was to create a cadre of officers for deployment in the final months of the war and to assist in restoring civilian governments in Europe. The men were sent to Oklahoma A&M.[5]

Less than a year after leaving the campus Hillerman was back there again. Little had changed since Hillerman had studied there the previous year, except that this time he didn't have to wash dishes or dig ditches. He had money in his pockets. The men took accelerated courses in math, science, and engineering and reported to the gym each day to retain their Fort Benning fitness level. Beyond that, they maintained the life of students, eating and living well, albeit dressed in uniforms. The ASTP patch on their shoulders featured the lamp of learning, which looked like a genie's oil lamp. Hillerman learned they were nicknamed "The Knights of the Flaming Pisspot" and that some said the program's initials stood for Always Safe Till Peace. "The scorn may have been more imagined than real, a product of the way we felt about ourselves," said Hillerman. But for sure, "coeds considered us slackers."[6]

Military commanders decided to end the program. Worried that there would be a critical shortage of infantrymen, especially following the anticipated invasion of Europe, they deemed the ASTP an unnecessary luxury. In February 1944, Hillerman traded his books for a rifle.[7]

Hillerman and seventeen other members of the Oklahoma A&M ASTP were sent south by train to Gainesville, Texas, just north of Dallas. On March 9, 1944, they were met at the station by trucks and taken to Camp Howze, a desolate infantry training facility that had been hurriedly assembled on 59,000 acres of the desolate Texas plains where longhorn cattle had roamed.[8]

The truck ferrying Hillerman and the other men cleared the gates and traveled down the camp's gravel streets lined with tarpaper barracks, pausing every so often, like a school bus, to drop off some of its charges at the various headquarters buildings. Hillerman's turn came at the one marked Company C, 410th Infantry, 103rd Division. Originally organized as a reserve unit in New Mexico in 1921, the 410th Infantry Regiment had been ordered into active service in 1942 and made part of the 103rd Infantry Division, whose troops were originally drawn from Arizona, Colorado, and New Mexico. Members of the 103rd wore a shoulder patch featuring a saguaro cactus. But the regiment to which Hillerman was assigned took as its symbol a blue shield with the Zia Pueblo sun symbol, the same one used on the New Mexico flag.

Hillerman climbed up the wooden steps and made his way into the clerk's office, where he handed his orders to a corporal who looked them over.

"Another quiz kid," he said to the nearby sergeant, referring to a popular radio program that had begun airing in 1940.

"Get him back to supply," said the sergeant.[9]

It was a sharp reminder to Hillerman of what he saw as "the standard us and them division of American society." The "us" were the ASTP men yanked from college campuses and the would-be-pilots sent down to fill out the ranks of the infantry. "We quiz kids and the flyboys were outside this fraternity—apparently forever," said Hillerman. The "them" in this case were the infantrymen who had trained and bonded together during months of drills and war games.[10]

Camp life was hard. Long days of drilling, marching, firing rounds of mortars, and performing maneuvers with blank and live ammunition were often followed by night patrol. Hillerman and the rest of the quiz boys soon proved their mettle. Under the August Texas sun, the men were sent out on one final ten-mile hike with all their new equipment. On his back, Hillerman carried about sixty pounds of gear—half of a pup tent, tent stakes, rations, clothes, and his mortar barrel along with a leather box containing the sight for it. A canteen and .45 caliber pistol were strapped to his side, and a steel helmet was on his head.[11]

The men began marching at a pace of three miles in fifty minutes, leaving ten minutes of rest before beginning the second hour. Then they began to alternate walking and running. By the third mile, the heat claimed its first victim, a sergeant collapsed in a roadside ditch. Others fell to the side. "On mile five it gets serious," said Hillerman. His company was known for singing while marching. But there were no songs left. "We trudge along in stony silence," he said, "looking for the telltale tilt to the right in the man ahead of us, which signals he's about to tumble." The ditch filled with dropouts.

Robert Lewis, a fellow ASTP member running alongside Hillerman, considered joining them. "Before we can decide," said Hillerman, "we are trudging away on mile ten. Finally, the end is in sight and it is too late to do the sensible thing." Later in the latrine, under the cool water of the shower, Hillerman and others realize that most of the men who completed the ten-miler were quiz kids. Commanders and infantrymen alike noticed it. The quiz kids won acceptance. "Some kidding still," said Hillerman, "but no more blatant disrespect."

In July, Hillerman was granted a furlough, one of many the army extended as combat neared. On the road outside the fort, Hillerman put out his thumb for a ride north. "Failing to pick up someone with his thumb out was antisocial," he said. "Passing up one in uniform was akin to treason." He reached Oklahoma City and was reunited with his mother and sister, who had moved into a boardinghouse after abandoning the Sacred Heart farm. As it was for thousands of other young men, this homecoming was filled with uncertainty. "There I received food, the farewell address and instructions younger sons get from their mothers with good-bye hugs," said Hillerman.[12]

At summer's end, the men were ordered to prepare their wills and send personal items home. The months of drills, long marches with heavy packs, and hours on the shooting ranges came to an end. "We were now battle-ready," said Hillerman. The men were ordered to remove their saguaro shoulder patches so that spies could not identify a regiment on the move. On the morning of September 20, 1944, after parading before townspeople and passing by the military brass for one final review, Hillerman and all the members of the 103rd were loaded into eastbound trains.[13]

With the exception of stops at quiet rural stations for calisthenics, the train clicked its way across the country while the men inside played cards, read books and magazines, and wondered what lay ahead. At last, the train journey came to an end at Camp Shanks, a bustling facility just north of New York City where as many as forty thousand soldiers a month spent their last days before shipping out for Europe. The soldiers called the spot "Last Stop, USA."[14]

The men trained with new rifles and pistols, listened to lectures on how to resist enemy interrogations, read pamphlets on insurance and money matters, and learned to climb down nets off the side of a ship. They also were given leave to go into New York City at night. Hillerman and three of his friends spent an evening in the city with three teenage women they met on the street. After the women departed, the four men decided to have more rounds of drinks. After downing a Singapore sling and several other concoctions from the bar, Hillerman tried to cut off a bite of a waffle sitting before him until the barkeep pointed out he was trying to slice into a picture on the menu. "It was a very important episode," said Hillerman, "because it taught me, I couldn't handle whiskey."[15]

Early one morning, the men assembled outside their barracks. In formation, the 103rd Infantry Division marched to the train station, the men sweating under their helmets from the weight of their field packs, loaded with fatigues, extra olive drabs, long underwear, and wool socks. Hanging from their packs were gas masks, canteens, tents, and a blanket roll. Their duffel bags had already been placed on their assigned seats, marked in chalk with a number matching the one chalked on their helmets. A little more than two hours later, the men and their gear stood on Hudson River docks with four troop ships moored before them.[16]

Hillerman climbed the gangplank with his duffel and pack, plus pockets full of change and dollar bills, surprise winnings from a farewell game of poker the night before. Basic training had transformed him into a passionate but usually losing poker player. Hillerman's company was assigned to the USS *General J. R. Brooke*. The 522-foot ship could carry nearly 3,500 soldiers and officers plus a crew of 500.[17]

The *General Brooke* and other troop-laden ships sailed out of New York harbor with an escort of destroyers, forming a convoy with other ships. Above, men in blimps kept an eye out for submarines, a constant worry for transatlantic traffic. Many men went topside and crowded the decks of the ships for one final look at the receding shoreline. The last structure to drop out of sight over the horizon was the parachute drop tower, moved to Coney Island after its service in the 1939 World's Fair at Flushing Meadows.[18]

The first days were pleasant sailing, although Hillerman remained trapped belowdecks on KP duty. The ships were mazes of bunks made from pipes and stretched canvas, stacked in tiers of four. The ill-vented chambers reeked of body odor, vomit from seasickness, tobacco smoke, and salt from the seawater showers.[19]

After more than a week at sea, Gibraltar appeared over the port deck and the convoy entered the Mediterranean. On October 20, 1944, the ships approached Marseille, where they were to disembark, and the men had their first sight of war's destruction. The Allies' bombing had done its share of damage, while the retreating German forces had destroyed bridges and docks, and left the harbor filled with scuttled ships whose rusted bottoms faced skyward.

When the *General Brooke* anchored, Hillerman and the other members of Company C clambered down the ship's side using rope nets like those they had practiced on at Fort Shanks, to reach tank landing ships bobbing up and down in the water below. More than one infantryman was injured when he lost his grip and fell into the waiting boat. By midday, the men were all ashore and began marching in pouring rain through what was left of the city. Young children yelled "okay" and made V signs with their fingers. Others, said one soldier, begged for *bonbons* and cigarettes *pour papa*.

After nightfall, the city suddenly plunged into darkness as sirens sounded. Ordinance men fired up smoke generators, enveloping the troops in fumes. The drone of an airplane could be heard in the distance and bright flashes of artillery lit up the night sky. When the "all clear" was sounded, the men resumed their march. At eleven that night, after trudging uphill for most of the day, they reached their assigned encampment spot. The rain was coming down so hard that they set up camp in and around large puddles. During the remainder of the night, thick mud flowed into the tents.[20]

For days, the men unloaded supplies from the ships and spent their nights in drenched, muddy tents. One evening, Hillerman and his friend Robert Lewis found a bistro where they encountered members of the 45th division from Oklahoma, famed veterans of the Sicily invasion and the Anzio landing. The men didn't hesitate to rib the newcomers. They shook their heads when learning that Hillerman and Lewis were mortar gunners. "Anzio horror stories followed," said Hillerman, "and the information that the life expectancy of mortar men in combat was something under fifteen minutes."[21]

On November 7, after more than two weeks as stevedores, the men were ordered to pack their duffel bags with all their personal items and items of value that would not fit into jacket pockets. Officers issued doubtful promises that the men would eventually be reunited with their duffels. Then, in tarp-covered trucks, the men headed north on war-torn roads through Aix-en Provence and Lyon to Dijon, where the men set up camp in the city's central park.

The next day, in the small Alsatian village of Docelles, the men learned that President Franklin Roosevelt had easily won re-election for an unprecedented fourth term with a new vice president, Senator Harry S Truman. Late that night the trucks delivered the soldiers to Epinal, sixty miles west of Germany and a day's march from what remained of German-controlled Alsace. Under General Dwight D. Eisenhower's plans, Allied forces would beat the Germans back from their defenses west of the Rhine River, cross over the waterway, and converge on Berlin. Hillerman's unit, as part of the Seventh Army, would be on the southern end of the massive eastward attack. Rain was again their companion as they made camp in another muddy field.[22]

When they woke on the morning of November 11, 1944, the men were issued ammunition. Twenty-six years after the armistice that silenced the fighting in the war to end all wars, nineteen-year-old Private Anthony G. Hillerman put on his raincoat, hoisted his pack and mortar onto his shoulders, and began marching toward combat. "What we had come for was about to begin."[23]

CHAPTER 4

◈ War ◈

In the swirling snow of a winter already being called the worst in four decades, Tony Hillerman and members of the 410th Regiment marched eastward in single file, each soldier holding on to the man in front. They carved an olive-colored line in the white landscape, leaving a brownish streak of trampled snow and mud in their wake. In the confusion of the falling snow, the 410th Regiment mistakenly walked past its destination. The men crossed into what was regarded as no-man's-land before being ordered to double back to the safety of the hills along the Meurthe River, a tributary to the Moselle running downward from the Vosges Mountains in Alsace. There, the men dug in as sporadic artillery shells fell. The Germans, only a few miles away, were letting them know their arrival had not gone unnoticed.[1]

Ahead lay the last remaining barrier to ending the war in Europe. Massed along a five-hundred-mile line west of the Rhine River was a numerically superior German troop force. By mid-November 1944, German soldiers knew Europe was lost but they continued fighting to keep Allied forces from crossing into the Fatherland. They had added new bunkers to the thousands already in place on the French-built Maginot Line of fortifications, along with new barbed wire and buried mines. For a GI on foot, the anti-tank mines could be spotted by the irregular bumps they left in the farm fields, but the shoebox-sized *Schützenmines* were almost undetectable. A field planted with these could reap a deadly harvest.[2]

Already the Germans had demonstrated the advantage of their defensive position. During one October fight American forces had lost one man every two feet as they crossed nine thousand feet of ground. By his own admission, General Dwight Eisenhower knew military logic dictated that he should now halt his forces to build up strength and avoid a wintertime battle. Instead, he ordered his soldiers to fight on.[3]

After several days in the bitter cold, Hillerman received his first combat orders. He and several other soldiers were to cross the Meurthe and conduct a raid aimed at hindering the flow of German supplies to Saint-Dié. The small French village was a key entry point to roads leading into the Vosges Mountains. The rugged and compact range rose more than four thousand feet upward from the Rhine Valley creating a defensive wall that would have to be breached to reach the Rhine and enter Germany.[4]

In the dark, a lieutenant led Hillerman's small squad along the banks of the Meurthe. They had been told the river was shallow, no more than three feet deep. But when the men waded into the frigid water, they discovered the river was so deep and rapid that one soldier was swept fifty feet downstream. "The lieutenant was as green as we were and had not yet understood the invincible ignorance of military intelligence," said Hillerman. The noise of the men splashing about alarmed another American platoon, which launched flares into the sky. But before either the Germans or the Americans could take aim, Hillerman and his soaking compatriots retreated to safety.[5]

At dawn the following day the men approached the river again. This time the Germans spotted them and fired rounds of artillery in their direction. The men scrambled back into their foxholes. "And now we are no longer virgins," said Hillerman. "We have been actually shot at." It was time to return fire. Hillerman and Robert Lewis, his fellow survivor of Camp Howze ten-milers, unshouldered their forty-two-pound mortar barrel. The $2\frac{1}{3}$-inch wide, 29-inch tall steel tube was one of the least complicated weapons of the war. Attached to a steel plate with an adjustable bipod, the tube could be angled so as to lob an explosive projectile. To fire the weapon, the gunner took a yellow rocket-shaped mortar and dropped it down the muzzle tail-first. When it hit the bottom, a firing pin detonated an explosive cartridge, sending the mortar airborne. To achieve greater distances, additional explosive packets were inserted into the slits of the eight aerial fins. "This weapon," *Popular Science* told its wartime readers, "is a simple but ingenious thing calculated to delight anyone who ever enjoyed playing with fireworks." But Hillerman and Lewis had little luck firing mortars their first time in combat. In fact, according to Hillerman, Lewis accidentally detonated some of the loose explosive packets and suffered burns on his face.[6]

Bumbling and inexperienced though they were, Hillerman and the reinforcements provided much-needed invigoration to the battle-weary soldiers of the Seventh Army who had long been in combat. Together, veterans and green recruits moved out in two columns across the open fields of Alsace. The pockets of the men's jackets were stuffed with cigarettes, candy, chewing gum, and packets of sugar. "With the jacket crisscrossed by your rifle belt and the bandolier straps," noted accompanying journalists, "you bulged out like Mae West on top and flared like her at the hips." Compounding the frigid rain, shells fell sporadically as the men marched at the pace the recruits had practiced in Texas: three miles every fifty minutes followed by a ten-minute rest. The new members had been warned not to tie their chinstraps lest they be strangled or decapitated if an explosive blast knocked their helmets backward.[7]

The soldiers soon reached the outskirts of Saint-Dié, their objective. The regiment ahead of Hillerman's met heavy resistance as it neared the city. When the infantry finally broke through and entered the city, elated townspeople, both adults and children, rushed out to greet the soldiers. The Germans had fled but not before setting fire to the city. That night, Hillerman bedded down on dry hay in a burned-out stone building. If this were war, it certainly did not seem as treacherous as the men in the Marseille bar had described it to Hillerman and Lewis. They had survived more than the promised fifteen minutes.

The next objective was Lusse, twelve miles to the east. It was the first of several villages the Americans would have to capture in order to cross the Vosges Mountains. As they set off, Hillerman experienced a new sensation. Before Saint-Dié, being in the army had seemed to entail a purposeless series of marches in some God-forsaken spots; long journeys in trains, ships, and backs of trucks; and waiting, endless waiting. Now, with each step, he felt he was playing a role in changing the map of Europe. "The grass ahead of me is occupied territory," he said. "The grass I have just trod upon is free."[8]

Heavy rain fell as they neared Lusse. The Germans pinned down the Americans with a barrage of rifle and machine gun fire. Hillerman and Lewis set up their mortars. Hillerman's first round soared over the German machine gunner dugout. After he adjusted his aim, the next three rounds landed on target. In the subsequent stillness, neither man wanted to climb up the hill and see their kills for themselves. "Unlike riflemen, we could keep our war impersonal—thinking of knocking out machine guns and not of killing the fellow teenagers behind them." Hillerman said. "As for me, it was here that I began thinking of myself as a bona fide and skillful mortar gunner."[9]

With Lusse taken, the men were permitted a short rest in captured houses. Afterwards, they set off into a high, forested area with the idea of bypassing German forces below. The snow and rain were gone, and the men rejoiced at marching under a warm sun. There was no sign of war, not even the distant sound of artillery fire. Rather birds sang in the trees around them and the men chatted and laughed.[10]

But when the platoon reached a ridge, a scout signaled them to take cover and the soldiers hit the ground. From his position, all Hillerman could see was a postcard-like view of a stone hut with a thin wisp of smoke coming from its chimney. "But it was not this spectacular view that interested our scout," said Hillerman. "He was pointing at something below us." Two men, dressed in long German overcoats, were strolling along a cow path. They were like two teenagers strolling in beautiful weather. One was even playing his harmonica. Hillerman calculated that the distance made the two Germans easy targets for a rifle platoon. It was too dangerous to try capturing the pair of soldiers because German machine gunners might be hiding in the woods behind. The platoon lieutenant instead gave the order to fire. Volleys of bullets rained down on the Germans, who turned and ran toward the shelter. Shattered shingles flew off the roof and tree limbs were severed in the fusillade, which ceased when the Germans gained the safety of the building. Seconds later, they emerged from a back door and the skilled American riflemen began firing. But, again, no shot hit its target.

"When we moved down the slope toward the cabin," said Hillerman, "I paced off the distance—a habit all mortar gunners form to improve their skill at estimating range."

"How far was it?" asked the lieutenant, who had noticed Hillerman marking off the distance.

"About 270 yards from where I was standing," replied Hillerman. "You think we need practice?"

"I don't think so," said the lieutenant, laughing. "I think we can blame it on the weather."

When the winter cold and snow returned, so did the fighting. Hillerman took cover and found himself lying near a wounded German soldier who called for water and cried out for his mother. When the skirmish ended, Hillerman and other soldiers approached the wounded man and gave him water, which they had been told one should not do for someone shot in the stomach. "But this man had also taken bullets through the lungs and elsewhere," said Hillerman. "His gray tunic was soaked red and he was far, far beyond being hurt by a sip of water."[11]

Five men in Hillerman's company were wounded in the brief exchange of gunfire. An amiable Chicago insurance salesman named Adolph A. Lucchesi was killed. It was the first death of a GI whom Hillerman knew personally. "After that skirmish," said Hillerman, "we were no longer quite so young."[12]

By the end of November, Hillerman's company had successfully crossed the Vosges. They came to the town of Itterswiller, an ancient Alsatian village on what had once been a Roman road. In the spring the half-timbered, steep-pitch roofed houses would be laced with window boxes brimming with flowers. Now the war-damaged buildings looked colorless in the snow. In the hills above Itterswiller, German tanks and artillery lobbed shells as US forces neared the town. Hillerman and his unit dug in and waited. Looking up from his foxhole, Hillerman saw Bob Huckins, the fellow Oklahoman he had met on the recruiting bus back home. Huckins told Hillerman that the sergeant had received word the Germans had pulled back from Itterswiller, and he wanted six volunteers to see if the intelligence was correct. Hillerman agreed to go. "Like most teenagers, Huckins and I knew we were immortal," Hillerman said. Besides, "Anything is better, when you're nineteen and confidently bulletproof, than cowering in a muddy hole trying to hide in your helmet."[13]

The sun made one of its rare appearances as Hillerman and the half-dozen soldiers approached Itterswiller, so they tried to use the surrounding hillside vineyards for cover. When they spotted the town's first building they relaxed. It looked to them as if the enemy had left. The sergeant moved to the corner of the building. Peering down the street, he saw trucks moving rapidly out of town followed by a column of German infantrymen. Hillerman, pressed against the wall as well, looked across the street, and spotted an old man peering down at him from a second-story window. He was holding a bottle of wine and gesturing for Hillerman to come over. Hillerman didn't dare move.

Confident the Germans were evacuating, the sergeant ordered Hillerman and the men back to rejoin the company. Company C later returned to occupy the town. Hillerman, marching with his fellow infantrymen, once again spotted the white-haired Frenchman. "He stood in his doorway displaying a huge smile, the wine bottle, and a glass," said Hillerman. "Now there was time for a glass."

Itterswiller had been a serene interlude. Death became commonplace. The men passed by corpses without nausea or even a glance. From the time Hillerman had landed in France, battle casualties had risen steadily, now reaching two thousand a day and rising. "Even in the quiet places there were reminders that the price of bad luck, or carelessness, was death and that beyond the woods lay the defended towns, where every building could house a machine gun nest," Hillerman said. "We really didn't know where we were or what day it was, just that we had to push on and work hard to stay alive."[14]

War revealed one of its worst horrors to Hillerman one afternoon as he lay sprawled by a road awaiting orders to move on. Two soldiers, escorting a pair of German prisoners about Hillerman's age, stopped to light cigarettes. Hillerman watched as the Americans pointed their rifles at the Germans and ordered them to run up the hill. "The two ran and were shot in the back," said Hillerman who, along with other soldiers, reported the incident.[15]

When it didn't snow, it rained. The ground was like a wet sponge, making it almost impossible to dig a foxhole. The hole would fill with water with every shovel of dirt heaved away. "When you got the hole dug, it was a mud puddle for you to fall in," according to one account. The cold weather gave the Germans the upper hand. They had been provided winter gear, including white uniforms and helmets, while Hillerman and his fellow soldiers remained in their highly visible olive drab uniforms, doubling up their shirts and underwear to stave off the frigid temperatures. Convinced the war would soon be over, commanders had been late in ordering woolen long underwear and shirts. As a result, less than half of the needed clothing reached the front, and that which did was often the wrong size. Boots, which had been fitted during warm weather at US training camps, became too tight and were useless in keeping feet dry. With the cold, wet conditions and inadequate footwear, a gruesome affliction known as "trench foot" reached epidemic proportions, especially among new recruits who didn't understand the need to take precautions. It was hideous and painful. The feet would swell, discolor, and sometimes become gangrenous. Thousands of soldiers had to be hospitalized.[16]

"The snows of the winter of 1944–45," said Hillerman, "made us citizen-soldiers wonder why West Point had not required an intelligence test for future generals, who apparently didn't plan on snow in northern Europe in the winter." According to Hillerman, the grunts who did the fighting deservedly held little esteem for military intelligence and upper ranks. "We doubted," he said, "if our Seventh Army headquarters had ever heard a shot fired, tasted K-rations, or even knew a war was going on!"[17]

There were no mess halls or mobile canteens on the route across the Vosges Mountains toward Germany. Sugar beets in a partially harvested field or sausages found on captured Germans were the only relief from canned C-rations, boxed K-rations, and wrapped D-bars, so bad some soldiers took to calling them "Hitler's Secret Weapon." The only hot meal Hillerman ate was on Thanksgiving Day 1944.[18]

The men could only dream of being clean again. The odor of wet clothing and unwashed bodies, worsened by widespread diarrhea known as the "GI shits," permeated the encampments to such an extent that cigarette smoke seemed like an air freshener. Once, and only one time since Marseille, a shower had been provided. Two tents were erected in a snowy field. In the first tent, the men stripped down to their underwear. Then, carrying their boots, they made their way along a boardwalk to the second tent. Inside they were handed a bar of soap and marched under nozzles of hot water. When they emerged clean, they were given clean underwear and socks but handed back their mud-caked, odiferous uniforms. There was no escaping the smell of war.[19]

For a nineteen-year-old farm boy who but a few years earlier had been playing war games with neighborhood children in the piles of cotton hulls by Sacred Heart's gin mill, the reality of Alsace was becoming a nightmare. "I was hungry, filthy, miserable, aware that war was not what I'd expected, at the absolute end of my endurance." At one point, Hillerman stood at the top of a slope and looked down at the road below. All he had to do, he thought, was jump down the hill. His weak ankle, which he had injured playing paratrooper in Sacred Heart, would certainly give way and he would be sent home. "Our company had at least two cases of men court-martialed for self-inflicted wounds, but a broken ankle wouldn't provoke punishment," said Hillerman. "Why didn't I do it? It had nothing to do with patriotism, or how badly it would hurt. I think it was because I didn't want to miss whatever lay ahead, or I didn't want to go through life knowing I was a sissy."[20]

CHAPTER 5

❖ Battle ❖

For Tony Hillerman the war paused on December 18, 1944, in Wissembourg, France, less than two dozen miles from the German border. When they reached the small town, the men dug foxholes, but at night retreated to a house that had been commandeered. Sitting in an overstuffed chair in a well-appointed apartment, Hillerman wrote to his mother. "Tomorrow night I may be sleeping in a foxhole," Hillerman told her, "but tonight I've got a silk bedspread."[1]

It wasn't the first time that members of Company C billeted in a house, barn, or even burned-out rubble. The liberating American forces regularly bedded down in buildings in towns deserted by the Germans and populated by war-weary French. Several days earlier, Hillerman's platoon had been given eight hours of leave at a mansion set on luxurious grounds that included a stable and racetrack.[2]

Along with Bob Huckins and Robert Lewis, Hillerman decided to explore the mansion. "The mysteries of what surprises a bedroom's bureau drawers contained or what a GI could find in a corner cupboard was all part of the mystique of searching and staying in homes," according to historian Seth A. Givens, who made a study of looting among US soldiers in World War II. Hillerman strolled by paintings, mostly scenes with horses, and examined the photographs on display. Among them were several shots of a well-attired man, presumably the absent owner, posing with German officers, along with inscribed prints of Joseph Goebbels, the Nazi minister of propaganda, and Hermann Goering, Hitler's second in command. If the owner had not been German, he was certainly a Nazi sympathizer.[3]

Hillerman and his compatriots uncovered a safe hidden behind one of the paintings. The men used a grenade to blow it open and retrieved a cigar box from inside. It contained a small number of high-denomination bills from the Weimar Republic, now unusable, and four thousand Reichsmarks issued by the Third Reich, a cache that would have been worth about $1,000 prior to the war. Their ransacking came to an end with the arrival of American commanders in the now-secure village. Hillerman and his compatriots were ordered to rejoin the troops who had resumed their march north. As they made their way in the sleet, the soldiers learned of the money Hillerman and his two buddies were carrying. "We improved our status," he said, "by handing out deutsche marks to the less fortunate."[4]

A jeep rolled up alongside and the trio was ordered to get in. The men were driven back to the mansion, where a major and two MPs were waiting for them. The major sat at the kitchen table with the cigar box from the safe. He told the soldiers to empty their pockets and take a seat. In his hand the major held a scrap of paper. On it, Hillerman could make out a number exceeding four thousand. They were in deep trouble, said the major, unless they returned the sum he had written down.

"Each of us counted separately," Hillerman said, "and when the three totals were added it came to a little over five thousand marks—each of us trying to fudge enough to cover our charity handouts and overdoing it." The major took the cash, put it in the box, and scribbled a new number on the paper. The men were dismissed and were taken back to their platoon. They escaped being court-martialed because superiors generally ignored looting of this sort. Hillerman had not been alone in being tempted by the spoils of war.

"Don't ever let anybody tell you that we didn't loot," recalled Alexander Gordeuk, who served in the 13th Armored Division. "The American Army were great looters." From the time they landed in Normandy, American troops were always on the lookout for war souvenirs. Houses were scoured for spoils, and soldiers used minesweepers to search gardens for hidden valuables. As the soldiers neared and eventually crossed the German border, the practice took on the additional rationalization that the purloined items belonged to the enemy. Watches, rings, field glasses, medals, flags, furs, and weapons, particularly German Luger pistols, were the most sought-after items. As for Hillerman, he would bring home a Nazi flag, autographed by platoon members, and a Luger.[5]

Hillerman and his fellow infantrymen didn't limit their looting to French and German homes, but also pilfered items belonging to the US Army. Once, for instance, Thomas Morick, a Pennsylvanian who had also been part of the ASTP college training, wandered around a captured town to do some "scrounging" with Hillerman, whom he considered to be among the best at it. "Tony remarked he sure would like to have a Tommy Gun," Morick said.[6]

When they passed by parked Sherman tanks, Morick told Hillerman that tanks often carried the weapon he was looking for. "Tony hopped on a Sherman, peered down a hatch, and pulled up a Thompson." Down the road the two then came across a Half Track with supplies tied to it. "We took out our knives and cut the ropes while some of the crew looked out a window about twenty feet away," said Morick. "Either two grimy looking infantrymen with grenades and weapons were too much or they pitied us. Either way back at the platoon we enjoyed the real bacon, butter, and goodies."

Jollification and pilfering soon came to an end. To the north, a surprise attack by the Germans pushed back the center of the Allied front line. The press dubbed the fight the Battle of the Bulge because of the round, protruding shape of the German advance represented in maps. The American forces had managed, at great cost, to halt the German advance and were taking steps to regain the lost territory.

As a result, the American forces to which Hillerman was attached were stretched to the limit. The 103rd Division was put on reserve in the tiny village of Bousbach and assigned to defend a three-thousand-yard open flank. The brigade was decimated by casualties and any reinforcements that might have replenished their ranks were sent north. Everyone manned a foxhole, including the cooks.[7]

When the sun went down each day, Hillerman and another soldier prepared for night duty on the perimeter. They emptied their bladders and, if lucky, their bowels. Putting on every bit of clothing they had, the two hiked to an orchard and relieved the day shift. Either Hillerman or his partner would begin the night at the bottom of the hole bundled in an inadequate sleeping bag searching for sleep. "The other," said Hillerman, "would stand behind the gun, watching, waiting, memorizing the shape of every bare tree in the orchard, the shape of the slope where it met the sky, noting where the stars were on the skyline so he would notice if someone in white camouflage blocked some, straining eyes for a sign of movement, imagining the worst, keeping the rifle unfrozen inside the sleeping bag since the frozen machine gun probably wouldn't work."[8]

At some point in the night, the men would trade spots. Conversation laced the long hours of darkness. "We talked of girls, of the meaning of life, of the death of this friend or that one, of why two of our high-ranking noncommissioned officers were never around when serious shooting started," Hillerman said. At last, the sky behind the German lines would take on a pink hue. The day shift would return, and Hillerman and his partner would climb from the hole and make their way back to Bousbach to eat, get warm, then return later for another night's duty.

Not all nights were spent in the frozen mud. Sometimes Hillerman slept in town, which the Germans had abandoned without having done great damage. Hillerman thought Bousbach, with its narrow cobblestone streets and snow-covered peaked roofs, looked like a Hallmark holiday card. The soldiers sang Christmas carols and, on occasion, were joined by an Alsatian family. For many of these men, this was the first time they had been away from family on Christmas. On Christmas Eve, Erwin King, a member of Hillerman's company, wrote in his diary that the men were exhausted from so many days on the front and longed for peace of mind. "This is a strange life," Hillerman told his mother. "Today we have a manger, tomorrow perhaps a hotel suite, perhaps a foxhole."[9]

The Germans' surprise attempt to push back the Allied troops in the Battle of the Bulge proved there was a lot of fight left among the Nazi troops and shattered any dreams of a rapid end to the war. "These were black days on the Western front," said a pair of GI scribes recording their battlefield experiences. Now, in January 1945, the Germans launched a duplicate offensive in Alsace, not far from Hillerman's location. Pitting crack SS troops against an overstretched American defensive line, the Germans rushed into the upper Vosges Mountains with the goal of destroying the Seventh Army and recapturing Strasbourg.[10]

Hillerman and his regiment had been held in reserve, safe behind the lines. But when the attack came, so did new orders. Hillerman and other soldiers were loaded into trucks and taken west toward the German border as sleet pummeled the tarp covers. At the Bois de Sessenheim, close to the Rhine, they joined American troops put in place to hold off the anticipated German assault. As night fell, Hillerman's platoon took cover in the woods. Cutting through roots, he made a usable foxhole and huddled in the bottom with his arms folded over his head, listening to the exploding shells landing all around them. When the sleet ceased in the morning, the men moved forward and once again took cover. "We dug in again and waited, and waited, and waited," he said. It was for Hillerman yet another reminder of the old adage that war was endless boredom punctuated by moments of abject terror.[11]

Soon gunfire resumed and mortar rounds flew. The expected rounds of American artillery, intended to provide cover for an assault, failed to materialize, but nonetheless, the men were ordered to climb out of their foxholes and attack. "Here you have another proverbial moment of truth," said Hillerman. "Would you prefer to charge out of our woods into that snow field and take a machine gun bullet or fail to do so and live with the contempt of your friends and the incurable damage to your fragile nineteen-year-old self-esteem?"[12]

Hillerman charged. The Germans, anticipating a retreat by the outnumbered Americans, were surprised, and Hillerman and the men were able to overrun the enemy's position. New foxholes were dug and Hillerman and his assistant gunner assessed their situation. Night was falling. Mud, fed by rain and melting snow, threatened to fill their foxhole. If the Germans regrouped, the Americans would be unable to hold their position. Before dawn, potato mashers—a kind of grenade mounted on a stick favored by Germans—began to rain down on the frozen and mostly defenseless Americans. From his spot, Hillerman could make out German soldiers rushing toward him, their white snowsuits visible in the fading darkness. He and his assistant gunner ran to where his captain and other soldiers were huddled. The captain ordered the men to line the embankment along the road and attempt to halt the oncoming Germans.

Hillerman pressed himself down into the dirt of the small slope. The embankment, not much more than two or three feet high, afforded little protection. No farther than fifteen feet from him, a young German soldier crested the road. Hillerman watched as the soldier crouched down and aimed his machine gun toward him. Hillerman had three bullets remaining in the chamber of his M1911 Colt semiautomatic pistol, the rest having been wasted shooting wildly during his run from the foxhole. He raised his pistol, pulled the trigger, and watched as a .45 slug slammed into the soldier's upper body, sending him backwards down the incline. "This was face-to-face killing of a man, not the impersonal killing we had done with the mortar," recalled Hillerman.[13]

There was no time for reflection. Voices speaking German rose from where the soldier had fallen. Soon a group of well-armed soldiers would crest the hill. Jerry Shakeshaft, one of Hillerman's best friends from infantry training, was also pinned down on the embankment. He was on his knees holding his carbine above his head and spraying bullets toward the Germans. Shakeshaft instructed Hillerman to roll a grenade across the road. But Hillerman had no grenades left on his belt.[14]

"Somebody throw Tony a grenade!" Shakeshaft yelled. A soldier tossed one over.

"Tony, roll it, don't throw it," Shakeshaft said. "Pull the pin and roll it."[15]

At such a short distance, the five-second fuse meant that the grenade might reach the Germans before detonating, giving the enemy time to toss it back. Hillerman pulled the pin and held the grenade. He counted to two and tossed it low so that it bounced upward as it reached the other side of the road. The grenade exploded just as it descended on the group of German soldiers. "We lay there for a few moments, Shakeshaft beside me now with a carbine, and listened to the screams of those blown away by the grenade fragments."[16]

Hillerman and Shakeshaft rose and ran across an open field toward a forest. The surviving Germans pursued, shooting at them. As the two made their dash for the safety of the trees, Shakeshaft remembered they had left behind their mortar guns, too heavy to carry when running. "God, that's all we need," he thought, "to be taken out by my own mortars." His fear seemed to be realized when a shell landed nearby. But no more followed.

Huffing and puffing, Hillerman and Shakeshaft staggered deep into the woods, where they found cover. They fell down against a tree and sat for a moment, safe from the Germans. Hillerman turned to Shakeshaft. "Did you stop to think over there what would have happened if they had found their grenade first?" he asked. The two men burst out laughing. Then Hillerman found himself engraving into his memory every minute of his encounter with the German soldier. "I always seem to remember his face, although the dawn light made that unlikely." The vision he formed would remain with him for the remainder of his life.[17]

Soon it was back to long days and nights in a wet foxhole. One night, Hillerman heard singing from the German lines. He could distinctly make out the words: "Oh, give me land, lots of land under starry skies above. Don't fence me in." The 1934 song had become a big hit back in the United States the previous year after Roy Rogers sang it in *Hollywood Canteen* and Kate Smith on her radio show. Apparently, the Germans had found a copy of the sheet music among the possessions of a captured American officer. Hillerman knew of the tune from letters but in one of the unusual vagaries of war was hearing it for the first time, sung with a German accent.[18]

Hillerman began running a fever and suspected he had come down with pneumonia. After a couple additional days in a wet foxhole, his fever grew worse. By the time he was able to see his unit's first aid officer, he had a temperature of 102. "That won't cut it," said the medic. "Last month they raised the temperature and now it has to be 103 before I can send you back." He prescribed that Hillerman chain-smoke a pack of cigarettes under the belief it would raise his fever, and handed him a pack. He did as he was told. But Hillerman could not determine if his temperature rose or if the medic simply decided it had. In any case, he was given a seat in a jeep with other patients and taken to the Army Medical Clearing Station at the 11th Field Hospital headquarters in Saverne.[19]

In November and December alone, twenty-three thousand US soldiers were hospitalized from cold-weather ailments. By February, when Hillerman fell ill, the number had risen above thirty thousand, particularly due to the increasing number of trench foot cases. "Combat exhaustion"—the term that had replaced World War I's "shell shock"—added to the number of soldiers being evacuated from the front for medical help. "Psychiatric casualties," a doctor told General Dwight D. Eisenhower, "are as inevitable as gunshot and shrapnel wounds in warfare." Even among those who didn't face gunfire or shells, the protracted Alsatian campaign was producing a number of casualties equaling six divisions of infantry.[20]

The hospital had been full since it set up operations in Saverne two weeks earlier. The staff, who wore an insignia featuring a bear's head created by Walt Disney Studios, tended to a steady flow of patients under makeshift conditions. Hillerman was given a bed between two soldiers with serious wounds. "Both of these neighbors had lucked out. Headed for the Zone of Interior with the Million-Dollar Wound," said Hillerman, referring to the kind of injury sufficiently serious to end a soldier's front-line service but not permanently crippling. "A wound or injury is regarded, not as a misfortune, but a blessing," according to a report from the Office of the US Surgeon General distributed by General Eisenhower to his combat units in Germany. "Something funny about the men you bring back wounded," one stretcher carrier said, "they're always happy."[21]

In Hillerman's case, however, hot food, showers, and rest in a clean bed cleared his lungs and his fever in a few days. Out of bed, outfitted with clean underwear, and back in uniform, Hillerman tried to find out when he would be sent back to his company. No one knew. So he checked himself out of the hospital and boarded a truck near the train station loaded with replacements heading to the front. The new recruits were full of questions, and Hillerman basked in the prestige of being a battle-hardened vet. By day's end on February 8, 1945, he was back with his company.[22]

As rain fell the next morning, Hillerman scurried around to borrow clean trousers, winter boots known as shoepacs, and a gas mask. Like most soldiers, he had gotten rid of his and used the case to store food. But on this day, full regalia was needed. General Anthony McAuliffe, who had famously replied "Nuts" to a German demand of surrender during the Battle of the Bulge, had arrived to review the troops and award medals. Hillerman was slated to receive a Silver Star, the third highest combat decoration, for his gunfight on January 29, 1945.

Hillerman sent his mother a photograph taken when he stood before McAuliffe on the wooden review platform. In the darkness of early morning, one can make out the troops and the forest beyond the reviewing stand. "I've lost all my love for woods like those behind me," Hillerman wrote to his mother on the back of the photo. "They can be most unpleasant at times."[23]

The army's press corps composed a valiant account of Hillerman's heroism. "He, with utter disregard to his life, gallantly remained at his post, armed only with a pistol and hand grenade," proclaimed the announcement from the headquarters of the 103rd Infantry Division. "He fearlessly stood up in the face of enemy fire, simultaneously shooting his pistol and throwing hand grenades into the midst of the onrushing foe."[24]

The end of February arrived and Hillerman's much-decimated company was positioned near Niefern, in northern Alsace, where German forces were still hunkered down. The town was little more than a collection of stucco farmhouses at an intersection, not much different than Sacred Heart, Oklahoma. As in other parts of Alsace, which had gone back and forth between French and German control over the centuries, it was not always clear where locals' loyalty lay.[25]

By this point Hillerman had been in combat in Alsace just short of four months. Winter's grip on the region gave little evidence of ending and Germans continued to stymie American advances. Many of the men with whom Hillerman had trained in Texas, had shared a rough sea passage, and had marched through rain and snow in France, now lay dead in Alsace. "The only way to get home alive," Hillerman came to believe, "was to be wounded seriously enough to no longer be repairable for return to combat." Aerial photographs revealed the fields surrounding Niefern were heavily mined. Before launching an assault, American commanders wanted to capture a German soldier to interrogate about the mines' locations. For the job they selected two rifle squads, both reduced in strength by casualties to half of their usual dozen members, and four mortarmen. Hillerman and his friends Jerry Shakeshaft and Bob Yager were among those chosen.[26]

Hillerman and the other mortarmen were assigned to carry stretchers to bring back the wounded, including possibly their prisoner should he get hurt in the operation. The nighttime raid was postponed for twenty-four hours, however, a worrisome delay as it might give locals time to tip off the Germans. Finally, on the night of February 27, the order to go was given. In near-complete darkness, Hillerman and the men reached the top of a hill above Niefern where Company B was dug in. Hillerman spotted a soldier he had known since his first days as a recruit.

"You guys are surely not going over there tonight, are you?" asked his friend.

"Yea," replied Hillerman.

"Hell, those guys over there have been working all day getting ready for you. They've been setting out mines, they have been zeroing in their mortars on sensitive spots, they've been doing everything."

"When you are told to go, you go," said Hillerman.[27]

The men began their descent toward Niefern, moving as quietly as they could toward the stream at the edge of town. When they got close to the village, most of the soldiers took to the road while Hillerman and a smaller group waded knee-deep through the freezing water. Explosions, machine gun fire, and screams shattered the night's stillness as they crossed a muddy snow-covered field close to the outskirts of the village. The men who had taken the road into the village were under heavy attack. Other Germans hidden at the entrance to the village now opened fire on Hillerman and his men. On their way in the Americans had carefully threaded past the concealed mines. Now they ran. "Enemy fire forced us to spread out into the fields and into the mines which exploded around and under us with devastation, killing, and wounding," recalled Thomas Morick.[28]

Hillerman ran, trying to place each step in the boot prints of the man before him. But one soldier near him stepped on a Schützenmine, known to Allied soldiers as a "shoe mine." Consisting of a hinged wooden box, no bigger than its namesake shoebox, this mine was simply engineered and difficult to locate with a metal detector. If stepped on, the lid depressed downward, detonating seven ounces of TNT. Hillerman and another soldier stopped running and lifted the wounded man onto the stretcher Hillerman had brought with him. The two men, now burdened with the weight of a third, ran for the cover of a barn. "You'd be amazed at how fast you can run carrying a stretcher when you are scared," said Hillerman.

But before they made it out of the field, Hillerman's left foot struck another shoe mine. A loud explosion and an incandescent flash rose from his feet. Lifted into the air, Hillerman feared he would fall onto another mine. Instead, he found himself face-down in the thick mud of the cow pasture. His face hurt and the skin on it burned. He could not see or hear anything. He knew the mines were designed to blow off the lower leg of anyone who stepped on one. "Judging from the victims I had seen, [they] usually did," Hillerman thought. He realized he was in trouble as he drifted in and out of consciousness. "No more pain," he said. "Just warmth, comfort, an incredible sense of peacefulness, or moving slowly through a passageway. Of being welcomed. Of God, or one of His delegates, welcoming me."[29]

When he came to, Joseph Christopherson and another soldier were rolling him onto a stretcher. Christopherson, his twenty-year-old rescuer, was from a town as tiny as Sacred Heart, where his father operated a butcher's shop. Christopherson grabbed the front of the stretcher, raised it up, and began guiding his partner on what he believed would be a path out. Only a few steps later, it was Christopherson's turn to step on a mine. The stretcher fell from his hands and Hillerman was back on the ground. More men rushed into the field to help the injured. Lyall Kniffin, a fellow Oklahoman, and Bob Yager lifted Hillerman up and draped him over the shoulders of one of them in a fireman's carry. This time the group made it off the field, through the creek, and back to awaiting vehicles. In all, four men were killed, two were missing in action and presumed dead, and a dozen were wounded, nine of whom received their injuries while trying to evacuate the wounded from the deadly pasture.

Hillerman was lowered into the back of a jeep. Briefly, he became aware of his surroundings and regained some hearing. "I'm lying there and thinking at least the war is over for me," Hillerman said. He recognized the voice of his captain but could not decipher whatever he said. Two miles to the south, the jeep unloaded the wounded men at a first aid station in Obermodern. There Hillerman received his first medical care. It was brief. His eyes were bandaged shut and antiseptics were applied to his wounds. After a shot of morphine, he was placed on the bottom rack of an ambulance. Christopherson, whose leg had been blown off, was lifted onto the rack above. As the ambulance made its way to a clearing station, warm blood from Christopherson's wounds dripped down onto Hillerman's chin and neck. "Then," Hillerman said, "morphine brought blessed oblivion."[30]

CHAPTER 6

◈ **Wounded** ◈

For the next few days, Hillerman drifted in and out of a morphine haze. The doses that deadened the pain also turned the passing world into a blur. He came to briefly while strapped to a cot in a hospital train heading south along the route that had taken him to the front one hundred days earlier. An orderly told him his legs were broken, his face was burned, but he would be okay. For Private First Class Tony Hillerman the war was at an end but he was alive. Joseph Christopherson, the man who had helped save him, had died.[1]

After a five-hundred-mile journey, the hospital train pulled into Aix-en-Provence, where medics and nurses unloaded their fragile cargo for transportation to the Army 3rd General Hospital on a hill overlooking the picturesque city, just north of Marseille. Originally built for psychiatric patients, the complex had been taken over in wartime by members of New York City's Mount Sinai Hospital.[2]

On March 6, 1945, a week after stepping on the mine, Hillerman awoke in one of the hospital's 1,800 beds, remembering little of the past days. His eyes were bandaged shut, and much of his body was wrapped in a cast. He made out the voice of a nurse, the first woman speaking English he had heard since leaving the United States. She assured him he would be fine but that details about his wounds would have to come from a doctor.[3]

When a doctor finally arrived at his bedside, Hillerman asked if he still had feet. The doctor assured him he did, but said that he would have to wait for an orthopedist to determine the condition of his lower wounds. The doctor then removed the bandages and pads covering Hillerman's eyes. They were swollen shut. The doctor lifted the eyelid of one eye then the other. Hillerman couldn't see. He was blind. "When you are nineteen and that realization hits," said Hillerman, "it's good to have jolly, jolly morphine in your bloodstream."[4]

Hillerman's eyes were burned and contained fragments from the explosion. Most of the fragments had been removed at the clearing station. The burns could be treated and the remaining shrapnel removed. The worrisome issue was that his eyes were infected. If the infection could be remedied, the doctor said, Hillerman should regain sight, at least in the less-damaged right eye. At first, Hillerman's doctor thought it might be best to remove the left eye and concentrate on saving the right one. Instead, he opted to make use of penicillin, which was being manufactured in vast commercial batches for the first time since its discovery as an antibiotic in 1928. Since D-Day as many as one hundred thousand servicemen had fought off dangerous infections with penicillin. Doctors were unrestrained in their use of this miraculous new infection fighter.[5]

Hillerman's eyes were bathed each day and every few hours a nurse gave him an injection of penicillin. The shots were so frequent that the nurse had to find fresh spots on his back and buttocks for the injections. Several days later the doctor removed the bandages. Hillerman opened his eyes. He could discern light, shadow, and the shape of his doctor's face through his right eye. Then the eye began watering up. "Jubilation. I am not blind." A few days later, he began to regain some vision in his left eye, which had been more severely damaged.[6]

Although he could now see, Hillerman remained bedridden with his legs in casts. To determine the extent of the damage done by the mine, Hillerman was wheeled to the X-ray room, a thick-walled cell that had previously housed violent psychotics. The walls of the room were scratched with drawings of all sorts. "The dominating motif seemed to fall back on Mother Nature as a source for inspiration for they were the weirdest drawings of animals we've seen—probably of the Picasso school," according to Dr. Ralph E. Moloshok, a member of the hospital staff.[7]

The X-rays revealed the damage to his legs. On his lower left leg, he had fractured the larger of the two bones, the one that carried his weight, and there was serious damage to the spot where that bone connected to the foot. The mine had also fractured the third bone in his right foot, but that was a lesser concern. Additionally, part of his left boot had been blown upward and cut bone-deep into the skin around his right knee and thigh.[8]

The doctors scheduled operations to repair the fractures and graft skin from Hillerman's rear end onto the right leg. But a shortage of anesthesiologists delayed the procedures. While waiting his turn under the knife, Hillerman was subjected to a custom developed by wounded soldiers on the ward. For each soldier headed to surgery, the men would hold a mock wake, extolling the patient's virtues and sharing tales of operating-room mishaps such as healthy limbs being mistakenly amputated.[9]

Once the surgeries succeeded in realigning the fractured bones, Hillerman could escape his bed by means of a wheelchair. "I would roll it outside," he said, "and sit in the soft spring sunlight of Provence, and dream my dreams." On one such day in May, Hillerman sat in his wheelchair and considered his future. "My career goal since high school had been simple—find a way to make a living which would get me off the farm," he said. He anticipated receiving a $200 disability payment and a $300 check when he was discharged. The money would not last and he, disabled, would return home to compete for jobs against healthy veterans. "I had always been an obsessive reader, especially historical stuff and fiction," he said. "The people who wrote that surely got paid for it. Maybe I could be a writer."[10]

Before the sun had set, Hillerman composed his first literary effort. "Cash in on the war, I thought. Lots of excitement, lots of emotional words, thrills, and so forth," he said. It would be "a short story about the sad fate of replacements—those poor fellows who were sent up to the killing grounds fresh out of training bases." To build the tale, Hillerman mined his experiences on the battlefield, his ride with replacement troops after his short hospitalization in Saverne, and his keen observations of nature. Unlike the city recruits, Hillerman rarely had a moment during the marches across Alsace when he had not spotted or heard birds like the racket from a murder* of crows coming from the woods "having characteristic crow disputes exactly as they did over our alfalfa field in Oklahoma."

Crows open Hillerman's story, as Sergeant Hubble rests against a stone wall "hoping that the crows would fly away from their nightly roosting place and this would somehow delay the coming of darkness." The sound of a German machine gun leads the seasoned officer to assume an inexperienced replacement soldier inadvertently made himself visible to the enemy. The death of another replacement by mortar fire is on Hubble's mind because he can remember the

---

*A flock of crows is often called a "murder" because of the bird's connection in folklore with their scavenging activities from the slaughter on a battlefield.

snow on the dead man's glasses but not his name nor even his voice. "He could hardly remember any of them, not the later ones," Hillerman wrote. "He could sort of remember, but not their faces and not their names. Not any names at all."[11]

At the end of the tale, Hubble meets a lieutenant fresh from the replacement depot in Saverne, where Hillerman had once been. The sergeant takes an envelope and pen from his pocket to write down the man's name. "'I like to remember names,' Hubble said, just glancing at the lieutenant. Lieutenant Eberwine smiled again, a warm and happy thing it was, and Hubble turned away from it quickly. He saw the crows were roosting now for the approaching night." Hillerman tucked away his story. Despite his clever use of crows, it was, like most first efforts from a writer, not a polished work. Yet, it was a beginning.

Eventually Hillerman graduated from a wheelchair to crutches. Wearing a blue bathrobe, in the company of two other similarly clad patients, Hillerman would walk down the hill into town and sit on a bench on a tree-lined boulevard, watching the now-liberated French amble by.[12]

But the nights were long. Many of the men rested on old French metal beds that had been left behind when the psychiatric hospital was relocated. "The groaning and squeaking springs were quite reminiscent of their former occupants," Dr. Moloshok wrote. The war also intruded into Hillerman's sleep. A shout would break the silence, soon followed by others. Screams of "Get down! Get down!" or "Go. Go. In trees. Over there" would echo off the ancient nineteenth-century stone walls. "The sound of combat had spread like a ripple down the double row of beds" Hillerman said, "bringing troubled dreams to the surface." The men called it "Night Music."[13]

In his own recurring nightmare, Hillerman was carrying his mortar gun through the woods. It was raining and he could hear the whistle of artillery rounds in the air and the explosions when they struck the trees. Looking down, he saw Sergeant John P. Arras staring up from a ditch where he lay wounded, muttering something Hillerman could not make out. It was a reprise of the moment, just before Christmas, when Hillerman had come across Arras, who had been blown from the road by an exploding shell. "His expression was stunned," said Hillerman, "but when I shouted to him, he seemed to be trying to laugh."[14]

Hillerman had seen a chaplain only a couple of times in the past four months and, by his own admission, had not attended mass since arriving at the hospital. The war had challenged his faith. The adage that there were no atheists in foxholes was an "absurd lie" now that he had seen the battlefront. "Where else could atheism better thrive than in the killing fields where homicide was honored?" he asked. Now Hillerman sought out a priest to hear his confession. He told him about killing the young German soldier who pointed a machine gun at him but did not mention those who died from the lobbed hand grenade. "He granted me absolution without comment—tired I'm sure of such accounts."[15]

Now ambulatory, Hillerman joined a poker game that began each day following breakfast. The men played seven-card stud, then the most popular form of poker, with a one-franc limit. The game was a welcome distraction from the tableau of mangled bodies and hours upon hours of boredom, and became an obsession for Hillerman and his fellow patients. The game even trumped attending a memorial service for President Roosevelt when word of his death reached the hospital. The game also made Hillerman a smoker. "I bitched and whined about the secondhand smoke, was persuaded that it wouldn't bother me if I smoked myself, was provided free Luckies, and quickly got myself addicted," he said.

As the days turned into weeks and weeks into months, Hillerman continued to heal. He switched from a crutch to a cane, from eye bandages to a single eye patch. At best, his left eye could only see at twenty feet what most people could make out at two hundred feet. In short, he would have been legally blind had his right eye not healed and returned to 20/20 vision. Hillerman questioned the treatment he had received. The infection in the left eye could have endangered his less-injured right eye, a condition doctors call sympathetic ophthalmia, which could have resulted in complete blindness. Hillerman concluded that not having removed the left eye to safeguard the other one and instead treating both with penicillin without his consent had been risky. "Even then, at nineteen, it seemed to me that this was betting a minor inconvenience against an almost total disability," Hillerman said. "But no son of August Alfred Hillerman was conditioned to bear a grudge."[16]

On May 8, 1945, German authorities in Berlin signed documents of surrender. In Aix-en-Provence the downtown below the hospital burst into celebration over the war's end "All the streets were ablaze with lights and wildly careening figures of the celebrating natives stopped all traffic," recalled Dr. Moloshok. "Our reaction was a happy one tempered with the ever-present thought that there was still fighting to be done on the other side of the world."[17]

Despite the momentous news, a clerk at the hospital managed to find the time to prepare Hillerman's papers for his return to the United States. Two days later, with signatures from three doctors and approval from the commanding officer, Hillerman was free to head home. Alsace had taken its toll. Few in his unit returned unscathed.[18]

On May 27, 1945, Tony Hillerman turned twenty. His brother, Barney, sent birthday wishes from Dachau, Germany, where after 511 days of fighting he and members of the Forty-Fifth Infantry Division had come to the end of their service in Europe. There were rumors, Barney told Tony, that the division would be sent to the Pacific. "This war can't last forever though and we'll all be together someday."[19]

A bureaucratic snafu delayed Hillerman's departure. But on June 10, 1945, he boarded a ship in Marseille. Reaching New York City after a sixteen-day crossing, he was taken to Camp Upton, on Long Island. The Red Cross had distributed vouchers to the returning wounded soldiers redeemable for a long-distance telephone call. He placed the first call of his life—there had been no phone in his Sacred Heart home—to the boardinghouse in Oklahoma where his mother lived and left a message that he was back on American soil.[20]

To care for the tide of returning wounded soldiers, the army had put together a fleet of hospital trains to transport the men to military hospitals around the country. Each train was equipped with a surgery room, library, kitchens, and a full cadre of nurses and doctors. Hillerman was put aboard a train headed for Texas. By the end of June, the rolling hospital pulled into Fort Bliss in El Paso, which sprawled over more than one million acres in Texas and neighboring New Mexico, and housed the William Beaumont General Hospital, one of the five oldest army hospitals in the nation.[21]

In July, Hillerman was granted a furlough to continue his recuperation at home. Before going to Oklahoma City, Hillerman wanted to stop in Sacred Heart. Reaching Konawa by bus at the end of a day, he bought a sack of hamburgers, took it, his duffel bag, and cane and limped to the road leading the last few miles home. A cattle buyer named Reid who lived in a neighboring town stopped to offer a ride. He said Hillerman looked like one of Gus Hillerman's boys. Glancing over at his passenger, Reid added it seemed as though Hillerman had "gotten buggered up some in the war."[22]

As they drove down Sacred Heart's bumpy dirt roads, Hillerman recognized trees and fence posts in the moonlight and heard the sound of the bullfrogs in Harper's pond. He noted that Pat Ackermann's house now stood empty and the Hidgon mailbox was missing from the cluster of mailboxes at the intersection near the house.

Reid dropped Hillerman off at the front of his family's old house, now uninhabited. The smell of dust permeated the inside. His path lit by the moon, Hillerman found his way around the first-floor rooms and up the stairs. In the bedroom he had shared with Barney he put his sack of hamburgers on his bed, sat down, and gazed out the window. Clouds drifted across the face of the moon, but when its light shone Hillerman saw that the old pecan tree was gone and the orchard was overgrown.

"Behind me the old house creaked as its timbers cooled and I could smell decay from my bedroom door and drought outside my window," said Hillerman. He knew that the farm was in shambles, fences down, terraces eroded, and Johnson grass overrunning the bottomland. "But I also knew that these were superficial changes, quickly made right again," he said. "The real change was in me, who had been seventeen and now, a moment later, was almost twenty-one."

CHAPTER 7

◈ Enemy Way ◈

"Then I was home," said Hillerman, "standing in our dirt driveway with the sound of Mr. Reid's car diminishing behind me. I had a feeling for a moment, not of coming but of never having been away." Contemplation would have to wait. Hillerman needed to get work. "In the United States in August 1945," he said, "not finding a job would have been downright impossible." A headline in the August 14 issue of the *Daily Oklahoman* read STATE FORECASTS WORK FOR ALL, and the paper bulged with employment advertisements. Accommodations, on the other hand, were harder to come by, at least until Hillerman was employed. Both his mother and sister were working as nurses but living in a rooming house while Margaret Mary's husband and brother Barney were still overseas.[1]

A visit to the state employment office yielded the address of a garage looking to hire. But before going to the place, he walked over to the *Daily Oklahoman*. The largest circulating newspaper in the state, it was housed in an elegant five-story corner building, classical in style, with columns extending its full height. Hillerman went in to meet Beatrice Stahl.

The forty-year-old Stahl had begun working for the newspaper in the 1920s, first as a clerk then as a receptionist. By World War II she was producing a series of features, called "Oklahoma Heroes," in which she wrote up accounts of bravery in war. Earlier in the year Stahl had received news of Hillerman being awarded the Silver Star and located his mother at St. Anthony's Hospital, where she was working. Borrowing the letters Tony had written his mother from the front, Stahl devoted an installment of her series to Hillerman. In HE STOOD FEARLESSLY, published on April 29, 1945, she used army publicity materials and the letters to render an account of Hillerman's January 19 roadside encounter when he shot the German soldier. The article featured a large black-and-white hand-drawn illustration of a GI, with a gun in his left hand, throwing a grenade at Germans in the woods. Stahl's prose elevated the drama of the moment. "The Nazis came pouring toward him, supported by all that they had. He couldn't tell how many. But it didn't matter now. Somehow, he knew that they must be stopped. And it was then that Hillerman no longer crouched beside his broken gun. He stood up."[2]

Stahl had told Lucy Hillerman to send Tony in to see her when he returned home. Hillerman found Stahl at work and the two chatted. Stahl commented to her young visitor how well written his letters were. Had he considered being a writer? "I'd never known one, seen one, ever heard of an actual live one," Hillerman said, recollecting his conversation. How did one become one? "One went to journalism school, she said. And thus the seed was planted," recalled Hillerman.[3]

The garage job did not work out. Hillerman, who retained a reputation of being mechanically challenged for his entire life, was ill-suited to replace brakes. The owner decided Hillerman would be more useful digging a basement at his home. Before Hillerman started on that job, he traveled out to Konawa, the town where he had attended high school. Larry Grove, his cousin, had returned from the war in the Pacific, where he had been wounded by a mortar that badly damaged one of his hands. "He sure was a happy boy to get home and see us and his girl," reported Larry's father. "Tony came down with him and did they talk. You know how they are. One of them couldn't wait for the other one to get a story through before he started telling one and those two boys have both found out a lot about what war is like."[4]

On August 14, 1945, the Japanese had surrendered and the war came to an end. Hillerman caught a ride downtown. "Not everyone was celebrating," he said. "I joined a Marine corporal sitting at a Main and Broadway bus stop and we talked about why we didn't feel happier." The two were not alone. For many veterans who had seen combat, the end of a war that had taken the lives of an estimated sixty-five million people was nothing to celebrate. Corporal Frank Bocchin, who was on furlough, had been eating dinner with his father, sister, and two brothers when the news came over the radio. "I recall that I had a sense of relief rather than joy. I also realized for the first time that all of us had just spent three of the best years of our lives in the service. Years that we could never get back." Hillerman and the corporal left unresolved the question about their mood and instead talked about what they might do now that the war was over. "Neither one of us knew but I spent a moment or two trying to imagine myself as a writer—whatever that might be."[5]

Two weeks into his furlough, Hillerman met a young woman at a USO dance who was planning on entering the University of Oklahoma in September. When he escorted her home, Hillerman was introduced to her father. He was in the oil-drilling supply business. He said he was planning on running a couple of truckloads of equipment to New Mexico where an old shallow well was being reopened. They were leaving the next day; would Hillerman be willing to drive one of the trucks? Hillerman agreed. He could use the money and he liked the girl, who said she would ride along.

"We formed a caravan of two worn-out trucks, credible only to those old enough to remember the days of gasoline and rubber rationing when vehicles were kept running with baling wire and hope," Hillerman said. The girl's father, a burly figure, drove the bigger of the trucks with a trailer loaded down with pipes and the drill stem used to bore through the ground. The convoy moved slowly, especially as the heavier truck could barely climb hills. They traveled through the day and night, taking short rests when they could. "We stopped for gasoline, to refill radiators, check oil, grab a loaf of bread and baloney," recalled Hillerman.[6]

At last they reached Albuquerque and needed to push only a bit farther west to reach their destination. The two trucks crossed the muddy and shallow Rio Grande and began an arduous slow crawl, of no more than eight miles per hour, up and over Nine Mile Hill leading out of town. Exhausted, Hillerman nodded off and his truck bumped into the other one. The pipes on the flatbed missed the windshield and no damage was done. Once they reached the crest of the hill, Hillerman saw a landscape unlike any he had seen in his life. Miles and miles of brown and red desert sparsely dotted with scrub bush opened before him. To his right rose the 11,305-foot dormant volcano called Tsoodził by the Navajos, whose nation stretched west and north from it, and later renamed by settlers after President Zachary Taylor.

Another ninety or so miles west, red cliffs began to run parallel to Route 66. Deep fissures in the cliffs made some of the formations appear like the bows of anchored ocean-bound ships. When they reached the hamlet of Thoreau, pronounced *thuh-ROO* by its sparse residents, the two trucks turned north on a dirt road toward Crownpoint and their final destination on the Navajo Nation, a territory the size of West Virginia.

As they drove on, Hillerman drew closer to what would be the most consequential encounter of his life. A group of Navajos on horseback came out from a piñon-and-juniper thicket and crossed the road. "The riders seemed to emerge as if by magic from that red cliff of pink-and-salmon sandstone that forms the southwest wall of Mariano Mesa," Hillerman said. Some wore ceremonial clothes and had their faces painted. One man carried a pole with something that looked like a flag at the top. "Had he been a Kiowa or Comanche, I would have called it a 'coup stick,'" said Hillerman, referring to the sticks used among Plains Indians connected to prestige in battle. On closer examination, he realized the stick carried a long-billed cap, probably from a Japanese soldier.[7]

A few miles later, while unloading the trucks, Hillerman asked the rancher receiving the equipment about the Navajos he had seen. "He tells me the delegation I saw was the 'stick carrier's camp' bringing some necessary elements to an Enemy Way ceremony," said Hillerman. "He's heard this was being held for a couple of Navajo boys just back from fighting the Japanese with the Marines."

When the United States had entered the war four years earlier, Navajos remarkably rushed to enlist. It had been the US government, after all, that had evicted them from their land in 1864. The forced march to Bosque Redondo in eastern New Mexico and the return on foot when the government relented on its relocation plan in 1868 resulted in the deaths of hundreds. The story of the Long Walk, as it became known, had been repeated to each generation ever since. Later this horror was compounded by the needless slaughter of their sheep and the virtual kidnappings of their children to be placed in boarding schools. Yet Navajos responded to the government's call to service by sending three thousand men and women to battle. One group of recruits eventually became famous as code talkers for developing a code based on the Navajo language as a secret means of communication. The large majority of the enlisted Navajo served with distinction as soldiers in all the branches of service. Upon their return, tribal members, led by a medicine man, would carry out an Enemy Way ceremony to help restore the combatants to *hózhó*, the Navajo term for personal harmony.[8]

As Hillerman continued to ply the rancher with questions, the latter suggested he simply go and watch the ceremony. "If the stick carrier was just getting there today it would be still going on through tomorrow night," the man told him. So, that evening, Hillerman took himself down to a bonfire surrounded by Navajos. He likely arrived at the point in the multiday event when the participants had moved to a campsite alongside a road several miles from the main ceremony. Hillerman heard the chants and watched the dancing to the beat of four drummers. He saw the two marines who, like him, were glad to be home. With an injured leg and an ill-functioning eye as constant reminders of the war and his wounding six months earlier, Hillerman took it all in. "I thought about all the people I knew who fought the Japanese and just hated them," he said. "What a difference this was from the way I was greeted coming home. More than any single thing, this chance encounter caused me to be attracted to the Navajo way.[9]

The dances and aspects of that night remained with him all the years since. "My imagination has transmuted them, as imagination does with good memories," Hillerman reflected years later. "Gradually accumulated knowledge of Navajo metaphysics has illuminated them, giving religious meaning to what I saw."[10]

The following day the oil equipment man paid Hillerman and told his daughter, who had apparently lost interest in Hillerman, to give him a ride back to Thoreau. "From there I hitched back to Oklahoma City to while away what was left of my self-esteem and furlough time."

Hillerman had unfinished business with the military. He needed to return to the hospital in Texas for another operation on his ankle and to complete his discharge. At Tinker Air Force Base, outside Oklahoma City, Hillerman began a series of plane rides over several days that left him running late and hitchhiking from Phoenix across southern New Mexico to the hospital near El Paso, Texas. He reached William Beaumont General Hospital four days past the end date on his furlough document, which Hillerman admitted to surreptitiously extending with some clever typing before leaving on furlough.

He presented his document to the officer of the day. "Four days AWOL then," said the officer. "What's the excuse?" Hillerman's training provided only one correct answer to such a question and he told him he had no excuse. "He is pleased to hear that, a good sign," said Hillerman. The officer adjusts the dates on the form and dismisses Hillerman.[11]

For reasons not given, the promised ankle operation did not occur and Hillerman was told to report to the headquarters building. There he received back pay, discharge money, an envelope of documents, and an offer to enlist in the Army Reserves, which he declined. "Thus, a few minutes after noon on October 16, 1945, I became a bona fide twenty-year-old unemployed civilian with a notion that I'd become a journalist—whatever that might prove to be."

Once again in Oklahoma City, Hillerman was reunited with his brother. The two drove out to Sacred Heart and briefly considered reopening the family farm. But they determined the economics were not promising and it might take years to break even. "Finally, I didn't want to be a farmer," said Tony. So Barney, Margaret Mary, Tony, and their mother, Lucy, gathered to make plans. Lucy would sell the farm. Margaret Mary would continue working as a nurse and await her husband's discharge from the military. Tony and Barney would use the GI Bill to attend the University of Oklahoma. "The decision," said Tony, "disconnected us forever from agriculture and, sadly, from Sacred Heart." But for the widowed mother, the war was over and her boys were home safe. With the proceeds from the sale of the farm, Lucy purchased a three-bedroom, one-bath, bungalow in Norman, one mile north of campus, where she and her two sons could live while the young men attended the university.[12]

CHAPTER 8

❖ University of Oklahoma ❖

L ucy, Barney, and Tony's move to Norman was well timed. Housing had suddenly become scarce in the city of fifteen thousand. The GI Bill had unleashed a torrent of more than one million veterans heading to college just in the first year after the war. At the University of Oklahoma (OU), the 7,406 arriving veterans raised the enrollment to 12,531 students, making the university the twelfth largest in the United States. "The campus was overrun with veterans whose only desire was to hurry up, make a C average, get a degree and get on with life," Hillerman said.[1]

OU president George Lynn Cross found the new crop of students more serious than students of the prewar years. Their grades were certainly better than the nonveterans. He also believed his GI Bill students were more philosophical about obstacles in their path. "This acceptance was probably due in part to the sobering effect of the war," Cross said.[2]

Passed by Congress in 1944, the GI Bill provided veterans who wanted to attend college with tuition, fees, school supplies, and a monthly stipend for up to four years, depending on the length of their service. For Tony, Barney, and their cousin Larry Grove, this translated to an all-expenses-paid college education and an allowance of $65 a month, more than sufficient for all other expenses. A college education that had seemed out of reach for Hillerman's generation of farm kids was theirs for the taking.[3]

The university accepted many of Hillerman's credits from his brief time at Oklahoma A&M as well as his time on campus as part of the Army Specialized

Training Program. In addition, he was granted advanced standing for his military service. His grades at OU were a marked improvement over his first dismal attempt at college prior to joining the army. In the summer he took his first three journalism classes: Fundamental Photography, Newspaper and News Writing, and Mechanics of Newspaper Typography. The future writer received a D in Advanced Composition, the lowest grade he would get during his time at OU.[4]

In January 1947, with three semesters successfully completed, Hillerman accelerated his pace of learning. He signed up for the maximum permissible course load while continuing to earn mostly Bs. His impatience to reach the finish line was shared by most veterans. "They have a sense of the urgency of tomorrow," as an Ivy League professor told a *Life* magazine reporter.[5]

Like almost all journalism students at OU, Hillerman's path through the curriculum led him to Professor Harold H. Herbert's classroom. A former Illinois newspaper editor, Herbert joined the university's faculty when the School of Journalism was established in 1913. Since then the school had grown from twenty students to four hundred. By the time Hillerman was one of Herbert's students, the professor had iconic status on campus. In fact, aside from one professor in Wisconsin, he had taught journalism longer than anyone else in the United States. Hillerman took three classes from the highly respected professor: Reporting Public Affairs, Editorial Interpretation, and Ethics and Laws of the Press, earning Bs in all three. Herbert's teachings on ethics found a receptive listener in Hillerman. "Whether or not it's legal, constitutional, or fair, a career in journalism carries power, Herbert told us."[6]

While Herbert inspired his student on matters of ethics, editorial writing, and public affairs, it was Professor Grace E. Ray who honed Hillerman's writing skills. Ray had studied under Herbert when she had obtained bachelor's and master's degrees at OU two decades earlier. She was a popular professor who used her extensive freelance work to find assignments for her students. She carried a passion for precision into her classroom. Ray was particularly intolerant of what she called "cornstarch" words that could be crossed out with no effect on the meaning of the sentence. "Like barnacles on a boat's bottom," Hillerman recalled Ray saying, "they slow down the sentence, reduce its force, make you sound like an English major." Studying under Ray, Hillerman developed a tight, spare writing style. She taught him, in his words, "to say precisely and exactly what one intended to say with no wasted words." It would prove a skill valued by the wire services, the mainstay of newspapers and radio news programs of the era.[7]

Less than a year after arriving on campus, Hillerman began writing for *The Covered Wagon*, the campus humor magazine. At the time, most college campuses supported a humor magazine. Yale University's *Record*, started in 1872, had been the first. The publications attracted many talented students with writing aspirations. F. Scott Fitzgerald worked on the *Princeton Tiger*, and James Thurber wrote for *The Lantern* at Ohio State University. Invariably the publications focused mostly on sex and drinking. *The Covered Wagon* was no exception. In that era suggestive cartoons, alluring photographs of female students, and bawdy jokes were a widely accepted staple of the publication. Typical of its humor were two staff-written jokes that appeared in the March 1947 issue just after Hillerman joined the magazine.

CO-ED: I had a date with an absent-minded professor last night.

FRIEND: How did you know he's absent-minded?

CO-ED: Well, he must be. He gave me a 'D' on my history test this morning.

And:

It's amazing what some women can get away with, and still keep their amateur standing.[8]

Hillerman introduced himself to *The Covered Wagon* readers in January 1947 with a short story about Walter Wenchless, a veteran who had come back to college. Daydreaming in class one day, Wenchless imagined himself hunting in the bush. "He heard one of the savages creeping toward him," wrote Hillerman.

Then a voice interrupted his catnap.
"Wenchless," the voice repeated. "Is Wenchless here?"
"Damn right, I'm here," Walter shouted. "Come and get me."
The professor laid aside his class roll sheet and eyed Walter coldly. "Young man," he said, "your being a veteran does not give you the right to speak like that. Get out of my class."[9]

Hillerman followed this story with "First Epistle to the Freshmen," in which he provided seven admonitions for dealing with advisers, professors, teaching assistants, roommates, and various aspects of campus life. "Lo, all ye miserable freshmen who enter through the gates of admissions into the land of knowledge promised ye by the Father in Washington, called G.I. Bill," wrote Hillerman, "hearken to my words: for I have dwelt in this land for many semesters and mine eyes have witnessed all manner of folly and woe."[10]

During the remainder of 1947, readers of *The Covered Wagon* grew familiar with Hillerman's droll pieces. "Tony Hillerman found a following for his 'Fifth Wheel' feature every month," reported one observer. For the October homecoming edition of the magazine, Hillerman penned caricatures of professors of law, botany, math, and English, complete with spoof footnotes such as "Charles Darwin believed Botany Professors to be descendants of monkeys" or "crocodile birds pick the crocodile's teeth but to our knowledge, no engineer has gone that far for a math professor." His description of the English professor was the cleverest of his four targets. They are descendants of ones brought by the Pilgrims, wrote Hillerman. "Many historians believe that the rapid westward movement of early American colonists was due to their attempts to escape the multiplying English professors, who they believed would not flourish in the forests."[11]

But Hillerman's most original contribution was the charming "The Night Santa Claus Got It" published in the holiday issue at the end of year. It followed OU psychology professor McDermott who, on Christmas Eve, is determined that his kindergarten-age son Bobby should not believe in Santa Claus. "He wouldn't allow a son of his to harbor any mythological delusions and as a result he could sleep late in the morning," wrote Hillerman. In his living room that night McDermott encountered a red-suited, portly man with a large sack, whom he presumed was a burglar. "I'll catch this bandit and end this boy's illusion for good," said the professor, retrieving his duck gun from the closet. When the bearded intruder dashed for the window, McDermott shot him dead.

"Sani Claw?" asked the boy upon seeing the body. No, replied the father. It is a man disguised like Santa to steal presents. The boy next looked out the window.

"Daddy," he said, "hosses in the garden."

"Nonsense," roared McDermott. "Go back to bed."

"Lots of horses," Bobby insisted, "eating your geraniums."

The professor strode angrily to the window, jerked back the drapes, and looked out into his garden lit by the bright moonlight. Six reindeer hitched to a sleigh were waiting there, eating his geraniums.[12]

At times during his student days, Hillerman felt left behind as his friends found girlfriends and wives. By the beginning of his senior year, half of his fellow veterans were already married, and all of the husbands were also fathers. Statistically, it was not easy for men to find female companionship at OU. Women made up less than 25 percent of the student body. "I was feeling way down and blue," said Hillerman, "rejected by young women, looking back at a wasted youth, looking forward to an infinite unknown of unpromising blankness." But Hillerman's luck changed on an October evening in 1947. He and his friend Robert Huckins, whom he had met on the bus after being drafted and had served with in France, decided to attend a dance sponsored by the university's Catholic Club in Newman Hall.[13]

The hall, built in 1926, was owned and operated by the Sisters of Divine Providence, a nineteenth-century Catholic order established in Germany. Despite its Catholic connection, the place was open to students of any faith. The thirty-six women residents maintained an academic atmosphere and frequently had the highest scholastic record among the residence halls. "Staying up all night to cram for exams and a lot of play after they are over is typical of the college life of the girls at Newman Hall," said one of the residents.[14]

By 1947, college dances had resumed the atmosphere of a meeting spot filled with hope rather than the sense of urgency that permeated the gatherings during the war years, when the partner with whom you waltzed could be sent overseas before the next dance. The music, as well, had grown optimistic. Gone from the airwaves were songs such as Kate Smith's rendition of Kermit Goell's "Wonder When My Baby's Coming Home." In its place, Francis Craig sang a new Goell tune, "Near You": "Make my life worthwhile," he crooned, "by telling me that I'll spend the rest of my days, all of those happy, happy days, so near you." Punch bowls became places where couples talked of their days to come.

For the occasion, Hillerman dressed in a cashmere sports coat he had bought for four dollars from a housemate at Oklahoma A&M before the war. It was still the only dress jacket he owned. At the dance hall, he leaned against the wall. He no longer wore an eye patch but still carried a cane when he went out. Dancing was a challenge. As he looked over the men and women dancing, he spotted a tall slender woman with shoulder-length wavy dark auburn hair parted on the side, laughing and enjoying herself. "I pushed myself away from the wallpaper," said Hillerman, "tapped her dancing partner on the shoulder, and asked if I could cut in." The two danced briefly as they made introductions. The conversation began poorly when he asked if she were a freshman. The senior overlooked the faux pas and told her dance partner she was Marie Unzner, a microbiology and education major from Shawnee. After a slow dance for which Hillerman had mastered the steps, he resumed his post against the wall and watched as other men took turns dancing with Unzner. The following day Hillerman found he could not stop thinking about the woman with the enchanting brown eyes.[15]

Marie Elizabeth Unzner had lived in Newman Hall for all four of her years at OU and was now its president. Popular and outgoing, Unzner was known for her willingness to help classmates with their studies or tend to friends who fell ill. "Anyone who needed help, she would help," recalled her younger sister, Teresa Sifford. "She loved everyone, and everyone loved her."[16]

In the days following the dance Hillerman took Unzner to the movies, armed with tickets from a friend who worked as a projectionist in a downtown theater. She took him to a basketball game. Hillerman, the would-be writer, offered Unzner, the would-be scientist, help with her English literature papers. She accepted and came to the *Covered Wagon* office, where Hillerman now served as features editor, to work on the papers together. Unbeknownst to Hillerman, it was the working typewriter that most drew her to the office. She was not an admirer of the magazine and its antics.[17]

Hillerman received a promising invitation from Unzner to accompany her to Shawnee to meet her family. While his connection to *The Covered Wagon* was off-putting, his personality and war service soon won over the family. In particular, the family was impressed with Hillerman's earnestness, Catholicism—both he and Marie had been educated by Sisters of Mercy—and modesty: "He never bragged on himself," recalled Teresa Sifford.[18]

With the help of one of his more worldly friends, Hillerman obtained an affordable engagement ring. Marie accepted the proposal in early spring and the two set a wedding date for the following year. Unzner's parents were relieved by the planned yearlong engagement because they hoped their daughter would first earn a master's degree. But as graduation neared, the young couple's ardor was such that they decided they couldn't wait an entire year. They informed the Unzner family while eating in a Norman steakhouse. The news so upset Marie's mother that she ordered apple pie à la mode as an entrée.[19]

Journalism students hoped to cap their studies during their senior year by assuming the leadership positions on one of the three student-run publications: *The*

Sooner Yearbook, the *Oklahoma Daily*, and *The Covered Wagon*. In the fall of 1947, Hillerman had worked briefly for the *Oklahoma Daily*, serving on several occasions as issue editor. Among the articles he filed was a profile of twenty-one-year-old senior Mary Ruth Souter. The history major, according to Hillerman, had logged two hundred hours of flight time since becoming the youngest woman pilot in the United States at age fifteen. Souter, reported Hillerman, "can't be convinced that flying is a man's game."[20]

Hillerman decided against remaining with the paper. Instead he persuaded the university publication board to appoint him editor of *The Covered Wagon*. Selecting the humor magazine over daily journalism provided Hillerman with a chance to publish his nascent fiction. He knew his post-college paycheck would come from a news-writing position, but he continued to dream of writing stories and novels. The editor's job also gave him an outlet to write about hijinks absent from his college life. There was a tension among veterans between their serious approach to schoolwork and their envy of the carefree college pleasures enjoyed by the younger students who had come directly to OU from high school. With one semester left, *The Covered Wagon* became Hillerman's last stop on his way into the world. He would make the most of it.[21]

In January 1948, Hillerman took control of the magazine. Joining him were his brother Barney as a photographer and cousin Larry Grove, who gave up being sports editor at the *Oklahoma Daily* to become Hillerman's associate editor. "We were to convert the prewar magazine into a postwar magazine," said Hillerman, "appealing to a campus swarming with mostly males just out of the Army, Navy, or Marines." The financial arrangement, according to Hillerman, was that the editors and staff were entitled to 10 percent of the profit, but the magazine had not made a profit in years. "We decided," Hillerman said, "we were going to make some money out of it and the way to do it was to stir up some interest."[22]

Driving up to Oklahoma City, he and Barney found the story they needed at the Club Jamboree. In December, plainclothes police officers had arrested club performer Evelyn West after she completed her number "Revelations of 1947." She was charged, according to the *Daily Oklahoman*, "with putting on an indecent dance, sans clothing."[23]

Tony, in words, and Barney, in photographs, prepared a two-page feature story on what they found. Their report portrayed the club and reviewed the provocative entertainment. After witnessing Bronya's striptease act, Hillerman described her costume's weight as diminishing from nine pounds to three-eighths of an ounce in the course of her dance. "Anyone caught within the Jamboree club during the floor show is in danger of severe eye strain," he reported.[24]

Hillerman said one performer claimed her nudity to be the cutest and was "ready to prove it at the drop of a G-string." Another's act, added Hillerman, required that the club host pass among the audience "collecting eyeballs in a dust pan." His tone was dismissive of the city's concerns about the goings-on at the club, suggesting the legal case revolved around "how much of Evelyn West's ample bosom could be exposed to the unsophisticated eyes of Oklahoma citizens without endangering their morals."

Barney's photographs caught the performers still clad but in suggestive poses with lots of leg showing. One of the five photographs was of Tony interviewing Bronya, seated with her skirt pushed back and her arm draped over him. "Well," wrote Hillerman in the accompanying caption, "you didn't think I'd put out my first issue without my picture in it, did you?"

A WAGON EDUCATIONAL FEATURE: CULTURE COMES TO INDIAN COUNTRY was published in the first week of February with a Valentine's Day cover. Accompanying the brothers' report on the Club Jamboree, the issue included articles lampooning the student newspaper and the university president's habit of not commenting to the press, along with pages of indelicate jokes. Even though it was a target of the magazine's humor, the *Oklahoma Daily* reported the issue "was generally considered 'tops' in the wagon history by the student body." The administration, however, found nothing to laugh at.[25]

Meeting on campus, the university board of regents took time from their planned agenda to discuss the content of *The Covered Wagon*. Afterwards, President Cross instructed the university's publication board, which had appointed Hillerman as editor, to consider the regents' objections to what they termed the "vulgar sexiness" of the Valentine's Day edition. After a closed-door meeting with a member of the board, Hillerman defended the content of the magazine. "Why, it was all in fun," he said. "I thought everybody would know that and get a big bang out of it." Hillerman even quipped about the regents' interpretation of the jokes. "Some of those gags must have had a double meaning I didn't catch." The tempest passed. EDITOR RETAINS POST AT OU, announced the *Daily Oklahoman* two days later. Hillerman, it reported, "was back at his desk pouring [*sic*] over copy and pictures for his forthcoming issue."[26]

The next issue showed no evidence of a retreat. The cover featured a female student in an oval tin bathtub, soap bubbles strategically placed and long legs reaching upward. Hillerman told readers that he and the staff had not been bothered by the regents' complaints until they were widely publicized. "As it stands now," he said, "we're damned if we do and damned if we don't."[27]

"If you can't find anything risqué in this issue," he told readers, "you'll think we backed down, turned yellow and so forth, and we've had it as far as you're concerned. On the other hand, if you do find anything risqué, we've had it, period, and hello Oklahoma A. and M." A further dig at the regents followed when Hillerman told readers that signed laudatory letters to the magazine are printed with the writer's name. "You'll notice we didn't print the names of any regent members," he said.[28]

On the evening of May 31, 1948, Hillerman and Unzner took their places among 1,714 seniors in a half-mile-long procession entering Owen Stadium for the largest graduation ceremony in the history of the state.[29]

In his final semester at OU, Hillerman had added a one-credit course to his six-class schedule. Taught by special assistant professor of zoology Mrs. A. I. Ortenburger, Marriage Orientation was based on a series of lectures "Looking at Marriage" that she had given to women students. The series of talks had proven so popular that students successfully petitioned to add it to the university curriculum.[30]

Now well trained as a journalist, engaged to be married, and perhaps suitably educated in matrimonial matters, Hillerman was ready to begin his quest for a spot on a newspaper staff. But what had been a surplus of journalism jobs when he began his studies was gone. "By the summer of '48 in America the surplus was unemployed young men home from the war, graduating from college, and eager to get on with it," he said. "All my applications drew blanks."[31]

CHAPTER 9

❖ Borger ❖

On an early June day in 1948, Tony Hillerman piloted his Ford sedan westward down Route 152 across the desolate Texas Panhandle toward the city of Borger. For most travelers, an ever-present black cloud in the distance signaled they were nearing the oil town whose newspaper's masthead proudly proclaimed it the Carbon Black Capital of the World. Produced by burning residue from the gasoline refining process, carbon black was used in rubber tires, as well as in paints and inks. Borger's plants worked overtime to meet demand, all the while pumping into the air a fine powder that rained down on the town like coal dust in a Victorian British city. Women in Borger would wipe down their clotheslines and check the prevailing wind each day before hanging their laundry out to dry. Boys who played outside would come in with legs black from the bottom of their shorts to their socks. Carbon black combined with the smell of sulfur and oil—described by town boosters as "the smell of money"—made Borger an industrial boil on the flat lands of the Panhandle.[1]

A telephone call had put Hillerman on the road to Borger. The caller, an editor from the *Borger News-Herald*, said he had gotten Hillerman's name from Oklahoma University professor Harold Herbert. Would Hillerman be interested in a six-days-a-week reporting job on the paper that paid $55 a week? It was a dollar less than the average wage for an American, but when a week's worth of groceries at Latimer Grocery or White Way Grocery No. 1 in Borger went for $11.05, it was good money for a first job out of college.[2]

The editor didn't know it, but there was no question regarding Hillerman's answer. Since graduation, Hillerman had only found one job. He had gone to work at an Oklahoma City advertising agency, penning commercials for Cain's Coffee Company, a brand much favored by Oklahomans, and for Ralston Purina Pig Chow, the choice of many farmers for their pig troughs. The job and Hillerman were such a mismatch that he feared his one-week trial period would end with a dismissal. The call from Borger had been a rescue line.[3]

Hillerman's Ford crossed the Hutchinson County line and entered the city, coming to a stop near the one-story *Borger News-Herald* building at 207 Main Street, completing its 250-mile journey from Norman. The *Borger News-Herald* published an afternoon edition during the workweek, ranging in size from four to eight pages, and a thirty-eight-page morning edition on Sundays. Typical of many small-town newspapers, the front page was dominated by international, national, and state news provided by the Associated Press and the Newspaper Enterprise Association. J. C. Phillips, who ran the paper, was obsessed with communism. He reserved a portion of the front page each day for hyperbolic reports and ominous warnings of the growing red menace, including a series of articles in the summer of 1948 written by FBI Director J. Edgar Hoover entitled Don't Be Duped by the Communist Party.[4]

Other than reports on the Hutchinson County Anti-Communist League meetings, local news rarely earned a spot on the front page. Rather, it was on the inside that readers could find out what was happening in city hall or at the county courthouse, who was running for office, or how the oil business was faring, along with chatty columns about the weather, gardens, rodeos, and the comings and goings of residents. Interspersed among the dense pages were comics such as *Our Boarding House with Major Hoople, Li'l Abner, Blondie,* and *Superman.* On Sundays, *The Katzenjammer Kids, Henry,* and *Flash Gordon* made their appearance.

The newspaper, like most businesses in Borger in 1948, was prosperous. Its pages were filled with advertisements touting chenille bedspreads for $5.00 and Stylespun nylons in 30 denier* for $1.49 at Anthony's; black-eyed peas, two cans for 25 cents, at Panhandle Associated Grocers; and Blatz beer for $3 a case at Star Liquor Store.

The *Borger News-Herald* building was new, as was every brick building Hillerman could see up and down Main Street. In fact, Borger was only a year

---

*Denier is a measurement of the nylon or silk; the smaller the number, the finer the weave. Dress stockings are usually between 10 and 15 denier.

older than the twenty-three-year-old Hillerman. Yet, as young as the city was, it had a storied history. In 1926, oil had been discovered on ranchland that made up most of Hutchinson County's treeless landscape bisected by the slow-moving Canadian River, a 906-mile-long tributary to the Arkansas River. Within three months oilmen and fortune seekers overran the spot some fifty miles northeast of Amarillo, bringing with them the usual retinue of bootleggers, card sharks, prostitutes, and other nefarious types. Asa Phillips Borger, known to most as "Ace," rushed over from Oklahoma, where he had developed two oil towns, and immediately bought up 240 acres of land. He persuaded the state to approve his Borger Townsite Company, drew up property lines, and published a map. Within six months every lot was sold. Before the end of the year, a city stood where a few months earlier cattle had grazed on little bluestem grass and eastern gamagrass.[5]

Corruption flowed through the city like the oil in the surrounding fields. The first mayor, in cahoots with his chief law enforcer Richard "Two-Gun Dick" Herwig, gave a free hand to a crime syndicate that ran the gambling rooms, dance halls, and brothels. The frequent murders and rampant corruption attracted the attention of the governor in Austin, five hundred miles to the south. He dispatched a detachment of Texas Rangers, who quieted the town for a short while. Finally, after the assassination of the district attorney, the governor imposed martial law. It worked. The city was freed from crime and corruption. However, Ace Borger did not live to see much of his town's spiffy new image. A rival murdered him as he picked up his mail at the post office. Some vestiges of the not-so-old days remained. Borger's assailant was acquitted despite having plugged the town's namesake with five bullets. By 1948, when Hillerman arrived, the town's early life was the stuff of bar tales and the forty thousand city and county residents enjoyed a mostly quiet and prosperous life in a town where front doors were rarely locked.

On one of Hillerman's first days at the *Borger News-Herald*, reporter and photographer Fred Lawrence took the paper's newest staff member out to show him the police station, sheriff's office, and other stopping points that Hillerman would need to hit each day as the paper's new crime reporter. A fire truck rushed by as Lawrence and Hillerman made their way down Main Street. From the radio, Lawrence learned of an explosion at the Phillips Petroleum Plant two miles outside the city, and they pursued the caravan of emergency vehicles.[6]

At the gate to the plant, security officers stopped their car while letting others through. "They know me and I can't get past them," Lawrence said. "But," he added, "they don't know you." So Hillerman exited the car. Joining the large crowd inside the gates, he took notes for the first time as a professional reporter. He learned that three workers had been sandblasting the ten-foot-diameter interior of a seventy-foot tank used for water storage. Witnesses to the explosion told Hillerman they had seen one body flying high in the air. Two workers had died and the third was being transported to the hospital in fair condition. The story, without a byline, made the front page of the paper. "My career," said Hillerman, "as professional journalist was thus launched."[7]

That the two dead men were fellow Oklahomans was not a surprise. Hillerman may have left his native state, but Borger was virtually an Oklahoman outpost. One early settler calculated as much as 90 percent of the settlers were from the Sooner state. "Everyone there was a wayfarer, moving through, headed someplace else," said Hillerman.[8]

Over the next weeks, Hillerman became acquainted with Borger. Each day, after checking in at the office, he and the other two or three reporters would stroll up Main Street for breakfast at the M. E. Moses five-and-dime. Then, following a few hours back in the newsroom, Hillerman would make his rounds. Reading law enforcement logbooks, clerks' notes on complaints, and reports of arrests were, as Professor Herbert had drummed into his students, the first duty of a reporter on the crime beat. In comparison to its raucous past, the city was quiet in the summer of 1948. But, like any American community, it had its share of crime, especially that perpetrated by transients. The man in charge of protecting Hutchison County citizens was Sheriff Hugh Anderson.

Standing six feet, one and a half inches tall, with trim physique, piercing blue eyes, a ruddy complexion, and never without his light-brown Stetson hat, Hugh Anderson was a dominant figure in Borger. He had begun his career in law enforcement eight years earlier when he was hired as a deputy at age thirty-one. Two years later, in 1942, he decided to run for sheriff but withdrew from the race to enlist in the Coast Guard as a criminal investigator during the war. At the end of the conflict, he returned to Borger and ran successfully for sheriff.

Although Borger had its own police force, the sheriff remained the chief law enforcer in both the city and county. Anderson projected confidence and had a reputation for honesty. But he was also known for administering his own personal form of justice when he felt a case called for it. In Hutchinson County young men apprehended for petty crimes were sometimes given until the end of the day to enlist in the armed forces. Conmen and grifters were provided a not-too-gentle ride to the county line, and suspects sometimes arrived at the county jail bruised and battered. Within two days of being on the job, Hillerman met Anderson.[9]

Three robbers had come down from St. Louis. The gang leader was twenty-six years old and his two accomplices were only eighteen. They had begun their crime spree in St. Louis when the two younger members hid in a department store ventilation room only to discover their partner had locked them in. Crawling through an air vent, the two made it into the store and got away with three pistols. With their newly acquired arsenal they approached a jewelry store. The pair of teenagers entered with their pistols, leaving the older member of the gang outside. The robbery was an instant failure. The jeweler took the gun away from one of the two and called for help. The other would-be robber got rid of his weapon and they both fled.[10]

The hapless gang left St. Louis by bus to Tulsa, where they stole a car and came to Hutchinson County. In the hamlet of Pampa, just east of Borger, they waved their pistol at Mrs. W. B. Simmons, who was behind the cash register of her family's store. Unlike their previous attempts at robbery, this time they made off with some loot, a modest take of the few dollars that had been in the till.

"At this point the gang ran into Texas law," wrote Hillerman in his first bylined front-page story. A roadblock was set up, but in their fast car the men escaped both it and a pursuit by Deputy Tex Cotter. "They had less luck when Sheriff Anderson spotted their speeding car on its way to Borger," Hillerman reported. Anderson gave chase, easily keeping up in his Ford Mercury Eight. When the engine rods of the robbers' car gave out, they surrendered without a struggle, having ditched their gun during the chase. "The fact that the three desperadoes chose not to fight it out with Anderson who was alone indicated their respect for Texas law enforcement," Hillerman told his readers, adding a quip from the gang leader that "these big-hatted Texas lawmen are liable to kill somebody."

Hillerman's story was headlined TRIO HAS RESPECT FOR TOUGH TEXAS OFFICERS. Its favorable account of Anderson's quick work may have been a reflection of Hillerman's training under Professor Herbert. Most reporters learn early that a flattering piece about an important source when beginning a new beat can pay dividends.

Afterwards, Anderson told the young reporter he was thankful to have made a rapid capture of the crooks. Not having done so, he explained, might have given the FBI time to take over the case and, in Anderson's mind, complicate matters. For Hillerman, the moment was an insight into the rivalry between local and federal law enforcement not often visible to the uninitiated. In the army, Hillerman had witnessed the same sort of friction between soldiers and West Point–trained officers. Even in Sheriff Anderson's world, there was the "us-versus-them" division that Hillerman had learned of in Sacred Heart, but this time it applied to those in the front trenches of law enforcement.[11]

Hillerman spent an increasing amount of time with Anderson, either in the sheriff's Borger office, which was also occupied by the highway patrol, or having pie and coffee at the Snack Shack, a few blocks from the newspaper building on Fourth Street. Anderson drove his own car, paid for his office and all his expenses using a line of credit, and billed the county at the end of the month. Such was the sophistication of rural American law enforcement.[12]

One day, while Hillerman sat at a table sorting out his notes, two teenage women burst into the office demanding that their father be arrested. They reported their younger sister had gotten the family's truck stuck. When she got her father to come help, he raped her. "She should have known better," said one sister. Anderson took out a complaint form, completed it, and handed it to one of the sisters for a signature. After she signed it, Anderson said he would go out and make an arrest.[13]

"Wow," said Hillerman, "I'm thinking. An incest rape. How do I handle this one without identifying the victim?"

Anderson, who had been watching Hillerman take notes during the two women's visit, asked if he was going to report this.

"Sure," said Hillerman.

"About an hour after I get their daddy locked up they'll be back telling they won't press charges," said Anderson.

"How do you know?" asked Hillerman.

"Because that's the way it happened the last three times."

And he was right. Events unfolded just as Anderson predicted. "I had met," said Hillerman, "a cop who tempered justice with a sort of humane wisdom." Two decades later, Hillerman would remember Anderson when he began creating a police officer for the first of his mysteries. The conflict between the FBI and local jurisdictions, which Hillerman first learned of in Borger, would also show up in the conduct of his fictional Navajo cops.

Working on a small-town paper, even with an assigned beat, Hillerman did all types of reporting. Under his byline, he told readers about recent Borger High School graduate Nettie Lott Lindsey's departure on a fifty-day, eleven-nation tour of Europe and traveled to Lubbock with the Borger Gassers minor league baseball team.[14]

Hillerman also did his share of reporting based on his own news gathering, what editors call enterprise journalism. In one piece he reported on how citizens could run afoul of odd, forgotten laws still on the books. "If you are responsible for any goose being loose within the corporate limits of Borger, you're trifling with the law, chum, and subject to a fine," wrote Hillerman. Furthermore, your goose could be sent to the city pound at a cost to the owner of $2.50 plus $1.00 a day for room and board. Another front-page story certainly gave readers a momentary pause when they learned that operating a beauty parlor in one's dining room was illegal, as was spilling water on a public thoroughfare. "Borger was a fine place to learn—about being a reporter and about myself," Hillerman said, looking back on his time in the city.[15]

One day he drove up to Stinnett, the county seat. Stopping in at the courthouse was a usual part of Hillerman's rounds. Outside the Spanish Renaissance Revival courthouse, with friezes depicting oil drilling and ranching, Hillerman got to talking with a young highway patrolman when a radio call announced a fatal car crash a dozen miles away. The two men regained their cars and sped northward.[16]

The accident scene was gruesome. The driver of one car had been impaled on the steering wheel, and blood, teeth, and tissue were splashed about, said Hillerman. The patrolman moved away from the site trying to control his nausea while Hillerman continued taking notes. The pale officer looked over at Hillerman in astonishment at his calm demeanor. "All I could say to explain it was that it's not so bad when the dead are not your friends."

The psychological scars of war that made Hillerman more impervious to blood and death than the patrolman were still tender. Hillerman's fellow members of Company C, almost all of whom had made a point to see each other within a year of returning home, also reported trying to rid themselves of recurring nightmares. "A deep, deep burn costs one the feeling in a fingertip," said Hillerman. "Perhaps seeing too much ghastly casual death does it to a nerve somewhere behind the forehead bone."

Despite succeeding in his first reporting job, Hillerman found Borger to be a lonely place. Marie Unzner remained at home in Shawnee, Oklahoma, a separation made more difficult because neither could afford long-distance phone calls. By their May graduation from OU the couple had already broken their resolve to wait a year before marrying. "We agreed to cut that to six months, getting married the following winter," he said. "By July, with much playing on her sympathy, I got that cut down to a month."[17]

As the chosen date—August 16—neared, Hillerman's bosses granted their young reporter the weekend off plus two extra days. In preparation for the wedding, he had gone to the hospital in Borger to have his blood drawn and tested, a requirement for the Oklahoma marriage license, and sent the results on. On the Friday before the planned Monday wedding, Marie's brother Charles phoned Hillerman in the newsroom. Oklahoma, he said, required that the blood work be done in state. Hillerman left the office and drove north over the Oklahoma border to a clinic in Guymon. The plan failed when he learned the test results would take a week. The wedding was now less than seventy-two hours away.[18]

In despair, he retreated to Borger. At day's end it was decided that the only way the test could be completed in time was for Hillerman to come to Oklahoma City and try the Catholic St. Anthony's Hospital, where his mother and sister had worked during the war. But before getting back into his Ford, Hillerman had to borrow money as the banks were now closed. Sheriff Anderson, coworkers, and city police all accepted IOU notes from the would-be groom in a panic.

Hillerman set off in the rain, clothes in the backseat and $61 in his pocket. But no more than thirty miles into his journey, his car slid in the mud, went off the road, struck a car entering the road, and came to a rest in a ditch. His mother's admonition over the phone earlier that day to have faith and to remember that nothing is impossible with the aid of prayer must have seemed dubious as Hillerman sat in his car nursing a bloody forehead, bandaged by the uninjured driver of the other car, as the rain continued to fall.

The Pampa police, amused and sympathetic, provided a cell for the night, and in the morning Hillerman resumed his journey by bus. His brother, Barney, now working in Oklahoma City, met Tony at the bus station and drove him to St. Anthony's. The hospital lab had been persuaded to remain open. The test

was completed. Now the results needed to reach the Pottawatomie County clerk
before the early-morning wedding on Monday

At sunrise on Monday morning, Marie woke in her family's well-appointed
Shawnee home and took to the piano to play her favorite tunes and savor her
happiness. Like Tony, Marie came from German Catholic stock. Her paternal
grandfather had settled in Oklahoma around the time of the 1877 land rush and
had married a German immigrant. He and Marie's father were leatherworkers,
known for their harnesses and saddles. In comparison to her future husband,
Marie had been raised in comfortable circumstances in what a boy from Sacred
Heart might have judged a city.[19]

Savoring her anticipation, Marie and her family, with the sole exception
of her brother Charles, had no idea of Hillerman's travails with blood tests, a
car accident, and his night's lodging in a police cell. They dressed and got into
their cars, with no doubt they would find the groom waiting at St. Benedict.
When the organist played "Here Comes the Bride," Tony was standing at the
altar dressed in a one-button white dinner jacket, a thistle-shaped bowtie, and
a rose boutonnière, a look popularized that decade by Humphrey Bogart in
Casablanca. By his side stood his best man, Barney. Marie's brother Charles's
many connections and owed favors had come through, and the blood test results
had reached the county clerk in time.

Tony watched as Marie's father, Charles, escorted his daughter down the aisle
clad in a duchess satin gown with Juliet sleeves, a basque waist overlaid with
lace peplum, and small covered buttons rising up the center of the dress to a
mandarin collar. On her dark coiffed hair rested a tulle veil. She was the first of
the three young women in the Unzner household to be married: the sisters Marie
and Teresa and cousin Gesina Clarkson, who had come to live with them as a
young child following her mother's death. Joan, as she was called, was treated
like a daughter.

The Unzner parents had been resistant to their daughters or niece being
married before they earned graduate degrees. Charles Unzner, in particular, had
ambitious professional aspirations for the young women, unusual for fathers in
that era. He strongly believed that women without a superior education would
have no choice but to assume a domestic role. When Marie agreed to the earlier
wedding date, it meant putting off graduate school. But her mother and father
acceded because of their trust in her choice of a husband.[20]

Later in the morning, the new Mr. and Mrs. Hillerman bade goodbye at a reception given by family friends, he in a dark suit and tie, she in a high-collared white jacket and dark skirt. As Tony's car remained in its inoperable state in the panhandle, Barney lent the couple his car, the entire back window of which had been painted with "Just Married." (There goes any chance of my getting a date, Barney quipped.) Following a twenty-four-hour honeymoon in Dallas, Tony and Marie returned to Borger. For their first home, Tony had rented an apartment at 410½ West Grand Street, a converted two-car garage on the dirt alley running behind Grand. Its tiny living room and bedroom were furnished with worn-out furniture Tony had purchased at an inflated price.[21]

Marie, who never let anything dampen her bright disposition, went about transforming their ramshackle dwelling into a home. White lace curtains went on the kitchen windows and she, like most Borger housewives, began her battle against the carbon black dust that seemed to find its way in no matter what. Soon after settling in, Marie moved the furniture out to properly scrub down the place. Having just finished her toil, she was still in her dust-laden clothing when Tony came through the door, having brought home the newspaper's editor to meet his new bride. An embarrassing moment soon turned into family lore.[22]

Marie landed a job as a seventh-grade teacher. She was given a difficult bunch to teach. "'They are good kids,' Marie would insist, who never saw one who wasn't," said Tony. Their simple life was filled with joy. Approaching the garage home after a day of work, Tony took comfort knowing, in his words, "Marie was in there waiting for me, ready to swap stories and turn the day's misadventures and disappointments into fun." On Sundays, Tony's one day off work, the newlyweds would begin their day by attending St. John the Evangelist, the only Catholic church among the town's twenty-two houses of worship.[23]

After six months at the paper, Tony had risen to city editor. The new responsibilities meant longer hours but no additional pay. As had happened when he was stuck writing commercial jingles, Hillerman received a providential telephone call. This time it came from Larry Grove, cousin and co-conspirator on the troublemaking articles published when Tony ran the University of Oklahoma's *Covered Wagon*. Larry had taken the job of sports editor at the *Lawton Morning Press* in Lawton, Oklahoma, and was calling with an invitation from the paper's management that Hillerman come north and take the city editor slot.

CHAPTER 10

❖ Feeding the Wire ❖

Veteran Oklahoma state capital correspondent Otis W. Sullivant spotted a new United Press (UP) reporter at the capitol one day in 1952. Little escaped Sullivant's attention. On the state legislative beat since 1927, the forty-nine-year-old reporter was said to hold such power that if he wanted an interview, he would simply summon the person. Indeed, that is how the new UP reporter, twenty-seven-year-old Tony Hillerman, found himself sitting in a chair by Sullivant's desk in the narrow and dim pressroom, steps from the rotunda still lacking a dome thirty years after the state ran short of money to finish its capitol building.[1]

Tall, wiry, unsmiling, and laconic, Sullivant began by asking Hillerman about his job with UP and where he had worked before. The journalist was known for taking an interest in young reporters and often helping them develop their skills. He said he'd heard Hillerman was a farm kid, and he wanted to know where and if he had chopped cotton, picked bole weevils, or castrated calves. "Satisfied on all those scores," Hillerman said, "Sullivant wished me well." To be noticed in such a manner by the dean of the Oklahoma press corps was a heady moment for Hillerman.[2]

Sullivant also introduced Hillerman to an old saw that he would cherish and frequently repeat. Hillerman had interviewed the state senate majority leader. "Otis read it, called me to his desk, tapped a finger on my byline," said Hillerman.

"You write this thing?" he asked.

"Yes, sir," Hillerman replied

"Kid, you want to know how to tell when a politician is using you?"

"Sure."

"When you ask 'em a question, watch their face. When their lips start to move, they're lying."[3]

It had been three years since cousin Larry Grove had called Hillerman in Borger, Texas, to let him know about the job opening at the *Lawton Morning Press*. General Newspapers Corp, which operated a chain of newspapers, had purchased the *Morning Press* in 1948. To compete with the more established *Lawton Constitution*, the company had gone on a hiring spree, picking up newly minted reporters from the University of Oklahoma's School of Journalism, including Grove and now Hillerman.

When the Hillermans arrived in Lawton in January 1949, they found a town that shared some traits with Borger. Lawton was also an instant city, born in the summer of 1901 when twenty-five thousand people came to bid on homesteading lots after an "agreement"—the polite term used by town fathers for seizing the land—had been reached with the Comanche, Kiowa, and Apache tribes who lived there. Although it was the same size as Borger, Lawton had shed its frontier coarseness. Wide streets laid out in neat alphabetic and numeric order gave it a citified sheen.

Instead of oil, the source of Borger's prosperity, Lawton owed its good fortunes to the military. It was home to the massive Fort Sill, where Hillerman had first gone as an army inductee in the summer of 1943. The war had been good to Lawton. The population had doubled in the past ten years, and the city could afford to build a new industrial park and complete a 4,750-foot runway at the airport. But Lawton's claim to fame was an annual passion play in the nearby Wichita Mountains, started in 1926. By the time the Hillermans moved to Lawton, the program drew more than 200,000 people each year and was seen in newsreels by countless more. Movie theaters in Lawton were readying to show the world premiere of Hollywood's version, *The Lawton Story of The Prince of Peace*, starring child actor Ginger Prince.

As they had done in Borger, Tony and Marie rented a garage apartment. This one, however, was on the second floor and accessed by a steep steel staircase, perhaps not the best option for a now-pregnant Marie. The couple obtained better quarters in a multiplex apartment building when Marie found work in a Fort Sill laboratory. Yet even these left much to be desired. The sound of tenants coming and going could be heard through the plywood walls. So thin were the walls, claimed Tony, he could hear "the sound of his neighbor's razor blade scraping off his whiskers." Diesel train engines idling nearby shook the poorly built complex. "First the pictures on the wall would shake, then dishes and pans would rattle, and soon the apartment would be filled with the sound of tinkling, clicking, and clacking," remembered Tony.[4]

The 184-mile journey from Borger to Lawton had liberated Hillerman from a dead-end job and put him behind an editor's desk with potential for advancement. The new hires like Hillerman were charged with filling the morning paper with local stories so as to leave only news crumbs for the *Lawton Constitution* by the time it reached the streets in the afternoon. The enlarged and ambitious staff made up for its inexperience with long hours and hard work. The paper increased the number of pages in each day's edition, added a sixteen-page Sunday magazine, and dropped advertising rates. "We were beating the staid *Constitution* on stories, our circulation was way up, the big advertisers were beginning to buy big advertising space," said Hillerman. As one observer noted, "The *Press* soon was waging an all-out circulation war against the *Constitution*." But the progress didn't last long. After the paper supported the losing side in a bitter mayoral election and the publisher who had invigorated the paper departed, the *Lawton Press* began hemorrhaging money.[5]

On May 9, 1949, Hillerman was working late at the city desk. Emmett Keough, the associate editor of the *Lawton Constitution*, appeared in the newsroom and went into editor Frank Hall's office. The clattering of typewriters ceased and conversations paused in midsentence. The idea of an editor from the rival newspaper stopping in was unthinkable. "There was no socializing between these papers," said Hillerman. "We ate at different coffee shops, drank at different bars, ignored one another at news conferences."[6]

After a while the door to Hall's office opened and Keough crossed the newsroom and left. Hall then came out and walked to Hillerman's desk. He handed him an announcement and told him to publish it on the front page. The next morning the headline read MERGER OF PRESS AND CONSTITUTION SCHEDULED SUNDAY. Under the terms of the deal, Hillerman's paper would continue to publish except on Sundays when the two newspapers would bring out a combined edition. Hillerman kept his job, as did Larry Grove, but he was bitter. "It finally seeped into our innocent skulls that we were the front-line troops in a fairly typical example of capitalism in action. Our goal was to cut the Constitution's profits deeply enough to make buying us out cheaper than competing," he said looking back on the merger.[7]

In July, Marie, six months pregnant, and Tony escaped the summer heat by driving to Santa Fe, New Mexico, with an eye to finding work there. Tony's fellow Oklahoman Lloyd Lacy worked for the *Santa Fe New Mexican*. Near Clayton, New Mexico, a few miles from the Texas border, Tony and Marie stood by their Ford and watched a high plains thunderstorm roll in. "The air, hot and humid across Texas, was suddenly cold and—for a flatlander—incredibly transparent," said Tony. "There was an artillery of thunder, a heady ozone smell, and a dazzling aftermath of rainbows that made the stormy sky luminous with color."[8]

In Santa Fe, the Hillermans stayed in Lacy's adobe house on the picturesque Acequia Madre. Tony visited the *Santa Fe New Mexican* offices, where he introduced himself to editor Will Harrison, a hard-drinking, seasoned editor well known in journalism circles. He took no interest in Hillerman. Unknown to Hillerman, the syndicate involved in the Lawton newspaper war had a financial stake in the *Santa Fe New Mexican* and was rumored to be trying to displace publisher Robert McKinney. "Thus, Harrison presumed I was a syndicate mole, assigned for either spying or sabotage," Hillerman wrote years later when he finally learned the reason for the prompt dismissal. Vacation at an end, it was back to Lawton. But the visit to Santa Fe planted the idea in Tony's mind that the colorful capital could be a great place to be an editor.[9]

In the meantime, the couple found a cozy and quiet house in Lawton suitable for their firstborn, whom Marie delivered on October 2, 1949, at the small Southwestern Clinic Hospital. Soon thereafter, Anne Margaret Hillerman was baptized at the Blessed Sacrament Catholic Church. The Hillermans were well settled in Lawton, except for Tony's job at the merged papers. He wanted to leave despite having received a pay raise. He did some freelance reporting for the *Daily Oklahoman*, both to earn extra money and to attract the attention of editors in the state capital. His efforts paid off when Carter Bradley, the manager for United Press in Oklahoma, called to offer him a job in the Oklahoma City bureau. "Now I had a job that might lead somewhere," Tony said.[10]

On his first day at the UP office, Hillerman found everyone on telephones or typing. He stood waiting for someone to welcome him, presuming he would be introduced to the staff. Instead, Bradley nodded his head toward an unattended phone that was ringing. Hillerman lifted the receiver.

"United Press," he said.

"Stockers," said the voice on the line, which immediately began listing cattle price quotations from the Oklahoma City Stockyard. Hillerman, grabbing a pencil and paper, madly copied down the stream of numbers. Bradley watched and then came over. "Use your head," he said. Instead of writing the information twice, he told Hillerman to type it directly onto the teletype. "The basic and all-important skill of being a journalist (as opposed to a writer) is information collection—and that was an area of Bradley's genius," said Hillerman. Bradley was also a product of the University of Oklahoma School of Journalism. A half-century later, Hillerman would give Bradley a highly complimentary cameo appearance in the last novel he wrote.[11]

Despite the disconcerting first hour, Hillerman was grateful for the post of staff correspondent. The hours were regular and the pay included a two-week annual vacation thanks to a contract negotiated by the American Newspaper Guild. By this point, two years after graduating, Hillerman had worked on three newspapers and covered stories ranging from weather disasters and sensational murder trials to contentious elections and sleep-inducing commission meetings. "I felt pretty good about my writing," he said. "But in the United Press bureau in Oklahoma City I had dropped into a den of bona fide pros."[12]

The pace of the work quickly determined which reporters were cut out for the wire service. United Press and Associated Press reporters were the workhorses of the industry. A newspaper reporting staff had the luxury of picking and choosing what they wrote about, knowing there was wire service copy to plug the news holes. As a wire service reporter, Hillerman had to cover everything.

Print reporters often view themselves as feeding copy to fill a cavernous daily news hole. Here, there was a deadline every minute. The slave masters of wire service reporters were the teletypes dedicated to national, state, sports, entertainment, and market news. "Each machine was delivering something that needed attention, was waiting in dreadful silence for you to feed it with something new, or was producing the Ding, Ding, which signaled the need was extremely urgent," said Hillerman. He soon became habituated to typing his stories directly into the teletype. As he composed a sentence the first words were already making their way down the wire. "It was an unorthodox way to learn English composition," mused Hillerman, "but it quickly conditioned the brain to manipulate the language and to zip through the stored vocabulary for those nouns and verbs that fit the need without a clutter of modifying adverbs and adjectives."[13]

The editors also wanted brevity. They often told him to cut 40 percent of the story while preserving all the important information. "Before long I learned to write a 500-word story in 275 words," Hillerman said.[14]

Two men helped complete Hillerman's unofficial postgraduate education in journalism. Phil Dessauer, who had worked on the staff of the *Daily Oklahoman* before joining UP, edited Hillerman's copy. "Dessauer, a fine writer himself, went about his duties with tact, understanding the tender egos of learners," said Hillerman. He would praise Hillerman for a submitted bit of reporting, then tell him to cut it in half. "Bad for the ego," said Hillerman, "but good if you're trying to learn how to master the language." The other mentor was Howard Wilson, who had been reporting from the capitol for thirteen years. Hillerman met him when he was reassigned to the capitol bureau. "Wilson was a genius at finding leaks, at getting politicians and bureaucrats to talk when their best interest told them silence was wiser, and at learning what (and who) the special interest lobbyists had up their sleeves."[15]

As a wire service reporter, whether in the bureau or at the state capitol, Hillerman was called on to write news copy on topics from political corruption to sports. He fed the wire with the doings of Governor Johnston Murray, who as an enrolled member of the Chickasaw Nation was the nation's first elected Native American; activities of political parties; and meetings of state boards and commissions, and of course, the legislature.

Hillerman followed corruption probes, writing information-laden ledes filled with atmospherics, what editors refer to as second-day stories. "An unprecedented series of politically poisonous investigations have strained the nerves of vote-conscious state capitol bureaucrats this summer, and the end of the probes seems nowhere in sight," reported Hillerman. Among the discoveries made by the investigators, Hillerman told readers, was the existence of a "shadowy 'flower fund' amassed from a two percent assessment on employees in the office of the Examiner and Inspector."[16]

Hillerman did his own excavating of malfeasance. He reported that further discoveries of misspending awaited investigators. "If Crime Bureau agents, now probing dealings of the State Emergency Relief Board, dig deep enough they'll find the office saw fit to spend $5.70 of the taxpayers' money for a case of Puss 'N Boots cat food."[17]

Hillerman was also called on to write sports stories. On a fall day in 1951 when winds were blowing an icy drizzle, he returned to his alma mater to cover the Sooners' football game against the University of Colorado. "Oklahoma's Eddie Crowder, the quarterback who 'couldn't pass,' knocked Colorado out of the Big Seven conference lead in 17 minutes Saturday with four straight touchdown tosses and then helped his team roll to a crushing 35–14 victory."[18]

During his off hours, Hillerman returned to the dream of being a writer that first came to him during his convalescence in the Aix-en-Provence army hospital. While still in Borger, he had again tried his hand at a short story. He unsuccessfully circulated to magazines a 2,900-word story, "The Cockroach in the Cast," about pranks pulled by soldiers in a military hospital.

Now, two years later, Hillerman tried again to publish a short story. This one was a Western, complete with cowboys, a gunfight, and a lady in distress. At the end, a sobbing woman runs into the arms of the hero who, after rescuing her, vows he will never run "errands" for her again. "But, as she pressed against him," wrote Hillerman, "he knew it wasn't so. He'd be running errands for Ellen for about the rest of his life."[19]

Hillerman's paycheck came from journalism but he dreamed of one day writing fiction.

CHAPTER 11

❖ Santa Fe ❖

When Tony and Marie Hillerman batted around ideas about their future together, he confessed his ambition was to edit a state capital newspaper, preferably in neighboring New Mexico, which he had first seen in 1945 when delivering oil equipment. In late September 1952, a path that could bring him closer to his goal opened. One night, when he showed up to work a late shift at the UP office, his boss told him the Santa Fe bureau chief had resigned. Would he want the job? he asked. The following day Hillerman was behind the wheel of his aging sedan rolling down Route 66 bound for New Mexico. Marie, always stalwart, remained behind to pack up and sell the house with their two-year-old daughter underfoot. And, as Tony had left with the car, mother and child had to take the train to Santa Fe when the Oklahoma City house was sold.[1]

For the fourth time in as many years, the Hillermans took to the road in pursuit of Tony's journalistic advancement. Now he and his hopes traveled the same route that two decades earlier had carried Okies away from the dust bowl. John Steinbeck, one of Hillerman's favorite authors, had enshrined Route 66 in the nation's consciousness. His 1939 *Grapes of Wrath* described the plague of dust, floods, and unscrupulous land dealers that drove people from their lands. "From all of these the people are in flight," wrote Steinbeck, "and they come into 66 from the tributary side roads, from the wagon tracks and the rutted country roads. 66 is the mother road, the road of flight."[2]

In 1952, a traveler would enter Santa Fe by way of College Avenue (later renamed Old Santa Fe Trail), which passed by the seventeenth-century San Miguel Chapel and led to the Plaza and the ancient Palace of the Governors at the heart of the city. The route was a quick introduction to the city's infatuation with adobe architecture. Bypassed by the railroads, Santa Fe remained unaffected by the modernization that usually accompanied economic growth. The city of twenty-seven thousand was as it had been for years, an exotic collection of aging adobe buildings along winding streets, many of which were dirt.[3]

The preservationists did have a gem to safeguard. Not only was Santa Fe picturesque, but it also possessed a storied history. Originally the site of an Indian pueblo known as Oghá P'o'oge in the Tewa language, the spot became the center of Spanish colonial rule in 1610 when it was designated the capital of the northernmost province of New Spain. The new rulers renamed it La Villa Real de la Santa Fe de San Francisco de Asís (the Royal Town of the Holy Faith of Saint Francis of Assisi), soon simplified to Santa Fe.

In 1680, Pueblo Indians rose up in rebellion and expelled the Spanish in the first successful war of independence in North America. In 1692, however, the Spanish returned and reimposed their rule. In the years following, Santa Fe served successively as the capital of Nuevo Mexico after Mexico's independence from Spain, then as the capital of the New Mexico territory after the United States won its war with Mexico. By the time Hillerman arrived, Santa Fe was marking its fortieth anniversary as a state capital, New Mexico having been admitted into the union in 1912. Not only could it lay claim to being the oldest capital city in the United States, but at seven thousand feet it was also the highest in elevation.

Several populations coexisted in the state. Pueblo Indians still lived in dwellings dating back almost a millennium, while Navajo and Apache peoples occupied large tracts of reservation land. Hispanos, denoting those who traced their lineage back to the conquistadors, dominated state politics, church life, and music. Completing the mix were newcomers like Hillerman, who were designated as Anglos. "The Hispanos, then, were the social cream," said Hillerman. "All others were Anglos, whether their origins were European, African, Asian, Samoan, or Turk."[4]

The departing UP bureau manager took Hillerman around to introduce him to useful sources. It took only a few handshakes before Hillerman got an earful about how Santa Fe had declined, particularly since the arrival of the Tejanos, the disparaging name locals had taken to calling wealthy Texans who were making the city into their summer playground. Despite those complaints, the city still had a large population of colorful, eccentric, artistic, and oddball characters.

"The situation in the autumn of 1952 gave tyro [beginner] political reporters such as myself scant time to enjoy them," said Hillerman. Feeding the insatiable demand of the UP wire came first.[5]

Hillerman's title as bureau chief meant he supervised a staff of one inexperienced reporter while the rival Associated Press (AP) bureau had a staff of six. Unlike in Oklahoma, UP was new to the state and a weak competitor to the AP. Hillerman would have to churn out reams of copy. He began each day with stops at the state government offices, looking for tips, gossip, and news. Even though it was a state government, the size and scope of its jurisdiction over fewer than 700,000 people was similar to that of a county government like those in rural Westchester, New York, or Milwaukee, Wisconsin.[6]

After completing his rounds, Hillerman would make his way to the office on Marcy Street, just a few blocks from the Plaza. Office might be a generous term. The UP bureau occupied a small room crammed with three teletype machines, a filing cabinet, a couple of chairs, but only one desk and one typewriter. Even reaching home at 6:30 in the evening did not mean an escape from work. His home telephone number was written down next to phones in state police headquarters and other offices. "It wasn't a job that allowed time for relaxing," said Hillerman.[7]

His post, however, gave Hillerman a chance to learn more about Navajo culture, which had gained his attention and interest during his 1945 encounter. In March 1954 he went out to Window Rock, the capital of the Navajo Nation that stretches across the corners of Utah, Arizona, and New Mexico. The Navajo Tribal Council was reconsidering its 1940 ban on peyote use following news that one out of every six members of the tribe was using it. Describing the "tiny, button-shaped cactus bean" as "the keystone of a strange religion," Hillerman filed an article quoting an Anglo pharmacist and an Anglo sociologist but no Navajos. "Since the bean is the key ingredient in ceremonies of the Native American Church," Hillerman predicted, "the issue will be freedom of religion."[8]

It was not long before his reporting was noticed by editors at the *Santa Fe New Mexican*, which occupied the building next door and was the state's leading political paper. Five months after starting work in Santa Fe, Hillerman wrote about a shakedown at the state penitentiary, following the fatal stabbing of an inmate, that had uncovered a stash of handmade knives and rope of sufficient length to scale the wall. State police officials were under orders from the governor to keep the results of the search "confidential" but Hillerman found troopers willing to talk. The *Santa Fe New Mexican* ran Hillerman's UP story on page 1.[9]

The following day correctional officials invited the press to the prison, where they offered supposed evidence, often contradictory bits of information, to disprove Hillerman's reporting. Even though he didn't work for the *Santa Fe New Mexican*, the paper came to Hillerman's defense. Referring to him as "an experienced and reliable newsman," the paper's lead editorial said it was "highly debatable" whether anything said by state officials "proved or disproved Hillerman's story." Any inaccuracies, if they existed, would not have been disseminated had the state been more forthcoming with details of the shakedown, opined the editorial board.[10]

After almost two years of nonstop work with UP, Hillerman's superiors reorganized the wire services operation in New Mexico and opened a bureau in Albuquerque. With no staff, Hillerman's already impossible schedule worsened. Robert M. McKinney, the publisher of the *Santa Fe New Mexican*, asked Hillerman to join his paper as news editor. Hillerman accepted the offer and, in July 1954, walked across the parking lot separating the UP office from the Santa Fe New Mexican building. For the first time in four years, Hillerman was back at work in a newspaper's newsroom, with its symphony of ringing telephones, dinging teletype bells, and clattering typewriters, the air thick with cigarette smoke laced with the smell of printer's ink wafting out of the adjoining press room.[11]

Established in 1849, the *Santa Fe New Mexican* was the West's oldest paper. McKinney, who had been a successful New York financier, had bought the paper in its centenary year for $560,000. Though not as large as its rival *Albuquerque Journal*, the *Santa Fe New Mexican* was widely read, well respected, and often had the scoop on state politics as the capital's newspaper. Politics was its life blood. "Its readership" said Hillerman, "depends on political news to approximately the same extent as that of *Playboy* magazine depends upon bare skin."[12]

"Most publishers, we believed, were easy to fathom," Hillerman said. "Robert McKinney wasn't." Nonetheless, the two men had a lot in common. They were tall, lanky Oklahoma natives and University of Oklahoma graduates—both of whom got in hot water as editors of campus publications—World War II veterans, and storytellers. In fact, before he became a newspaper publisher, McKinney had published a book of his poetry with Henry Holt and Co. "We knew that well-used language was important to him—a value sadly rare among publishers as a class," Hillerman said.[13]

At the same time McKinney's aristocratic airs were off-putting to Hillerman's country-boy sensibilities. On several occasions Tony and Marie dined with the McKinneys in their resplendent home in Nambe, to the north of Santa Fe. Marie fretted whenever the invitation came, and for good reason. Shawnee and Sacred Heart upbringings left them ill prepared to sup in a candlelit dining room, furnished in English antiques, with a uniformed server hovering about. McKinney paid a great deal of attention to the running of his newspaper, much to the chagrin of his employees. The newsroom staff found McKinney to be abrupt, demanding, and often tactless. When the publisher was appointed ambassador to Switzerland, Hillerman was said to have joked, "We've never had trouble with Switzerland before, but this might be the start of it."[14]

Hillerman's seven years of reporting, especially his time with UP, made him a valuable member of the paper's staff. When not at the editor's desk, he supplemented the modest-sized staff's output of hard news stories and wrote bylined features on such topics as a couple training a bloodhound for rescue work, a profile of a state supreme court justice, how the state government watched over its fleet of cars, and even a little sports copy.[15]

In January 1957, a storm coming up from Mexico blanketed northern New Mexico with up to six inches of snow. For a water-starved state, the storm brought welcomed relief. But when a second storm arrived on its heels, a good thing turned dangerous in some of the state's isolated communities.[16]

The *Santa Fe New Mexican* got a tip that a freight train on the Denver and Rio Grande Western Railway, which had been built across the southern portion of the Rocky Mountains in the 1880s, was stranded atop Cumbres Pass on the Colorado border. The railway was trying to keep a lid on the story, after it had failed to halt trains crossing the 10,022-foot pass at the height of the storm. A rescue train was now also stuck in the snow. In addition to the crew members trapped in trains, section men who had been working on the rails were also marooned at the top. In all, as many as sixty men were now in need of rescue.[17]

The story was too good and too close by for Hillerman to remain at his desk. He reached the small village of Chama at the same time as a detachment from the army's Mountain Winter Warfare School and Training Center in Hale, Colorado. The men brought two M29 weasels, small vehicles designed for cold-weather use in World War II, with treads like gigantic rubber bands that could travel over soft ground and snow. The weasels had not returned from their initial rescue attempt by the time Hillerman filed his first dispatch. Instead, he reported on conditions and what he could learn about the stranded men.[18]

He put his story on the front page and it was sent out on the AP wire, a source of pride for any news reporter. But after coming all this way, Hillerman was still reporting from the sidelines. At last Hillerman talked his way into a ride on one of the weasels. With the reluctant consent of the commander of the army detachment, Hillerman set off through the snow. Watched by a crowd of sixty onlookers, the two machines pulled out of Chama and roared down State Route 19, now a snow trail. Four miles out the weasels began their climb up to the pass, past snow-filled canyons and buried cabins.[19]

"Further up, four elk, led by an antlered bull, could be seen floundering slowly through the trees," observed Hillerman. "They moved behind a stand of fir without a glance at the noisy weasels below them." The drivers decided to turn back after the engine of one of the weasels died. A failed attempt to tow the disabled vehicle back caused the group to crowd into the other weasel. Spending the night in subzero temperatures was not an option. As they neared Chama, they picked up an exhausted CBS cameraman who had tried to ski up to the stranded trains. The following day Hillerman's words and photographs dominated the paper. Soon the last of the stranded men was rescued with the functioning weasel, and plow trains began to cut a path to reopen the pass. Eleven months later, Hillerman's coverage took second place in the straight news category of the New Mexico Press Association competition.[20]

In his role as the editorial page editor, Hillerman could shed the writing straight-jacket he wore when working on the news pages. McKinney gave Hillerman full license to represent the paper's opinion, particularly on local items, reserving commentary on national and international events for himself. At first, Hillerman wrote staid commentary on such topics as the beauty of the aspens in the fall, traffic safety, and the March of Dimes. But over time, he developed a quiet folksy style salted with occasional bits of humor and vitriol.

While his tone was often droll, Hillerman also used the page to chastise the behavior of public officials. School Superintendent Irving P. Murphy ran into Hillerman's literary buzzsaw when he forbade a reporter from viewing records, as permitted by law, to learn whether athletes were getting an academic break. "We hate to spoil the fun, but to confess that those mysterious 'certain persons' to whom Mr. Murphy refers aren't representatives of the Mafia—they are just us," Hillerman wrote. "We are the sneaky fox causing the cackling in the chicken coop. But honest Injun, Scouts Honor, we don't intend to blackmail anyone, break up any homes, or make an assault on the 'human dignity and worthwhileness' which the superintendent avows to protect." The superintendent quit his job the following year and Hillerman's editorial took second place in the New Mexico Press Association contest.[21]

Perhaps inspired by his stint as editor of the University of Oklahoma's humor magazine, *The Covered Wagon*, Hillerman enlivened the editorial page by mischievously enlisting the help of a Mrs. H. Pincus, a Texan who summered in Santa Fe. She had first appeared in the pages of the *Santa Fe New Mexican* in the spring of 1954, while Hillerman was still working for UP. Her one-sentence letter to the editor came after news reports that the city was considering paving over the Acequia Madre, a centuries-old irrigation ditch. "If you people in Santa Fe cover the Acequia Madre," she wrote, "I'll never come back."[22]

The acequia was not paved and Pincus returned to Santa Fe, at least judging from the letters to the editor in 1957. But, according to reporter Lew Thompson, a classmate who coincidentally had preceded Hillerman as editor of *The Covered Wagon*, Pincus did not exist. She was the invention of a previous editor. It was now Hillerman's turn at playing Cyrano de Bergerac of the press by penning letters for a fictitious Mrs. Pincus.[23]

In her new letter, Mrs. Pincus complimented the city for paving streets but complained that no improvements were being made to College Street. "The main entry to your city from Texas—and we're the people who keep you alive—is disgraceful," Pincus wrote. "The city should condemn all those dirty mud buildings and make the street wide enough to handle traffic." In this brief missive Pincus hit two hot-button issues: Santa Fe's antipathy toward Texans and its almost religious reverence of adobe.[24]

Readers took note. Artist Gustave Baumann offered up a poem chastising Pincus for wanting to make New Mexico into another Texas. He was followed by the owner of a brown mud building on College Street who asked, "Why, oh, WHY do you keep coming to Santa Fe? . . . Please, hereafter, stay in Texas. No other place in the world could endure you."[25]

Several months later, after more missives from Mrs. Pincus, one reader questioned the authenticity of the letters. "I suspect that Mrs. Pincus is a fictitious creation of some local citizen who is resorting to trickery in an effort to sway the local populace while others railed against her," wrote H. Winneng of Los Alamos, New Mexico. If, Winneng added, Mrs. Pincus were for real, then an ordinance ought to be passed banning her, and other Texans like her, from coming to New Mexico.[26]

"People would get up in arms about it," said Thompson. Over the years, Mrs. Pincus's letters would return at regular intervals. In 1959, for instance, she belittled yet another cherished aspect of Santa Fe. Penned in a style that hinted at it being a spoof, Pincus's letter complimented the city for awarding prizes before "the date when people put out those messy incendiary *luminarios* and *farolitos*." She hoped "a true-blue American tradition of up-to-date electric lights will undoubtedly be another of those dangerous and unsightly customs your people seem to cling to in spite of everything."[27]

In her final appearance in the paper, she praised construction projects opposed by many residents, such as the drab new Federal Building. She told readers to ignore Indian complaints about a proposed statue honoring the Spanish governor who reconquered New Mexico after the Pueblo Revolt, and tossed in a comment that the state would have never amounted to much had Indians been in charge. An accompanying editor's note all but gave away the ruse.[28]

"We had been informed that Mrs. Pincus, a frequent summer visitor in Santa Fe in past years, had died in a Fort Worth hospital last September," wrote the editor, likely to have been Hillerman. "We are pleased to note that the obituary in the *Dallas Morning News* was exaggerated."

Mrs. H. Pincus never reappeared in the pages of the *Santa Fe New Mexican*, although a Miss Lulu Maud Pincus of Dallas sent in a letter several months later. "Our family never did like that dirty old mud Governor's Palace," she wrote, adding it ought to be redesigned to look like the Alamo. "A chip off the old block."[29]

As much as Hillerman enjoyed humor, especially his own, he had his limits. For instance, when he became managing editor, he put a stop to a newsroom practice of appending funny tales or jokes to the end of copy to amuse the composing room staff. Hillerman told the newsroom that when he worked in Oklahoma one reporter wrote up a funeral adding "and a good time was had by all." No one caught it until it was published in the newspaper.[30]

Santa Fe fed Hillerman's yearning to write fiction. The UP bureau, his first worksite in the city, was just up the street from where territorial governor Lew Wallace had written *Ben Hur*. In the newsroom of the *Santa Fe New Mexican*, where

Hillerman worked next, columnist Oliver LaFarge's *Laughing Boy* had won the Pulitzer Prize, and nationally renowned poet Winfield Townley Scott served as books editor. On the Plaza, at the grocery, even in the jail's drunk tank, Hillerman ran into people who made a living writing fiction. He reckoned if those people could do so, so could he.

Hillerman began to consider obtaining a master's degree to expand his writing opportunities. In the spring of 1959, he contacted the dean at the School of Journalism at the University of Missouri. The dean told Hillerman it would be possible for him to work part-time, helping oversee the school's commercial daily newspaper, and earn a degree in two years. Nothing further came from the discussions. In the end, a confrontation with death convinced him to follow his dream to be a writer.[31]

On the night of January 7, 1960, Hillerman drove out to the state penitentiary on the outskirts of Santa Fe, where a prisoner was scheduled to be the first executed in the state's gas chamber. In the company of other reporters, Hillerman was taken to a cell holding David Cooper Nelson, convicted of killing a man who had picked him up while hitchhiking. "I feel wonderful," Nelson told the reporters. "Do any of you believe that you will live forever?" An episode of *Johnny Staccato*, an NBC private detective series, played on the cell's television set. A guard turned the volume down. Hillerman watched as Nelson stretched out on his bunk and continued his expansive philosophical chat about what might come after death. The warden announced an end to the visit and the reporters filed out. As Hillerman looked back he saw Nelson gripping the bars of his cell. "God bless you," said the prisoner.[32]

Twice before, Hillerman had covered an execution. His first time was in 1954 when Frederick Heisler was put to death by electrocution. Hillerman had been horrified by the spectacle of more than one hundred police officers, politicians, and others who had come to witness the event, many with alcohol on their breath. "I had the feeling some of those guys were having orgasms," Hillerman said. "It was just a sickening spectacle." A few months later, state lawmakers passed the "Hillerman bill," limiting the number of spectators at future executions.[33]

On this 1960 night, Hillerman, his colleagues, and official witnesses took their places in the observation room whose plate glass window looked into the newly built gas chamber. Nelson, strapped in a chair, smiled and winked at the reporters he had spent time with earlier. Hillerman listened as the warden counseled the condemned man. "When you first smell the fumes, take a deep breath Dave," said the warden. "Don't try to fight it." Minutes later thick fumes rose from a bucket of acid into which a pound of cyanide pellets was poured. "Nelson's white shirt tightened across his bulky chest as he inhaled," wrote Hillerman in his front-page story. "He gasped convulsively for several minutes." Eight minutes later Nelson was pronounced dead. Hillerman could not shake the memory of that night, of Nelson's hands on the bars and his smile through the gas chamber window. "It caused me to think seriously for the first time about writing fiction," Hillerman said. "How could one report the true meaning of that execution while sticking to objective facts?"[34]

In November 1962, after serving as managing editor for three years, Hillerman was given the newly created post of executive editor, overseeing all aspects of the newspaper. At long last his aspiration of running a state capital newspaper had come to pass. But during the climb to this position a different dream had taken root. Instead of news, Tony told Marie, he wanted to pursue his on-again, off-again longing to write fiction. Now fourteen years into a journalism career, Hillerman was burned out. "I felt like I was writing the same story over and over," he said.[35]

On November 24, 1962, Hillerman placed a sheet of paper in his typewriter. "Dear Mr. McKinney," he began, "I have decided to resign from the New Mexican."[36]

CHAPTER 12

❖ Back to School ❖

A telephone call from the University of New Mexico (UNM) had sparked Hillerman's sudden November 1962 resignation letter. The caller asked Hillerman to come to Albuquerque for a meeting with university president Tom L. Popejoy. Hillerman already knew what lay behind the invitation. He had recently heard from Keen Rafferty, the chair and founder of the university's Journalism Department. With only two faculty members and forty-five students, it was the smallest accredited program in the nation. The sixty-two-year-old Rafferty was preparing for retirement and wondered if Hillerman might want to pursue a graduate degree and, once properly credentialed, be his successor.[1]

The plan offered an escape from the grind of daily journalism to a world in which Hillerman could pursue his goal of writing fiction. But it would only be feasible if he found a way to make a living during the anticipated two-year transition. "If Marie was dismayed by this economic problem, she didn't show it," said Tony. "Marie had more confidence in my writing than I did." Supportive of her husband's literary ambitions, she told him she would return to work if need be. The offer, however, was financially unrealistic because her salary alone would be insufficient to support the family, especially as there were now five children to care for.[2]

After the birth of their daughter, Anne, in 1949, Marie had undergone a hysterectomy, then a widely prescribed procedure to treat prolapses or, in rarer circumstances, cancer. "When destiny ruled that Anne was the only offspring nature would provide us, Marie and I decided to finish building our family by adoption," said Tony. Marie had grown up with relatives who had been adopted but Tony, as was his habit, approached the topic by reading books, articles, and newspapers. "They just wanted to have a family," said Marie's sister Teresa Sifford, who had five biological children and one adopted child.[3]

While living in Oklahoma City, Tony and Marie had made their first attempt to adopt. They resumed their efforts following their move to Santa Fe in 1952. "After months of braving hostile suspicion and smiling our way through various interviews, reference checks, and home inspections, the call finally came," Tony said. In February 1954, Tony, Marie, and five-year-old Anne drove to Albuquerque, picked up nine-month-old Sherry Diane from adoption officials, toured the city's zoo and, to Anne's great delight, bought ice cream. "And then we didn't ever take her back," Anne recalled. "And I remember waiting. We're in the car, we're going to Santa Fe. I don't know if I actually said it, but I remember thinking, *What's this baby doing here*?" Sherry, who was renamed Janet Marie Hillerman, wept for several days before adapting to her new family. The *Santa Fe New Mexican* welcomed the addition to the family. "She is just the right size to enjoy the services of Anne Margaret Hillerman who is five-years-old."[4]

A year later, the Hillermans adopted a six-month-old boy, whom they named Anthony Grove Hillerman Jr. His sisters Anne and Janet were thrilled to have a little baby in the house. When he grew to school age they walked him to school holding hands. He was, by all accounts an easy but shy boy who rarely complained. However, Marie had to adapt her cooking as young Tony turned out to be allergic to milk, wheat, and other common foods. Tony's adoption was followed by the addition of Stephen August Hillerman. The family of four grew again in 1960 when Monica was adopted. The three-year-old girl had fibular hemimelia, a rare birth defect that gave her a left leg shorter than her right and a left foot with four toes. For her first years Monica practically lived at the Carrie Tingley Hospital for Crippled Children in Truth or Consequences, at one point spending seven months in traction as doctors lengthened her leg bone by breaking it and leaving a gap for new bone growth to fill.

All these months the Hillermans would drive down from Santa Fe, and later from Albuquerque, to visit Monica. The young girl was bewildered when the couple standing by her bedside would call themselves her parents. The journey through foster care and medical care had been all she had known. "Hospitals, in fact, seemed to be her favorite residence, and homes merely places she stopped off between them," said Tony.[5]

With Monica, the Hillermans believed they were done with adoptions. "Three daughters and two sons seemed about right," said Tony, who remained at work sixty hours a week. It fell almost entirely on Marie to care for the children, and she dedicated herself to the task.[6]

Thomas Lafayette Popejoy, the UNM president Hillerman was to meet, was the first native New Mexican to take the helm of the seventy-three-year-old university. Born in Raton in the northeast corner of the state, he had begun working at UNM in 1925 and had remained with the university except when he took a federal government post during World War II. In the fourteen years he had been president, Popejoy had greatly enlarged the university's programs and student body.

In 1962, however, leaders of the American Legion in New Mexico were causing trouble for Popejoy. In a new hue of the red menace, Legion leaders charged that some UNM professors were disloyal to the United States because they informed students they did not have to sign a loyalty oath appended to National Defense Education loans. The legionnaires were pressuring Popejoy to fire the professors. Rather than be cowed, Popejoy went to the legion's annual gathering in Carlsbad, New Mexico, and told the legionnaires he would fight to defend the academic freedom of his faculty and students.

Many of the state's newspapers sided with, or at least tolerated, the American Legion's campaign, except for the *New Mexican* whose editorial page was managed by Hillerman. "Our compliments to Mr. Popejoy for so squarely confronting the issue which he could have skirted," wrote Hillerman. "It was an act of intellectual courage and one which certainly should be reassuring to his faculty." Quoting the French philosopher Voltaire, Hillerman told his readers that the liberty to think, criticize, and argue is crucial in a university. "Any inhibition of this liberty of thought—such as certainly would be caused by real or implied limits on freedom of speech—would cripple the university." Highly satisfied with his defense of Popejoy, Hillerman entered the editorial in a newspaper contest. Popejoy so liked the editorial that he wanted its author to work for him.[7]

When Hillerman drove down to Albuquerque for his meeting with Popejoy, armed with a freshly typed résumé, he found the UNM president held the missing piece to the transition puzzle.[8] The two men met in the president's office in Scholes Hall, a splendid example of Pueblo Revival style at the center of the campus designed by architect John Gaw Meem. At the time, running a university with an enrollment of seven thousand students was a rather low-key affair. Popejoy maintained an open-door policy, and all sorts of people came calling, including prospective students.[8]

Two of the top three administrators joined the meeting. Popejoy, Hillerman, and the men chatted about that year's legislative session. No other topic came up. One by one the men left for other appointments. Finally, Popejoy rose from his chair, handed Hillerman an envelope containing an employment contract. "Thus, ended the job interview," said Hillerman. "Not a word had been spoken about what I would be doing."[9]

The contract was vague, as was the official announcement subsequently issued by UNM. Hillerman, it said, would serve as an assistant to the president and "work at first on some institutional studies and publications" connected with the office of the president and those of other members of the administration. The post came with a salary of $9,240. "A pay somewhat higher than Marie and I had decided we had to have," said Hillerman. In fact, the salary was twice the median income for a man in 1962, at a time when a hamburger at Lota Burger Stand on Washington Street sold for thirty-nine cents, a dozen eggs fetched thirty-five cents at Boy's Market on Isleta Boulevard, and a carload could see John Wayne in *The Comancheros* at the Tesuque Drive-In off Route 66 for seventy-five cents.[10]

He signed the contract. On Saturday, November 24, 1962, Hillerman sat at his typewriter to explain his decision to *New Mexican* publisher Robert McKinney. "I believe you will understand and appreciate my motives," wrote Hillerman. He made no mention of his new job, but rather told McKinney he was moving to Albuquerque to begin work on an advanced degree. "I recall very vividly an afternoon in your office some three years ago when you told me of your own yen to study, and teach, philosophy," Hillerman wrote. The decision to leave was a hard one, he confessed. "If I delay making this break, I'm afraid I never would."[11]

On December 7, 1962, the paper published the news of Hillerman's resignation and his plans to pursue more schooling at UNM on the front page but made no mention of his new job with Popejoy. It wasn't until the following day, when the rival *Albuquerque Journal* carried its own story, that Hillerman's new employment became known.[12]

On a chilly Wednesday, January 2, 1963, Hillerman settled into his new office in the Journalism Building on the Central Avenue side of campus. He stepped into a vastly different kind of domain with an unhurried pace unlike anything he had known in the deadline-driven world of journalism. "I went from a six-day workweek and getting a story written every minute to an environment of thinkers. Time no longer mattered," said Hillerman."[13]

Hillerman's primary duty, as far as he could determine, was to be what he called a "doer of undignified deeds" for Popejoy. Within a week, Hillerman was riding in a car with the president and other members of the administration up to Santa Fe for the annual meeting of the state legislature. "Because of his Capital City background of several years," noted one newspaper, "Hillerman has a wide circle of friends among the legislature who appropriate college funds." He was soon a regular member of the lobbying crew showing up at the capitol for days at a time.[14]

One day, the president told Hillerman to expect a telephone call from the sheriff of Sandoval County, a large county north of Albuquerque. According to Hillerman, the sheriff called to say he was in need of about a dozen mattresses to replace ones burned at the jail in an inmate-set fire, and he believed the university might be able to help. "Fresh from handling political news in Santa Fe," Hillerman said, "I didn't need to be told the name of the sheriff nor his kinship with a member of the state senate." In the world of New Mexico politics, movers and shakers worked a network of family ties in which IOUs were traded like currency. The favor was later remembered by a state senator when a crucial vote came up on Popejoy's plan to open a medical school. "Thus," said Hillerman, "the evildoers in the Sandoval jail got mattresses and New Mexico got an incredibly expensive medical school.[15]

In Hillerman, Popejoy had a trusted and valuable assistant. In fact, when three UNM students were wrongly arrested in Quito, Ecuador, in connection with a drug investigation, the president selected Hillerman to quietly extricate them. Flying first to Miami, Tony and Marie, who had valuable Spanish-speaking skills, traveled on to Quito under the pretense of inspecting the University of New Mexico Andean Center. "I was to meet with a Quito attorney, place an envelope full of money in his hands, and arrange to spring the three UNM students from jail and get them back to New Mexico," said Hillerman. "The mission was accomplished. The three students came home and the university avoided bad publicity."[16]

Settled in on campus, Hillerman turned to his academic plans. He applied for admission as a graduate student in English. To Hillerman's good fortune, several professors had established a creative writing program. At the time, the now-famous Iowa Creative Writing Program was considered an experiment, recalled Paul B. Davis, a member of the UNM English faculty. The plan at UNM was to permit established writers to become credentialed by writing a creative thesis rather than the customary academic treatise on a dead poet. Members of the old guard in the Department of English were skeptical of the idea. Among the upholders of tradition was Franklin Miller Dickey, a medievalist who was serving as acting chair. Hillerman called on Dickey to be admitted to the graduate program. The professor was unimpressed with Hillerman's academic record, his work as a journalist, and his recounting of the books he had read. "Here," intoned Dickey, "we pronounce that Yeah-ts."[17]

Dickey gave Hillerman a list of undergraduate courses and requirements to complete before he could begin his graduate studies. Hillerman immediately registered for a class in Shakespeare's tragedies, normally taken by freshmen twenty-three years younger. This was followed by a summertime correspondence course—what later would be called an independent study—on the history of the English language and a class on Milton. By September he also completed two exams testing his knowledge of early and late English literature. In pursuing his master's, Hillerman took a traditional sequence of English courses: Milton, Chaucer, Whitman, and Dickinson, along with creative writing, contemporary fiction, and American humor. He earned A's in all his classes, except for a B in a class on the poet William Carlos Williams. Where he deviated from the norm was in following a suggestion for a master's thesis topic from Morris Freedman, an iconoclastic professor who recognized where Hillerman's talents lay.[18]

The professor, only five years his senior, was unlike any Hillerman had known in college in Oklahoma. Raised in a Yiddish-speaking home of Eastern European Jewish immigrants in New York City, Freedman had been an unmotivated student until he became enamored with literature and Latin while in high school. He graduated from City College of New York, served in the Army Air Force during World War II, and earned a doctoral degree at Columbia University.[19]

Freedman was content to live in Albuquerque and teach at the non-prestigious public university. "I was born, raised, and earned my living in New York," he wrote, "but the finest hour for me was when I picked up my hat and said, Farewell, my unlovely." In the eight years he had been in New Mexico, Freedman had explored all parts of the state and he shared Hillerman's fascination with the Land of Enchantment. He was, as the *Chicago Daily Tribune* described him, "a genuine intellectual who has happily moved to Albuquerque."[20]

One day, in his advanced creative writing class, the professor asked Hillerman why he stayed clear of first person in the essays he wrote. "I told him," Hillerman said, "journalists are conditioned to be invisible, to be what Walter Lippmann called 'the fly on the wall,' seeing everything and feeling nothing." Freedman took the answer as an excuse. "He wouldn't let me write to my strengths, which I wanted to do. He forced me to write first person all those things you hate to do when you're a journalist," said Hillerman. "I found the *I* on the typewriter."[21]

Hillerman composed a nostalgic sixteen-page first-person essay. Freedman asked him to read it aloud to the class. "Looking back, and looking back has sometimes been my weakness," Hillerman began reading to his fellow students, "I think that my coming of age would have been delayed a few minutes had the mockingbird, too, been gone. But that night as I walked up to our empty house, seeing it for the first time in almost three years, I was glad to hear him singing his familiar, erratic song on the ridgepole."[22]

In a measured pace and with a richness of telling details, Hillerman related his return to the abandoned Sacred Heart family farm as a wounded combat veteran on leave at the end of the war. The reader—or listener in this case—could feel the night air as he hitchhiked after disembarking from the bus in Konawa. Discursive passages recounted his childhood among Benedictine monks, Sisters of Mercy, and Pottawatomie Indian girls, and how he coped with the loss of his father and eventually the farm, as well as the coming of the war.

When he reached the farmhouse, Hillerman told his classmates, "the mockingbird was continuing the same quarrelsome monologue with the night from exactly the same perch on the ridgepole. The whippoorwills were repeating themselves in Mr. Mann's woods exactly as usual. And the sultry night air was carrying the same thousand summer smells of alfalfa, of oak leaves and of dust." With a Thomas Wolfe–like conclusion, Hillerman ended the essay by contrasting the reparable decay of the farm with the unalterable changes in him caused by the war. Freedman gave Hillerman an A. The direction Freedman urged his student to follow—the mining of memory, the use of details in creating scenes, and the deliberate employment of ambiguity to allow readers to form their own conclusions—opened a new path for Hillerman.

Freedman became chair of Hillerman's master's thesis committee. To complete the committee the professor enlisted two young colleagues, Davis, a professor of British and Irish literature, and Hamlin Hill, a renowned expert on Mark

Twain. Freedman proposed that Hillerman fulfill this final requirement for his degree by composing a series of nonfiction stories about New Mexico, its places, and its people in a style suitable for a popular audience. While it was an unlikely topic for an English thesis, the idea made sense to Freedman, who admired the writing in *Life* and other popular magazines and was fascinated by the charms of New Mexico. He also knew the stories Hillerman might write could perhaps later be sold to magazines, providing welcome additional income to his student.[23]

Hillerman set about mining his decade in Santa Fe journalism for much of his material. He wrote five essays—more like nonfiction short stories. For the title piece, he selected a botched bank robbery in Taos. In November 1957, two armed men, one clad in women's clothing complete with high heels, stood in line at the First State Bank. The disguise, especially as the man had neglected to shave, did little to hide the cross-dressing robber's gender, and customers in the bank began to stare at the pair. The would-be bandits fled, fearing they had been discovered. Their getaway pickup truck, borrowed from a friend, crashed into a car driven by the pastor of the Brethren Church, who sped after them until the robbers fired on him, encouraging him to give up the chase and call the police.

A reporter at the time, Hillerman couldn't resist the tale, even driving to Taos to cover the chain of events. "Act three of the First State Bank's comic opera 'intended bank robbery' dragged along today with three FBI agents and a swarm of other officers patiently poking through Taos for the principal comedians," Hillerman reported in his front-page story.[24]

Eventually the culprits were apprehended, providing fodder for an editorial. Calling the tale as hilarious as a Gilbert and Sullivan opera, Hillerman claimed that had the robbery been attempted anywhere else, it would not have been funny and someone would likely have been shot. "But at Taos, where Taosenos don't take mundane affairs such as bank robberies very seriously, it was bound to be ridiculous. Long live Taos and may she never grow old and stodgy." Three months later, a grand jury gave the affair an ending matching the delight it had provided to Taos. It refused to indict the pair, classifying the event as a practical joke.[25]

Now, as a student of creative writing, Hillerman returned to the event to write it in a manner unrestrained by the corset of journalistic conventions. He called it "The Great Taos Bank Robbery." He began with a telephone call to the *New Mexican*'s city editor from a Mrs. Ruth Fish, who announced the bank would soon be robbed. How did she know this? asked the editor. Because, she replied, the robbers were in line at the bank.

"But, persisted the city editor," Hillerman wrote in the opening scene, "how was it possible to predict that these two persons intended to rob the bank?"

"This presumption seemed safe. Mrs. Fish said, because one of the two men was disguised as a woman and because he was holding a pistol under his purse. Whereupon she said good-bye and hung up."

In a leisurely, almost dawdling, pace like that of a porch raconteur, Hillerman told the story of the failed robbery, the bumbling getaway, the manhunt, the eventual capture of the men, and the grand jury proceedings that failed to indict the miscreants. It was an event that locals came to compare to a flood for which there is no record:

> Thus The Great Bank Robbery was denied the official federal imprimatur of indictments and was left as the sort of thing Alice's Mad Hatter might call an Unfelonius Unrobbery. Still, if you happen to be in Taos on Veteran's Day and the man on the next barstool happens to be an Old Taos Hand, you're likely to hear something like this:
>
> "You know, tomorrow is the anniversary of our Big Bank Robbery . . ."
> Or maybe he'll tell you about The Great Flood of 1935.

The compact tale was pitch-perfect and written in an understated manner evocative of Mark Twain.

In addition to "The Great Taos Bank Robbery," Hillerman penned four other tales about an archaeology dig, the bubonic plague, an odd episode in New Mexico politics, and a profile of a small northern New Mexico town. "They seek instead to create an interest and impart some knowledge," he wrote in the introduction to his thesis. "Thus, an overriding goal in each has been to engage the reader's interest and to hold it throughout."[26]

In his essays Hillerman adapted some of the techniques he encountered reading the works of Rebecca West, particularly *The Meaning of Treason*, her highly regarded 1947 account of the trials of William Joyce and John Amery for treason during World War II. In it, West makes extensive use of observable details, such as the carvings in the courtroom's judicial bench. Hillerman seized on this approach. "I have attempted," Hillerman told his committee members, "to isolate the significant details and use them to recreate in the imagination of the reader the scene and the action."[27]

As Hillerman worked on the pieces for his thesis, he honed a more creative style of writing. The thesis was also a storehouse of polished articles with which he could launch a professional career, as Freedman had intended. When Hillerman was only one year into the program, Freedman contacted his well-connected New York literary agent to see if she could place some of Hillerman's articles. She said yes.

CHAPTER 13

❖ No More Excuses ❖

With the tangible promise of a writing career, Tony Hillerman longed for a meeting with Professor Freedman's literary agent. The opportunity presented itself on June 2, 1964, when Hillerman and daughter Anne joined a nineteen-member delegation led by the governor that traveled to New York City for the World's Fair. A portion of the state's five-building pueblo-style exhibit comprised a photographic exhibit assembled by UNM, and Hillerman was to represent the university when the fair celebrated New Mexico Day later that week. From the Essex House, where the delegation was going to lodge, it would be an easy walk to the agent's office.[1]

With more than two decades of publishing experience, Ann Elmo ran a successful agency and was known by most book editors in the tight-knit world of New York City publishing. Hillerman reached her office on Fifth Avenue, near the city's magnificent public library, in time for his appointment. Ushered into Elmo's office, he found the diminutive, dark-haired agent behind a desk stacked with manuscripts. When she looked up from her work, Elmo appeared puzzled until Hillerman reminded her of Freedman's introduction.[2]

She agreed to take a look at the stories Hillerman drew from his briefcase and assured him she would phone him at his hotel. "On the way out," said Hillerman, "I noticed that it was now four minutes after eleven—about an hour and fifty-six minutes less of her time than I had expected." It turned out that the brevity of the meeting was Elmo's style, not an inauspicious sign. Later, when she made the promised telephone call, Elmo told Hillerman she thought she could sell two or three of his stories.[3]

By July, Elmo got her first nibble. It came from *True* magazine, one of several magazines competing for the male reader in the mid-1960s. Unlike its rivals *Penthouse* and *Playboy*, *True* had no photographs of unclad women. What caught the editors' interest was Hillerman's article on an outbreak of bubonic plague in New Mexico. To New York magazine editors, the distant lands of New Mexico, its ancient people, and its Spanish colonial heritage possessed a romantic, exotic allure. Mixing in the Black Death could make for an enthralling article. But Dick Adler, one of *True*'s editors, told Hillerman the story would need considerable revision. "We see the piece as a detective story," he said. "Can you make more of the ending, building up the climax so it has all the excitement of a classic denouement?" Adler provided a list of specific demands. The major revision was to recast the work so that biologist Bryan E. Miller was given "almost a Sherlock Holmes treatment" in his pursuit of the villainous bacteria *Pasteurella pestis* that causes the plague. "With these changes," he said, "I think you will have a saleable piece."[4]

The editor's instructions challenged Hillerman, who had been trained to reveal as much as possible as early as possible in a story—the so-called inverted pyramid of news reporting. In the writing he had done for Professor Freedman he had not strayed far from a traditional expository style. With the summer ahead of him and free from his studies, Hillerman agreed to try. He retained much of his original reporting, including the dramatic moment when the "dusky cyanotic color" of sheepherder Amado Ortega's nails and lips raised alarm at St. Vincent's Hospital in Santa Fe. "To be exact," wrote Hillerman, "they were the color of the Black Death. Had a physician of the fourteenth century seen these signs he would have evacuated the city." But for the remainder of the piece, Hillerman shuffled and tweaked his copy to make biologist Miller's pursuit of the source of the infection the narrative thread.[5]

In previous instances, Miller had been lucky enough to easily pin down the point of origin. But the place where the dead sheepherder had contracted the sickness was in the Pecos Wilderness, a spot frequented by thousands of campers and visitors. "Children love to chase chipmunks, golden mantle squirrels, and other small mountain animals," explained Hillerman. "Sick animals are easily caught, and they would be captured at a time when the fleas they carry were loaded with plague bacilli."[6]

Miller's detective work grew more pressing when another fatal case surfaced that might have come from prairie dogs near Santa Fe. He suspended his Pecos search, obtained reinforcements, and rushed to Santa Fe. Summer days passed and Miller remained no closer to finding the origins of the plague in either place. But a doctor in Pecos, aware of the plague outbreak, correctly diagnosed the hard, discolored, walnut-sized bumps surrounding the groin of one of his patients as a symptom of the bubonic plague. He administered the appropriate antibiotics and saved the man's life. This case gave Miller the break he needed. "A man who has been touched by *Pasteurella pestis* and was still alive to talk about it," wrote Hillerman.[7]

Miller and his crew, using information from the survivor, set traps and performed field autopsies on the captured rodents. "The monotonous work continued," wrote Hillerman, "and as it continued, fear grew that Miller's X on the map merely marked a bad guess." But then Miller spotted an irregular pattern of dark spots on the spleen of a ground squirrel. More squirrels were caught and tested. The origins of the plague had been found. The infected population of ground squirrels was trapped and killed. When the next summer came, the plague did not return. The article closed with children in Pecos singing "Ring around the Rosy," unaware that the song came from the Middle Ages and "we all fall down" had the lugubrious meaning of mass death. Miller and his colleagues had won this time. "But the Black Death is still in the mountains," Hillerman warned.[8]

By September, Hillerman's revisions approached the desired mark. Adler had been correct. Putting biologist Miller at the center of the search for the source of the Black Death made for a better story. "His education had made him a biologist," wrote Hillerman, "his profession had made him a hunter." The magazine's managing editor, upon reading the new draft, told Adler, "This guy is a good writer and he is really almost there." Hillerman made yet one more round of revisions, adding yet more detective-style drama. In October the article was accepted for a payment of $1,000. After taking out Elmo's $100 agent's commission, the check was like receiving a 10 percent salary bonus. But Hillerman, unused to the heavy-handed editing typical of magazine work, complained to Elmo about the revisions he had been required to make. "I know how hard you worked on the article, getting it through so many revisions to please *True* editors," Elmo wrote back, "but it's heartening that you managed to satisfy them."[9]

Despite his grumblings to his agent, Hillerman was changed by the experience of reshaping the article. It revealed to "an old wire-service man" that while facts were not malleable, the writing of nonfiction could be. The detective approach to his story had worked as an effective way to introduce tension and retain the reader's interest. It might be used again.

The sale was Hillerman's first to a major national publication. It made him eager
for more, but he had to keep up with his studies in order to obtain his master's
degree before the chair of the Journalism Department stepped down. Showing
no aversion to repurposing his writing, Hillerman lengthened and improved his
1948 effort at a short story about the antics of wounded soldiers in a hospital. It
earned an A-. He even rewrote some old newspaper stories, including one tale
of partisan politics in which the protagonist learned that "sometimes you have
to sacrifice a knight to save your queen."[10]

Hillerman completed his coursework at the end of the spring semester of 1965.
He let Elmo know he had only a year of work remaining to complete his thesis
and earn his degree. Hearing the news, the agent hoped that Hillerman would
soon be free to work on his own writing. "I have no doubt whatever material
you turn out will be highly marketable," she wrote.[11]

True editor Robert J. Shea asked Hillerman if he might be willing to do a
profile of George Agogino, a Paleo-Indian archaeologist who the summer before
had found a circular pit that Clovis people may have used as a water well around
11,500 BC. Instead, Hillerman suggested the magazine commission him to follow
up on a lead he had obtained from Frank C. Hibben, the most famous member of
the university's highly respected Anthropology Department. A big-game hunter
whose kills adorned his house built in part from stone blocks from Ancestral
Pueblo ruins, Hibben had shaken up archaeology at the young age of thirty-nine.
In the 1930s and 1940s, in the Sandia Mountains overlooking Albuquerque, he
had uncovered artifacts that suggested inhabitation by humans twenty-five
thousand years earlier, thousands of years prior to the Folsom people then the
earliest known inhabitants of the New World.[12]

Hibben told Hillerman about the promising work being conducted by Jerry
Dawson, one of his students, who was sifting sand on the outskirts of Albuquerque's urban sprawl where developers' bulldozers had gridded fifty-five thousand
acres of open land west of the Rio Grande for a new community being called
Rio Rancho. Hillerman drove out to see the work. When he reached the site,
Hillerman found the area marked off into ten-foot quadrants with white string
tied to wooden pegs and spotted Dawson by a plume of dust rising from a sifter
frame he was shaking. Eager to talk of his work, the archaeologist ran his calloused finger through the debris of gravel, stone, and a bewildered scorpion
on the wire mesh. Holding up a thin chip of stone, no larger than a fingernail,

Dawson explained the bit of flint had come off a stone being chiseled into a lance point by a Stone Age hunter in pursuit of a long-horned bison.

Hillerman prepared a two-page pitch for Shea. The magazine's editors conferred and, without promising to publish the piece, invited Hillerman to "take a crack at it." This time, *True* wanted Hillerman to imitate the style of the *New Yorker* magazine's "Reporter at Large" column. The big discoveries were less important to the article than describing the work itself. "In other words," Shea told Hillerman, "a sort of picture of archeologists at work—an interesting, romantic sort of job, but a tough one as well." It would be hard work to pull it off. "But judging by your Black Death piece," he added, "you should be able to put a lot into it."[13]

It was late summer when Hillerman finally got to work in earnest on the article. His passion for fishing had gotten the better of him. In his decade in Santa Fe, Hillerman had regularly escaped for a day along the rivers and streams of northern New Mexico and southern Colorado. Since 1955, when Woodrow "Woody" Wilson, a journeyman printer at the *Santa Fe New Mexican*, first introduced Hillerman to the almost inaccessible Rio Brazos, a moderate-sized stream that feeds the Rio Chama north of Santa Fe, it had been his favorite spot to fish. On occasion he would take one of his children along. Teenaged Anne watched her father cast his line into brooks swollen with spring runoff. "He looked so happy that I felt happy too, despite the mosquitoes," she recalled. "If the fish were biting, we'd eat the wily trout he'd hooked. If not, we'd have crackers and Vienna sausages out of the can with a Hershey bar for dessert." Living in Albuquerque added an hour or more of driving, but the waterways still beckoned. "To be frank," Hillerman told Shea when reporting on his lack of progress, "a tipster in the Game and Fish Department told me of some beaver ponds in the San Juan National Forest which should have some big trout in them. They did."[14]

When fall arrived, Hillerman was still not ready to submit his finished article. "It doesn't satisfy me and I'm confident it wouldn't satisfy *True*," he told Andrew Mills, who had replaced Shea as editor. In November, after yet one more visit to the dig site, Hillerman sent "The Hunt for a 10,000-Year-Old Hunter" to Mills. A month later Hillerman opened a letter from the editor that appeared to be a rejection letter. "We have come to the conclusion that the piece, in its present form, is not right for *True*," Mills wrote, "For some other magazine, yes, but not for us."[15]

As Hillerman read on, he learned to his relief that the magazine was not killing the piece. Instead the editor wanted a substantial revision that included a new beginning and more speed and action. "That doesn't mean that we don't like what you've done so far," said Mills. "As a matter of fact, we like it a lot." As proof of his interest, Mills said the magazine would advance $500 toward the promised $1,000 payment for the article.

Through the Christmas and New Year's holidays, Hillerman polished the piece and cut 1,500 words. He labeled it *Revision of Rewrite*. "After reading through both versions last night," Hillerman reported to Mills, "I'm forced to admit that my own prose, like bad whiskey, improves with cutting." He opened the piece with a description of Dawson moving about on the barren expanse outside Albuquerque, pausing here and there to scrutinize the ground. Then Hillerman had Dawson reappear with a pickup truck, tools, and food and water. Carefully digging at spots and sifting the soil through a boxed mesh screen, he examined tiny chips of flint that to the untrained eye looked no different than other bits of stone. But they were. "Dawson's shovel had cut through ten thousand years of time and uncovered the hunting camp of Folsom Man," wrote Hillerman.[16]

Writing extensively in the first person, a novelty for him, Hillerman made himself into a literary foil who drew out Dawson to explain his work and its potential significance. The complicated and scattered story gained a soothing explanatory tone, almost as if Hillerman were telling it from a porch rocker. When he had started work on the article, editor Shea had issued a warning. "Bringing off something like this," he said, "is going to depend a lot more on what you can put into the piece than we can tell you." Hillerman succeeded.[17]

With his thesis all but complete, Hillerman began the next phase in his journey to become a writer. By this point, he had given more than two years of service to the university as an assistant to President Popejoy, then as associate director of the Information and Publications Office. Popejoy delivered on his 1962 promise, and the job in the Journalism Department materialized. In February, Hillerman was named associate professor of journalism effective beginning in September. By summertime he was selected as chair of the university's modest Journalism Department, staffed by one associate professor, two assistant professors, and two visiting lecturers.[18]

The move to an academic post with the accompanying job security and salary hike was well timed. Tony and Marie, who thought they were done with bringing children into their family, found themselves adding one more child to the household. Visiting the adoption office in downtown Albuquerque to straighten out some paperwork regarding Monica's records, the couple were told of a boy who was suffering from neglect in foster care. He had spent the first six to nine months of his life in an orphanage and for the past two years had been confined in a playpen in the confines of a cruel woman's house where no one had held him, played with him, or even talked with him. The child was one of many in need of a home in New Mexico. When the Hillermans adopted their first child in 1954, the waiting list for children was long. By 1966, the situation had reversed for a variety of reasons, including an increase in what were then called "illegitimate" births. There were now more parentless children than parents seeking to adopt.[19]

The boy was in the office, said the social worker. Would the Hillermans like to meet him? The Hillermans agreed. "He clung fearfully to the leg of the woman who brought him in for introductions," said Tony, "a handsome toddler who, once we had seen him, had no chance for escape." They named him Daniel Bernard Hillerman, the middle name in honor of Tony's brother. When they brought him home, the years of neglect became apparent. The lawn in the family's backyard was the first grass on which the boy had ever walked. "I think one of the early nights after they adopted me, if not the first night, we had hamburgers," recalled Daniel. "And later that night, my mom was tucking me in, and she noticed that my cheeks were kind of bulging. She looks in my mouth, and I still had some hamburger in my mouth, wondering when my next meal would be."[20]

Even though Hillerman now had administrative duties and classes to teach, many of the constraints that had kept him from writing were lifted. When he had been at the *Santa Fe New Mexican* the demands of his job had always been his excuse for not writing. "If you work with words all day at the office, it's tough to work with them at home," he said, thinking back on those days. "Each day you get older with nothing literary to show for it except a few more pages of false starts." Now it would be different. "For the first time in my life," he wrote Elmo, "I'll have time to write and no more excuses if I can't produce."[21]

For years he had longed to leave what he called "the hard rock" of journalism and "move into the plastic of fiction." Now doing so was at last possible and the potential awed Hillerman. "Working with facts, as a journalist must, is like working with marble," he said. "Truth has its beauty but it does not bend." Fiction gave the writer license to create facts. If bad weather or a sunset is needed, then the writer in godlike fashion can create a downpour or move the sun across the sky.[22]

Hillerman decided to put on hold his ambition to write an American *War and Peace*. "That would run maybe 250,000 words, a lot for a fellow who had been conditioned to describe the Texas City disaster* in a page and half." Instead, Hillerman began to consider other forms of fiction. "I would write something shorter, and something with a shape," Hillerman decided. He tried but soon gave up on a novel using the Potawatomis he had known in his childhood. Instead he looked to try his hand at a mystery.[23]

"The crime novel has a form, a structure," he said. "It can be serious lit." Freed from the classical detection tradition, Hillerman thought the mystery form had enormous advantages. "You can do anything you want with it," he said. "I think it is a lovely form for anybody who wants to write a novel." The genre had come a long way since Edgar Allan Poe penned *The Murders in the Rue Morgue* in 1841, which Hillerman had read while at Konawa High School. The cozy style of mysteries, such as those written by Agatha Christie and Dorothy L. Sayers in the golden age of mystery fiction, had been eclipsed by more hard-edged novels featuring flawed detectives and corrupt police, and laced with alcohol, violence, and sexual tensions.[24]

In making his decision to pursue mystery writing, Hillerman was influenced by three writers he had grown to admire: Eric Ambler, Raymond Chandler, and Graham Greene. "The ones," he said, "who demonstrated the rich possibilities of the form." British thriller writer Eric Ambler, widely credited with elevating the genre to literature, most impressed Hillerman with his versatility. "He never wrote the same book, or anything like the same book, twice," said Hillerman.[25]

Born in 1909, Ambler came to fame with the publication of his fifth novel, *The Mask of Dimitrios*, when he was only thirty. The work established him as a master of the spy novel. In it, and in his other novels, the main character was not a professional spy. Rather Ambler selected everyday protagonists—like a writer, an engineer, or even a petty criminal—all of whom were out of their depth but

---

*The Texas City disaster occurred on April 16, 1947, in the Port of Texas City at Galveston Bay, when a ship loaded with ammonium nitrate exploded. Nearly six hundred people were killed in the United States' deadliest industrial accident.

somehow by the end outwitted their opponents. Certainly, one feature of *The Mask of Dimitrios* didn't go unnoticed by Hillerman. The main character was a university professor who made a success of writing detective stories.

Hillerman considered American-born Raymond Chandler a better writer than Ambler. Born in 1888, Chandler created the prototype of a hard-boiled city detective in Philip Marlowe, a private eye at work in the dark recesses of 1930s and 1940s Los Angeles. To Hillerman, Chandler created masterful scenes that summoned all the reader's senses, and no scene was better than those in his fifth novel. "Reading *The Little Sister*," said Hillerman, "should make anyone aware that the mystery form, applied with craftsmanship and talent, can be literature."

In his examination of model mystery writers, Hillerman reserved special praise for Graham Greene. Born in 1904, the English novelist struck Hillerman as possessing even greater versatility than his British colleague Ambler. Greene's more than two dozen novels were a mix of suspense works, such as *The Third Man* and *The Confidential Agent*, and literary novels such as *The Power and the Glory* and *The End of the Affair*. For Hillerman, who sought to write a great American novel after practicing on a mystery, Greene's work offered a model. "How can anyone who wants to be a storyteller read *The Third Man* or *The Comedians* and not feel the urge to try the feat?" asked Hillerman.

As Hillerman began to consider where to begin, he made a fateful decision. "Since I was uneasy about my ability to plot, but cocksure about my ability to describe," he said, "I would play out my tale against an exotic, interesting background, á la Ambler, Greene, et al."[26]

By March 1966, Hillerman was well into a draft of his first murder mystery. Four months later one of the most respected editors of suspense novels provided well-timed and critically important encouragement that Hillerman had made the right choice. The July issue of *The Writer*, which since 1887 had proffered advice to aspiring writers, featured an article on the editing of mystery novels by Joan Kahn, who had launched the Harper Novels of Suspense department in 1947.[27]

"A mystery novel is a novel," Kahn declared. Mysteries, she explained, possess a form with infinite variations and provide the writer with whatever room is needed. When done right the present-day mystery achieves a high standard of writing and tests the boundaries of storytelling. "She elaborated what I believed to be true," said Hillerman, "and explained the things that had lured me into the mystery field." It was as if Joan Kahn had written a letter directly to Hillerman, validating both his decision to begin with a murder mystery and inviting him to push the boundaries of the genre. Now, he also knew of an editor and book series that might be receptive to his nascent novel.[28]

"The terrible moment had arrived," said Hillerman. "Naked and exposed. Nothing left to hide behind. No more excuses. . . . Either you can write fiction or you can't."[29]

CHAPTER 14

◈ The Birth of Leaphorn ◈

If editor Joan Kahn's 1966 article extolling mystery writing inspired Tony Hillerman, his duties as professor and department head silenced his typewriter for long stretches of time. And when he did return to his manuscript, doubt drove Hillerman away. "It would occur to me in these periods of lucid reality that no publisher would ever print the stuff I was writing, no one would ever read it, what I was doing was an unconscionable waste of typewriter ribbon," he said. "At such times I would put the book on the closet shelf to collect dust until the urge revived itself." Yet slowly the stack of pages grew.[1]

For the protagonist of his mystery, Hillerman created Bergen Leroy McKee, an Anglo anthropologist from UNM. Hillerman was well acquainted with members of the actual Anthropology Department, housed on the west side of campus a short stroll from his office. It had been Professor Frank Hibben, after all, who led him to the story about the search for early Americans that Hillerman wrote for *True* magazine. In creating McKee, Hillerman added familiar touches of academic life, such as the contents of McKee's faculty mailbox. After nearly five years on campus, Hillerman knew the culture of academia. He also mixed in real elements by adding the actual names of seven faculty members along with his fictional ones.[2]

In keeping with his plan to set his book in an exotic locale, Hillerman moved McKee off campus onto the Navajo Nation. The approximately twenty-seven thousand square miles of the modern Navajo homeland, larger than the state of West Virginia, stretched across the vast open expanses of northwestern New Mexico, northeastern Arizona, and portions of southern Utah. Navajos trace their arrival to a time when, according to their creation story called Diné Bahane', First Man, First Woman, and the Diné (or "people") emerged onto the Earth's surface after three previous worlds were destroyed. Archaeologists, in contrast, believe Navajos, as well as nearby Apaches—descendants of Athabaskan-speaking tribes in the far north—emigrated from western Canada in perhaps the 1400s. By the 1700s the Navajo were well established in the lands they called Dinétah. This made them latecomers to the Southwest in comparison to the Pueblo people whose settlements dotted the landscape. Hopi, Acoma, Zuni, and Taos Puebloans, to name but four groups, had inhabited stone and adobe structures in city-like villages since at least 1100, and were descended from Ancestral Puebloans who went back centuries earlier.

When he had worked at the *Santa Fe New Mexican*, Hillerman had met members of the well-established Santo Domingo, Santa Clara, San Juan, and San Ildefonso Pueblos. "In other words, town boys," he said. "Great people, but the country boys were for me." Rural Navajos were more accessible and an easier choice for character development than the more reclusive Puebloans who guarded their lives, culture, and religion from outsiders. Navajos also struck Hillerman as familiar. "When I walk up to the trading post at Two Grey Hills or someplace in the boonies and there's a bunch of guys sitting on the front porch," Hillerman told a friend, "I *know* these people. They are the same people who sat on the front porch at my dad's store."[3]

Hillerman wanted to populate his book with an assortment of Navajos in trading posts, curing rituals, and hogans (traditional dwellings). "I thought that the Navajos and the Navajo reservation were so intriguing that even if my plots weren't so good, the background would be interesting," said Hillerman. He was confident in his ability to write vivid descriptions of the rugged landscape and compelling portraits of the people from his years as a journalist. But plotting a mystery was entirely new to him. He was counting on his use of a Navajo backdrop to carry the story along.[4]

In his choice of a setting, Hillerman may have been influenced by two authors. When he lived in Santa Fe, Hillerman had become acquainted with *Santa Fe New Mexican* columnist Oliver La Farge. An anthropologist and advocate for Native Americans, La Farge had written the novel *Laughing Boy*, set on the Navajo Nation. Certainly, it had not escaped Hillerman's attention that a book written by a white author with Navajo characters earned a Pulitzer Prize. Also, by his own admission, Hillerman was inspired to create literary landscapes like those penned by Arthur Upfield. The writer of detective stories set in Australia featured a half-indigenous inspector with the memorable name of Napoleon "Bony" Bonaparte. Hillerman recalled having read Upfield's stories as a child when he sold magazine subscriptions. However, none had been published in the United States at that time. Rather, it was when he lived in Santa Fe that Hillerman came across the writer's work. At the public library he found *The Bone Is Pointed*, Upfield's eleventh novel, as well as several subsequent ones. He was spellbound by the author's descriptions of the landscape in the outback and the portrayal of what was then referred to as aboriginal life. "I cannot say that when I set about to write my own version of the mystery novel Arthur Upfield was consciously in my mind," said Hillerman. "Subconsciously, he certainly was."[5]

Despite his brief encounter with Navajos in 1945 and his years as a reporter in northern New Mexico, Hillerman's knowledge of the Navajo way of life was insufficient if their world was to serve a critical role in his book. He became a frequent visitor to UNM's Zimmerman Library, a massive Pueblo-style edifice designed by John Gaw Meem with hand-carved vigas holding up lofty ceilings in cathedral-like reading rooms. There he found approximately two dozen works of ethnology and anthropology to provide an authentic feel to his work. Particularly useful was *The Agricultural and Hunting Methods of the Navajo People*, by his friend and university colleague Willard W. Hill. In it he found drawings and explanations for using the deadfall to trap a kangaroo rat that he used in the opening lines of his manuscript.[6]

> Luis Horseman leaned the flat stone very carefully against the piñon twig, adjusted its balance exactly and then cautiously withdrew his hand. The twig bent, but held. Horseman rocked back on his heels and surveyed the deadfall. He should have put a little more blood on the twig, he thought, but it might be enough. He had placed this one just right, with the twig at the edge of the kangaroo rat's trail. The least nibble and the stone would fall.[7]

The scene transported the reader away from the urban milieu of detective novels by Raymond Chandler, Ross MacDonald, and other masters of the form that Hillerman admired. The landscape he painted was unlike any that mystery readers would have encountered, with perhaps the exception of the Upfield books. By using Navajo place-names—or inventing ones such as Many Ruins Canyon—and mixing in Navajo nomenclature, Hillerman told of thunderheads outlined by the Bearer of the Sun above the expanse of the Kam Bimghi west of the Lukáchukai Mountains. Ravens noisily took to the sky, their caws replaced by the whistling of the horned lark. And canyons were redolent with the smell of wet dust and rain-blessed grass.[8]

To add touches of authenticity Hillerman included passages of Navajo spiritual songs from the various reference works he found in the Zimmerman Library. Songs, or chants, are a central feature of Navajo life and, broadly speaking, are used in blessing ceremonies to ensure continued fortune, and in healing ceremonies. A paragraph into his manuscript Hillerman has his Navajo hunter, Luis Horseman, sing a chant drawn verbatim from one of the anthropological tomes he had taken down from the shelf.[9]

At the end of the opening chapter, Luis Horseman appears doomed after he believes he has seen a Navajo Wolf. Forty-two pages into the book, his body is discovered. Hillerman's protagonist McKee, a student of Navajo witchcraft, learns of Horseman's mysterious death when he meets up with Navajo Police Lieutenant Joe Leaphorn. The two had been students together at Arizona State University, and Leaphorn provides McKee with leads of apparent sightings of Navajo witches. Soon McKee and his UNM colleague J. R. Canfield are drawn into a deadly adventure surrounding the Navajo's death that plays out in the canyons of the Lukachukai Mountains.[10]

Despite being introduced early in the novel, it is not the Navajo police officer who does the majority of the sleuthing in Hillerman's first attempt at writing a mystery. Instead that role falls to McKee, who, though younger, shares a number of traits with the author. They both had rural upbringings, were war veterans, worked as UNM professors, and were drawn to Navajos. But as Hillerman shaped his story, he encountered a common phenomenon in writing fiction. Characters turn out differently from the original conception, almost as if they take on their own life. In McKee's case, Hillerman said, "He was not really the sort of fellow I had intended him to be, less heroic and more academic."[11]

Rather, as he wrote, another figure grew in importance. "An officer of the Navajo Tribal Police," said Hillerman, "whom I had intended to be nothing more than a cardboard device for passing on information to the reader, had also taken on three dimensions and was clamoring for a bigger part." In short, the groundbreaking introduction of a Native American sleuth into the world of mysteries had been an afterthought, almost an accident of plot making. And the character might not have even been a Navajo.

For a brief time in the early stages of plotting, Hillerman had considered using an Apache police officer. He had gotten the idea from a front-page story about the death of a Jicarilla Apache tribal officer published in the *Santa Fe New Mexican* while he still ran the paper. Ishkoten Koteen had been shot and killed after he encountered someone stealing gasoline on the reservation. The thief had been gathering what was known as "drip gasoline" formed by condensation on natural gas pipelines. As Depression-era children, Hillerman and his brother, Barney, had done the same in Sacred Heart. "The circumstances stuck in my mind and I thought when the time comes that I am going to write a novel of this kind of stuff, I'm going to use an Apache tribal policeman," Hillerman said.[12]

But as he considered the idea further, Hillerman decided Navajos were more suitable for his plans. "They are such a big tribe and such an important tribe," he said, "and their religion and their metaphysics [are so] attractive to me, complicated, rich, that I decided to make it a Navajo." In passing, he invented the name Joe Leaphorn for his Navajo tribal policeman. It came to him from the pages of Mary Renault's 1962 novel *The Bull from the Sea*. "It was in the book I was reading, where Mary Renault was writing about Cretans jumping over the bull's horns," said Hillerman. "So, I stick it in, even though there's no Navajo in the world named Leaphorn!"[13]

"Besides," Hillerman thought, "the policeman wasn't going to be that important anyway, the anthropologist was going to be the main character." He would later regret his naming decision.[14]

Before the start of the 1966 fall semester, he mailed Ann Elmo his opening chapter along with several others he had completed for what he called his "Navajo Reservation cliff-hanger" to get the agent's thoughts. She got back to him after reading the scant pages. "I am intrigued all right," she said. "I am especially attracted to your story background and your Indian characters." But the story moved too slowly for her and had too many characters, she told Hillerman. "It would be easier I suppose, if you re-focused your story say, around McKee (isn't he the person who eventually gets at the bottom of the mystery?)" She also worried that the opening chapter, focused solely on Horseman, could mislead readers. "But," she added, "it would be difficult, and unfair too, to pass judgement now since there is very little story to base a decision on." That would have to wait until Hillerman had something approaching a complete manuscript, or at least a solid plot outline.[15]

For months on end Hillerman worked on the story whenever he could find time. "When I was sitting in those dreary faculty meetings," said Hillerman,

"I was looking intelligent and listening, I was really in chapter nine, getting a reputation as a good listener and working on my book." But mostly the book was created in the Hillermans' Texas Street house in Albuquerque. In the early evening, the family would gather for dinner around a large kitchen table. Sometimes Hillerman paused to eat but not for conversation, he admitted. "Wife senses 'lost in chapter' condition and leaves problems for later." Marie made meals of beans and rice, chicken, and other budget-conscious dishes. "She was really good," said their son Tony, "but it was the sign of the cross, amen, then it was all hell broke loose as far as getting what you wanted to eat." When the food carnage was complete, the children did the dishes and the table was pushed back against the wall.[16]

Hillerman would then retreat to a worn-out couch where he took out two decks of cards and played spider solitaire. Marie would keep the children away. "Don't bother your dad," Marie told their daughter Anne, "he's working." Since the beginning of their marriage, Marie had done everything she could to free Tony to pursue his journalism career. Now that he was taking this midlife leap into fiction, Marie continued in her supportive and protective role. "She made my dad's career possible because she was the one that kept everything going on, so he could be able to write," recalled their son Tony.[17]

In Marie, Tony had an extraordinarily well-read partner and he valued her writing advice. Somehow—between running a house, tending children, attending daily mass, and volunteering—Marie found time to read stacks of books. At the time Tony was working on the manuscript, Marie was making her way through a selection of literary authors that was the equal of any graduate school reading list. It comprised, among others, Albert Camus, Anton Chekhov, Fyodor Dostoevsky, Graham Greene, Oscar Wilde, Wallace Stegner, and D. H. Lawrence. Her nonfiction choices included C. S. Lewis, Edward Abbey, Henri Troyat, Teilhard de Chardin, and Dag Hammarskjöld. Almost no author escaped Marie's attention. Short story collections, literary tomes, biographies, and mysteries were all of interest to her.[18]

She recorded all the books she read in pocket-sized notebooks, writing brief summaries and reviews in neat handwriting. "The book made me wonder about my own inherent prejudices," Marie wrote when she put down Jonathan Kozol's *Death at an Early Age*, a devastating account of racial injustice in Boston public schools. Thornton Wilder's *The Eighth Day* drew great praise: "One of the best novels I've ever read." With a husband at work on a detective novel, Marie also included classic and contemporary mysteries in her selections, exclaiming when she finished Dashiell Hammett's *The Thin Man*, "don't know how I could have missed it for so many years." But Marie's notebook entries were not always complimentary. She read Edward Abbey's *Desert Solitaire*, a Thoreau-like meditation on the desert, just after it was published. "It seems to me that anyone loving nature as much as he seemed to would have more compassion and love for his fellow men," she wrote. "He disappointed me." For her husband, Marie became a valued critic, applying her perceptive literary skills to his writing. "She knows how to criticize my work to tell me what she thinks of it without hurting my feelings," Hillerman told an interviewer. "She is the brains of the family."[19]

As he played solitaire each night, Hillerman developed the scenes for his novel. "He would get this look on his face," recalled his son Tony. "He would get up and go into the bedroom and sit down and start writing." The process would repeat itself: more cards and more writing into the night. "Sometimes in those dark hours I would realize that the scene I had finished was bad, the story wasn't moving, the book would never be published, and I couldn't afford wasting time I could be using to write nonfiction people would buy." He would then put the pages into a box and back on a closet shelf for days and weeks until the urge to tell the story returned.[20]

After three years of work, Hillerman enlisted the help of Mary Dudley, a graduate student in anthropology who worked part-time for him. Hillerman's growing confidence in his writing convinced him to pay her with his own money to type the penultimate draft of his book after work on an office typewriter using the back of UNM presidential stationery left over from the seventy-fifth anniversary of the university in 1964, when Hillerman had worked in the president's office.[21]

By the spring of 1969, Hillerman neared the end of his efforts. He believed the scene in the book where McKee escapes a killer in the darkness of the fictitious Many Ruins Canyon was some of the best writing he had ever done. But, on the whole, he remained insecure. "The book," he said, "wasn't nearly as good as I'd intended." Particularly the ending. He chose one of three he had written and tacked it on. He had come to the point where he was unwilling to continue working because he had grown tired of the manuscript after three long years of toil.[22]

Like most New York City book editors, fifty-four-year-old Joan Kahn received a daily deluge of letters and manuscripts from authors and agents. She could hardly complain, as she herself had opened the spigot by penning articles in *The*

Writer that gave hope to aspiring authors. Lacking a college degree, notorious for being incapable of typing, and a poor speller, Kahn had nonetheless risen from an entry-level job at Harper & Row after World War II to running her own imprint. Her desk on the top floor of Harper & Row's six-story brick building on East 33rd Street was littered with paper. "A mound so high you could hardly see her if she was sitting down at the desk," recalled her colleague Hugh Van Dusen.[23]

On an early April day in 1969, Kahn found a letter bearing a New Mexico return address in her stack of mail. The writer—either genuinely earnest or stealthily cunning—wanted her to arbitrate a literary dispute. "Ann Elmo (whose agency had placed magazine non-fiction for me)," began Hillerman's letter, "and I are currently disagreeing over whether a suspense novel manuscript I sent to her is ready to be submitted for publication."[24]

Hillerman explained he had written a novel with Kahn's Harper Novels of Suspense series in mind. It featured an anthropologist in a plot laced with Navajo witchcraft and werewolf superstitions. The problem, Hillerman continued, was that Elmo felt the material relating to Indian ritual slowed the action and should be cut. "I would, therefore, deeply appreciate your editorial opinion," he said. "It is not that I am trying to make you a referee," insisted Hillerman. He and Elmo viewed their difference of opinion in a friendly manner, he said. "It is simply that I consider you the premier authority in this field, and Ann, I believe, agrees with me."

Kahn was apparently persuaded, flattered, or sufficiently intrigued. Within two days of receiving Hillerman's letter she requested a copy of the manuscript. On April 10, Hillerman mailed the manuscript, which he titled *Monsterslayer*, one of the two Hero Twins in the Navajo origins story and the nickname given to McKee by his students. "I couldn't think of anything better," said Hillerman. When it arrived, Kahn gave it a quick read and asked her sister Olivia, who often read manuscripts for her, to look it over as well. Both were impressed, particularly with what the two sisters referred to as the "Indian stuff." Within days, Kahn turned to her typewriter. "I'd want to reread it before giving you all my thoughts on revision," she wrote to Hillerman, "but unlike Miss Elmo, the parts I'd want to keep are the Indian lore and ritual parts." What needed work, she said, was the ending and the development of several of the lesser characters. "Anyhow," she concluded her note, "if we agree after we've talked further and when I've reread, I hope you can revise and we can publish."[25]

Part of the appeal of Hillerman's manuscript to Kahn was timing. There was a growing interest among New York publishing houses in Native American culture. The year before, Kahn's own company had published the breakthrough novel *House Made of Dawn* by Kiowa writer and poet N. Scott Momaday. Set on a pueblo modeled on the Jemez Pueblo of New Mexico, the novel went on to win the Pulitzer Prize for Fiction that spring and would come to be regarded as the first major work of the Native American Renaissance.

In Kahn's domain, that of mysteries, memorable characters and settings had grown in importance and Hillerman's use of Navajo culture and a Navajo police officer seemed promising. "I do prefer people to puzzles," Kahn wrote in February of that year. "I get tired of games pretty quickly and doubt I could have spent as many years in the business as I have, if the whodunit had not turned into the suspense novel when it did."[26]

As Kahn's letter made its way west to New Mexico, Hillerman was flying east to New York City for a meeting of the American Council on Education for Journalism. He called Kahn while in the city, as one did in an age of long-distance telephone rates.[27]

"Haven't you got my letter?" she asked.

"No," he replied. "I've been away."

"Well, we want to publish it if you can write a better last chapter."

"I can," Hillerman promised.[28]

From New York, he drove north to Amherst, Massachusetts, to visit his daughter Anne, who was completing a semester exchange program at the University of Massachusetts. In a rental car, the two battled East Coast traffic, a novelty for them, to visit Plymouth. It was Tony's first trip to New England. Anne reveled in having her father all to herself and being with him after he had received the encouraging news from Kahn. Six years after leaving the paper, five years after getting an agent, and three years after completing his master's thesis, Tony Hillerman was on the verge of reaching his dreamed-of moment.[29]

Kahn had a reputation as a tough editor. "You have to stand by your authors," she told *Publishers Weekly* that year, "but you do them a disservice by publishing everything they write even if it's not good." She sent Hillerman a two-page list of necessary editorial changes. He eagerly undertook the revisions. "One's attitude toward a manuscript changes when one learns it's likely to be published," he said. In addition to richer secondary characters, Kahn wanted more Leaphorn. She also urged Hillerman to get rid of the clichéd action. "We had too many rocks clenched in McKee's good hand and too many tied up trees, etc." said

Kahn. Lastly, Kahn made it clear, the conclusion Hillerman had slapped on the end of his manuscript in frustration was inadequate. "The whole ending has the feeling that you were in sort of a hurry to get the book done. You rush past everything—don't let it grow as you've done with the rest of the book," she wrote. "And if you'll rework the ending, I'll start a contract through."[30]

Hillerman got to work on the revisions as Elmo and Kahn settled on terms. The contract provided a $2,000 advance and a standard royalty scale of 10 percent for the first 5,000 copies sold, 12.5 percent for the next 5,000, and 15 percent thereafter. The money was equal to 25 percent of Hillerman's annual salary. More important to the author was that the manuscript was now an incipient book. "Gone was the notion that this was wasted time, that I was only indulging myself," he said.[31]

Hillerman followed Kahn's lead and greatly expanded Leaphorn's role. "I beefed up the role of this relatively minor character in the book and gave him a much more important role, because I was beginning even then to see what I might do with it." For instance, in the early pages of the book, Hillerman eliminated Belasandro Ortiz, who wrote an important letter to McKee about witchcraft. Instead he made Leaphorn the letter's author, establishing his friendship with McKee and his role as explainer in the remainder of the book. Hillerman also reworked pages to carve out an additional chapter for Leaphorn. In it, Leaphorn's inner monologue contrasts Navajo thinking with that of *bilagáana*—white people—and produces a breakthrough in the Horseman murder case.[32]

By May 22, Hillerman had completed most of the revisions, except for the ending. He worked on several versions, all intended to slow down the pace. "The book's too good to let the end go rushed and sloppy," Kahn had admonished. Hillerman confronted a common problem for mystery writers. It is one thing to write an intriguing plot, it's entirely another problem to bring it to an end in credible fashion. Hillerman resolved it with his wounded protagonist contriving a homemade weapon, Leaphorn making a timely arrival, and a suicide. The manuscript was improved sufficiently for Kahn, but both editor and author knew the ending was the weakest part of the book.[33]

Kahn worked meticulously to give the manuscript its final polish. She had a keen eye, inserting missing clues and fixing inconsistencies. Kahn, a city woman, even corrected Hillerman's mistaken references to the constellations, his inaccurate description of a hawk's beak, and goldenrods blooming in the wrong season. She was, however, confused over trucks and campers. "Out here," Hillerman told her, "'camper' is an almost universal term for a pickup truck with a covered living arrangement fitted into the pickup bed."[34]

In one instance, Kahn questioned whether a person could be tied up face-down on the back seat of a car in the manner that McKee found himself. "I tried it," reported Hillerman, "sans rope, because I wondered myself. It's possible but a strain." At another point in the manuscript, Kahn sought to alter the word "emergence" to "divergence" used in a phrase describing Leaphorn "grating on his ingrained Navajo conviction that any emergence from the human norm was unnatural and—therefore—unhealthy." Hillerman dissuaded her. "It's the despair of Indian school teachers that the smart kids resist emerging from the mass due to this attitude," Hillerman scribbled in the margin.[35]

The proposed book title *Monsterslayer* did not sit well with Kahn. She sent Hillerman a list of ideas she had drawn from the manuscript: *The Male Game*, *The Dark Horn*, *The Man in the Wolfskin*, *To Keep Me Safe from Witches*, and *The Blessing Way*. On July 2, Kahn pronounced Hillerman's revisions satisfactory and left on vacation. In her absence a problem surfaced. Harper & Row permissions editors wanted to know the source of what they called the "Navajo poetry," the chants Hillerman used in his book. Even the smallest bits of poetry are protected by copyright and Hillerman had used verbatim excerpts throughout the work. He promised to return to the library to find his sources.[36]

There he located all the books he had begun with more than four years earlier and submitted the citations for all but the ones at the beginning of his manuscript. He was mostly on safe ground as the books were old and had fallen into the public domain. But in the case of the first two chants in the book, he wrongly believed he had rephrased a translation from UNM Professor Hill's work, whose copyright was still in force. He did not seek permission from the Navajo Nation. In any case, he had a solution that would get around both potential copyright and permission problems. He rewrote the unattributed songs into what he called "a synthetic Hillerman version of Navajo chants." He told the editors, "I wrote these last night with no question of infringement on someone else's translation. I like to do my sinning on the side of safety."[37]

On June 2, 1969, Hillerman's mother, Lucy Grove Hillerman, died in Mount Kisco, New York, where she had been living for a while with her daughter Margaret Mary Chambers. She was eighty-three and, in recent years, had required care because of her worsening memory loss. Four days later, the siblings Tony, Barney, and Margaret Mary gathered for a requiem mass at Christ the King Catholic Church in Oklahoma City. Afterwards, they drove to Sacred Heart and laid her to rest next to her husband, August, in the small cemetery in front of the church on the hill just up the road from the family's old farm. It was a mild early summer day for Oklahoma, with temperatures in the eighties. "The Zoeller pear orchard below still in bloom. Mockingbirds performing in the old cemetery cedars, and the songs of meadowlarks accompanying the graveside prayers," Hillerman said. "I remembered how Mama had loved days like this. And a host of other things about her that I was now old enough to begin understanding."[38]

More than his father, who had remained a distant figure until his death when Hillerman was only sixteen, Hillerman's mother had been the source of life lessons he retained as an adult. Her adventurous youth as a homesteader had inspired Hillerman to seek adventure in the world beyond the small village of his youth. Her most important legacy was not to be afraid of anything. "Since God loves us, there is no rational justification for fear," Hillerman said his deeply Catholic mother taught him. "If we do our part by using the good sense He gave us, He's not going to let anything happen that isn't somehow or other for our own good."[39]

A stern but loving mother, Lucy Grove Hillerman passed on a stoicism from her hard life on the plains of Nebraska and Oklahoma. When Tony was only five or six years old, his father was carrying home a Black Diamond watermelon that he had tended all summer long. At the gate to the house, the watermelon slipped from his hands, wet with sweat, and shattered on the ground. When his mother comforted Tony, he heard for the first of many times his mother's favorite aphorism: "Blessed are those who expect little. They are seldom disappointed." Thirty-two years after his mother's death, Hillerman would title his memoir *Seldom Disappointed.*

The book at Harper & Row, now retitled *The Blessing Way*, was done and ready for publication. Readers would be unaware of the fact, but Hillerman had come full circle. The book set in the Navajo world would be in stores twenty-five years after he viewed an Enemy Way one night on the Navajo Nation at war's end. Neither Hillerman nor his editor had any idea what the publication of this book would start. And, like any author, Hillerman knew the fate of another book would rest greatly on the success of the first. "Harper and Row," he wrote to a friend, "is publishing my first novel (and maybe my last one, for that matter.)" Now the only thing forty-four-year-old Hillerman could do was wait.[40]

Tony (right end of front row) poses with his classmates at St. Mary's Academy in Sacred Heart, Oklahoma, in the early 1930s. His brother, Barney, is second from the left in the front row. The mission school for Potawatomi girls run by the Sisters of Mercy admitted a sprinkling of boys whose parents wanted them to partake in the academically oriented curriculum. (Sacred Heart Monastery)

Barney, Margaret Mary, and Tony Hillerman put on their Sunday best for a family portrait in the early 1930s. (Karl Hillerman)

On most days Tony Hillerman's father, August "Gus" Hillerman, could be found behind the counter of his general store until ill health and the Great Depression forced him to close the business. Gus died on Christmas Day 1941 when Tony was only sixteen. (Hillerman Estate)

A stern but loving mother, Lucy passed on a stoicism from her hard life on the plains of Nebraska and Oklahoma. She was the source of life lessons Tony retained as an adult. Her youthful experience as a homesteader inspired him to seek adventure in the world beyond the small village of his youth. (Hillerman Estate)

Hillerman (standing with cane) at the Army 3rd General Hospital in
Aix-en-Provence in spring 1945, where he recovered most of his eyesight
and use of his left leg after stepping on a land mine. While recuperating,
Hillerman first began considering a career as a writer. (Janet Grado/CSWR)

At the end of World War II, Barney (left) and Tony (right) reunite with
their mother Lucy shortly before entering the University of Oklahoma in
January 1946. Tony took off the eye patch he still frequently wore and set
aside his cane for the photograph taken by their cousin Larry Grove who,
like Tony, returned from the war wounded. (Janet Grado/CSWR)

Hillerman arrives on the campus of the University of Oklahoma in January 1946 full of hope and ambition, like many other returning veterans whose tuition and expenses were paid by the GI Bill. (Janet Grado/ Hillerman Estate/CSWR)

Tony Hillerman and Marie Unzner marry on August 16, 1948, in her hometown of Shawnee, Oklahoma, shortly after graduating from the University of Oklahoma. Marie, a brilliant student of microbiology, met Tony at a dance during their senior year. A stylish dresser who took great care for her appearance, Marie was camera shy and came to avoid being captured in family photographs. (Hillerman Estate)

Hillerman put in long hours in the 1950s as a wire service reporter and eventually as editor of the *Santa Fe New Mexican*. The volume of copy he produced and the deadline pressure honed his writing skills. A chain smoker known to have a cigarette smoldering in the ashtray while lighting another, Hillerman gave up cigarettes after a cancer scare in the late 1960s. (Hillerman Estate)

In 1958, Tony poses with his growing family after celebrating the baptism of its youngest member at St. John the Baptist Catholic Church in Santa Fe. From left to right are Janet, Steve, Tony Jr., and Anne. Not pictured here is Daniel, who was adopted in 1966. (Marie Hillerman photograph/Hillerman Estate)

Hillerman takes a break from his work as an administrator and professor of journalism at the University of New Mexico, where he obtained a master's degree and began writing his novels in the late 1960s. (Hillerman Estate)

In the summer of 1971 Hillerman and his first book editor, Joan Kahn, spend time together while she visits New Mexico. She recognized the significance of Hillerman's use of Navajo culture and people, and her support of his work launched his career. (Hillerman Estate)

Larry Ashmead and Tony Hillerman share a moment at a writing conference. Ashmead took over editing Hillerman's books after Kahn left Harper & Row in 1980. Hillerman's relationship with Ashmead became the longest-lasting, most profitable, and most successful he had with any editor. (Hillerman Estate/CSWR)

Hillerman enjoys a laugh at his regular poker party. The weekly gatherings were so important to him that he turned down a dinner invitation from Robert Redford in order not to miss a game. (Steve Northup Photographic Archive, 2012-237/4, Dolph Briscoe Center for American History, University of Texas at Austin)

Barney (left) and Tony spend a rare moment together in 1980. A decade later
the two brothers jointly produced *Hillerman Country*, a coffee table book with
Tony's text and Barney's photographs. Just before the book's publication, however,
Barney died from a heart attack. On the front door of his photography studio in
Oklahoma City, a sign was posted: "Bernard (Barney) Hillerman 1/27/23–10/7/91.
Gone to photograph another area. (Good shooting.)" (Janet Grado/CSWR)

Hillerman and members of the Navajo Nation Tribal Police line up for the camera in
1994. Over the course of writing eighteen novels Hillerman became popular among
members of the police force. From left to right are Marlon Tolberson, Randy W.
John Sr., Leroy Desla Jr., Billy Hillgartner, and Sam Ahkeah. (Hillerman Estate)

Hillerman visits the set of *A Thief of Time* in 2003 to make a cameo appearance in Slick Nakai's revival tent scene. Here he poses with Brandi Ahmie, a member of the Laguna Pueblo, who was a film extra. (Alice Fernando-Ahmie photo.)

In 2003, newly elected Navajo Nation president and Hillerman fan Joe Shirley Jr, with his wife, Vikki, examine a Navajo rug with Hillerman. Shirley praised Hillerman's books because they encouraged Navajo children to read. (Don Strel photograph/CSWR)

New Mexico governor Bill Richardson (second from left, back row) hosts a gala to celebrate the 2003 PBS broadcast of "Coyote Waits." Attending the event were Rebecca Easton, executive producer (to Richardson's right), Pat Mitchell, president of PBS (to Richardson's left), and actor Wes Studi, who played the role of Joe Leaphorn. Sitting with Hillerman on the couch is Jane Fonda. (Linda L. Carfagno photograph)

Hillerman leans back against his favorite pigeonhole desk, which he obtained from an old hotel office. Above his desk he hung an AAA map of the Navajo Nation, like the one used by his fictional police officer Joe Leaphorn. (Hillerman Estate)

CHAPTER 15

❖ Professor Hillerman ❖

The thermometer read ten degrees the morning Tony Hillerman drove to campus for the first day of the spring semester, January 5, 1970. He steered his dark-metallic-green 1970 Ford Maverick—the first new car he had ever owned—down Louisiana Boulevard to Interstate 40. When the smog above Albuquerque abated, the place offered Hillerman an expansive view westward. "It is exactly at this spot and at this moment that Mount Taylor comes into view," he said. "It is my favorite mountain, and the gateway to my favorite places."[1]

To most commuters, the panoramic vista was just one more in a state filled with geographic splendor. But to Hillerman the view of the mountain now took on a meaning shaped by four years of studying Navajo culture. Tsoodził, as the Navajos called it, was one of the four sacred peaks delineating the boundaries of Dinétah, the Navajo homeland. To the north and west of Tsoodził lay the land that had served as the setting for the novel waiting to go to press in New York. "My map tells me the Turquoise Mountain is 62.7 miles from this noisy intersection," said Hillerman. "In another sense the distance is infinite."[2]

The day would afford little opportunity to think about that distant land or his book. Students were streaming back onto the campus. Enrollment in the Journalism Department had grown by 20 percent during the last year. Hillerman had to prepare for three courses: Advanced Reporting, Newspaper Practice, and Media as a Social Force. In addition, he was planning for a new course in editorial writing in the fall and had tedious administrative responsibilities as department chair. His office was on the southern edge of the campus in one of the university's ubiquitous adobe buildings that had once served as a residence for women students.[3]

Hillerman usually arrived on campus in an ebullient mood. "Have you seen the clouds today?" he would ask Mary Dudley, who worked briefly in the office. "If I didn't give a convincing *yes*," she recalled, "he would insist that we go out and we'd stand on the lawn of the Journalism Building and look at the clouds come over the Sandia Mountains." Ever since he was a child growing up in Oklahoma during the Dust Bowl. Hillerman had been a cloud watcher.[4]

When Hillerman had first begun teaching at UNM four years earlier, he had inherited the basic journalism classes such as News Writing. Instructing future journalists harkened him back to his days as a student at the University of Oklahoma after the war. "It was a wonderful time to be teaching," said Hillerman. The students struck him as eager to learn and they took to his folksy pedagogy. The avuncular professor wore the narrow ties that were fashionable then, but loose with an open collar, with jackets and pants carelessly matched. "There's none of the professorial moss about Tony," noted a reporter who stopped by the campus that spring. "There is a disarmingly casual air about him."[5]

In class, students were treated to tales from the trenches of daily journalism. "He was always warm, humorous, generous, droll, with an anecdotal style of teaching, using lots of illuminating examples, many from his own experience," according to former student Sharon Niederman, who became an author and journalist. Hillerman's recollections were his tools of teaching, journalistic parables that also served to inspire. "We wanted to get out in the world and turn experience into prose," said another former student, George Johnson.[6]

Like the much-admired Professor H. H. Herbert at the University of Oklahoma, Hillerman wanted his students to understand the power and the accompanying responsibilities that came with being a reporter. "From him, the students learned about real-life examples of proper journalism ethics," recalled one student. Hillerman was not averse to using his own experiences to show the consequences, often unforeseen, of the news business. The topic was also on his mind in the 1970 spring semester. In his typewriter at home was the beginnings of a new novel in which journalistic ethics would play an important role.[7]

Inspired by William Strunk Jr and E. B. White's *The Elements of Style*, Hillerman offered a set of writing rules to guide the willing students. At home, he was putting them into practice in his fiction. "Writing is writing," Hillerman told his students.

"Whether fiction or non-fiction, poetry or prose, most of the same rules apply, most of the same devices are effective, most of the same flaws will kill you."[8]

Concision was paramount: "As sentences get shorter, they generally get stronger," he said, paraphrasing the famous guide to writing. Active voice should be a habit: "It makes for forceful writing." Concrete and specific nouns and verbs were preferable: A *welder* rather than a *laborer*, a *begonia* instead of a *flower*. Echoing the instructions to remove "cornstarch words" that Professor Grace Ray had given when he was in college, Hillerman offered his students a lesson in *wordectomy*. The sentence "The animals' faces expressed pleasure as they consumed their food" became concise, concrete, specific, and active when written as "The hippos grinned as they chew their carrots." For Hillerman, writers were verbose because they lacked a command of the vocabulary. Conciseness does not demand short sentences, he said, "It requires simply that every word tell."[9]

The placement of words and clauses should be deliberate: "Use the phrase, or word, you wish to emphasize, at the end of the sentence or paragraph." Also, a word or clause gains attention if used at the beginning of a sentence when it is not the expected subject. For instance, "Bad manners, she could never tolerate" or "Reckless drivers, these Armenians." Writing with nouns and verbs achieved economy: *the elderly man walked slowly by* is made better by using the word *plodded*. "When you use adjectives choose them carefully," he admonished. "If you pick the right noun or verb you probably won't need them."[10]

Hillerman pushed his students to make their writing reveal rather than tell and to weave their material together. In his class on persuasive writing, aspiring journalist Susan Walton struggled at first with shedding the linear way she had been taught to write. "I wasn't synthesizing well. I was really regurgitating," she said. "And he wasn't interested in that. He wanted to see a process of consideration and thought, coming out." He pushed the students to use observations to develop a point of view. Drawing on his experience writing editorials at the *Santa Fe New Mexican*, Hillerman demonstrated his method. If, for instance, city maintenance was failing, Hillerman figuratively walked the reader down the street to the fence lined with trash, by the drain with cockroaches, and past the unfilled pothole. Now that he was a professor, he instructed his students to leave campus to hone their observation skills.[11]

Compare the crowds at the airport and bus terminal, he told them. "If you think they represent different socio-economic classes, let me see enough to lead me to the same conclusion." Visit bars frequented by homosexuals and a bar playing country-western music. "What do you see that identifies them?" Attend a trial and look for a bored member of the jury. "Show me what you saw that caused you to think that." Hillerman argued observation and detail were the keys to a good journalistic story, according to one student. "Hone in on every detail so that you could set a stage around a story." If the stories the students brought back were good enough, Hillerman offered them to the *Albuquerque Journal*, which occasionally published some.[12]

Papers assigned are papers in need of a grade. When it came to the many essays and articles submitted by his students, Hillerman applied an idiosyncratic approach. He evaluated the students' work on a ten-point scale and was not hesitant to provide an opinionated reaction, though gentle in his criticism and invariably encouraging. One of his talented students, George Johnson, broke up with this girlfriend just before the final assignment of the semester was due. "I was up late drinking beer and spewing out pages of typewritten angst, which I submitted the next morning." Hillerman returned the work with an A+. "You write better drunk than most students do sober," he wrote on the top of the paper. "That was all the encouragement I needed," said Johnson, who went on to become a *New York Times* editor, science reporter, and author.[13]

On major assignments students received lengthy typed evaluations. For instance, Hillerman wrote a one-page, single-spaced commentary praising and encouraging a young woman who had submitted chapters of a novel in a creative writing class he taught. "None of this has anything to do with the grade," he wrote. He explained that she came to the class with a lot of talent and some bad habits and left with a lot of talent and some progress. "I rate that as *Satisfactory Performance* which earns you a C," he concluded. "Had I been a better teacher for you it could have been a B at least." To another student named Felipe, he wrote, "I think I will give you a B, which reflects a grade but not my judgment of your talent, which is remarkable."[14]

His dedication to his students prompted him to spend time selecting paragraphs from their work, typing them up on a stencil, and running them off on the office mimeograph machine. The blue-inked sheets were then distributed in class for group discussion. Typically, Hillerman Socratically pushed the students to apply his writing rules. "You say 'obviously drunk,'" he might say, "What made it obvious?" Along with samples of their own work, Hillerman typed up more stencils with brief excerpts from the works of Joan Didion, Tom Wolfe, Gary Wills, Barbara Goldsmith, Ken Kesey, and Gay Talese, among others.[15]

Hillerman was certain he could teach most of his students to write. "There are some who can't be taught to write," he admitted, "just as I can't be taught to whistle thru my teeth." He disliked many of the bromides about the craft. It was, for instance, "sheer nonsense" that writers write for themselves. "You have to write for someone otherwise you're like a man at a telegraph key talking into a vacuum. It's totally sterile and self-defeating," said Hillerman. The point is to send and receive, "translating," in his words, "the image inside your skull into symbols and launching it at a target."[16]

Teaching nonfiction while exploring the writing of fiction after-hours caused Hillerman to reflect considerably on the differences between the two. "The differences between fiction and non-fiction are more apparent than real," he wrote. Nonfiction, which he had been trained to write and now taught, was less pliable than fiction and more craft-like. Fiction demanded more creativity resting on material either made up or from one's memory. "The facts are crafted in your imagination," Hillerman said. "They are glossy, persuasive, rich in symbolism, redolent of universal meaning, glittery, sordid, perfect, polished facts—the stuff of art."

Despite the demands of being department chair and the late-evening hours consumed by his own writing, Hillerman always made time for students. He wanted to provide instruction on how to write but give encouragement as well, as Professor Morris Freedman had done for him. "He himself was an author, which impressed me," said Hillerman, "and he saw promise in my work—which impressed me even more."[17]

Jim Belshaw was one of many aspiring journalists who experienced Hillerman's devotion to students. After being discharged from the Air Force, Belshaw registered for classes at UNM in September 1970. The clerk handed him a small slip of paper with the name of his adviser. "I looked at the name and thought, well, I don't know who Tony Hillerman is, but I know how to report." When he reached Hillerman's office, the professor looked over Belshaw's test scores, particularly the ones for math. "Journalism, right?" asked Hillerman.[18]

Hillerman guided Belshaw to an undergraduate degree in journalism and on to a career as a reporter and columnist. While working at one of his first jobs on a Las Cruces newspaper, Belshaw sent his former professor the manuscript of a book that had been rejected by a publisher. "The reason you sent it to me is because you lack confidence," Hillerman wrote back. "Go to the library and pick any novel (not the great classics) and read it. You will find that you write as well as most, and better than some."[19]

Once Judy Redman stopped by his office. Hillerman was her adviser and she wanted to show him a creative writing paper on which she had earned an A. Another professor overheard the conversation and stuck his head in the door. He jocularly told Hillerman that students studying creative writing in the English Department will hurt their ability to do journalism. "I disagree," replied Hillerman. "Good writing is good writing." Redman went on to become a reporter and book author.[20]

Hillerman, however, believed journalism was the best training ground. Carmella Padilla, a Santa Fe native, was uncertain what career she might want to pursue when Hillerman asked her about her goals. "I was thinking I wanted to be a physical therapist," she recalled telling him, "but I don't know, maybe I want to major in English."[21]

"Yeah, but what do you want to do?" persisted Hillerman.

"I want to write, I think."

"Or do you want to teach?"

"Well, I think writing is more becoming to me than teaching."

If that were the case, Hillerman advised her to stay clear of the English Department. He continued, according to Padilla, to say something to the effect: "If you really want to learn how to write, and learn the discipline of writing, which is what it's all about, you'd be better off in the Journalism Department."

"That really sunk in. I won't be so bold as to say that Tony Hillerman directed me to be a journalist, but he certainly opened my eyes to that as an option." After completing the journalism program, Carmella Padilla became one of New Mexico's most distinguished authors and an editor of work devoted to the Hispanic art, culture, and history of the state.

The dedication Hillerman showed his students, his willingness to guide them, and his irrepressible and engaging classroom storytelling made him an immensely popular professor. One student, however, ran up against a unique problem taking one of his classes. His daughter, Anne, made the mistake of enrolling in her father's early-morning class. Her eyelids grew heavy and she dozed off to the sound of the voice that had once put her to sleep reading bedtime stories.[22]

CHAPTER 16

◆ The Great American Novel ◆

Tony Hillerman had no intention of waiting for a verdict on his first novel before setting to work on his next one. *The Blessing Way* had been intended as a warm-up act. "The time had come to quit stalling and actually write *The Great American Novel*, which would concern journalists and politicians and have nothing to do with Indians," he said. "Now it was time to tap a fifteen-year accumulation of journalistic memories to write the important book." In the final months of 1969 and early months of 1970, Hillerman set to work on a novel, the kind that had been his goal when he left journalism and returned to school.[1]

He had written 146 pages so far on a tale of power, corruption, and journalism. He told his editor Joan Kahn, "All I can guarantee is that—since I spent ten years covering politics—the detail will be accurate." No time-consuming cultural research was needed. This was a world he knew firsthand. And, unlike *The Blessing Way*, for which he worked out the plot over the course of writing the book, Hillerman knew the story he wanted to tell. "Or at least I thought I did," he said. "But when I got into it, I found my storytelling instincts were at war with my urge to give the reader a truly realistic view of the professional life of a political reporter." Storytelling prevailed.[2]

At the novel's center is John Cotton, a reporter who stumbles on a conspiracy among high-level officials in an unidentified midwestern state where he worked as a capital correspondent. Hillerman wrote rapidly, mining his reporting experience in Oklahoma, his exposure to government corruption in Santa Fe, and his familiarity with fishing streams in northern New Mexico.

If Hillerman had begun with the intention of penning a work of literature, he soon changed his mind. "As I began writing it, getting into it, the more it became not what I had intended it to be but a mystery-suspense novel," said Hillerman. "I found I liked to write it better that way." He built this second novel much like the first. Both begin with a violent death, feature angst-ridden white protagonists who fall for the only woman in the book, and depend on a timely contrived weapon, what some in literary circles might call a deus ex machina. Also, in a strikingly similar fashion, Hillerman takes the reader deep into an unfamiliar culture. In *The Blessing Way* it is Navajo culture. In *The Fly on the Wall* it is the world of journalism.[3]

In the opening pages, one of Cotton's colleagues falls from the sixth floor of the capitol rotunda. Hillerman weaves a tale of political corruption tied to the death. Exposing the plot could bring down powerful politicians and might have deadly consequences for the reporter. Instead of a police procedural novel, where a detective would have searched for a killer, *The Fly on the Wall* becomes a journalistic procedural novel in which corruption is the crime and murder a consequence.

A notebook left behind by the dead reporter contains tantalizing clues of a scheme to bilk the state of highway construction funds. Hillerman details every aspect of the mundane and exhausting work of investigative reporting and extols the virtue of the journalist's creed. The setting was modeled on the capitol building in Oklahoma City, where Hillerman worked for United Press. "For some reason which has never seemed sensible in fiction, "Hillerman said, "I seem to need to sort of memorize the places in which my plots take place. For *The Fly on the Wall*, I had driven back to Oklahoma and prowled the echoing old corridors to refresh the memories collected in my reporting days."[4]

The corruption, however, was imported from his experiences in Santa Fe. In the decade during which he worked as a newspaperman in New Mexico's state capital, Hillerman wrote news stories of blatant corruption now suitable for his fiction. A favorite story the *Santa Fe New Mexican* pursued biannually was the commonplace practice of giving cash payments to voters. In May 1962, Hillerman dispatched an employee of the circulation department with a Minaflex camera about the size of a cigarette lighter to document the action at one polling place. "Phil DeBaca went out to take pictures of vote buying yesterday," Hillerman wrote in his front-page story, "and ended up with 14 crisp new $1 bills, a 50-cent piece, and a strong impression that politicians are careless with their money." His impression was correct. DeBaca never had time to vote.[5]

Hillerman ran into plot difficulties after John Cotton received a death threat. Cotton was not a police officer. He was only a reporter and writing stories that could get him killed was not part of the job description. Dropping the story would have been the prudent path. "I hit on having him flee to New Mexico, go fishing at my favorite little stream in isolated Brazos Meadows," said Hillerman, "and realize the death threat was merely a ruse to get him away from the state capital to somewhere he could be murdered quietly."[6]

Again, for this scene Hillerman needed no research. The Rio Brazos north of Santa Fe had been his favorite fishing spot for years. Hillerman used the spot to put Cotton in an almost inescapable position, copying a plot device from *The Blessing Way*. In that novel Bergen McKee had been trapped in a cave and had to contrive a weapon to ward off his would-be killer. Here Cotton makes his fly-fishing pole into a weapon. Attaching a heavy fishing lure with two sets of barbed hooks, Cotton snares his killer's jacket and pulls him off his unsteady perch on a log into the fast-moving stream. A fly fisherman who read the novel might be puzzled that Cotton had heavy lures in his tackle box, but Hillerman preferred to fish with them.[7]

A change in Hillerman's personal life spilled onto the pages of his new book. A few years earlier, after he had finished most of the manuscript for *The Blessing Way*, a doctor-ordered X-ray had revealed an ominous growth on one of his lungs. Since taking up smoking during World War II, Hillerman had maintained a two-pack or more daily habit. Sometimes he would have one cigarette smoldering in the ashtray while lighting the next. Once a colleague stopping by Hillerman's office spotted three cigarettes going at once. Marie gathered the children around the bed in the parents' bedroom. "They found a spot on Daddy's lungs," she said. Then each night the children knelt around the bed, said the rosary, and prayed for their father. When the time neared for surgery, the spot was gone. "Mom attributed it to our prayers which I do, too," said daughter Janet.[8]

The scare, however, caused Hillerman to give up his cigarette habit. On his desk at UNM, among the piles of papers, Hillerman placed a small rack with six smoking pipes based on the then-common but mistaken belief that they were safer than cigarettes. Pipes were certainly more professorial.[9]

In *The Blessing Way*, both McKee and Leaphorn were smokers like himself. But now Hillerman made Cotton a man who had recently quit. In an early chapter, Cotton is tempted to take a cigarette from an open pack on the table. "But then Cotton would be back on two and half packs a day by tomorrow," wrote Hillerman. "And eighteen days of misery would be wasted."[10]

On March 11, 1970, *The Blessing Way* was released. "After writing for more than a quarter of a century I was now, formally, officially, and incontestably an author," said Hillerman. For the cover, Harper & Row had turned to Mozelle Thompson, an African American Pittsburgh native who was a well-known album cover designer. Considered a pioneer in his field, Thompson had also done some book covers such as the one for the 1963 paperback edition of *A Clockwork Orange*. Sadly, the *Blessing Way* cover was one of the last works he completed before committing suicide in December 1969. For Hillerman's novel he placed a black silhouette of a Native American with an aquiline nose and a wolf headdress against a dark lavender background. The title appeared above in graffiti-like red letters. Hillerman first saw the cover when a Harper & Row sales representative who made calls on Albuquerque bookstores had a dust jacket in his briefcase.[11]

Of the nearly thirty thousand books published that year, three hundred were mysteries. Hillerman's was among a select number that gained attention from critics. The early reviews for *The Blessing Way* proved that it had been a wise decision to use a Navajo background and introduce a Native American police officer. The influential pre-publication reviews in both *Publishers Weekly* and *Kirkus Reviews* praised the Navajo aspect of the book. The *New York Times Book Review* compared Hillerman to Arthur W. Upfield and applauded his "well-developed presentation of Indians." Joe Leaphorn and the Navajo setting upstaged the novel's protagonist. "What makes this first mystery by Tony Hillerman outstanding is the wealth of detail about the Navajo Indians—customs, rites, way of life—with which he has crammed his pages," opined the *Saturday Review*. "These are not the Lo-the-Poor Indians such as those envisioned by city dummkopfs who wouldn't know a bear claw from a squash blossom," proclaimed the *Los Angeles Times* in full journalistic hyperbole. "They are today's Indians, on and off the reservations, modern as atomic energy and ancient as the sun."[12]

Within the first two weeks of the book's publication, Harper & Row had sold 6,300 copies. "Should go on rapidly from there," said Kahn. In April, Dell Publishing purchased the rights for a mass paperback edition to be released in 1971, providing an advance of $7,500 with a $5,000 bonus if the book were optioned for a movie, in expectation of selling a hundred thousand copies at newsstands, drugstores, train stations, and airports. Of the Dell advance, Hillerman received

$3,375, half of the amount minus his agent Ann Elmo's 10 percent commission. In addition, she sold the rights for editions in Japan and the United Kingdom.[13]

By June, Harper had sold close to ten thousand copies of *The Blessing Way.* "Very nice," Kahn wrote. These were good numbers, well above the seven-thousand-copy mark expected for a first-time novelist under the Joan Kahn–Harper Novels of Suspense imprint. But the sales paled in comparison to popular titles on the bookstore shelves that summer. Top sellers included John Fowles's *The French Lieutenant's Woman,* Mario Puzo's *The Godfather,* Graham Greene's *Travels with My Aunt,* and a slim Harper & Row novel by Yale professor Erich Segal. His *Love Story* was on its way to selling more than five million copies.[14]

Now that he had a published book, Hillerman had visions of success on the big screen. Kahn and Elmo did little to dampen his hopes. "As I guess you know," Kahn wrote, "every moving picture company is calling up about the book—and surely one of them will option it." One did: Warner Brothers Movie producer Eleanor Timberman called Hillerman. He succumbed fully to movie fever. After talking to Timberman, he excitedly reported to Elmo that the studio "definitely intends to make the film of *Blessing Way.*" Additionally, he took to mind that he might write the script. "We left it with her promising to send me a copy of one," he said, "upon which I would let her know after I saw what was involved." Not much, it seemed to him. After reading two scripts by James Agee—"The African Queen" and "The Blue Hotel"—he felt confident he could do what was required.[15]

"We'll do the best we can if screen writing really interests you," Elmo assured Hillerman. But she also told him it was unlikely he would be recruited to write the screenplay. Producers preferred to use a screenwriter rather than the author, she explained. She was correct. In the end, Warner assigned the script to Arthur Rowe, who had written for the television series *Gunsmoke* and *Death Valley Days.*[16]

She assured a worried Hillerman she saw nothing in the film contract that barred him from continuing to use the Joe Leaphorn character. "By all means use the Navajo cop and if any objection arises a name can be changed easily," she wrote. That would later prove to be a $22,000 mistake.[17]

In August 1970, after a year's work, Hillerman delivered the manuscript of *The Fly on the Wall* to his editor. Kahn could not mask her initial disappointment. "Political intrigue," she said, "is always good material for a novel (though not as unusual as the material in *The Blessing Way*) and I hope you'll retackle the book."

She and others who had read the manuscript found the opening unenticing. Then the endless parade of characters, many of whom appeared only once, were bound to leave the reader bewildered. In one case, Hillerman had two politicians with short names beginning with R and ending with K. "By page 63, fifty names have appeared," she said, "and most of *them* are just names and never reappear."[18]

Hillerman annotated her critique, giving himself instructions such as "better setting early" and "more Cotton personality early," and immediately let Kahn know he would make the necessary adjustments. "What we'll have when you re-approach the novel," Kahn replied, "is a good Hillerman and a good book." It took all autumn, but in early December Hillerman delivered a greatly improved manuscript. Still, Kahn insisted on additional changes that consumed two more months. She was not one to send a book into production before it met her exacting standards. After all, the title page of her books now read "A Joan Kahn–Harper Novel of Suspense."[19]

But not Elmo nor Kahn nor even Hillerman yet recognized the potential for a Navajo mystery series. Despite the promising sales of *The Blessing Way*, Elmo remained cool to the concept of a Navajo setting and characters. "You have done well with *The Blessing Way*," she conceded to Hillerman, "and maybe I am wrong in expecting perfection in every manuscript I submit." Of course, she had never actually submitted Hillerman's manuscript. He had engineered that himself. Even Kahn, who had sought to retain the Indian elements of *The Blessing Way*, was at this point listening attentively to Elmo's pitch for a nonfiction book built on the anthropological pieces she had sold to *True* magazine. A nonfiction proposal could net a substantially larger advance than fiction, Elmo told Hillerman, benefiting both author and agent. Kahn confirmed her interest in the project. "That should make a *very* good book, she told Hillerman.[20]

But Hillerman's yen for fiction was winning out. Even before he completed *The Fly on the Wall*, the book he had planned to be his great American novel, he began longing to return to Joe Leaphorn and the Navajo Nation. *The Fly on the Wall* had convinced him of his affinity for writing mysteries, and the success of *The Blessing Way* had revealed the value of Navajo culture. *The Fly on the Wall* was not the direction Hillerman wanted to take. "While I was writing it," Hillerman said, "my imagination kept going back to the Navajo reservation and I kept regretting the missed possibilities, seeing what I could have done with that first book had I started it out knowing what I was up to." Now, more than merely an intriguing background, Hillerman recognized that the Navajo landscape, religion, and culture could play a role in his novels as important as a character might assume.[21]

He told Kahn and Elmo his next book would bring Leaphorn back, but this time as the main character. "This one was going to be my apology to the generic American Indian for the mistakes I had made in *The Blessing Way*," he said. "As far as tribal culture was concerned, this one was going to be just right."[22]

CHAPTER 17

◈ Leaphorn Returns ◈

Early in December 1970, Tony Hillerman drove on Interstate 40 across the Rio Grande and up Nine Mile Hill. In his rearview mirror, the towering Sandia Mountains rose up like a stone wall on Albuquerque's east side. With each mile he headed west, the snow-covered Mount Taylor ahead grew into the landscape's most dominant feature. The mountain rarely looked the same each time he looked at it. "Sometimes," Hillerman said, "a stark indigo outline against a garish sunset horizon, sometimes white, sometimes only a hazy, hinted mountain, sometimes wearing its clouds like a blowing scarf, sometimes piling them into stratospheric thunderheads."[1]

Instead of turning north into the Navajo Nation, Hillerman continued west on a search. He needed the right place to set his next book, which he hoped would "revive the Navajo Sherlock Holmes." More than selecting the right landscape, Hillerman was seeking a certain cultural backdrop. Initially, he considered setting this new novel around the Hopi people in Arizona. Surrounded on all sides by the Navajo Nation, the Hopi live in twelve villages on three mesas where they have farmed and maintained a traditional lifeway dating back centuries. To Hillerman, a pueblo setting would offer readers an unusual opportunity to see the often-impenetrable Pueblo culture through Joe Leaphorn's eyes. "He's an outsider, just as I am," said Hillerman, "and he doesn't know a thing more about them than I do." But the Hopi were traditional enemies of the Navajo. As a result, Hillerman decided Zuni Pueblo might be a better candidate.[2]

Zuni is one of twenty surviving pueblos, nineteen of which are in New Mexico. Descendants of the ancient people who had inhabited Chaco Canyon and other cliff dwellings in the Southwest, traditional Pueblo peoples live in compact, permanent settlements, sometimes in multistory houses, and sustain themselves by farming. Zuni at the time had a population of approximately four thousand. Its history, its isolation, its language unrelated to any other native tongue, and its cultural and religious practices were perfect for Hillerman's purposes. They met his original concept when writing *The Blessing Way*—that an exotic backdrop would hold up his books if his plots failed to do so. Zuni's proximity to the Ramah Navajo Reservation, an isolated portion of the Navajo Nation, also provided a legitimate reason for Leaphorn to be involved in solving a mystery set on Zuni land.

Hillerman reached Zuni on December 4, 1970, in time to witness the annual Shalako ceremonies, said to be one of the most complex Native American religious observances still in existence. The multiday event reached its apex with the arrival of the giant birds known as Shalako, the "Messengers of the Gods." Men impersonated the messengers by strapping on ten-foot wood frames draped in blankets and donning a mask adorned with eagle feathers. The pueblo was teeming with activity by the time Hillerman took his place among the spectators. As an outsider, he was hardly alone. Curious Navajos, tourists minus their cameras—per strict rules against photographing the ceremony—and pot-smoking young men and women from a nearby hippie commune waited in the cold by the stone footbridge that crossed the Zuni River. "The Shalakos are coming. The Shalakos are coming!" yelled a member of the crowd. Six towering masked figures emerged from the smoky haze from piñon-fired bread ovens and fires. In the front of the group stood Shulawitsi, the fire god personified by a young boy whose body and mask were painted black with yellow, blue, red, and white spots. He stepped onto the bridge and led the Shalakos past the crowd.

A reporter from Arizona watched as they walked by. "Perhaps it's part of the magic, the night of the Shalako dance, that nothing can prepare the visitor for the impact of first hearing those primeval chants and seeing those ghostly figures stepping to some ethereal cadence across the sacred foot bridge and into this tiny village," she later told her readers. Hillerman looked down from a rooftop as the Shalakos entered the pueblo, separated, and made their way to newly built houses or additions designated for the occasion. Upon reaching the assigned house, each Shalako entered to the sound of drums, rattles, and songs as a priest sprinkled cornmeal on the ground before him. Descending from their rooftop perches, Hillerman and others went from house to house throughout the freezing night, with temperatures in the teens, to peer through windows for glimpses of the ceremonial dancing and religious rituals. "Even as a visitor, one is part of a chain of the magic nights of the Shalako that stretches back through the centuries," noted the reporter.[3]

The following day, Hillerman took his place on the north side of the Zuni River among the sleep-deprived observers. Sitting with his back against the corner post of a sheep pen, his legs on the frozen ground, Hillerman watched the Shalako dash back and forth on the field across the river in a complicated and elaborate closing ceremony, the last act before returning to Kothluwalawa, their resting place until the following year. Exhausted, Hillerman saw little reason to remain to the end. "I have found what I need. Indeed, my drowsy head is full of it," he said. The plot was unclear but he had the setting he wanted and, perhaps even more importantly, a title. He would call the book *Dance Hall of the Dead*, the rough English translation of Kothluwalawa. "Since my plot concerned a neurotic Navajo boy who wanted to become a Zuni and go to their heaven it was a natural for the book," he said.[4]

By placing much of the action in the Zuni world, Hillerman would introduce readers to the enchanting pueblo as well as the kachina spirit world. "One thing such folks would certainly learn," said Hillerman, "is that Navajo and Zuni traditional religions, social/political structures, and value systems are no more similar than are those of traditional Buddhists and Presbyterians." The idea appealed to Hillerman because he was vexed by the public's ignorance about Indians and the widely shared presumption that they were all alike. "I set about to dent this ignorance by moving Leaphorn a hundred miles south to the Zuni Reservation," he said.[5]

The research for the book was daunting. First, the reading and work Hillerman had done to prepare for writing *The Blessing Way* was inadequate if Leaphorn were now to emerge as the protagonist. "When I decided to continue writing Navajo mysteries, I found I didn't know as much as I thought I did," Hillerman said. Furthermore, the Zuni's complex religion and culture were highly guarded, making it particularly difficult for an outsider to learn about it.[6]

Hillerman also strove for accuracy in other ways. In a pivotal scene, Leaphorn is shot with a tranquilizer dart. In research for *The Blessing Way* Hillerman had climbed into the back seat of a car to see if one could be tied up in the way his character was. For this novel he went to the Albuquerque Zoo, where he learned that there were a variety of places where darts, guns, and tranquilizers could be purchased. He followed up his visit with the zoologist by talking with pharmacologists at the UNM Medical School. "I was able to get a pretty good reading on the kind of hallucinations it causes and its paralyzing effects and how long it lasts and all that stuff," he said.[7]

In April 1971, Hillerman met with Harper & Row editor Joan Kahn in New York City. She was keeping her fingers crossed, she told him, because she had learned that *The Blessing Way* had been nominated for the Best New Novel prize awarded by the Mystery Writers of America. Hillerman's novel did not win. Instead the prize went to *The Anderson Tapes* by Lawrence Sanders.

In the summer the first prepublication reviews of *The Fly on the Wall* appeared. They were not especially strong. *Kirkus* offered a short and lukewarm assessment: "It will do, even if he did better in *The Blessing Way*." *Publishers Weekly* was kinder, complimenting Hillerman on a "credible story line" and some "exciting and frightening chase sequences." When the book reached stores in mid-September, the *New York Times Book Review* called it "a highly credible book, full of action, flawlessly plotted." Alice Cromie, the mystery reviewer for the *Chicago Tribune*, found little more to say than that the book had a "timely plot." Her lack of excitement may have reflected disappointment. When *The Blessing Way* had been published, Cromie had highlighted the Navajo material and the "new breed of western lawman," adding, "It is hoped that Hillerman will keep him in business."[8]

Mirroring the lukewarm reviews, the six thousand copies of the novel sold in the first two months were more modest than sales for *The Blessing Way*, which was now on newsstand racks in a Dell edition. (The cover of the seventy-five-cent Dell paperback featured a young woman with a mass of blonde hair pinned up, her safari shirt straining at the buttons, being led away from apparent danger.) If Hillerman was disappointed he didn't show it. But two errors gave him grief. One of his characters refers to the *Oregonian* newspaper as having folded. The *Oregonian*'s managing editor wrote to Hillerman, letting him know the paper was still very much in business. "I guess what I meant to write was the *Houston Press*," Hillerman replied in an apologetic letter, referring to the Scripps-Howard paper that had ceased publication in 1964. He assured the editor his mistake "was no Freudian death-wish for your paper."[9]

The other mistake was discovered when readers pointed out that John Cotton had removed his shoes in a nighttime visit to the capitol, so that the men chasing

him would not hear his steps on the marble floor, but he never put them back
on. He then walked through streets wet with sleet, took a cab ride, and arrived
at the final scene in the house of the Democratic Party state chairman, all in
stocking feet. Over time, Hillerman came to be fond of this mistake, frequently
sharing it with readers.

By the time 1972 began, Hillerman had his characters chosen and the plot mostly
worked out for *Dance Hall of the Dead*. But his teaching and work as department
chair slowed his writing. By April, Hillerman figured he was no more than 20
percent done. "The writing is going very slowly because I'm still involved in
research," he told a friend. Explaining the delays to Kahn, Hillerman warned
her, "I don't intend to rush it because I want this one to be really top-flight."[10]

Leaving his struggles with the manuscript, Hillerman invited his daughter
Janet to come with him on a business trip to New York City as a combination
high school graduation and birthday present. Janet was excited because she
had never spent time alone with her father. The journey also made her nervous.
"I am not very interesting, and Dad's around interesting people all the time,"
she remembered thinking as the plane sat on the tarmac waiting for a delayed
departure. "But Daddy was really good because he loved to talk. And so, I just
listened."[11]

In New York City, Hillerman took Janet to his meetings, including one at
Warner Brothers, which held a film option on *The Blessing Way*. As was his and
Marie's habit, Tony and his daughter arrived early. He frequently repeated to his
children what his father had told him. When you're late, you make people think
you think you're more important than they are, and you're not. "That was kind
of the motto of our family," said Janet. "'The first shall be last, and the last shall
be first,' and that's the way they were."[12]

In the reception room high in the skyscraper, the receptionist informed the
early-arriving father and daughter that Warner executive Elaine Timberman was
eating lunch downstairs with "Dusty" Hoffman. "Would you and your daughter
like to go join them? She just went down not too long ago, and it's right there on
the corner," Janet recalled the woman asking.

"Oh, no, no. We'll just sit here," replied her father.

After about ten or fifteen minutes, Tony turned to his daughter and asked
about Timmerman's lunch companion. "Why does that name sound familiar
to me? Why does that ring a bell?"

"Well, Dad," said Janet, "I think she meant Dustin Hoffman, the actor. *Little Big Man. . . . The Graduate.*"

A few more minutes passed.

"Oh, well, hell, you probably would have liked to have done that."

"No, that's okay, Dad. I'm happy just sitting here with you." And I'm thinking, "Oh, well, so close yet so far."

Looking to find uninterrupted time to complete *Dance Hall of the Dead*, Hillerman struck on the idea of finding a place in Mexico for the summer, far from Albuquerque and the demands of work. The Instituto de Allende in San Miguel de Allende, Mexico, offered him a guest lectureship. The art school, established in 1950, offered a wide array of undergraduate courses for which students could obtain transferable credits. The program attracted American students in droves. "The *instituto* as far as I could tell was run as a place for the affluent to send troublesome college-age offspring and for older folk to amuse themselves," concluded Hillerman. The institute had no salary to offer him but could provide accommodations in the picturesque city a four-hour drive north of Mexico City. "Strange as it seems to be saying it, I don't really need a paycheck for a while (bless book clubs and movie options!)," Hillerman wrote to the institute's director. "Frankly, my number one goal is to get far enough from our campus to be beyond convenient reach of the telephone caller."[13]

In early June, Tony and Marie packed four of their children into the family's seafoam green 1968 Ford Country Sedan station wagon, leaving behind Anne and Tony Jr., who were now old enough to fend for themselves, and crossed the border at Juarez. At San Miguel de Allende they settled into a hillside house that had been last used by the managing editor of the *Chicago Daily News*. On a cobblestone street in the Atascadero section, the house had an entry courtyard filled with bougainvillea and a driveway that went through the center of the house. This delighted Dan and Steve because they were given a bedroom on the ground floor with easy egress beyond the sight of nosy parents. Especially as it had no telephone, the house offered Hillerman the peace he sought to work on his Zuni novel.[14]

On Sundays the family went to mass in the old church by the marketplace. To the right of the altar was an enormous blue canvas that hid cloistered nuns. Janet, who had once aspired to be a nun, watched during Communion as the priest would walk over to the partition and open small flaps in the canvas. "And tongues would come out," recalled Janet, "and Father would give the cloistered nuns their Communion like that."[15]

San Miguel de Allende offered the parents a rare moment alone. One night, Tony and Marie ate supper in an old colonial building. They were the only diners and the rain, as frequently happened, had caused the electricity to fail. The musicians with an audience of two, sang Tony's requested *La Paloma Blanca* and for Marie, facile in Spanish, *corridos* from the Mexican Revolution. "How good it is to be with the woman you love on such a rainy night," recalled Tony.[16]

The summer in Allende was a success. Returning to the United States in the fall, Hillerman had a nearly complete manuscript. When Kahn read the pages, she would find Hillerman had used an almost identical opening as that of *The Blessing Way*. In both, a lone Native American confronts death in a scene laced with otherworldly overtones that ends with his presumed death. At the end of the opening of *The Blessing Way*, Navajo Luis Horseman runs from a Navajo wolf. In the shorter opening section of *Dance Hall of the Dead*, a twelve-year-old Zuni boy is nearing the end of a dusk run on the open land surrounding the pueblo, where he was expecting to meet up with a fourteen-year-old Navajo schoolmate.

In tightly scripted opening pages, Hillerman masterfully combined key elements of Zuni religious beliefs: the anticipation of blessings from the Shalako, and the possibility of a taboo violation with serious consequences. The heart-stopping conclusion follows when the unnamed boy confronts what he believes is a Salamobia, a warrior wearing a birdlike mask who maintains order. "And he remembered that Salamobia, like all the ancestor spirits which live at the Zuni masks, were visible only to members of the Sorcery Fraternity and to those about to die."[17]

The copious amounts of blood found by the Zuni police lead them to believe the Zuni boy was murdered. But because the other boy, potentially a suspect, was Navajo, Leaphorn is brought in to investigate his disappearance. It also makes him the center of the action. Over a period of six days leading up to Shalako, Leaphorn searches for the missing boy and the dead boy's killer on a path that takes him to an archaeological dig, a hippie commune, the Zuni Pueblo, and the Ramah Navajo enclave. The climax of the pursuit takes place in the midst of a snowy night during the noisy arrival of the Shalako dancers to the pueblo, equally cold as the night when Hillerman observed the Shalako in 1970.

Now that Leaphorn had assumed a central position in the new manuscript, Hillerman needed to develop his character. He began by giving Leaphorn a clan identification. Clans, built around kinship, are of great importance to Navajos. In their matrilineal and matrilocal society, each Navajo belongs to four clans. The first and most important clan is the mother's, second is the father's, third is the maternal grandfather's, and fourth is the paternal grandfather's. Clan membership determines whom one can date—sex between members of the same clan is regarded as incestuous—and establishes familial obligations to take care of relatives, even ones considered distant under western kinship systems. Almost any introduction among Navajos includes sharing the maternal clan, to whom one is born, and often the paternal, for whom one is born.

Hillerman used *Dance Hall of the Dead* to establish Leaphorn's kinship. "Leaphorn came from the Taadii Diné, the Slow-Talking People Clan," he wrote. "The father of his mother was Nashibitti, a great singer of the Beautyway and the Mountainway, and other curing rites, and a man so wise that it was said the people of Beautiful Mesa added Hosteen to his name when he was less than thirty—calling him Old Man when he was far too young to be a grandfather." A distinctly different and far more Navajo-like introduction to the man than the one Hillerman crafted in *The Blessing Way* when the police officer meets an eighty-two-year-old singer conducting an Enemy Way ceremony. "'I am called Joe Leaphorn,' the young man said, 'and I work for Law and Order.'"[18]

However, as Hillerman worked on making Leaphorn into a more authentic Navajo, he drew on his *bilagáana* (white person) past to account for Leaphorn's personality, particularly his approach to law enforcement. Even after more than two decades, Hillerman still retained admiration for Hutchinson County, Texas, sheriff Hugh Anderson, whom he had covered as a cub reporter on the *Borger News-Herald* in 1948. "He was smart, he was honest, he was wise and humane in his use of police powers," Hillerman said, "my idealistic young idea of what every cop should be but sometimes isn't." He passed on those traits to Leaphorn.[19]

For the archaeological site central to the plot of *Dance Hall of the Dead*, Hillerman constructed a fictional version of the one he had visited for his 1967 article on the Folsom Man in *True* magazine. In the article he had described Jerry Dawson, as a graduate student working for UNM's world-famous archaeologist Frank Hibben, sorting debris through a screen box. "The residue caught on the wire included an assortment of twigs and roots, half a dozen dried antelope droppings, a large badly confused scorpion, and several hundred bits of small gravel." In *Dance Hall of the Dead*, it was now Ted Isaacs, a graduate student working for Professor Chester Reynolds, who ran a callused finger through the debris in his screen box. "Within three minutes nothing was left on the screen except an assortment of pebbles, small twigs, old rabbit droppings, and a large scorpion—its barbed tail waving in confused anger."[20]

Hillerman sought and collected details like these from real life to use in his writing. If you want to make a point of the hard life of diggers, he told his students, "you look at the blowing dust, the sticker weeds, the scorpion, the sunbaked earth, the sand in the drinking water." The smell of rain, the sight of buffalo grass in the light of a setting sun, the warm feeling of freshly baked bread, the clammy coolness of a table surface, and the arrogant stare from a restaurant hostess all went into his notebook. "I've been doing this for years," Hillerman said when he was sixty-two, "stripping down people and places, dissecting their looks and their mannerisms, filling the storage bin of imagination with useful parts; doing the same with street scenes, with landscapes, with the weather." The details, he was convinced, did more than bring the reader into the scene, as in the moment when the anthropologist flicks the scorpion away. "It gives him insight into the character of the man who owns the calloused fingers."[21]

But with the fictional dig he placed near Zuni, Hillerman went a step further in having his art imitate life. Central to the plot of his novel was the possibility the professor was salting the site. In other words, he was planting items that his unsuspecting student would uncover and thus credit the professor with solving one of the great mysteries of anthropology. This was the same accusation facing his UNM colleague Hibben. In the years since Hillerman had written his article about Hibben's Folsom hunter dig for *True* magazine, it had become widely believed that the archaeologist had salted the Sandia Cave dig upon which his reputation rested.

As he plotted his third mystery, Hillerman discovered he was better off without outlines and detailed planning. "From the abstract distance of an outline, with the characters no more than names, nothing seems real to me," he said. "I can get a novel written to my satisfaction only by using a much freer form and have faith that—given a few simple ingredients—my imagination will come up with the necessary answers."[22]

In November, Hillerman completed the final chapter of *Dance Hall of the Dead* with an ending inspired by Sheriff Anderson's favoring of remedies outside of a court system or normal law enforcement procedures. Joan Kahn was pleased and sent Hillerman's agent a contract with a $4,000 advance, again increasing Harper & Row's up-front payment. In March 1973, Kahn returned the edited manuscript to Hillerman for a round of final changes. "I still like the book," she wrote, launching into one of her notoriously breathless paragraphs. "I'll admit that it might be better if the reader had been able to meet the villain for himself, and, alas, I'm not exactly sure if I can understand the plotting, including the dart that plants itself in Leaphorn; but I trust that everyone, including the critics, will enjoy the book enough not to look at the plot too closely."[23]

Once again, an interesting backdrop trumped plot. But with this work, Hillerman had finally created a fully realized figure in Leaphorn, despite his decidedly non-Navajo name, and put the policeman on center stage.

CHAPTER 18

◈ The Edgar ◈

With *Dance Hall of the Dead* in production at Harper & Row in the spring of 1973, Tony Hillerman turned to the pressing task of finding a new literary agent. He had grown dissatisfied with Ann Elmo. In the almost ten years he had been working with her, the New York agent had sold Hillerman's articles to national magazines, handled the sale of three books to Harper & Row, and negotiated a movie option with Warner Brothers. Yet Hillerman had not forgotten Elmo's original objections to *The Blessing Way* and her unwillingness to sell it until he made his own contact with Joan Kahn. The personalities and style of the two also didn't mesh. "We just don't seem to communicate, never have, and never would," Hillerman told Carl Brandt, a well-regarded agent he approached based on a recommendation from Joan Kahn.[1]

Brandt was one of four agents Kahn told Hillerman she thought "are better than the one you have." In endorsing Hillerman's plan to part company with Elmo, Kahn was transgressing the accepted rules of publishing. Going around the back of an author's agent was widely considered improper. Her actions did show, however, the trust that had developed between Hillerman and Kahn.[2]

When the spring semester ended, Tony and Marie went on a child-free getaway to New York City and stayed at the Commodore, the elegant but massive hotel near Grand Central Terminal. During their stay in the city, Tony met with Brandt. The agent agreed to take him as a client but not until he completed his next manuscript. At this point in his career as a novelist, Hillerman was still only offered contracts on finished books. Miscommunication torpedoed the plan. Hillerman failed to tell his new agent that Elmo had already sold the

German rights to his previous books. When Brandt instructed his foreign rights representatives to do so, they soon found out. "I had caused embarrassment to him and his foreign rights people in Europe," said Hillerman. The mistake ended the plan of working with Brandt.[3]

Hillerman began to make his own book deals, while not entirely terminating his relationship with Elmo. He teamed up with photographer David Muench to do a coffee table book about New Mexico to be published by an Oregon company. "I handled it directly with the publisher without even notifying my agent," Hillerman told a friend. He earned $4,000 for thirteen thousand words used entirely as captions. He also negotiated a deal with the University of New Mexico Press to publish two books.[4]

The first would contain the essays he had written for his master's thesis, including the two articles Elmo had sold to *True* magazine, under the title *The Great Taos Bank Robbery, and other Indian Country Affairs.* The second, called *The Spell of New Mexico,* would be a collection of essays by prominent writers. The latter idea grew out of lunches Hillerman shared with UNM Press editor Jack Rittenhouse at the University Rexall Drug Store on Central Avenue across from the university. "At these, we fell into the habit of remembering what famous folks, from D. H. Lawrence to Karl Jung, had written about New Mexico," Hillerman recalled. The two men were curious about the appeal of the state to writers. "Finally, it occurred to us to go directly to the source," said Hillerman. "Why not allow the writers and artists to provide their own answers in their own words?" By the end of their rumination, the writer and editor decided to include essays by Mary Austin, Conrad Richter, D. H. Lawrence, C. G. Jung, and Ernie Pyle, among others.[5]

For Hillerman, the experience of serving as his own agent seemed promising. "I'm going to do the same with my next novel of suspense," he told his friend. "I've *had it* with agents.[6]

Dance Hall of the Dead was published on October 10, 1973. Reviews proved Hillerman's and Kahn's literary instincts had been correct in the eyes of critics. "The story's not the thing, it's Hillerman's anything but wooden Indians and the way in which he informs their way of life with affection and dignity," said *Kirkus.* The *New York Times* reviewer decided, "It will be a dull reader who has not figured out the murderer halfway through—but that, somehow, is not important. Hillerman knows his background well, and is skillful enough to make it an integral part of the action." The *Chicago Tribune Book World* was equally taken: "Hillerman novels are so noteworthy for background and characterization that the excellent plots are strictly a bonus," said its review. Early sales were also promising. Within a week of its publication, 6,680 copies had been shipped to bookstores which, said Kahn, "means it should dash on from there."[7]

Hillerman pondered his next move. He had three ideas for a new novel, one of which came from the front pages of the newspaper. Earlier in the year, members of the American Indian Movement had occupied the town of Wounded Knee, South Dakota, in protest. They leveled corruption charges at the Oglala Lakota tribal president as well as protesting the federal government's treatment of Native Americans. Hillerman told Kahn he was considering the idea of trying a straight novel rather than another mystery. "It might involve hostages and a notable place by Indian militants (as at Wounded Knee) with a mixture of occultism-mysticism and fanaticism," he said. "Maybe it could use Joe Leaphorn again."[8]

On an April evening in 1974, Tony and Marie Hillerman entertained visitors from Tucson, Betty Lou Baker, an author of historical fiction set in the Southwest, and Don Schellie, a columnist for the *Tucson Daily Citizen*. "It wasn't until a couple of beers had been downed that Hillerman mentioned casually that his mystery was one of five finalists for the Edgar," said Schellie. "When pressed, Hillerman blew his Joe Cool cover, grinned, and admitted that he was a bit edgy about it."[9]

The Edgar, named after Edgar Allan Poe, was the highest prize the Mystery Writers of America gave each year to the best mystery novel and other mystery-related books, films, and plays. This was Hillerman's third try. His first book, *The Blessing Way*, had been nominated three years earlier. Hillerman's second novel, *The Fly on the Wall*, had also been nominated but lost out to Frederick Forsyth's *The Day of the Jackal*. The competition for the top prize this year was tough. "It was a vintage year for good mysteries," said Alice Cromie of the *Chicago Tribune*, one of the six-member judging panel.[10]

For Hillerman the stars were aligned. Cromie was likely an advocate for the new Leaphorn novel. When she had reviewed *The Fly on the Wall*, she had urged Hillerman to return to Leaphorn. The other four nominated authors, P. D. James, Victor Canning, Jean Stubbs, and Francis Clifford, were all British writers. The panel met in Santa Fe and two of them, mystery writer and reviewer Dorothy Hughes and former Mystery Writers of America president Martin Stern, resided in town. There would be no New York City bias in selecting a winner in a year when the events at Wounded Knee brought Native American issues to the fore.[11]

Harper & Row flew Marie and Tony to New York for the awards banquet held May 3 at the Essex House along Central Park in Manhattan. At the end of dinner, the award winners were revealed. *Dance Hall of the Dead* was proclaimed the best mystery novel of the year, and Hillerman flew back to Albuquerque with a nine-inch porcelain statuette of Edgar Allan Poe. As one observer put it, "Four British authors chosen as Edgar finalists, and Tony Hillerman blows through musty manor halls with a breath of Southwestern desert air."[12]

Upon his return home, Hillerman took a literary victory lap. "The Golden Age of Detective Fiction—saints be praised—is dead, dead, dead," he wrote in an article for a New Mexico newspaper. "To the average readers this simply means narrative fiction has escaped from the snobbish cult which once wrote its rules." The boring and unrealistic settings of manor houses with servants and bloodless murders were no longer holding readers' interest. True, Dame Agatha still had hundreds of thousands of readers, but her books had not abandoned an antiquated convention of rules like those of a game, he said. "It is basically a different ball game these days. Escape is—generally speaking—out. Realism is in."[13]

With three novels published, one of which had won a significant award, Hillerman decided at age forty-nine to give up his role as chair of UNM's Journalism Department and inch closer to a writing career. Among the reasons he gave to his predecessor who had recruited him was that the fifteen to twenty hours of work each week, mostly paperwork (which he hated), was overwhelming and took away from teaching (which he loved). But more important, Hillerman said, "I want some time for thinking."[14]

Work on a new novel, however, would have to wait its turn. Hillerman had to fulfill his commitment to produce the three nonfiction books he had promised UNM Press and the Oregon publisher, as well as freelance writing assignments he had secured.

At the end of 1974, Gwyneth Cravens, an editor at *Harper's Magazine*, one of the nation's premier magazines along with *The Atlantic* and *The New Yorker*, thought the magazine ought to publish an article on contemporary Indian problems. John Fischer, a retired editor of the magazine who was a native Oklahoman, University of Oklahoma graduate, and Rhodes Scholar, suggested Hillerman. Apparently neither he nor Cravens considered looking for a Native American writer. Cravens and Hillerman talked, and he went to work on an article comparing the deep connections Navajos felt to their homeland to that of Jews toward Israel. When he finished the piece, he found that Cravens had left her post. Lewis H. Lapham, the renowned editor, delivered disappointing news. "There are some interesting things in the piece, but I'm sorry to say that my colleagues and I feel it doesn't work for *Harper's*." Vexed and crestfallen, Hillerman reminded Lapham that Cravens had contracted for the piece. "My objections to your article had to do with my lack of interest in its subject," Lapham bluntly explained. Lapham was a deity of the magazine world and ran *Harper's* like a dictator. So, his lack of interest was a death sentence. Hillerman left no clue to how he felt about the rejection.[15]

The cultural gap between Hillerman's world and the rarified air of New York publishing was wide, and the author knew it. Editors regularly sent him queries about his work that reflected ignorance about life west of the Hudson River. "What does LDS stand for?" asked one editor about the abbreviation for the Church of Jesus Christ of Latter-day Saints, the formal name of the Mormon Church. "What is 'fry bread' and did you mean to write it that way?" asked another about the Native American staple. And yet one more editor changed the spelling of "chamisa," a bush common to the Southwest, to "chamiso" when he couldn't find it in a reference book. "When Southwestern writers do pierce the thicket of stereotypes fencing the Southwest, they have frequently been told their work is not of national interest," said David King Dunaway, coeditor of *Writing the Southwest*.[16]

When the 1975–76 academic year began, Hillerman still found it hard to work on his next novel. "I have a weakness for promising more than I can produce," he admitted to one editor. In the fall he taught while working to finish the last of the freelance writing projects he had agreed to do, including one for *Fodor's Old West*. For this book by the well-known travel guide company, Hillerman wrote a lengthy entry "Folklore, Music, and Tall Tales." Despite the title, it focused primarily on songs, cowboy songs in particular. "When I was a boy," Hillerman recalled, "the neighbor we called Old Man Mann was already very old. And the song he most liked to sing in his cracked, breathy old voice was much older." *All year o'er the prairie alone I do ride / Not even a hound dog to run at my side.*[17]

In January, William "Bud" Davis, UNM's new leader, brought Hillerman back to work in the university president's office. In return for serving as Davis's assistant, Hillerman's teaching responsibilities were reduced to one class. The change in university leadership and an end to freelance projects finally opened a way for Hillerman to make progress on giving Leaphorn a crime to solve. Actually, as it would turn out, several crimes.

On May 23, 1976, Hillerman stood before the seventy-eight members of the Zuni Pueblo High School graduating class, accompanied by seven hundred parents, relatives, friends, teachers, and others seated in the school gym with the colorful Zuni Thunderbird mascot painted on the wall. After being introduced, he expressed surprise the students had selected him to be their commencement speaker and told them he assumed it was because of his authorship of his most recent novel *Dance Hall of the Dead*, which was set in Zuni, and his success in publishing *The Boy Who Made Dragonfly* (1973), one of the pueblo's most cherished stories.

Six years earlier, Hillerman had come across the dragonfly tale while he poked around Zuni in the course of researching *Dance Hall of the Dead*. "I was charmed by it," he said, "told it to some of my own children and found them extremely interested." The story concerned a time long ago when the village ostentatiously wasted an abundant crop of corn, the staff of the pueblo's life. The Corn Maidens, whose breath brought the rains and summer sun, were saddened by such behavior. They entered the pueblo disguised as beggars. Even though they looked tired and hungry, only two children were kind enough to offer them sustenance. When a drought forced the Zunis to evacuate the village the two children were accidently left behind. The boy constructed a dragonfly from cornstalks to distract his hungry sister. The dragonfly came to life and fetched the Corn Maidens, who fed the children. When the adults returned, they found their fields fertile again. The boy, having been visited by the gods, was made the Corn Priest and guided his people to change their wasteful ways.

The oral story, passed down by generations of Zunis, had been written down and published by Frank Hamilton Cushing in 1883, an anthropologist who had lived in the pueblo. One winter night around a campfire, his Zuni companion kept him up until dawn telling the tale of how the Corn Priest came to be. Cushing's version read like a biblical tale in stilted English. Hillerman wanted to make it more readable and explained his approach to Ann Elmo. "In my transcription," he said, "I cut some material, expanded some sections, and converted it to my own ideas of how it should be worded for a juvenile audience."[18]

Hillerman was so taken by the story he decided he could make it a book for young readers. Kahn thought a children's book idea might appeal to the firm's juvenile division, headed by Charlotte Zolotow, a legendary children's book editor who had begun as a stenographer at Harper & Brothers in the 1930s. Within a week of getting back home, Hillerman submitted the first pages of his rewrite of the myth. Zolotow was pleased with the initial work and agreed to consider the whole work when completed. Hillerman went to work.[19]

At the time, Hillerman's wholesale use of the Zuni story would not necessarily have been considered improper. The term "cultural appropriation" was only just coming into use. At first the criticism had been directed against colonialism. By the late 1960s it began to be used in regard to race and ethnicity. For instance, in 1968 the author Harold Cruse complained that whites were making money from African Americans "through the simple practice of cultural appropriation of aesthetic ideas not native to their own traditions." Later in life, Hillerman would have to defend his own body of work from the charge. But for the time being both *The Boy Who Made Dragonfly* and *Dance Hall of the Dead* were accepted by Zunis, Navajos, and other Native peoples. In fact, the books found a ready audience.[20]

Now, speaking to the Zuni students, Hillerman talked of the significance of publishing the story. Cushing had had a hard time finding someone to publish it, Hillerman explained. "He found out that white men weren't interested in the Zuni people." So why was Harper & Row, ninety years later, so eager to publish the tale? "The story hasn't changed," he said. "What has changed is the world outside Zuni." The white man has killed millions in war, developed the hydrogen bomb, and wasted the world's natural resources, certain his was the right way. "He didn't think he had anything to learn from an old Zuni lesson," Hillerman said. But the white man is realizing there is something wrong with his ways. "He's learned enough to know that he's got something to learn from a society like your own—because he's just beginning to become conscious of what your people have done that his people have not been able to manage." As with his adulation of Navajos, Hillerman professed unabashed admiration for the Zuni. "I urge you," he said, "if you leave the Zuni reservation, not to leave the ways of the Zuni behind you."[21]

After the speech, Hillerman was escorted to the school principal's office. There he found six members of the pueblo's governing council, waiting to talk with him. One of the elderly men held a copy of *Dance Hall of the Dead* in his hands. "They had a whole list of questions prepared, most of them asking where did you get this information or that detail," said Hillerman. "What they were doing was trying to find out whether anyone in the village had been talking to me." For the Zuni, like for other Pueblos but perhaps even more so, guarding religious knowledge from outsiders is essential. The secrecy revolving around their religion plays a crucial role in socialization, is an important element of social control, and is central to their identity as Zuni. An old Zuni proverb speaks to this devotion to protection. "Power told," it is said, "is power lost."[22]

Hillerman told the council that no member of the pueblo's kivas had revealed anything sensitive to him. "I cited my sources, most of them from scholarly publications, some from attending various ceremonial dances, from watching the personifiers of the Council of the Gods coming down Greasy Hill to enter the village, from chatting with those feasting on the goodies provided for visitors in the Shalako House," he said. The answer satisfied the elders. The moment also confirmed that for an Anglo author, the Navajo were a more tolerant subject.[23]

Not long after Hillerman returned from Zuni, his eighteen-year-old son Steve was arrested for possession of marijuana with the intent to distribute and was sent to the New Mexico Boys' School in Springer, New Mexico. Since his adoption, Steve had been a challenging child for Tony and Marie. "He had tactile issues and he had outburst issues and he had lack of control issues," recalled his sister Janet, five years older than Steve. His teenage years included heavy drinking, breaking and entering into homes, an incident with a knife, and altercations with the police. "Mom and Dad felt so bad for him, more than for any of the rest of us. And they put everything they had into Steve," Janet added.[24]

Steve's closest ally in the family was his sister Monica. She was now married and living apart from the family. But when she had been there Steve and she were, in her words, "the black sheep of the family." The lack of connection to the family brought them together. The years Monica had spent alone in the hospital being treated for her birth defect had taken its toll. It was hard to feel part of a family after spending so much time apart. Four years earlier when she was caught after sneaking out at night, her mother told her to remain in her room until her father came home. "My dad got home, came downstairs, and with that look of disappointment and anger, he proceeded to say, 'Do you know you're hurting your mom?'"[25]

"I don't want to hurt her," Monica recalled saying through her tears. "Then I blurted out maybe I should move out. Well, Dad took those words to heart and the next thing I know I was gone and went to a juvenile center first then was transferred to a group home." That night when Janet set the table, she remembered asking if she should set a place for Monica. Marie remained silent and Tony said no. "And that was pretty much it," said Janet.[26]

Out of house but not of mind, Tony and Marie kept track of Monica, and at one point, Tony interceded with her group home to make sure she received proper care. "I always felt like somebody was really watching out for me," Monica recalled. "Like, I don't know if Dad had people, but I always felt like somehow I was okay." Three years later, when Monica turned eighteen and left the group home, she fell in love with army veteran Douglas Atwell, whom she met at the Alibi Inn bar in Albuquerque, owned by his parents. When he proposed, she rushed to a pay telephone to call her parents. Both her mother and father attended the wedding, held in the foothills of the Sandia Mountains, and the reception that followed at the bar. Even though she had been sent away, Monica said she had always remained certain of her parents' love. "I really did even though it was different," she said looking back. "I did know that in my heart."

With Steve confined to a correctional facility, only twelve-year-old Dan remained at home. Tony Jr. now held a job as a mechanic. "Tony was one of those mature teenagers parents can leave in charge of things (including themselves) with absolute confidence," recalled his father. Janet, who worked for the city's Parks and Recreation Department, was preparing for her August wedding. Anne had completed her college degree as well. She was married and lived in Santa Fe, working as a reporter for her father's old paper the *Santa Fe New Mexican*.[27]

At no time did Tony and Marie give up on any of their brood, according to each member. They made the long trek north to visit Steve, as they had driven south for Monica when she was confined to the hospital in Truth or Consequences. In fact, unknown to them, Tony always carried a joyful tale about each of his children to share when he saw his UNM colleague Dick Pfaff.[28]

"My parents stressed to Jan, Tony, Monica, Steve, and Dan that their adoption made them special, much loved, chosen children," recalled Anne. "Families have more to do with common memories than common genes. They're more about sharing experiences than sharing blue eyes or curly hair," wrote Anne looking back to that summer nearly a quarter century later. "When I open my metaphorical treasure chest these days, I realize my parents' investment in love paid dividends that any princess would cherish."[29]

CHAPTER 19

◈ Trouble with Leaphorn ◈

In August 1976, fifty-one-year-old Tony Hillerman checked into the Holiday Inn in Kayenta, just south of Monument Valley, whose awe-inspiring landscape dotted with buttes and spires drew sightseers from the world over. Traveling with him was Alex Etcitty, one of his three most reliable Navajo advisers Hillerman used in the course of researching his novels. Hillerman had met Etcitty in 1961, years before he had considered writing a Navajo mystery, when he stopped and picked him up hitchhiking about twenty miles east of Crownpoint. On the reservation, where a working car is beyond the reach of many, hitchhiking was common.

"From the time Alex Etcitty thumbed a ride with me on the road to White-horse Lake until his death he was a hugely helpful bridge between the scholarly dissertations on Navajo mythology and the Way of the Diné I was reading, and the current world of sheep camps, bootleggers, and the shaky assimilation of teenagers," Hillerman said.[1]

On this summer night, the two men readied for bed after watching the 10:00 P.M. television newscast. Events in Israel prompted Etcitty to recall a moment when he had been a student at St. Michael's, the Catholic boarding school just outside Window Rock, capital of the Navajo Nation. His Bible history teacher compared the Navajos' Long Walk and exile from their homeland in 1864 to the captivity of the Jews in Babylon. "He told us," Etcitty related to Hillerman, "no one could understand the Jewish culture without understanding Zion any more than they could understand us Navajos without knowing what Dinétah means."[2]

The comparison appealed to Hillerman because it had been the one he had tried to make in his article for *Harper's* that was spiked. Despite being a resolute Catholic, Hillerman understood Navajo identity and spiritual beliefs as being inseparable from their land. "Like Zion, *Dinétah* is the Holy Land of its people," Hillerman said. "It is also a way of life for the Navajo."

The next day, Hillerman and Etcitty set off in search of a "listener," one of several types of Navajo spiritual leaders called upon to assess an illness that cannot be easily diagnosed. Most commonly a woman, a listener tries to find the cause of an illness. Usually she begins by meeting with the sick person then retreats to a solitary spot where, in a meditative state, she "listens" for what ails the patient. Such a listener would play a key role in the new novel Hillerman had begun.

Etcitty had a cousin who was a listener, and the search for her had taken the pair from Moenkopi, near Tuba City on the western edge of the Navajo Nation, to Ganado and up north to Kayenta. "We had driven through a landscape as empty as any in America," said Hillerman. The drive prompted Etcitty to talk of his family, Navajo ceremonialism and, recalled Hillerman, "how a Navajo content on the lonely landscape of *Dinétah* learns the meaning of loneliness in the crowds of Phoenix."[3]

When they surmounted a rise on the road leading through the Chinle Wash, the men pulled over. Before them was an expanse of sunbaked stone, red clay, and gray caliche through which water from snow runoff and summer monsoon storms drained northward to the San Juan River. "It was spectacular under the morning sun, and the only color lacking was the green of growing things—the color that means money to agrarian people," said Hillerman. An Anglo mapmaker might label the spot Desolation Flats, Hillerman told Etcitty. "We call it Beautiful Valley," replied his friend. That moment became one of Hillerman's most often repeated anecdotes pertaining to the difference between how Anglos and Navajos look at nature.[4]

Etcitty's help gave Hillerman what he needed for his next novel. But he did not yet know where the listener would appear in the book. His indecision reflected his approach to writing novels. Having given up on trying to outline his books, his strategy was to create the characters and problems. "The real mystery," said Hillerman, "is how I'm going to finish the book." He began his new book with a chapter in which one of the story's two villains escapes FBI surveillance in Washington, DC, by setting up the FBI agents to follow the wrong person. This ruse has the pace and suspense of a Robert Ludlum thriller. Hillerman considered it "the best 5,000 words I've ever written." Unfortunately, he placed the episode in a time far too early relative the book's central action to work as an opening chapter. Hillerman put the pages aside to reassemble later as a flashback in what would be chapter 12.[5]

Instead, Hillerman decided to start the story in the hogan of an aging widower being visited by a listening woman. Setting the scene in a traditional Navajo dwelling, Hillerman believed, would establish the isolated lives most Navajos lead on the vast reservation. The old man confessed to the shaman that he had broken a cultural taboo. This was a quintessential Hillerman clue, in that the FBI agent would think it insignificant but for Joe Leaphorn it would become an important clue in solving the case. The first draft, however, struck Hillerman as dull. "In fact," he said, "it was *awfully dull*."[6]

So Hillerman brought the murder, planned for chapter 2, to the opening pages. This created a new problem. To eliminate witnesses, the murderer would also need to kill the shaman along with her niece. But for the plot to work, Listening Woman would have to remain alive. Considering what he knew about Navajos and their high rate of glaucoma, Hillerman realized he could make Listening Woman blind. Then he placed her some distance from the hogan in a spot where her niece had left her alone to give metaphysical consideration to the sickness besetting the widower.[7]

It worked. "The niece gets killed, and now you have a double murder done while the blind woman is away at a quiet spot having her trance," Hillerman said. "You also have an opportunity to close the chapter with a dandy non-dull scene in which the blind woman, calling angrily for her newly deceased niece, taps her way with her cane across the scene of carnage."[8]

In his car on the way to work, Hillerman puzzled over chapter 2, his distracted driving triggering a blast from a car horn as he made a left turn from the right-hand lane. At the point where he paused working on the manuscript to go teach a class, he had been trying to introduce Leaphorn and provide the reader with a glimpse of the main villain. Throughout the day, between lectures and committee meetings, he picked a setting for the two men to meet. It would be on a stretch of US Route 160 that he knew well enough to recall its vistas in a setting sun and its desert fragrances, the kind of touches he loved to add to a scene. Freed from his last committee meeting and heading home, while his driving brought more honking from fellow commuters, Hillerman dreamed up an internal monologue for Leaphorn driving across the barren land.

At home, Hillerman went to his desk, itching to develop that day's harvest of ideas. He reread his new opening chapter and dug into chapter 2. He started with the internal monologue he had concocted on the drive home. But it seemed stilted so he let the manuscript sit while he joined the family for dinner. "Wife senses 'lost in chapter' condition and leaves today's problems for later." Fed and back at the typewriter, Hillerman decides to introduce a memorable and extremely clever young sheep thief in handcuffs to turn Leaphorn's thoughts into conversation. "He turns out to be wittier than I expected," said Hillerman. His sympathetic portrayal of the young Navajo in cuffs may have been inspired by his son Steve, to whom Tony had remained loyal throughout his ordeals with the law.[9]

Retreating to the living room couch and dealing rounds of spider solitaire, Hillerman meditated in silence about the scene. "As many writers do, I imagine myself into scenes—seeing, hearing, smelling everything I am describing," said Hillerman. "I've been for years a reporter, so I write everything in scenes."[10]

Back at his typewriter, Hillerman reconstructed his imagined scene with the sound of Leaphorn's boots on the gravel, the red flashing light of the police car bouncing off the windows of the Mercedes, and finally, the face of the driver. "I think," said Hillerman, "you won't know this man's name for a long time—until the end of the book, practically. So, I've got to tag him so I have something to call him, some way to identify him, so I have him wear gold-rimmed glasses."[11]

The technique fit wonderfully for a plot set in the Navajo world, where family names such as "Manygoats" and place-names such as "Two Grey Hills" are common. In *Dance Hall of the Dead*, Leaphorn referred to a man on the commune as "Hair in Bun," and in *The Blessing Way* one of the villains was known as "Big Navajo." In the new work, "Goldrims" would become the moniker of the criminal mastermind. Nicknaming a character by means of an attribute grew into a signature trait of Hillerman's style.

With the opening chapters set, Hillerman moved on to construct the plot. For Hillerman, it was the writing of scenes that brought important elements to the surface. "I have gradually learned that this sort of creative thinking happens for me only when I am at very close quarters with what I am writing, only when I am in the scene, in the mind of the viewpoint character, experiencing the chapter and sharing the thinking of the people in it," he said.[12]

By December 1976, Hillerman had a complete draft of the book. He dropped his initial title "The Painted Cave" and renamed the manuscript *Listening Woman*.

This novel was more tightly plotted than either of his first two Navajo mysteries, with three seemingly unrelated but interlaced crimes. The plot also focused more on police matters, such as the cultural and procedural conflicts between the tribal police and the FBI. Leaphorn's investigation of the murder in the hogan that opens the book leads to an action-filled climax where a gang of Indian militants who pulled off an armored truck robbery are holding eleven Boy Scouts, whom they intend to kill in retribution for a century-old massacre of Kiowa youth.

In a sophisticated twist, *Listening Woman* also mirrors an aspect of the Navajo origin story that Hillerman had been studying. In the tale, the Hero Twins, who protect the Navajo, represent the traits of intelligence and aggressiveness. In his book, Hillerman contrasts two brothers who are central to the plot in a similar fashion. One of them becomes a Catholic priest and the other, an Indian militant. "I wanted to explore the dichotomy of human nature that the Hero Twins represent by closely examining the personalities of these two brothers," Hillerman explained.[13]

In a first for the author, the book includes bits of humor in the character of trading post owner John McGinnis, making his initial appearance in Hillerman's books. McGinnis's folksy wit and observations, perhaps inspired by Hillerman's own father who ran a rural store, provide a sympathetic Anglo view of the Navajo. McGinnis points out that Navajos don't engage in premeditated murder. "That's one kind of white man's meanness the Navajos never took to. Any killings you have, there's either getting drunk and doing it, or getting mad and fighting. You don't have this planning in advance and going out to kill somebody like white folks. That right?"[14]

"Leaphorn let his silence speak for him," wrote Hillerman. "McGinnis had been around Navajos long enough for that. What the trader had said was true. Among the traditional Diné, the death of a fellow human being was the ultimate evil. He recognized no life after death. That which was natural in him, and therefore good, simply ceased. That which was unnatural, and therefore evil, wandered through the darkness as a ghost, disturbing nature and causing sickness."

Kahn was pleased to receive a new Hillerman manuscript after nearly five years. But when she read it, she knew it was a long way from publishable. In her view, the complicated plot Hillerman had devised was flawed, and she urged him to write out a plotline. It might show where the manuscript needed "a helping hand," she first wrote Hillerman. Then she crossed out "helping hand" and replaced them with "strengthening." This suggestion was followed by two pages listing the needed changes if he were to meet her standards. Among the problems Kahn spotted was inconsistency in the protagonist's behavior. "The strength of our detective Leaphorn is that he's not only a policeman, but an Indian policeman to whom the Indians will talk," Kahn said. Therefore, why did he not know about the existence of the painted cave nor that one of the two important characters had gone to Rome to become a priest? As she always did, Kahn urged Hillerman to argue with her about the changes she sought. "I *do* want to do a first-class Hillerman—without, of course, driving the author up the wall," she said.[15]

By March Kahn was sufficiently happy with Hillerman's progress to offer a contract. "The Listening Woman is ready to begin listening," she told Hillerman. But Hillerman's final revisions stretched deep into 1977. It was not until September that he sent off the edited manuscript. "You'll note when you get it that I adopted virtually all the copy alterations," he wrote to Kahn. "I think the editing strengthens it and I'm generally satisfied that it's a good one."[16]

Hillerman's on-and-off relationship with Ann Elmo came to a crashing end a few weeks later. Four years earlier, when *Dance Hall of the Dead* was published, she had negotiated a film deal with Bob Banner Associates, a successful television production company that included the *Carol Burnett Show* among its credits. Hillerman received four payments of $2,500 for the option, more than twice the advance he received for the book. But in the interval, Hillerman became concerned that Elmo may have ceded the rights to Leaphorn as a character. Tom Egan, a producer with Banner Associates, believed this was the case. "It was the intent, in our conversations, that Bob would acquire the rights to produce a television motion picture and/or pilot based on *Dance Hall*, with the right, if the pilot sold, to produce a series based on the character 'Joe Leaphorn.'"[17]

Hillerman was furious. He told Elmo that giving the rights to Banner so angered him he would now refuse to cooperate with Warner Brothers' option on *The Blessing Way*. "And in view of the unhappiness I feel about my own misunderstanding of the Banner option renewals," he said in regard to the document assigning character rights, "I am going to either handle my own business arrangements in the future or work through another agency."[18]

Hillerman remained true to his word and accepted Kahn's invitation to negotiate a new contract without using an agent. "I don't think you need one right now unless you'd like to have one," she had told him. In promising her author that she and he could work out a contract on their own, Kahn was violating the norms of publishing and exposing Harper & Row to a potential lawsuit. "It's just not a place an editor should put her house in legally," said one veteran literary agent.[19]

There remained one problem from the debacle with Elmo—Joe Leaphorn. A frustrated Hillerman pondered his options. "It may become very important to me to stop using Lieutenant Joseph Leaphorn and use instead Corporal Charley Begay, another Navajo cop, who is younger, single, more inclined to irreverence, etc.," he told Kahn. If it came to that, Hillerman said he could switch the names in *Listening Woman* in three days of work. Kahn decided it was not necessary, but Hillerman had begun to think Leaphorn had run his course as a character.

"Frankly," he confessed to Kahn, "Leaphorn has a bit too much rank for my liking, and his name wasn't as well chosen as it would have been had I known that I was going to be using him more." Perhaps it was time for a new tribal officer.[20]

CHAPTER 20

◈ The Invention of Chee ◈

Even though he professed to be perfectly happy without a literary agent, Tony Hillerman continued his search. He knew literary representation was necessary if he were to succeed as a commercially viable author. After the debacle with Carl Brandt, Hillerman tried Claire M. Smith at Harold Ober Associates, whose client Sheila Burnford's book *The Incredible Journey* had been turned into Walt Disney films. She declined to take Hillerman on.[1]

In the summer of 1977, however, his luck changed. He had been invited to speak at the Mystery Library Writers' Conference at the University of California, San Diego. His editor, Joan Kahn, was among the speakers, as was his new friend John Ball, author of *In the Heat of the Night* and a fellow Edgar winner. During a lunch break at the conference, Hillerman was introduced to Perry Knowlton. Four years younger than the fifty-two-year-old Hillerman, Knowlton had risen to become president and owner of Curtis Brown, Ltd., a literary agency that had its start in England with such clients as D. H. Lawrence, C. S. Lewis, and A. A. Milne. The agent was "a fierce advocate for his clients, a gentleman of high standards, and a charmer with real wit," according to Alan J. Kaufman, general counsel for Penguin Books.[2]

Knowlton attended writers' gatherings in search of clients. "Any agent, like any publisher, is after new talent," Knowlton told a reporter at the International Congress of Crime Writers. He was entirely unlike the Oklahoma-raised Hillerman. The product of a prep school and Princeton education, the suave agent had been a teacher, editor, sailor, licensed airplane pilot, scuba diver, and beekeeper. He knew of Hillerman's books and represented another New Mexico writer, John

Nichols, the author of the 1974 novel *The Milagro Beanfield War* and a Hillerman fan. A couple of years earlier, Nichols had sat down at eleven at night with a copy of Hillerman's *Dance Hall of the Dead*. "It kept me up until 3:30 going straight through without taking a breath," Nichols wrote to Hillerman. "Wonderfully written and terribly exciting, and also truly authentic."[3]

Over the course of lunch, Hillerman listened as the agent expounded on the joys of sailing. "I learn that Knowlton's sailboat is twenty-eight feet long," said Hillerman. "Even a landlubber knows that's a lot of boat. And writers who have yet to write that breakout book want to have agents who can afford such luxuries." Knowlton asked Hillerman if he had an agent. When he learned he did not, Knowlton offered his services and Hillerman accepted.[4]

Back in New Mexico, Hillerman resumed work on his fourth Navajo novel. A trip to Texas to see his brother Barney, with whom he had remained close, gave him the seed of an idea for a plot. During their early years in New Mexico, Tony and Marie had made regular summertime pilgrimages back to Oklahoma to visit Barney and their mother Lucy. A geologist, Barney was in the Lone Star State logging an oil well, a process that identifies information about the various strata of rock along the bore hole. The work his brother was doing inspired Tony to have a fictional geologist keep secret his logging discovery of uranium-rich pitchblende from others at the well. It was typical of Hillerman to turn something that intrigued him into a plot device. "I liken the writer to the bag lady pushing her stolen shopping cart through life collecting throwaway stuff, which, who knows, might be useful some way some day," Hillerman often said.[5]

A story he picked up in the course of doing some freelance writing gave him the second of three key elements for his plot. Despite his growing literary success, Hillerman had continued to accept writing assignments of all sorts. "I had six children and a faculty job," he said. "If you've ever been on a faculty, you know you don't make any money." He accepted an offer from the Albuquerque National Bank to write a biography of its late president Charles Frederick Luthy. The son of an Albuquerque mayor, Luthy had built the bank into New Mexico's largest and had become a prominent figure.[6]

In the course of his work Hillerman learned that in 1938 Luthy had accompanied then bank president George Kaseman to a Hobbs, New Mexico, oil-drilling operation to which the bank had loaned money. Luthy and Kaseman went to witness a "shooting" operation by which an explosion in the well fractures rocks to increase oil flow. But as the oil workers removed the nitroglycerin-filled bomb from the truck, it detonated. "All of a sudden there was a flash," said Luthy, who stood about 150 yards from the well. "I first thought of my wife and boy. I then tried to get to Mr. Kaseman to see if I could help him." But Kaseman and seven workers were dead. The blast was so powerful that initially the only clue to identifying Kaseman's body was a tattered business card. Luthy suffered injuries that blinded him.[7]

Hillerman repurposed the accidental nitroglycerin blast into an intentional one meant to hide the secret of a rich uranium deposit that his criminal intended to tap later. Eventually, he went to Hobbs and drove around to see drilling operations, refreshing his childhood memories of Oklahoma oilfields. To complete the plot, Hillerman devised a murder weapon to silence Navajos who might figure out what had been done. He discussed his murderous idea with his California writing friend John Ball, then excitedly shared his plans with Kahn. "It involves what John Ball and I believe is a unique murder weapon," he said. But Hillerman decided to keep it secret from Kahn until she received the manuscript. The mysterious weapon was central to the book's plot, even revealing it to his editor before she read the manuscript would be like identifying the guilty party in a whodunnit before the end.[8]

By spring of 1978, Hillerman was about 60 percent done with what he was calling *People of Darkness*, telling the *Albuquerque Journal* that it would again feature Joe Leaphorn. The draft began in Miami, Florida, far from the dry, desolate landscape of his previous novels. Contract killer Alfonso Silk is getting his shoes shined without exchanging a word with the man at his feet. Vigilant and hyper-careful, Silk receives no mail or telephone calls at his apartment, nor any visitors except for the occasional call girl. On a pay phone at a Rexall Drugstore, Silk is instructed by someone identified as "Major" to kill a Navajo with a bomb. Except for this one reference to the target's ethnicity, readers might rightfully think they had stumbled onto a spy thriller rather than a Hillerman mystery. The chapter didn't work.[9]

Increasingly, Hillerman had found that first chapters could not be written first. "No matter how carefully you have the project planned, first chapters tend to demand rewriting," Hillerman said. "Slow to catch on, I collected a manila folder full of perfect, polished, exactly right, pear-shaped first chapters before I learned this lesson. Their only flaw is that they don't fit the book I finally wrote."[10]

The action and setting in subsequent chapters were more in keeping with Hillerman's style. Lieutenant Joe Leaphorn is driving up the slope of Mount Taylor to the impressive B. J. Vines* mansion, reputed to be not only the most expensive home in New Mexico but also the work of Frank Lloyd Wright. Hillerman got the idea for the house from an unfounded rumor that the famous architect had designed a house near Grants, New Mexico, for his granddaughter, the Academy Award–winning actress Anne Baxter. Hillerman had his detective remember the same rumor but moved the house to Mount Taylor. For its inhabitant, said Hillerman, "I wanted something that signified not only wealth but also taste and intelligence."[11]

Moving the house was also important because Hillerman planned to set his tale in what was called the Checkerboard area on the eastern side of the Navajo Nation. Its unusual name grew from the implementation of the 1887 Dawes Act that carved out plots of land for Navajos to farm in the style of European subsistence agriculture. Unassigned portions of land were then sold to Anglos or given over to the Santa Fe Railroad. The result, years later, was a hodgepodge of Navajo and nonnative landownership in a pattern like the board on which one plays checkers. "It's really a mixed-up culture," said Hillerman. "I wanted to set the story in that environment and put my Navajo in close contact with white materialism."[12]

But Hillerman found that Joe Leaphorn, who had originally been intended only as a secondary character, was limiting his plan. "I had been troubled by the fact that I had made Joe Leaphorn too old and too sophisticated and too wise in the white man's ways to do what I wanted to do," said Hillerman. "I was thinking this guy's not what I need. I need someone younger, more traditional, more into his religion, more amazed by white ways." At first, he toyed with the idea of setting the book earlier to make Leaphorn younger. "I didn't like the idea," he said, "I didn't think of him as a younger man, so I needed a young character." The new character would be, Hillerman decided, "still intensely curious about the white world with which he knows he and his people must operate in harmony if the *hózhó* of the Navajo way is to be maintained."[13]

Using his pencil, Hillerman began to cross out Leaphorn's name in his draft chapters, putting in its place first Sergeant Tso, then Joe Chee, and finally Jim Chee. Hillerman said he briefly considered naming the new policeman Jimmy

---

*Hillerman found that the original name he had given this character, B. J. Tanner, was also the name of a trading post, prompting a last-minute substitution of "Vines."

Begay, a common name derived from the Navajo *biye*, which means "his son." By tradition, Navajos do not share their ceremonial names with outsiders. "So, when boys were sent to BIA boarding schools and asked their names, they would often reply 'George Begay,' meaning 'George his son,'" according to author Douglas Preston. Other names were developed under similar circumstances when boys offered descriptions of themselves such as Yazzie for "short," Tso for "big," and Tsosie for "slim." "It's amazing how many Navajos you know are named Begay or Tsosie or Joe or Billy or something like that," said Hillerman.[14]

If the book were going to have a new police officer, Hillerman was not going to repeat his mistake of inventing a name that had no connection with Navajo, as he had done with Leaphorn. Instead he adopted the very common Navajo surname Chee. At this point, Hillerman took great care in naming his Navajo characters, regularly consulting the Navajo Communications Company telephone book and tapping a treasure trove of names he came across while visiting KNDN radio station in Farmington. The station, which featured an all-Navajo format, had two microphones in its lobby for listeners who wanted to broadcast a message. On a typical day the messages heard included:

> The squaw dance for Frank Woody at Ojo Encino has been postponed. . . .
>   And to anyone who's listening, Elmer Bigben would like the people of Red Mesa to leave messages at the chapter house.[15]

Before taking to one of the microphones to air their announcement, Navajos filled out a form. "I collected out of a wastebasket a whole stack of these," said Hillerman. "I went through them and wrote down names."[16]

The younger and more inquisitive officer who came to life on the page pleased Hillerman. Jim Chee provided a means to highlight the cultural differences made evident by the close proximity of Anglos and Navajos along the Checkerboard portion of the reservation. "Chee's curiosity about it, as about all things in the white man's world, was intense," Hillerman wrote describing his new protagonist's reaction to the Vines mansion. Spotting a tombstone with an unusual epitaph, Chee was again puzzled. "But then everything about the white man's burial customs seemed odd to Chee," Hillerman wrote.[17]

Creating a new central character required more than a name change. Hillerman had to frontload his book with details in order to introduce his readers to a new protagonist. In rapid sequence, Hillerman disclosed Chee's young age, his clan—Slow Talking, the same as Leaphorn—his view that Navajos had no religion in the manner which white people had, and that he was studying to be a *hataalii*, a traditional medicine man. For Chee's personality, Hillerman drew on the idealistic students he had taught during the Vietnam era. "These people were actually reading Hermann Hesse with pleasure," he said. "That is Jim Chee."[18]

Jim Chee was not Hillerman's only departure from previous books. In this work, he created an unrepentant villainous figure unlike any of his previous ones. Hillerman had used a contract killer before in *The Fly on the Wall*. But he had gotten away with a Chicago murder-for-hire man seemingly drawn from central casting because the character was not central to the book. Here, Hillerman planned on writing large portions of the novel from the killer's point of view. "The plot required a professional hit man," Hillerman said. "Since it seems incredible to me that anyone would kill for hire, I was finding it hard to conceive my character." The memory of a real-life murderer whose execution he had covered as a reporter in Santa Fe came to the rescue. Hillerman had not forgotten how the inmate said he had not seen his mother since he was twelve years old and had no idea where she was.

Hillerman renamed and recast the contract killer Alfonso Silk, from the discarded opening chapter, into Colton Wolf and made him suffer maternal abandonment like the death row inmate. A loner, Wolf used the money he made to pay a detective to search for his mother, ironically unaware that the private eye was conning him. He had no home and lived on the road. Where didn't matter, wrote Hillerman. "Until he could find his mother. Then there would be no home place." Wolf was the executed inmate "reincarnated as he might have evolved if fate had allowed him to live a few murders longer." Attending the execution of the murderer in 1960 had prompted Hillerman to consider writing fiction. Now the moment, long remembered, inspired his fifth book of fiction. "I thought I had that guy motivated properly and made a very believable character. People would say, 'This guy's a sociopath,' and they understood why." He was right according to readers. "Colton Wolf was the character who fascinated me because you made him a real person rather than just a 'psychopathic' killer," wrote a California fan. "He was very human, very believable."[19]

For the man who hires the killer, Hillerman turned to yet another memory, this one from his time at Oklahoma A&M as part of his military training during World War II. There an unscrupulous son of a banker had tried to enlist him into conning a pawnbroker with a ruse involving an allegedly stolen diamond stickpin. He also used Hillerman's army serial number when picked up for being absent without a pass. In this classmate's view, the world was divided into prey and predators. "He showed me a side of humanity I hadn't known," said Hillerman."[20]

In April 1978, Hillerman was back on bookstore mystery shelves with *Listening Woman. Publishers Weekly* complained about its slow opening but decided the book "picks up speed and hurtles to a very exciting conclusion, involving militant American Indian terrorist activities." *Kirkus* loved the action and last-second twists and proclaimed "Hillman's overdue return (five years since *Dance Hall of the Dead*) should draw murmurs of contentment from all sides." The *New York Times* mirrored the sentiment of most reviewers. "*The Listening Woman* ranks even with Mr. Hillerman's *Dance Hall of the Dead*, and that is praise indeed."[21]

But still no national book tour was in the offing. Rather, Hillerman spoke to such gatherings as the National Secretaries Association chapter meeting in Albuquerque or the El Corral de Santa Fe Westerners' Christmas party. Despite a growing legion of loyal readers, as his fan mail testified (much of which he personally answered), Hillerman remained a regional author in the minds of his publisher and bookstores.

His lengthy hiatus from bookstores also contributed to his relegation to a regional writer. With a third published Navajo mystery, Hillerman now had a series. Normally this was a desirable thing in the world of books because as new readers pick up the latest installment, they often purchase the earlier volumes. On the other hand, readers of series come to expect regular and predictable installments. Five years was a long absence from stores that Hillerman did not want to repeat. He kept his new manuscript in his briefcase at the ready for when he had a moment away from teaching or working in the university administration building. The breaks, however, were few and far between, especially when it came to his now four-year-long job as an assistant to President William "Bud" Davis in addition to teaching a journalism class each semester.

On a March 1979 day, Hillerman picked up the telephone on his office desk. On the line was a sports writer from the *Albuquerque Journal*. As the press-savvy member of the administration, it usually fell to Hillerman to answer potentially tricky queries from the media. This was certainly one. The reporter wanted to know why representatives from the National Collegiate Athletic Association, the organization that regulates college athletics, had just completed their third recent visit to campus. "I presume they're looking for recruiting violations,"

Hillerman told the reporter. "We don't know if it's a big deal or not because the NCAA never tells you anything."[22]

Hillerman was close to the mark. By the end of the year, the Lobos' promising season as one of the nation's best college basketball teams came to an end. The NCAA and the FBI had uncovered a grade-fixing scheme. The Lobos' well-known coach, Norm Ellenberger, was suspended, then fired. The only court the basketball coach saw for a while was one with a judge in it. He was eventually acquitted in federal court but convicted on twenty-one charges in a state trial. The press and public were skeptical that President Davis, once a coach himself, had not known about the cheating. "More painful for me, they found it hard to believe that I, Davis's gofer and an experienced investigative reporter, was as ignorant of all this as I insisted," said Hillerman.[23]

That year Hillerman, the spokesperson for UNM, was quoted in more than five hundred press accounts. Hillerman, the author, was confined to a few dozen mentions. Despite the lack of press for his new novel, *Listening Woman* improved Hillerman's standing. It was a selection of the Book of the Month Club and his new agent, Perry Knowlton, sold the rights in Germany, Sweden, Denmark, and England. The novel also became one of five finalists for the Mystery Writers of America Edgar Award. In March, Tony and Marie attended the awards ceremony in New York City, as they had for *Dance Hall of the Dead*. But unlike that year, Hillerman's book lost to Ken Follett's *The Eye of the Needle*.[24]

At summer's end, Hillerman delivered *People of Darkness* to Kahn, completed in the free moments while meeting his extensive UNM obligations. It was his fourth Navajo mystery and one that would premiere a new character. In mid-October, after an unusually long wait, Hillerman heard back from Kahn. "Word finally on *People of Darkness*—which I think is close to being one of your very best—but I see some problems—which I am sure you can handle," she wrote. Then, as she usually did, Kahn unsparingly laid out what needed repair. She focused particularly on the criminals. The disguise and actions of the leading villain lacked credibility, motives were unclear, and the hired killer, she said, "is good and scary—but seems to come from another book." But she was happy with the Navajo material, the mining dangers, and the new leading man and lady.[25]

Until now women and romance were uncharted territory for Hillerman when it came to writing. *The Blessing Way*'s protagonist is attracted to a young woman, and the ending of the book hints at a potential relationship. Again, in *The Fly on the Wall* Hillerman's main character is attracted to a woman but fails to act on his feelings. In *Dance Hall of the Dead*, Hillerman produced an undeveloped female character that both he and Kahn found lacking. Joe Leaphorn's marriage was revealed in the first book when Emma was mentioned by name twice in passing but she had not appeared in any book since.

In *People of Darkness*, Hillerman introduced Mary Landon who would become the first of Jim Chee's three romantic relationships. Chee's would-be girlfriend appeared first in a scene in the draft manuscript where Hillerman seemingly forgot Leaphorn was married. In the early drafts of the book, before Chee replaced Leaphorn, Mary Landon's encounter with Leaphorn was suggestive. When Hillerman crossed out Leaphorn and inserted Chee, he retained the scene but changed the rank of the man offering coffee. "The first time she had looked at him she had been inspecting a Tribal Police sergeant. Now she was looking at a man asking her out for coffee. It was a different sort of inspection."[26]

Landon accompanies Chee as he pursues his investigation. Acting like an investigative partner, as did Janey Janoski in *The Fly on the Wall*, Landon faces danger and helps Chee when he is wounded by the contract killer. But Hillerman's uncertainty about Mary's future as a character remains evident in the draft he submitted to Kahn. By the end, Chee doesn't think of Mary again, despite having put her in dangerous spots. It was one of several faults Kahn spotted in the manuscript. To fix her complaints, Hillerman undertook extensive revisions. After the winter holidays, Kahn announced she was pleased and sent the manuscript to her copyeditor Marjorie Horvitz (later Saul Bellow's preferred copyeditor) and a contract to Perry Knowlton. It was Hillerman's fifth book with Kahn, yet he still needed to complete a manuscript to Kahn's satisfaction before she would issue a contract. Hillerman still had not reached the stage in his writing career when publishers would offer contracts on yet-to-be-written novels.

People of Darkness marked Hillerman and Kahn's last collaboration. In May 1980, the editor informed her publisher that she was resigning after thirty-five years at the helm of Harper & Row's mystery series. In October, she accepted a position with Ticknor & Fields, an old publishing house revived by Houghton Mifflin. "I left Harper with my heart breaking, but it was changing," she said. The company's growth had disturbed her. "Since the only thing I really give a damn about is authors, and they weren't being taken care of, I thought I'd better go and find a place that would love them more."[27]

She hoped to bring her authors with her. "Some have already said yes, but I don't think I'd better say which," she told a reporter at the time of her departure. Hillerman and Knowlton, however, decided to remain with Harper & Row. It turned out to be a fortunate decision. Harper & Row executives assigned his books to forty-eight-year-old Larry Ashmead, a talented editor who came over when the company bought Lippincott, a venerable publishing house. It would become the longest lasting, most profitable, and most successful relationship Hillerman would have with any editor.

Like Hillerman, Ashmead was a consummate storyteller, although his tales often involved fresh gossip and were sometimes bawdy. "He could also be catty, and that was part of his charm," said legendary editor Tim Duggan, who worked with Ashmead. When the New York branch of Santa Monica's famous Michael's restaurant opened in New York, two blocks from the publishing company's office, Ashmead took to eating lunch there every day. The restaurant was always full of media figures, agents, and editors. "And they always had a table for him there, the same table, and he just kind of held court and told stories," said Duggan. "Unlike other people at Michael's who were all about, kind of, New York power and status, he was not."[28]

In the midst of the changing of the editorial guard, Harper & Row began shipping copies of *People of Darkness* to stores. Advance orders were higher than any of Hillerman's previous books. "Hillerman is once again among the New Mexico Navajos, but Joe Leaphorn isn't the sleuth this time," said *Kirkus*. "Instead it's Jim Chee, a young Navajo reservation detective who's also an up-and-coming tribal medicine man." *Publishers Weekly* dispatched Patricia Holt to Albuquerque for an interview with the author. Holt predicted that Hillerman's growing reputation as a mystery writer would reach even further with this new book.[29]

CHAPTER 21

❖ Two Stories, Two Novels ❖

Remarkably, in the fall of 1980, before his new editor, Larry Ashmead, even had a chance to work with Hillerman on the fifth book in the series, the author announced he wanted to abandon Leaphorn and Chee, at least for a while. Instead Hillerman proposed his next book be a mystery built around the unsolved 1949 murder of Cricket Coogler, the Las Cruces, New Mexico, waitress whose brutal death and the subsequent coverup cost the Democrats the governor's seat. It would be called *The Death of the Party*.

Ashmead discouraged the idea. *People of Darkness*, which his predecessor had edited, had already sold 9,300 copies, and Harper & Row was ordering a second printing. It was the best launch of any of Hillerman's books so far. He and Perry Knowlton, Hillerman's new agent, told their author that to do an "out-of-category novel" would require time and planning. "Meanwhile, we all agree it's best to continue on with the new Chee novel." Hillerman gave in for the time being. "I will start on the next one," Hillerman told the two men, "which will involve revenge, the dispute between Navajo and Hopi on the Joint Use reservation, and either Leaphorn or Jim Chee amid the Hopi Kachinas and their Two-Hearted witches."[1]

In the meantime, Knowlton contacted Alice K. Turner, who had recently assumed the job as *Playboy* magazine's fiction editor. He asked if she might consider buying a short story by his new client. Since its inception in 1953, the men's magazine had published such noted authors as Saul Bellow, John Irving, John Cheever, Anne Sexton, John Updike, and Isaac Bashevis Singer. According to one writer, the pages between photographs of naked women were "second only to *The New Yorker* in prestige as a place for serious writers to display their talent."[2]

Turner, a Bryn Mawr College graduate and holder of an advanced degree in English literature from New York University, agreed to consider a Hillerman story. Short stories, however, were not among Hillerman's strengths. The ones he had written during his years as a journalist had all been rejected. Nonetheless, the opportunity pleased him. "I was delighted because no one ever liked my stories," he said.[3]

Hillerman mailed Turner "Chee's Witch," a 3,800-word story written in 1979 that he had submitted with no success to *Alfred Hitchcock Mystery Magazine*, owned by the same company that published *Ellery Queen Mystery Magazine*. He wrote the tale to try out something he had learned about Navajo beliefs that he thought might work in his next book. According to Navajo lore, witches make "corpse powder" from the skin of a dead person's fingertips, palms, soles of the feet, and toes. When ingested, the powder produces physical or mental illness. It is believed that the whorls on the skin in those spots mark the entrance of the animating winds that first gave life to Navajos when they reached the earth's surface. What intrigued Hillerman is that removing these portions of skin could also hinder the identification of a corpse. Here he had an otherworldly practice that was perfect for criminals hiding their tracks.[4]

But aside from containing this intriguing aspect of Navajo culture, Hillerman's story fell flat. Turner told Hillerman she loved the Navajo-related material about clans and witchcraft, as well as the descriptions of the desert. "What I don't like is that there isn't any movement to the story," she said. Turner invited Hillerman to make it more of a story, even a different one if he wished, but to preserve the death and the corpse powder angle.[5]

Hillerman's second try produced no better results. "She found the new version loaded down with extraneous material, strained connections, and detective work that fell outside the action. For Hillerman the short story format itself was difficult to adopt in writing about Navajos for non-Navajo readers. The long, often fascinating, discursive passages about Navajo culture, religion, and lifeways were both a necessity and a strength of his novels. Short stories could not accommodate such an approach. But without it, the writing lacked authenticity. "Mostly the story has too many *things* in it," Turner said. "It might work very well expanded to novel length, but a short story is a different medium." That is just what Hillerman did. The witch material, a jewelry theft, and a card trick developed for the story were just the right ingredients for a second Chee novel.[6]

When Tony Hillerman got writer's block, Marie would often suggest a drive out to the Navajo Nation. The two frequently made these trips together. Marie would have maps open on her lap as they navigated the often-unmarked roads. She also advised her husband on botanical matters and geology. "I'd say Marie, what kind of grass is that over there near Chaco Canyon, she'd say well it's some Grama grass and some Cheat grass. So, I don't make as many mistakes as I would otherwise."[7]

"I have to go to the reservation, to the spot I'll be writing about, to get comfortable with it," Tony said. "I like to feel at home in my mind with the spot I have on the page." To get there, Hillerman depended on the Indian Country Guide. A map created by the Automobile Club of Southern California, it was the same map that Joe Leaphorn used. "I've worn out three road maps of the Navajo Reservation," Tony said.[8]

Now that Tony was having trouble expanding his short story into a book, he and Marie got into his aging Datsun pickup and headed west. "Shouldn't we make reservations?" asked Marie. "Ah, this time of year, there's nobody out there," said Tony. The expert on Navajo land was wrong. When they reached Kayenta five hours later, the Holiday Inn was full with a movie crew filming a western. Two more towns later, they still couldn't find a room and spent the night curled up on the front seat of the truck and trying to sleep. "There was a night watchman at the filling station," said Tony. The man had a pistol and fired off two or three rounds into the air. "What was that? What was that?" asked Marie, awakened by the sound. "I hated to tell her it was the night watchman trying to scare us off by letting us know he had a pistol," recalled Hillerman.[9]

In the morning they drove an hour to the Hopi reservation and found lodging at the Cultural Center. After settling in, Tony picked up a copy of a weekly newspaper and read how someone had vandalized a windmill used to pump water. It struck him as strange that anybody would vandalize a windmill, especially in a desert. "Before we left the Hopi Reservation, I could already see how I had to rewrite the book and how the windmill was going to be the linchpin that held the whole book together because it gave [Chee] a reason to be where he had to be."[10]

Research animated Hillerman's writing as he worked on his second Chee mystery. For the fiery demise of a drug-smuggling plane in Wepo Wash near Black Mesa, Hillerman persuaded a friend to fly him along the path his fictional Cessna would take, right up to the spot where it was to crash. For the depiction of the

Burnt Water trading post, which would play a central role in the story, Hillerman spent time visiting the real one, housed in a Quonset hut. By the end of his digging around, he had all the elements he needed. A quartet of seemingly unrelated crimes involving the damaged windmill, the plane crash, stolen trading post jewelry, and a murdered Navajo would display Chee's maturing investigative skills and produce what by now had become a trademark Hillerman climactic ending.[11]

Hillerman's research about the Hopis led him to learn about the long-standing animosity between them and the Navajos. Since the nineteenth century, the two tribes had jointly owned land near northern Arizona's Black Mesa. Congress had decided to partition the land and under the plan, 2,091 Navajo families would be relocated. Calling it "one of the largest peacetime evictions in American history," Hillerman took to the editorial pages of the *Los Angeles Times* in the summer of 1981 to write a lengthy criticism of the federal solution, taking the Navajo side.[12]

Hillerman successfully converted his short story into a novel and delivered it to Ashmead. Hillerman titled it *The Dark Wind*, a reference to the Navajo term for an evil force. For the opening chapter, Hillerman had taken an almost identical approach as he used in *Dance Hall of the Dead*. In the former he set the murder on the Zuni Pueblo, outside Navajo Land. In the new book, a body was found on Hopi land. In both cases the placement of the crime provided Hillerman with an opportunity to introduce Puebloan spiritual beliefs, which were more closely guarded and thus would be more exotic, to the reader. In *Dance Hall of the Dead* the first chapter insinuates the murder has been perpetrated by a Zuni spiritual warrior. The discovery in the opening chapter of *The Dark Wind* that the corpse's feet and hands have been mutilated suggests a killing by a witch. In Jim Chee, Hillerman had a tribal officer far more suitable to serve as a Virgil guiding the reader through the layers of the Navajo spiritual world.

The Dark Wind was published in the spring of 1982. "A few nice twists, with Hillerman's moodily fine prose in full Southwest regalia," said *Kirkus*. "But this time the darkness is murky as often as it's chilling—in the slowest, most relentlessly introspective case yet for the Navajo Tribal Police." United Press International, for which Hillerman had worked, reported that its former reporter "does a masterful job of setting the scene and capturing the beauty and mysticism of the area he writes about." Alice Cromie at the *Chicago Tribune* pronounced Hillerman was in "peak form" and that Chee was "a joy to follow as he tracks evildoers in the Southwest." At least one reviewer couldn't resist trotting out

Indian stereotypes, the kind Hillerman despised, to praise the book. "Put your ear to the ground, Kemosabe, and hear the sound of three, maybe four movie sales approaching." In fact, it was a prophecy that would come true by the end of the decade.[13]

Chee, appearing in his second novel, was undoubtedly a critical success. "The beauty and uniqueness of Hillerman's work are summed up in Jim Chee himself," noted the *Baltimore Sun*. The publishing world also took notice. Lee Goerner, a rising editor at Alfred A. Knopf, wrote Hillerman a fan letter and asked Ashmead if he would be willing to send over some books in trade for Knopf titles.[14]

In late June, members of the Western Writers of America poured into Santa Fe for their annual convention. Writers, publishers, historians, and college professors filled the Inn at Loretto for panel discussion, meals, and awards. The meeting promised to be contentious. A group of authors was planning to use the gathering to publicize their complaint that the real story of the West was being eclipsed by East Coast publishers' devotion to shoot-'em-up novels. "Western literature exists in the myths of the East," said Stan Steiner, an author with a passion for chronicling the lives of everyday westerners.[15]

The schism between those authors who created romantic tales of cowboys and those who sought to publish a more realistic view of western life that included women, Indians, Latinos, and others became evident during the five-day meeting. "I don't see any Chicanos or Indians here today," critiqued filmmaker Juan Salazar, who was in the audience for the panel on "The New Western—What Is It?" featuring Hillerman, Norman Zollinger, Stanley Noyes, Tony Mares, John Nichols, and Peter Decker. Salazar's remarks, according to a reporter who was present, "soon gave way to a near free-for-all, with charges and counter charges flying across the room."[16]

In the moment, Hillerman, ever the diplomat, told the assembly he viewed himself as an entertainer. "I'm writing to amuse not to shed divine light upon society to tell them which way to go and how to behave," he said. Nichols, who previously had told Hillerman of his admiration for his work, didn't buy it. "That's a cop-out," he responded. "A lot of what passes for entertainment brain washes people on how the rules of society run." In Nichols's view, cultural genocide was the theme of most Westerns. "Westerns have been classed as entertainment but they created a racist view of society in which Indians, Chicanos, and Blacks were on the bottom and the white-hatted cowboy was on the top."

Hillerman's *aw-shucks-I-am-just-an-entertainer* response was disingenuous. He very much wanted his work to change American attitudes toward Native Americans, which he believed was a monochromatic view that all Indians were alike. "It's a dirty shame that Americans (including Navajos) know so little about the Navajo culture," he wrote to a friend that year. Only a month prior to the WWA meeting, he had told a *Los Angeles Times* reporter, "I try to open the window for the readers and let them look in at these cultures." The form of his work might be that of a mystery, but its mission was greater than providing a diversion. "People who really intended to buy a mystery find themselves surrounded by what I know about Navajos."[17]

"It seems to me that this is how the game must be played," Hillerman explained to a pair of New England professors, who had published a scholarly article on his work. To share cultural information with the reader successfully it must be made germane to the plot, he said. "It must be made a natural part of the narrative story line, part of the way the crime is solved, part of the reason the crime is committed, part of the path toward understanding of character, part of the motivation for an action."[18]

That fall, Hillerman worked on a third Chee novel, matching the number of Leaphorn books. But he was pestered as usual with tending to his academic duties. "Unfortunately, I can't seem to get the next one finished, but I'm plugging away," he reported to a friend. The idea for the book first came to Hillerman the year before while exploring the reservation of the Cañoncito Navajo Band (now known as To'Hajiilee), a noncontiguous section of the Navajo Nation in the Checkerboard region that had been the backdrop for *People of Darkness*. He came across an abandoned stone hogan at the bottom of Mesa Gigante. Inspecting the building, Hillerman found a hole had been created on the north wall of the structure. He knew the hole had been created to remove the corpse of a person who had died inside. The hogan lay abandoned because it was believed the *chindi* (ghost) of the deceased remained trapped inside, causing ghost sickness to anyone who entered. "But why," Hillerman asked himself, "had the dying person not been moved outside before he died, so the *chindi* could escape?" The question stuck in his mind.[19]

In Hillerman's hands, Navajo taboos around death became a means to illustrate the cultural blinders that prevented the FBI agents from seeing clues obvious to Leaphorn and now to Chee. This was one of Hillerman's favorite techniques, used to great effect in *Listening Woman*. Devoted readers recognized it whenever the FBI was called in. In the new work, Chee spotted inconsistencies in the burial of the Navajo who had been removed through the corpse hole. While the corpse's moccasins had been intentionally put on the wrong feet so that his ghost would be confused by his footprints after death, other customs, such as properly washing his hair, had been ignored.

As Chee followed his separate investigation, the clues took him to Los Angeles, Raymond Chandler country. For the second time in his novels, Hillerman wrote about urban Navajos, descendants of families relocated in the 1940s and 1950s, trapped in limbo between the Anglo and Navajo worlds. He used the setting of West Hollywood, a place he had come to know when he and Marie visited her paternal aunt Isabel Ross when she was in ill health. The theme of cultural identity grew in importance and Hillerman played it out in Los Angeles, on the Navajo Nation, and in Chee's relationship with Mary Landon, the girlfriend Chee gained in *People of Darkness* but was absent from *The Dark Wind*. In a series of flashbacks, readers learn Chee and Landon's relationship is in trouble, as he is drawn to stay in his homeland and she fears her identity will be subsumed by his culture if she remains and marries him.

The abandoned hogan serves to highlight Chee's own search for identity. He stands before it, aware of the taboo on entering a hogan where a person has died, debating whether he should search for clues inside. "To the Jim Chee," wrote Hillerman, "who was an alumnus of the University of New Mexico, a subscriber to *Esquire* and *Newsweek*, an officer of the Navajo Tribal Police, lover of Mary Landon, holder of a Farmington Public Library card, student of anthropology and sociology, 'with distinction' graduate of the FBI Academy, holder of Social Security card 441-28-7272, it was a logical step to take." But to do so would run contrary to being a traditional Navajo, to which Chee aspired. In selecting attributes to illustrate the non-Navajo side of Chee, Hillerman used his own social security number and gave a literary nod to the Farmington Public Library, which had issued a card in the identity of Hillerman's fictitious police officer.[20]

As usual, Hillerman's cutting room floor received a healthy share of pages. At one point he had an idea to kill off the criminal in the Blue Door Bar, a fictional location just outside the Navajo Nation. The bar was described as notorious for supplying liquor to Navajo bootleggers who would carry it onto the reservation where alcohol was not permitted. Because Navajos are taught not to enter structures in which someone died, Hillerman thought setting the murder there would result in the bar being closed. He ran the idea by Sam Bingham, a journalist friend who taught at the Rock Point Community School north of Chinle on the Navajo Nation. Bingham submitted the idea to his students and asked them to write an essay on it. "They said, yes, a devout Navajo would avoid the bar if someone had been killed there," Hillerman said, "But, they added, a devout Navajo wouldn't go into a bar anyway and those Navajos who would frequent a saloon wouldn't care if someone had died in the place or not." Hillerman killed the plan.[21]

A final element of the plot came from one of the two still-unpublished short stories Hillerman had written for *Playboy*. In the story, Hillerman played with fooling law enforcement officials by switching the identity of a person placed in the witness protection program. He had found no use for the ruse in *The Dark Wind*, but it became the kernel from which this new novel grew. Still the first-chapter problem, which frequently bedeviled Hillerman, surfaced again. He began by placing the key victim's death by gunshot in West Hollywood. "It proved to be exciting, full of tension, etc., but it joined my thick file of first chapters that didn't make it because it bent the book out of shape," Hillerman said. Next he tried writing a scene in the Chuska Mountains on the Navajo Nation several days after the victim's death. On his third try, Hillerman penned a shootout between two Navajos in front of the Shiprock Economy Wash-O-Mat. One dies, the other is wounded and escapes in his out-of-place rented Ford. "The driver was Navajo, but this was white man's business." The short chapter worked. "I'm never sure how much such intangibles are measured," said Hillerman, "but it seems to be right."[22]

A lot of work remained ahead if Hillerman was to have this sixth Navajo murder mystery ready in time to maintain the desired publication pacing for a series. This installment might finally set him free to pursue writing full time. "Sales of my books had been moving up, slowly but steadily, in a puzzling pattern," Hillerman said. Southwestern states accounted for most of his sales but he was now finding readers in the Bay Area of California and the Northeast. At signings these new readers told the author they were not normally murder and crime fiction fans. An author and professor at the University of Massachusetts told Hillerman his were the only mystery novels he had ever read. "Usually they bore the hell out of me, but yours are so clearly more than mystery novels that I count them as a wholly different genre." The merging of geography and anthropology, the professor concluded, was unique in American letters.

"It occurred to me that I had tapped into a mass of American readers who suffer from the same workaholic problem that besets me," said Hillerman. These readers found reading a book for mere amusement made them feel guilty. "My books, like a sausage sandwich spiced with anti-acid tablets, give absolution along with the sin."[23]

For his part, Ashmead was confident that Hillerman and his series had proven its potential. "Now he's no chance at all," he said. "We know we'll make money every time. His setting, his characters, they've established a sure market." Sales of Hillerman's new and existing novels, including those published abroad, were generating substantial royalties. His newest book, *The Dark Wind*, sold sixteen thousand hardback copies before Avon Books published the mass-market paperback editions. Avon had also printed five thousand more copies of his first book, *The Blessing Way*, now more than ten years old. The idea of giving up teaching and its $41,000 salary in order to write full time, something about which Hillerman increasingly mused, was becoming a financial possibility.[24]

CHAPTER 22

◈ Character Identity Crisis ◈

Tony Hillerman left behind his duties at the University of New Mexico on a temperate day in April 1984 and made the familiar hour or so drive north to Santa Fe. He drove past the downtown and its historic plaza, where years before he had spent so much time, and up the incline leading to St. Catherine Indian School. Perched above the Santa Fe National Cemetery and Rosario Cemetery, the ninety-year-old Catholic boarding school had invited Hillerman to speak to an assembly. Visiting the school was a journey back to his childhood when he had been a student at St. Mary's Academy, the mission school for Potawatomi girls run by the Sisters of Mercy in Sacred Heart, Oklahoma. His books, adopted by the Sisters of the Blessed Sacrament for English classes at St. Catherine's, had become popular among ninth- through twelfth-grade students. He rewarded their loyalty by announcing that a fictional student from the school would play an important role in the third Jim Chee novel he was writing.

His choice of a St. Catherine's girl was more than a matter of creating a cameo role for the students. Rather, the engaging and courageous young girl Hillerman invented provided a narrative thread drawing together the action from the Navajo Nation to Los Angeles and back. The girl, Margaret Billy Sosi, would have fit in easily among the girls at the assembly. Like many of them she had been taught the Navajo Way by her family and now navigated the Anglo Way at the school. In the novel the bright and appealing Sosi became an effective foil to Chee's fears at entering the hogan he believed contained a *chindi*, the ghost of the dead.

In a marked change from previous books, that month Hillerman had signed a contract with Harper & Row for this new Chee book even though it was a long way from being finished. With increased sales, as well as continuing sales of his other five novels, Hillerman was emerging as an asset to Harper & Row. His agent, Perry Knowlton, made sure his client was rewarded accordingly.

In June, John Carr, an author whose most recent work was *The Craft of Crime*, arrived from New Orleans to write a profile of Hillerman. As he frequently did when journalists and writers came calling, Hillerman led his guest to his Isuzu Trooper II and drove out of town. A little more than an hour later, they stood on top of the 365-foot-high mesa at Acoma Pueblo, where Puebloans had lived for centuries. In the 102-degree heat, Hillerman and Carr walked through the ancient graveyard in front of the mission church San Esteban del Rey. "The landscape that lies below is a perfect setting for a conversation," recalled Carr. "The very topography seems an allegory of the struggle between Good and Evil." Looking over the wall, Hillerman pointed to the outhouses below, each with a padlock on the door. "Witches," said Hillerman.[1]

Back in the Isuzu, Carr asked, "Can you tie those padlocks to witchcraft?"

"I think I can draw certain conclusions, yeah," replied Hillerman. "At Hopi they call them sorcerers instead of witches, but it's the same notion. Most outhouses at Hopi too have padlocks—and I don't know any other reason why you would have a padlock on an outhouse—is that they don't want sorcerers to get their excrement and use it against them."[2]

As they drove east, the sun casting long shadows before them, Hillerman provided a short lesson in what he had learned over the past two decades about witches, particularly among Navajo. For the Diné, Hillerman explained, Changing Woman and Talking God had taught that those who turn away from trying to live in harmony become witches. "Traditional Navajos just can't believe that a town Navajo, especially one who's an alcoholic, is anything but a damned witch," he said. "Other Navajos at one level or another believe in witches the way a lot of us whites believe in evil."

The explanation struck Carr, a careful reader of Hillerman's books, as revealing. From the first novel onward, witchery and evil had always been present. Early in *The Blessing Way*, a healer asks Leaphorn if he believes in witching. He answers by recounting how witchcraft came into the Fourth World according to his father's teaching. "You didn't tell me whether you believe it," says the healer. Smiling slightly, Leaphorn replies, "My grandfather, I have learned to believe in evil."[3]

"Beyond its use as plot engines," Carr later wrote, "Hillerman is fascinated with witchcraft because he is a Catholic moralist who is awed, even fascinated, as Milton was fascinated, by raw evil, by falls from grace: man from God, Navajos from *hózhó*, a child from the love of his parents." In Hillerman's words, evil is "the absence of good, the way darkness is the absence of light."

For Hillerman, many of the Navajo practices he encountered were "dangerously Christian." Not the kind of Christianity he saw practiced in the United States, but the type he hoped would be followed. Years later, in his final novel, Hillerman offered a compact description of the affinity he saw between Navajo beliefs and his Christianity. "The Diné taught its people to live in the peace and harmony of *hózhó*, they must learn to forgive—a variation of the policy that *bilagáana* Christians preached in their Lord's Prayer but all too often didn't seem to practice."[4]

At summer's end, Hillerman and his editor Larry Ashmead met as Harper & Row began production of the third Chee mystery. Ashmead rejected the title Hillerman favored, *The Door into Darkness*, and renamed it *The Ghostway*. As the two men chatted, Ashmead brought up a problem. Hillerman had written a scene to demonstrate the cold-heartedness and shrewdness of a killer. Doberman dogs, which he planned to poison, guarded the intended victim's house and were trained to attack silently. To confirm this, the killer Eric Vaggan tosses a cat over the fence and watches the animal's silent demise. "This is offensive," Ashmead told Hillerman. "They'll be protesting you at book signings." Hillerman noticed that among the many knickknacks stuffed into his editor's office was a statuette of a cat and there were feline portraits on the wall as well. "But I defend my need for the scene, and he lets me win my argument for literary art-over-humanity." When the book was published a customer at a book signing told him his insensitivity to animal cruelty was offensive. "I said Ashmead had warned me that cat owners would object," Hillerman said. "She said, 'To hell with the cat. I raise Dobermans.'"[5]

Nonetheless, Ashmead was excited about *The Ghostway*'s potential. The prepublication reviews were promising. But a reading by another person turned out to be the most influential factor in the fate of Hillerman's sixth Navajo novel. Harper & Row had recently appointed William Shinker as its new director of marketing and paperback publishing. Shinker, who had begun his working life at Barbara's Books in Chicago, had a keen sense for sales especially after several years with Warner Books. "He fell in love with the Hillerman books," recalled Ashmead, "and said that it was time to put a stop to this tiny cult business." Harper & Row decided to do some national marketing and persuaded the Book of the Month club and the Mystery Guild to make *The Ghostway* an alternate selection. "This is a real break," Hillerman's agent wrote. "I think the sales will reflect it and the next book should benefit immensely." Knowlton was right. Within days of its February 1985 publication, Harper & Row shipped more than ten thousand copies and within weeks ordered second and third printings, the best sales ever for Hillerman.[6]

The book received glowing reviews. The *New York Times Book Review* gushed, "*The Ghostway* moves alertly along, has all the flavor and exoticism one associates with Mr. Hillerman and is one of the best in the series." To Hillerman, his future as an author seemed promising and university life correspondingly less appealing. After a fall semester of continued frustration over balancing writing with university responsibilities, Hillerman had grown restless. His patience for the much-transmuted university life had diminished. "The joy of learning had seeped out of students," he said. "With it went the joy of teaching."[7]

After fifteen years as a journalist and nearly twenty years of teaching journalism, Hillerman had had enough. "One dreadful day," said Hillerman, "I delivered a lecture that was so bad that even I recognized it was boring and I decided to quit teaching." He would turn sixty in May. "I feel kind of burned out," he told the student newspaper. "And when you feel burned out, you ought not teach for a while." He had spent the past twenty-two years on the University of New Mexico campus, nineteen as a professor. It was the longest stretch of employment in his life. But for the past several years it had been becoming increasingly difficult to balance his writing life with teaching and he had begun neglecting the latter. He had, for instance, ceased to update his lectures. Sherry Robinson, a student in his Ethics of Journalism class, noticed his examples had become dated. His lectures remained engaging, she said. "But he wasn't giving 100 percent."[8]

In June 1985, Tony and Marie attended the wedding of their youngest son Daniel at St. Bernadette Catholic Church in Albuquerque. On August 16, Tony and Marie would celebrate their thirty-seventh anniversary of their own wedding. In the years since, they had lived in five cities and reared six children. Anne had been married in 1974, Monica in 1975, and Janet in 1976. Tony Jr. would marry in 1987 but Steve would remain single. Steve said he never heard his parents utter a cross word to each other. The often-taxing efforts of rearing the children, especially the two for whom life's beginnings had been harsh, were mostly behind Tony and Marie. The five-bedroom ranch-style house on Texas Street now seemed empty.[9]

With three Leaphorn books and three Chee books published, Hillerman felt confident about the success of his new police officer. But the character shift created some confusion. One reviewer forgot entirely about Leaphorn, saying Chee had been the protagonist in all six detective novels. At a signing in one bookstore, a woman asked, "Why did you change Leaphorn's name to Chee?"

Hillerman was flummoxed. "It took a split second for the significance to sink in. A dagger to the heart. I stutter. Search around for an answer, and finally just say they're totally different characters."

"'Oh,' says she, 'I can't tell them apart.'"

Hillerman compared the moment to St. Paul's thorn in his flesh. "It wouldn't go away," he said. "I decided to put both characters in the same book to settle the issue for myself."[10]

Pairing the two police officers created more opportunities for Hillerman to highlight traditional Navajo customs and use them in his clue dropping. For instance, hiking with a Navajo one day, Hillerman noticed the man avoided stepping in the water when they crossed a ravine. "It shows respect for the water," Hillerman said. He put this knowledge to use in a scene when Chee explains to Leaphorn that the man they are pursuing is Navajo. "When he walked down the arroyo, he took care not to walk where the water had run. And on the way back to the road, a snake had been across there, and when he crossed its path he shuffled his feet.' Chee paused. 'Or do white men do that too?'

"'I doubt it,' Leaphorn said."[11]

To Hillerman these Navajo habits were the equivalent of the Anglo aversion to stepping on sidewalk cracks. "Step on a crack, break your mother's back," according to the adage. "This is an example of those peculiar cultural things that I'm always looking for an opportunity to include in my novels," he said.[12]

Hillerman turned to the commonly held Navajo belief in witches to contrast the different upbringings and beliefs of the two detectives. Usually referred to as "skinwalkers," witches were thought to possess the ability to change into animals and were believed to cause illnesses from which the victim could only be cured with a healing ceremony. "A skinwalker is a rather complicated Navajo traditional view of a witch," said Hillerman.[13]

Bergen McKee, the protagonist Hillerman created for *The Blessing Way*, researched witchcraft with occasional help from Leaphorn, his classmate at Arizona State University. In Hillerman's second Navajo mystery, the topic of witches came up during a conversation between Leaphorn and Father Ingles, a Catholic priest. Ingles passed on the rumor that a missing boy's mother had been living with two witches. "You believe in witches?" asks the priest. "That's like me asking you if you believe in sin, Father," Leaphorn says. "The point is you gradually learn that witch talk and trouble sort of go together."[14]

Talk of witches also surfaces in *Listening Woman*, the last of the three solo Leaphorn books. "'At first, I thought I would be maligning the Navajos by making them more witchcraft-ridden than they were,'" Hillerman said. But instead he discovered that Leaphorn's rational rather than spiritual approach to witches hurt the credibility of the books. A Navajo whom Hillerman had known for years told him, "The one thing that bothers me about your books, and I think is false to the culture, is that Leaphorn is so skeptical about witches. I've never known a Navajo, educated or not, who was skeptical about witches."[15]

From his earliest days of learning about Navajos, Hillerman had encountered tales of skinwalkers. For instance, he heard of a young white man who late one night pulled into the service station at Mexican Hat, a small town on the northern end of the Navajo Nation. Under the moonlight, shaking and stuttering, the young driver tried to recount how he had seen a big man running and motioning him to stop his truck on one of the dark roads. A student at the University of New Mexico told Hillerman about seeing a skinwalker while helping his grandmother tend the sheep when he was eleven. "Two legs like a man," he said, "but bent way forward and a head like a dog." Over time, Hillerman found that the most frequent version of a sighting was the "witch on the roof." In such accounts, the father is usually away and one of the children is awakened by a sound on the roof made by a skinwalker trying to drop corpse powder down the smoke hole.[16]

Up until this moment, Hillerman had only mentioned skinwalkers in passing in three books. Now he made the Navajo belief in skinwalkers the center of his new book. Bringing Chee and Leaphorn together in pursuit of a murderer who was a skinwalker, or was thought to be, offered Hillerman a chance to explore the tribe's spiritual cosmology through the eyes of a believer and a non-believer, both Navajo. "Leaphorn is the opposite of a fundamentalist," Hillerman said. "He sees their mythology purely as a metaphor, as a poetic way of saying, 'Stay in harmony, don't struggle against the current, everything that happens has a purpose." Ever the rationalist, Leaphorn has no tolerance for those who believe in the literal existence of skinwalkers. This angers Chee.[17]

Hillerman's Chee looked at the Navajo genesis much as non-fundamentalist Christians looked at their origin story. The stories were to teach lessons and the specifics about the size of the reed through which the Holy People emerged were unimportant. What mattered were the lessons the imagery taught. "Let him believe whatever he wanted to believe," was Chee's reaction to Leaphorn's disbelief. "The origin story of the Navajos explained witchcraft clearly enough, and it was a logical part of the philosophy on which the Diné had founded their culture. If there was good, and harmony, and beauty on the east side of reality, then there must be evil, chaos, and ugliness to the west."[18]

As usual, the first chapter was a challenge for Hillerman. But the content became clear to him when he woke one morning in a Tucson hotel during his book tour for *The Ghostway*. First and last chapters complete, Hillerman submitted the complete manuscript of *Skinwalkers* to Ashmead in March 1986. In turn Harper & Row sent Knowlton a two-book contract with the best terms Hillerman had yet been offered. The publishing company would provide an advance of $60,000 with the proviso that he deliver his next work in July of the following year. Ashmead and his boss, William Shinker, were thrilled by the conjoining of Leaphorn and Chee. Shinker told an executive at Waldenbooks, then a national chain of mall-based bookstores, Hillerman would "break out" with *Skinwalkers*. Ashmead sent a copy of the galley pages to Ursula Le Guin, a renowned science fiction and fantasy author. "I was just finishing *The Ghostway* when it arrived," she told Ashmead in her thank-you note. "The only mysteries I read are Tony Hillerman's. . . . Is that a blurb or isn't it?"[19]

"They are sure cranking up for this book," Knowlton told Hillerman. "Harper reps all over America dropped everything they were doing to settle down with your new book," wrote one California sales representative. "We're all looking forward to selling it." Seemingly on the path toward commercial success, Hillerman again brought up the idea to his editor of doing a mainstream novel. Again, Ashmead talked him out of it. "It would really be best for everyone if we can follow *Skinwalkers*, leap to new heights with another Indian novel," Ashmead said.[20]

Having turned over *Skinwalkers* to Ashmead, Hillerman agreed to use his free time to participate in a venture called the "Tony Hillerman Mystery Weekend." A company called Festival Ventures wanted to tap the growing success of mystery weekends, in which fans of the genre gathered to solve an original whodunit. The firm paid Hillerman to devise a murder mystery for a May weekend at the new and luxurious Eldorado Hotel in Santa Fe. Under the plan as many as 150 participants would watch a film about the victim and the suspects on the first night. Then, the next day they would prowl the streets of the historic city in search of clues while Hillerman would be on hand to provide additional hints. On Sunday, the participants, in teams of ten, would present their solution, after which Hillerman would reveal the actual murderer. "The murder," Hillerman promised, "will involve the Santa Fe industry—museums, art collectors, and artifacts. Probably some Native American stuff too."[21]

The weekend was costly, ranging from $195 to $395, depending on the accommodations. Reservations trickled in, but by May it was clear the number of confirmed participants was too few to proceed. Hillerman's star power was not yet sufficient. The organizer told his creditors there wasn't enough money to provide refunds and filed for bankruptcy. "If you know anybody who needs a good script, I've got one," Hillerman told a reporter.[22]

Hillerman also used the time to put out a new edition of *The Boy Who Made Dragonfly*. He had been dissatisfied with the illustrations in the first edition of the Zuni story, published by Harper & Row in 1972 when he was working on *Dance Hall of the Dead*. In his view, the features of the Zunis drawn by artist Lazlo Kubinyi were more Central European than Puebloan. "I felt that was a cultural slight," Hillerman said. He recovered the rights from Harper & Row, and the University of New Mexico Press agreed to publish a new edition. He turned to his daughter Janet, a talented artist who had chosen to stay home with her children rather than pursue a professional career.[23]

"I never liked to say no to Dad," Janet recalled. She was also well suited to the project. As a teenager, Janet had spent stretches of summers at Zuni Pueblo with a childhood friend who had moved to there when her father went to work for the Bureau of Indian Affairs. Janet executed fifteen pencil illustrations. "I had no money and had very little supplies," she said, explaining her choice of medium. Her precise, delicate, and animated illustrations were notched into the text, and a dragonfly drawing was placed at the beginning of each chapter. Hillerman directed that 60 percent of the royalties from the book go to Janet, a much-appreciated gesture that helped her and her husband meet expenses such as their children's Catholic school tuition. In a nod to changing sensibilities, the new edition no longer credited Hillerman alone as the author, reading instead "A Zuni Myth Retold by Tony Hillerman."[24]

Skinwalkers was officially released on January 1, 1987, though the publisher had permitted stores to start selling the book in November to capture Christmas sales. *Kirkus* was impressed. "Haunting backgrounds, quietly disturbing incidents, tautly orchestrated tensions: another indelible Navajo-world imprint from the author of *The Ghostway* and *People of Darkness*," it said. Reviewers from Arizona to Maine predicted it would be a best seller.[25]

The widely popular detective writer Martin Cruz Smith penned a long review for the *San Francisco Examiner*, praising the new book: "We have no one else like Hillerman," wrote Smith, whose mother was a New Mexican of Pueblo descent. "He has yet to achieve a 'breakthrough' book, but every time he writes he produces one of the ten best mysteries of the year." Readers in the Bay Area wouldn't have known, but six months earlier Hillerman had written an equally long and positive review of Martin Cruz Smith's *Stallion Gate*, accompanied by an interview with the author, for the *Albuquerque Journal*; and an equally laudatory one for the *Los Angeles Times*. Smith's choice to review Hillerman's *Skinwalkers* was a practice frowned on by most book review editors. "It was our rule as early as that—no mutual backscratching or revenge-taking allowed," said Dennis Drabelle, longtime mystery editor for the *Washington Post*. "Smith should have recused himself."[26]

Skinwalkers featured an entirely different style of cover. The seven previous covers were a hodgepodge of inconsistent designs, some lacking in sophistication. In light of Hillerman's growing success, Harper & Row turned to twenty-nine-year-old Peter Thorpe, a highly sought-after cover designer. The publisher sent him a copy of the manuscript. "I remember being just blown away by the atmosphere of the Southwest and then also the descriptions of the Navajos," Thorpe said. After completing his reading, Thorpe visited the Picture Collection of the New York Public Library on Fifth Avenue. He asked for materials related to Navajos and sandpaintings. "When I got to the sandpainting file, I said, 'I got to use this somehow. This is so wonderful, these designs.'"[27]

Sandpainting plays an important role in Navajo curing ceremonies. Created by pouring colored sand, the resulting imagery represents different traditional stories selected to be told together with certain chants. Hillerman had included sandpaintings in five of his novels, including the most recent one. In it, Hillerman described Chee's ability to remember as "the recall of a People without a written memory, who kept their culture alive in their minds, who train their children to memorize details of sand paintings and curing ceremonies."[28]

Harper & Row added another print run for *Skinwalkers* and sent Hillerman on a book tour to twelve cities. Los Angeles was his first stop, and the poet and journalist Lewis MacAdams was among those granted an interview. "Tony Hillerman sprawls his gangly frame across a chair, stares out at the winter-blue L.A. sky and allows that he is vaguely uncomfortable in this $185 hotel room," reported MacAdams. "But with an itinerary five pages thick and a month of promo visits with every book editor, feature writer, and radio gab-show host between San Diego and Montpelier, Vermont, looming ahead, Hillerman better get used to it."[29]

The pairing of Leaphorn and Chee within the same cover was paying off. *Skinwalkers* sold more than 140,000 copies by the end of the year. Hillerman's previous book, *The Dark Wind*, soon to be released in paperback, sold 120,000 copies. In San Francisco, Hillerman told a reporter that he was a bit awed by his reception in the Bay Area. "I'm absolutely overcome," he said. "I expect to get a crowd around a reservation in Arizona or New Mexico but, in Berkeley, damned if they don't have a reading room that seats 100 and they're packed in the aisles." By the end of January 1987 *Skinwalkers* was number four on the list of best-selling titles at Waldenbooks.[30]

Skinwalkers caught actor-director Robert Redford's attention. He was spending much of the spring of 1987 in the sleepy village of Truchas in northern New Mexico directing *The Milagro Beanfield War*, based on a novel written by Hillerman's friend John Nichols. The project was generating press as the first major motion picture told from a Hispanic point of view. In his downtime, Redford had picked up several Hillerman novels. "What they did," said Redford, "was actuate my interest in the Navajo culture."[31]

Redford's fascination with Navajos predated his reading of Hillerman mysteries. In the early 1940s, when Redford was five or six years old, his mother took him on her annual drive from Los Angeles to visit her family in Austin, Texas. "It was during the war years and there were no babysitters or anything like that," recalled Redford, "so my mom would take me along." When they reached Gallup, on the western edge of New Mexico, young Redford spotted Navajo women wearing pleated velvet skirts and wrapped in colorful blankets. "I thought," said Redford, "'Well, what is that? That's interesting.'" He asked his mother to stop the car. He got out, walked over to a group of women who were standing bundled up, and touched their clothes. "That's all I did," said Redford. "They smiled at me and that was that. Right then I became interested. What is it with this culture? What's the mystery of this culture? I kept that with me for quite a while." Now, some forty-five years later, Redford was reading his first Hillerman books. "Ah," he thought, "this looks like a place you could go to unlock at least some of the mystery of that culture, so I got really connected to him at that point." Redford wondered if he could bring Hillerman's books to the screen as he had just done with Nichols's *The Milagro Beanfield War.*

Despite Redford's courtship, Hillerman remained a skeptic. Since the publication of *The Blessing Way*, producers had made various attempts to turn Hillerman books into movies and television shows. In fact, the cover of the 1972 Dell paperback edition of *The Blessing Way* had been emblazoned with "Soon To Be a Major Movie!" But each project had failed and Hillerman's distrust of Hollywood had grown when he found himself having to pay more than $20,000 to buy back the rights to Joe Leaphorn, which his agent had sold off. But to Hillerman, Robert Redford seemed different than previous moviemakers. "I've been dealing with the scumbags out in Hollywood for twenty years," Hillerman said. "Redford is the exception that proves the rule." Hillerman was convinced that Redford wanted to try remain true to his vision for his books. "I think what attracted him to those books was the dignity they show in the Native American culture—the dignity, the strength, the values," Hillerman said. "He wants to break away from the old stereotypes of Indians and show a culture as it really is: a good strong people."[32]

The potential earnings from a movie were less important to Hillerman than they had been in 1970. His advances, royalties, and overseas sales had grown sufficiently to provide a living. Rather, Hillerman hoped that in Redford's hands the appreciation of Navajo culture contained in his books would be exponentially larger on-screen "I think it's a shame that so few Americans understand these cultures, and think of them anything except primitive—think of them in very simplistic terms, and they tend to generalize about 'Indians,' as if they are all alike, and of course they're terribly different." But, after meals eaten and documents signed, Hollywood grew silent. Once again, overtures from Tinseltown seemed hollow.[33]

When Hillerman reached New York at the end of his successful tour, his editor Larry Ashmead and his agent Perry Knowlton invited him to lunch. The two men told him he was on the verge of reaching the *New York Times* Best Sellers list, a "breakout book," as the industry called it. "*Skinwalkers* came within a fraction of making the *New York Times* Best Seller list," said Hillerman.[34]

Earlier while traveling through Arizona, Hillerman had spotted a poster intended to stem the robbing of artifacts from archaeological sites. The eye-catching poster was the idea of Donna Schober, who worked for Arizona governor Bruce Babbitt. She found an unspent $1,000 in her office budget as the fiscal year drew to a close. Influenced by the documentary "Thieves of Time" that she had seen on television, she spent the money on a poster displayed in state and national parks.[35]

Hillerman saw the poster. "It had written on the bottom of it, 'A thief of time,' and I thought, 'What a great title for a book.' All I've got to do now is write it."

CHAPTER 23

◆ Breakout ◆

Tony Hillerman stood on the northern bank of the San Juan River on July 13, 1987, a few miles from the tiny community of Bluff in southeastern Utah. On his desk back in Albuquerque, his eighth Navajo novel neared completion. Before him now were five Cherokee inflatable kayaks, a large inflatable raft, and three wooden dories. Hillerman hoped the river might provide what he needed to complete the book.[1]

"Specifically," said Hillerman, "I needed an isolated Anasazi ruin where my characters could do their illicit artifact digging unobserved and where I intended to have one of them murder the other one." The idea for the river trip surfaced when Hillerman consulted his friend Dan Murphy, a naturalist and archaeologist who had extensive experience working for the National Park Service. The forty-seven-year-old native of Buffalo, New York, had been a carpenter, done a tour in the Coast Guard, worked at the United Nations, and learned to fly before getting his driver's license. His sense of adventure had brought him to the Southwest, and he shared Hillerman's passionate reverence for the region.[2]

Murphy told Hillerman that not only did he know the perfect isolated Ancestral Puebloan ruins for the story but he also had a way to get there. His friend Charlie DeLorme, who operated Wild Rivers Expeditions out of Bluff, was looking for two people to entertain sixteen passengers on a seven-day journey down the San Juan River, whose banks were dotted with ruins. "Thus, Murphy and I signed on to float down the San Juan as natural historian and yarn-spinner, respectively," said Hillerman.

At this stage in his writing process, Hillerman was like a movie director looking for a location. He had worked out most of the plot about illegal Indian pothunting. But he was stymied by the lack of a setting. "Since the anthropologist, the pot hunter, and the crime would be pure fiction, it would seem logical that the cliff dwelling could be fictional as well," said Hillerman. "But logic doesn't apply when I am trying to write a book. For some reason I almost need to memorize the landscape I write about."

Under the hot July sun, the flotilla drifted downstream, propelled by the river's muscular current. Small waves in the stretches of modest rapids splashed against the gunwales, delivering refreshing sprays of cold river water to the sunbaked passengers. Soon, Hillerman and the others spotted abandoned cliff dwellings, Moki steps (footholds) carved into the sandstone, and petroglyphs scratched in the dark manganese oxide varnish covering rock outcroppings. The river became a gateway to the past.

Not far downstream, the group beached the crafts on the north side of the river for a visit to River House, once an Ancestral Puebloan settlement. The group hiked past thorny tamarisk and Russian olive trees, invasive species stealing precious water, and up a small incline to a sandstone alcove sheltering a set of dwellings possibly dating as far back as AD 900.

"It was cool on the earthen floor of River House, and quiet—a place to sit and think bookish thoughts," recalled Hillerman. On the whole, the ruins around him were remarkably intact. Some holes indicated pothunters had come through. A vandal as well had left his mark. The raft crew told Hillerman they suspected a Navajo youth with emotional problems was the culprit. "And so," said Hillerman, "while I sat in River House looking at the damage the boy has done, a possible first chapter took shape." In it, a Navajo boy would witness the murder and would later help Joe Leaphorn solve the crime.

The River House, however, would not work for Hillerman's opening chapter. It was too near the San Juan and there remained Murphy's tantalizing promise of a more remote set of ruins. So, the flotilla took to the river again. As it passed sandstone cliffs and steep willow-lined shores, Hillerman watched a lone egret take to the air. "It flew slowly," said Hillerman, "no more than six feet above the water, a graceful shape gleaming white against the shadowed cliffs ahead."

The next stop was on the south side of the river, or "river left" as the boatmen called it, where the ninety-mile-long Chinle Wash reached the San Juan. The arroyo, miles wide at some points, was carved by water running from Canyon de Chelly, miles to the south in Arizona. As Hillerman bedded down for the night and the campfire began to die, the missing components of his novel became clearer to him. "The egret would have its place in it somehow," he said, "and the thought that its solitary presence had provoked seemed to be turning the tale of action I'd intended into a novel of character." Later that night, as the moon rose, illuminating the cliff tops, Hillerman listened to the croaking of frogs, the howling of coyotes, and the flutter of bat wings. "I make notes of all of it, using reality to spare my imagination," he said.

In the morning, Murphy led Hillerman on a three-mile hike up the wash. Unlike the other shore, which was controlled by the Bureau of Land Management, this land belonged to the Navajo Nation. As the arroyo narrowed, they passed Ancestral Puebloan pictographs that caught Hillerman's attention. In particular, he examined an etching of Kokopelli, a flute-playing figure thought to be a fertility deity, scratched into the manganese oxide patina on rocks throughout the Southwest. Hillerman saw his first Kokopelli figure in the late 1960s on a visit to Canyon de Chelly. "Kokopelli is everywhere," he said, "with his humpback and little round head, in various shapes, forms, and positions—but always playing what looks like a clarinet."[3]

Thinking about the petroglyph, Hillerman began to wonder how he might work it into the still-elusive first chapter. "Specifically," he said, "I was considering how eerie it would seem if my foredoomed anthropologist, aware of the presence of these figures, hears the piping of music in the canyon's darkness." Murphy pressed Hillerman farther up the canyon to a small Ancestral Puebloan ruin on a western cliff, where they examined a large pictograph of a figure holding what appeared to be a red shield. Modern travelers had nicknamed the pictograph "Baseball Man" because it looked like the figure was holding a chest protector of the type worn by a home plate umpire. Yet another detail into Hillerman's notes.

The men crossed back over the dry creek bed and up an incline to a shelf on the sandstone mesa. They finally reached their destination, a cavernous arch with ruins on its various ledges. "They were far better than anything I could have imagined." A seep dribbled water that fed moss and ivy and, when it flowed more vigorously, filled a shallow pool at the entrance to the alcove. "The pool had produced its own swarm of leopard frogs, and watching them provoked thoughts." Now Hillerman possessed all the elements he needed. His anthropologist, illegally digging, hiding in the darkness would hear frogs and flute music.[4]

The snowy egret that had lost its mate would become a harbinger of loss. "Gradually," said Hillerman, "as I sat in that cool shade among the frogs, my Navajo Tribal Policeman became a widower." Readers first learned about Joe Leaphorn's wife, Emma, in *The Blessing Way* when Bergen McKee briefly recalled spending evenings in their house. She did not reappear until *Skinwalkers*, the seventh book in Hillerman's series. But despite her prolonged absence, Hillerman's effective use of flashbacks made Emma a key to understanding Leaphorn. "His mother had buried his umbilical cord at the roots of a piñon beside their hogan—the traditional Navajo ritual for binding a child to his family and his people," Hillerman wrote in *Skinwalkers*. "But for Leaphorn, Emma was the tie. A simple physical law. Emma could not be happy away from the Sacred Mountains. He could not be happy away from Emma."[5]

Now in *A Thief of Time*, Hillerman brings her life to an end. It is revealed that her close escape from death due to a brain tumor turns out to have been short-lived. A post-surgery blood clot kills her. In elegiac prose, Hillerman has Leaphorn remember their life together from their meeting on the campus of Arizona State University to her traditional Navajo burial. When Leaphorn's investigation of pot thievery takes him to New York City, he remembers an earlier visit with Emma when they had come across Picasso's sculpture of a goat outside the Museum of Modern Art. "Perfect for us Diné," she'd said. "It's starved, gaunt, bony, ugly. But look! It's tough. It endures." And she had hugged his arm in the delight of her discovery, her face full of the joy, and the beauty, that Leaphorn had found nowhere else."[6]

Losing Emma humanizes Leaphorn and makes him more accepting of the traditional Navajo Way that Emma personified. As the book closes, the rationalist older policeman turns to his younger officer:

> "I hear you're a medicine man. I heard you are a singer of the Blessing Way. Is that right?"
> Chee looked slightly stubborn. "Yes sir," he said.
> "I would like to ask you to sing one for me," Leaphorn said.[7]

Returning to Albuquerque, Hillerman tossed out ten chapters and began rebuilding his novel along the lines of the decisions he had made on the river trip. The pause along the northern shore of the San Juan also solidified Hillerman's intention to base a key character on a prominent Mormon of the region. A few weeks earlier, Doris Valle, who operated Valle's Trading Post in Mexican Hat, had told Hillerman about Calvin "Cal" Black, one of San Juan County's most prominent figures who had acquired a fortune from uranium mining and land development. (He was reportedly the inspiration for Bishop Love in the 1975 Edward Abbey novel *The Monkey Wrench Gang*.) Federal agents had raided Black's home the year before and carted off boxes of artifacts that they claimed to be looted Ancestral Puebloan pottery.

Near River House a road cut through a rocky ridge, built using only hand tools by wandering Mormons who settled in this part of Utah in the 1880s. The remarkable feat impressed Hillerman. "For me it was an ordeal to huff and puff up the traces of that old exploit burdened with nothing heavier than a canteen." The hike inspired Hillerman to include a Mormon in the book. "For my purpose," Hillerman said, "that was perfect material for the sort of red herring subplot I'm always needing." Hillerman had already spent more than a year on the book and was now running behind schedule. At least the river trip had provided him his usually elusive first chapter.

In early September Hillerman joined more than a hundred thousand people heading to Window Rock for the annual Navajo Nation Fair. For forty years the nation's capital had hosted an annual multiday gathering with rodeos, horse racing, powwows, food stands selling fry bread and mutton stew, agricultural exhibits, rock and country-western concerts, and contests such as the one for Miss Navajo Nation. The competition for this honor reflected the fair's efforts at preserving Navajo culture. The contestants had to be fluent in Navajo, participate in butchering a sheep, and display characteristics of First Woman, White Shell Woman, and Changing Woman.

The Navajo Nation Tribal Council, the legislative branch of the nation's government, selected this moment of cultural celebration to take the unprecedented action of honoring a *bilagáana*. Hillerman was escorted down to the middle of the rodeo grounds, where he was presented with a wooden plaque designating him as a "Special Friend to the Diné" for "authentically portraying the strength and dignity of traditional Navajo culture." Following the presentation, Hillerman was asked to ride a horse in the parade. Thinking the horse might be too spirited for him, the feted author asked to travel in the convertible with Miss Navajo. The moment produced Hillerman's Navajo nickname, "Afraid of his horse."[8]

Coming two decades after he began writing *The Blessing Way*, Hillerman felt more honored by the Navajos' celebration of his work than by the publishing prizes he had earned. "That means more to me than just about anything else," he later explained. "I was very touched because it expresses what I've been trying to do in my books all these years." In short, it conveyed what Hillerman craved for his writing—authenticity.[9]

At long last, in October 1987 Hillerman sent Ashmead the manuscript. "*A Thief of Time* is splendid in every way," Ashmead told Hillerman. "What a good, good book, Tony. Worth the wait and many thanks from everyone here at Harper & Row." From the editor assigned to write the catalog copy to the publisher of the trade book division, William M. Shinker, the staff was certain Hillerman had delivered a winner. Shinker talked by phone with Ashmead from the Frankfurt Book Fair. "I could hear in his voice that this book was something special," Ashmead told Hillerman. "I think it's a real breakthrough book for you."[10]

Hillerman had heard the same prediction for *Skinwalkers* from Shinker the year before. But since then, the British media lord Rupert Murdoch had acquired Harper & Row for $300 million. His dramatic entry into American book publishing breathed new life into Harper & Row, which in comparison to other publishers had lacked financial resources. "Rupert has deep pockets, and he's shown a willingness to back up his convictions with cash," said Brooks Thomas, the chairman and chief executive of Harper & Row. The new cash would support an ambitious plan for Hillerman's new book. The company planned a fifty-thousand-copy initial press run and set aside $75,000 for marketing. Ashmead also told Perry Knowlton the company was prepared to increase its advances to Hillerman for three more Navajo mysteries. "To have a secure and predictable $130,000 per book for the next three of these might be comfortable for you," Knowlton said to Hillerman. Already, he could count on more than $150,000 in income due him in 1988. The struggle to earn a living by writing was over for the sixty-two-year-old.[11]

As the editorial work drew to a close, Tony and Marie traveled to Grenoble, France, in October to receive the prestigious Grand Prix de Littérature Policière for the best mystery novel written by a non-French author. Presented at the Festival International du Roman et du Film Noirs, the prize honored *Dance Hall of the Dead*, the French edition of which had been published the previous year by Rivages.

Dance Hall of the Dead had been translated by thirty-eight-year-old Pierre Bondil and his wife, Danièle Bondil. Pierre had taught English in French schools before becoming a translator for major French publishing houses in 1981. By the time Hillerman was awarded the prize, *Là où dansent les morts* had sold more than eighty thousand copies, a figure Hillerman had only recently achieved in the larger American book market. Teaming with the Bondils, and later with Pierre alone after he and Danièle divorced, helped establish Hillerman's success in France, unmatched in the nearly twenty countries where translations of his novels would eventually be released.

Harper & Row called again on Peter Thorpe to create the cover for *A Thief of Time*. As he had done with *Skinwalkers*, Thorpe combined a sandpainting-inspired style with bold type and a single object. In place of the skull on the cover of *Skinwalkers*, Thorpe placed a pot featuring Kokopelli. "We are all quite pleased with the concept," reported Joseph Montebello, Harper & Row's art director. "The type is quite strong and bears a resemblance to *Skinwalkers* which our marketing people think is a good thing."[12]

The process of working with Thorpe, however, triggered last-minute confusion. The materials Harper & Row sent to Thorpe referred to the book as "The Thief of Time" rather than *A Thief of Time*. Thorpe decided the latter was the correct title and sent in a mockup of the cover that Montebello approved. "A week later, I get this angry call from Montebello, saying, 'You put the wrong title!'"[13]

"What? What are you talking about?" said Thorpe.

"It's supposed to be *The Thief of Time*."

"But, Joe, the manuscript says *A Thief of Time*."

"All right. We're going to contact Tony."

Montebello reached Hillerman in France, where he and Marie were traveling. The author confirmed he preferred *A Thief of Time*. Montebello got back to Thorpe and told him to stick with the title he put on the mockup. "I hang up the phone," said Thorpe. "I didn't even realize I was making this major editorial decision. I just went with the title that looked better to me for the cover."[14]

In January 1988 Hillerman put aside work on the new novel on his computer—in which Leaphorn and Chee find themselves in the nation's capital—and joined other mystery writers in Florida for the Key West Writers Seminar. For the first time the topic was unrelated to Key West's fabled literary heritage. "Whodunit? The Art and Tradition of Mystery Literature" attracted many of the nation's top mystery and crime-fiction writers, including Carl Hiaasen, Elmore Leonard, Donald Westlake, Mary Higgins Clark, and Robin Craig Clark. Otto Penzler, a leading mystery editor, told the large audience that gathered in the Tennessee Williams Fine Arts Center on Stock Island that mysteries were "holding the line on storytelling as mainstream fiction becomes ever more self-absorbed and inscrutable."[15]

Having assumed the presidency of Mystery Writers of America from Mary Higgins Clark, Hillerman had become the genre's de facto spokesperson and took the same message to reporters. "They keep saying the novel is dead—and in a way it is if we are dealing with the fad of minimalist fiction," he told the *Fort Lauderdale News.* "The mystery is such a free form now, you can do anything. Look at Scott Turow's *Presumed Innocent.* It is an important novel by any estimation, and it's a mystery." Between sessions, Hillerman took time to go outside and take in the Florida weather. He leaned up against a wall with his hands in his pockets and face upturned. Marilyn Stasio, who was starting to review mysteries for the *New York Times,* stepped out of her hotel on Duval Street and spotted Hillerman. "That looked good to me, so I joined him," she said. "Faces warmed, we drifted into conversation about Ernest Hemingway, whose novels, I pertly noted, were anathema to me because of their sexism."[16]

Hillerman resisted arguing. Instead he suggested Stasio walk over to the Hemingway Home and purchase a copy of *To Have and Have Not.* If she wanted to talk further about the author's attitude toward women, they could resume the conversation after she had read the book. Stasio complied, settled into the Hemingway Home garden with its famous six-toed cats, and had, in her word, an epiphany. "The next time I saw Tony, I tried to tell him what a jerk I had been and to thank him," she said. "He had his reward, he said, in bringing another reader to one of his favorite authors."

As the July 1, 1988, release of *A Thief of Time* neared, the various elements of the arcane art of bookselling were ready to work in his favor. The paperback edition of *Skinwalkers* had sold more than one hundred thousand copies, building anticipation in the trade for Hillerman's newest. *Publishers Weekly* was swept away with enthusiasm about the book. "Once more, Hillerman's artistry ensures that his latest cannot be easily classified as murder mystery or thriller or anything except a fine novel," read its review. Demand from stores proved

Harper & Row's fifty-thousand-copy press run inadequate and another eighty thousand books were ordered up. A $150,000 marketing plan was devised, with a multi-city whirlwind of bookstore events that for the first time included cities east of the Mississippi River. NBC's *Today* show agreed to book the author and *People* magazine planned a summertime two-page interview with Hillerman. Harper & Row's publicity machine had done its job. The author and his wife joined company executives in Anaheim, California, for the annual trade book show, where the busy schedule included a party on the *Queen Mary*, lunches in high-end restaurants, and an autographing session for booksellers. "If this one doesn't sell a lot," Hillerman said a few weeks prior to publication, "It will be my fault and not theirs." But readers responded.[17]

On his stop in Tucson, Arizona, Hillerman's guide was twenty-nine-year-old Gabe Barillas, who had been hired the previous year as a Harper & Row sales representative for New Mexico, Arizona, and Southern California. The temperature reached 103 degrees as the two men drove to the murder mystery store with the unusual name Footprints of a Gigantic Hound, a tribute to Sir Arthur Conan Doyle's *The Hound of the Baskervilles*, where Hillerman was scheduled to talk and sign books from noon until 2:00 P.M.[18]

As Hillerman was meeting readers and fans, the store phone rang. It was Hillerman's editor, Larry Ashmead, who asked to speak to Barillas. When he got the sales representative on the line, Ashmead announced that he had learned Hillerman's book would debut on the *New York Times* Best Sellers list at number fifteen the following week.

"I'm really excited and I got to tell him," Ashmead said.

"I'll tell him," Barillas replied.

"No, no, I want to tell him."

So Barillas brought Hillerman to the store's telephone and put him on the phone with Ashmead. When the call was over, said Barillas, Hillerman did not seem all that impressed. When they got back into the rented automobile to eat a baloney sandwich and drive to The Haunted Bookshop for a late-afternoon book event, Hillerman asked Barillas to explain why the *New York Times* Best Sellers list was so significant. Hillerman, whose previous books had been on such lists in other cities, was unaware of the sales power of the *New York Times*. Barillas, who had once worked in Vroman's Bookstore in Los Angeles, told Hillerman that stores used the list to make buying decisions. Not only would they want to be sure to have ample stock of *New York Times* best sellers, but they would also display these books up front, spurring more sales.

A *Thief of Time* appeared at number fifteen on the fiction list on July 10, along with works by mystery and thriller writers such as Robert Ludlum, Robert B. Parker, Clive Cussler, and Elmore Leonard. Hillerman continued on his tour, conducting media interviews and book signings in San Diego, Los Angeles, Phoenix, San Francisco, Seattle, Denver, Fort Collins, Colorado Springs, Chicago, Washington, DC, Boston, and New York City. By the end of his tour, the book had moved up to eighth on the list.

Manhattan was Hillerman's last stop before returning home for a rest. He sat down for an interview with Don Swaim at WCBS. Swaim produced a nationally syndicated series called *Book Beat*. As the host got started, the two men chatted about the book tour. It had been successful, but Hillerman admitted he was glad to be heading home and cease, at least for a while, living out of a suitcase. The bag's contents would keep Marie busy with laundry as Hillerman was a notoriously messy eater. Hillerman told Swaim that at the hotel the night before there was not enough time to get his suit cleaned, but he managed to get it pressed. "So, they're pressing in the gravy stains," he said, "but at least it won't have wrinkles in it."[19]

On August 16, 1988, Tony and Marie celebrated forty years of marriage. Ashmead made an anniversary gift of a specially boxed edition of *A Thief of Time*. The book now had more than a hundred thousand copies, in print earning him at least $300,000 in its first few months out. Also in the mail was a postcard from Sue Grafton, congratulating him on making the *New York Times* Best Sellers list. She had just completed *F is for Fugitive* in her alphabet series of mysteries, which would become her first *New York Times* best seller. "Teeeerific. You're one of those writers whose success we can all applaud," she wrote. "You're doin' good, kid."[20]

CHAPTER 24

◈ Leaphorn and Chee Go to Hollywood ◈

In the spring of 1989, Tony Hillerman learned that his work might yet make it to the big screen. Three years after Robert Redford first picked up a Hillerman book, some encouraging news was coming from Wildwood Enterprises, the actor's film making company. The first draft of a screenplay based on Hillerman's *Dark Wind* had been completed, and the company was selecting a director.[1]

Generating interest in Hillerman's work among film studios had proven more difficult than Redford had expected. "The thing never went anywhere because at that time Hollywood, the mainstream industry, was simply not interested in that culture," said Redford. "We have always looked at that culture in almost purely symbolic ways to satisfy Hollywood movies—where the Indians are going to be the bad guys against the cowboys, the good guys."[2]

Lacking mainstream support, Redford obtained funding from Carolco Pictures, Inc., an independent motion picture production company that had made a fortune from two Rambo films based on books by David Morrell. He also signed movie producers Midge Sanford and Sarah Pillsbury. The two women had succeeded in the virtually all-male industry by holding power lunches in yogurt shops and saving on messenger fees by delivering scripts themselves.[3]

To scout for a suitable location, Redford, Sanford, Pillsbury, and film executive Bonni Lee came to New Mexico in April 1989. The group, along with Hillerman, piled into a rented station wagon with Redford at the wheel. Pillsbury sat with a pile of maps, trying to track where they went while the actor insisted on keeping the windows down and driving at a terrifying speed, recalled Lee. She imagined she would be the unknown woman in a headline describing their end: REDFORD,

Hillerman, Sanford, Pillsbury, and Unnamed Woman in Car When It Collided and Burst into Flames. For his part, Hillerman later told Tony Jr. he had been impressed with Redford's driving because he never used the brake. "It was kind of fun, once you get over your nervousness," Hillerman said.[4]

During the long drive to the Navajo Nation and around the Hopi villages, the group discussed how they might make the first of several anticipated movies. "Getting in a car's a good place to get acquainted," Hillerman said. But he remained mostly quiet, speaking in a measured, quiet fashion punctuated occasionally by his dry humor, according to Lee. "The problem as Redford chewed it over for us," said Hillerman, "was capturing the attitudes, the innate courtesy, the dead-pan understated humor which characterizes the Navajo culture." Using Navajos and the desert landscape would help. "We want to make it all seem to be seen through the eyes of a Navajo, as in your books," Redford told Hillerman. "And all this while we're telling a complicated story about murder, greed, and revenge. It's not going to be easy." During the ride they debated which book to start with. The decision came down to either *A Thief of Time* or *The Dark Wind*. When the latter was picked Hillerman was pleased because the book featured both Navajos and Hopis. "It seemed to me," said the author. "that since so many people who go to the movies are the kind of people who think all Indians are alike, it would be good to put two quite different tribes in."[5]

At the end of the long day, they made one last stop to see the ruins of the Kuaua Pueblo just north of Albuquerque, which Hillerman urged because they could descend into a restored kiva, a subterranean ceremonial chamber. The group was exhausted, especially Redford who had done all the driving. As Lee watched the actor drinking coffee from a paper cup, a female British tourist came up and asked if he might be Robert Redford.

"Yes, I am," he replied.

"Oh, what are you doing way out here among the ruins?"

"Ma'am," he said. "I am a ruin." And with that he sipped his coffee and walked away quietly.

Time that had been Hillerman's to spend as he wished now became crowded with visits from movie stars, public appearances, and demands for blurbs. He discovered his success created new impediments to writing. "Making the *New York Times* Best Sellers list changes your life whether you like it or not," Hillerman told his old friend Jim Belshaw. "Look at this," he said, grabbing his appointment book. On its pages were appointments with journalists for *USA Today*, *Newsweek*, and other publications. "I'm not really complaining," Hillerman said, "but it makes getting any writing done a lot harder."[6]

He gave up on answering much of his fan mail, which now came in at a rate of at least a dozen letters a day, but continually felt guilty about neglecting it. In addition, Hillerman's mailbox on a typical day that year contained a request from the French education minister for a video that could be used in English classes, an invitation from the United States Information Agency to join a three-week trip to India, Polaroid photographs of Navajo children in the Lukachukai Boarding School, and a typed letter from an FBI agent who wanted Hillerman to call his place of work a bureau not an agency.[7]

The Hillermans' home telephone number, connected to an old-style rotary-dial telephone, had long remained listed. But one day, Tony and Marie answered twenty-three calls from strangers before the morning was out. A man from New Jersey said he learned Tony drove an Isuzu Trooper II and wanted a recommendation for a mechanic for his upcoming trip to New Mexico. When he hung up, Tony called Mountain Bell and obtained an unlisted telephone number.[8]

As Hillerman would say on several occasions, being a writer made it hard to write. Yet in between book events and endless interviews, he had managed to deliver another manuscript to Ashmead in January 1989, fifteen months after turning in *A Thief of Time*. In a proud nod to modernity, the technologically challenged author delivered *Talking God* on two floppy disks in ASCII format that he converted from his Word Perfect files on a Leading Edge computer. "I find computers strange and mysterious," he said. "I write on a word processor, but I do so uneasily." Hillerman had also begun to use e-mail as well. His address was Leaphorn@abq.com.[9]

Harper & Row rushed to publish the new novel so as to ride on the coattails of *A Thief of Time*. But unlike his previous eight Navajo mysteries, Hillerman decided to place most of the action away from the Navajo Nation. Twice before his investigators had traveled far, but only briefly. In *The Dark Wind* Chee went to Los Angeles and in *A Thief of Time* Leaphorn had gone to New York City. But for this book, Hillerman made Washington, DC, the center of the action.

Both Chee and Leaphorn use their vacation time to come separately to the nation's capital but for different reasons and without knowing the other was also there. Chee makes the journey when Janet Pete, a Navajo lawyer and potential love interest, seeks his help on a case involving her client Henry Highhawk. Leaphorn arrives after a corpse turns up along the railroad tracks near Gallup,

New Mexico. The dead man had a piece of paper mentioning a Yeibichai, a nine-day Navajo curing ceremony. Leaphorn uncovers some clues that bring him to Washington where a Talking God mask, like those used in the Yeibechai, will soon be on exhibit at the Smithsonian. The threads of the two investigations unite in a climactic but contrived fashion that includes an assassination attempt involving a foreign power.[10]

Hillerman had no first chapter problem this time. In fact, the opening of *Talking God* ranks as one of, if not the, best beginning of all his books. Catherine Morris Perry, a blue-blooded lawyer and spokesperson for the Smithsonian Institution, has been defending the museum's collection of Native American remains, which under the Native American Graves Protection and Repatriation Act are supposed to be returned to Native peoples. According to the *Washington Post*, Perry believes "the reburial of the museum's entire collection of more than 18,000 Native American skeletons was 'simply not possible in light of the museum's purpose.'" Arriving in her office she finds a mysterious box on her desk containing the article from the newspaper, a letter, and some objects in wrapping paper. The letter begins:

Dear Mrs. Perry,

You won't bury the bones of our ancestors because you say the public has the right to expect authenticity in the museum when it comes to look at skeletons. Therefore, I am sending you a couple of authentic skeletons of ancestors. I went to the cemetery in the woods behind the Episcopal Church of Saint Luke. I used authentic anthropological methods to locate the burials of authentic white Anglo types—

Digging deeper into the box, to her horror she unwraps bones and a skull belonging to her grandparents. "I received 'good-for-you' applause from about twenty tribesmen for that one," Hillerman said.[11]

After rejecting such titles as *Yeibaichai's Mask*, *Night Chant*, and *The Masked Gods*, the author and editor settled on *Talking God* because a Yeibichai becomes a central element of the plot. But Hillerman had never witnessed a Yeibichai. A new Navajo acquaintance came to his assistance as he was almost finished with the manuscript. In the fall of 1988, while attending a lecture at the University of New Mexico by a visiting professor, Hillerman had met forty-two-year-old Austin Sam, a Navajo from the Arizona side of the Nation. Later Sam spotted Hillerman doing research in the library and the two chatted. Hillerman complained that he needed to visualize chanting or rituals in order to write about them but was frustrated by not having seen a Yeibichai. It just so happened, Sam told Hillerman, that his sister-in-law was having one, and he offered to take him to it if he wished.

Late on a December day, Hillerman picked Sam up in Window Rock. As Hillerman would explain in his new book, "The Yeibichai can be performed only after the first frost, after snakes have hibernated, only in the Season When Thunder Sleeps." Traveling in Hillerman's Isuzu Trooper, the two men drove north to Ganado, through Chinle, and to Many Farms, where the Yeibechai was in its last day. In the cold darkness, Hillerman took a seat outside the family's hogan. "There were lots of people—they had built a kitchen, and booths to sell things, sawed telephone poles for the uprights," he said. "I'm not sure what the phone company thought about it."[12]

Hillerman sat quietly on a log and took notes as the ceremony unfolded in front of him. At 1:20 in the morning, Hillerman turned to Sam. "We've finished the book," he said, and the two drove back to Window Rock. Later, in his Albuquerque study, Hillerman reconstructed the scene in his manuscript just as he had witnessed it. "The screen of blankets had been dropped over the doorway of the patient's hogan now and all the curing activities were going on in privacy," he wrote. "The bonfires that lined the cleared dance ground burned high. Spectators huddled around them, keeping warm, gossiping, renewing friendships. There was laughter as a piñon log collapsed and the resulting explosion of sparks routed a cluster of teenagers. Mr. Yellow had built a kitchen shelter behind the hogan, using sawed telephone poles as roof posts, two-by-fours and particle board for its walls."[13]

Talking God was released on June 1, 1989, and immediately made it onto the *New York Times* Best Sellers list, where it remained for fifteen weeks, rising at one point to number two. At the beginning of the book tour, while in an elevator in Washington, DC, John Michel, of Harper & Row, had made a bet with Hillerman as to how high up the list the book would go. Neither could remember the exact bet. "But I think you were being modest and shunning anything higher than five," Michel told Hillerman when the book became the second best-selling novel on the list. "I guess it's not a bet you mind losing."[14]

But despite the novel's commercial success, the weakness of Hillerman's decision to set the story in Washington became apparent. Reviewers and readers noticed that, unlike Hillerman's intimate knowledge of the Navajo Nation built over more than two decades, he was obviously unfamiliar with the nation's capital. This led to embarrassing mistakes: His taxi cabs had meters, when it was well known they used a tariff system based on zones; Silver Spring was called Silver Springs; an embassy was in the wrong place; and Chee visited a Walgreens pharmacy when none yet operated in the city, as well as providing a 266 telephone prefix when all of Washington used 202, among other errors. An Illinois reader wrote, "As I was reading, I kept muttering aloud, 'Hillerman you should have stayed in New Mexico.'"[15]

The complaints, however, had no effect on book sales. Within weeks of *Talking God*'s release, Harper & Row went back for a third printing, bringing the total number above two hundred thousand. More printings would follow. "Remember when 25,000 was the first printing?" Ashmead asked Hillerman.[16]

In the midst of Hillerman's second commercial success, staff members from the University of New Mexico Zimmerman Library Special Collections arrived at his house. They had gathered up sixteen boxes of manuscripts, page proofs, correspondence, and lecture notes from Hillerman's teaching career. He had kept everything, including all the drafts of his earliest novel, editorial correspondence, contracts, and correspondence with fans, even caustic complaint letters. It was only the first set of materials to be transferred.[17]

Since retiring from teaching and leaving campus, Hillerman no longer needed to write at night or on weekends. Instead, after breakfast, he headed to the couch and the coffee table, where he continued his writing-life-long habit of playing spider solitaire, a kind of literary foreplay before tapping keys. "It does help me keep my sanity," Hillerman said. "And it's such a boring game, I find myself drifting away from it and turning to the plot."[18]

Hillerman's two *New York Times* best-selling books, *Talking God* and *A Thief of Time*, differed from his previous works and some devoted fans noticed. Among them was Edward J. Sparks, a New York City corporate executive. "To put it bluntly, I think you have lost your way," Sparks wrote to Hillerman. "What made you unique and a thrilling writer was your ability to present the reader with the mystery and grandeur of the west and more significantly, Indian culture."[19]

"Your last two books," he continued, "have reduced this to murder mysteries where cleverness has replaced culture and flavor. This is a shame. There are plenty of writers around who can do this; but few have your talent to go that next step."

Aware or not of this complaint, Hillerman took the path back to his original formula for his next book. He submitted to Shinker a four-page outline for a Leaphorn-Chee book set on the Navajo Nation and full of witches and taboos. The Harper & Row executive was relieved. "I think a novel that is set totally back on the reservation is a good idea as a follow-up of *Talking God*," he told Hillerman.[20]

Hillerman, however, had not given up on writing a non-Navajo novel. In fact, he had already traveled to the Philippines to do research for a novel he had been thinking about since his days as a reporter in Santa Fe. "I kind of feel like I've paid my dues, and if I want to write a Philippines novel, I'll do it," Hillerman told a journalism friend. A tug-of-war of sorts developed between the author and his publisher. Harper & Row was eager to sign him to a three-book contract for more of his best-selling Navajo books. But from Hillerman's point of view, such an agreement would again postpone his chance at writing a mainstream novel and would also make him a slave to deadlines. "I think God damnit I've earned a little independence," Hillerman told two Iowa professors. His writing process required time, and getting it right was important to him. "That motivates me without the *get-on-the ball* call from my editor."[21]

Shinker told Hillerman he was disappointed by his decision to decline the offer. But he gracefully added, "I want you and Marie to be happy and comfortable with your obligations and deadlines." Ashmead and Shinker also knew their much-valued author could easily go to another publisher who might readily agree to let him write a non-Navajo book. The name Hillerman was one any New York house would want on its list. A month later the editor and executive capitulated. "I know you are thinking about writing one or two novels that will not feature Jim Chee and Joe Leaphorn, and we would like to hear more about them whenever you want to talk. Tony, very simply, Harper's wants to publish *everything* you write."[22]

In late January 1990, Hillerman delivered his new Navajo Nation–centered novel. John Michel, who had taken over editing Hillerman's manuscripts, returned it with a laundry list of inconsistencies, mistakes, and confusing sections needing repair. The extensive list was not unusual, as Hillerman did little or no copyediting of his manuscripts. Trained as a newspaper writer on deadline, he retained the tendency of banging out a story and immediately passing it on to the editor. Polishing prose was not among his writing habits. But, once again, the story was in top form. "Tony, you've done it again!" said Shinker just back from vacation in Mexico. "*Coyote Waits* is one of the most complex plots you've ever done, and the love interests for both Joe Leaphorn and Jim Chee are wonderful."[23]

Coyote Waits would be Hillerman's tenth Navajo mystery, his eleventh novel. The murder of a Navajo Tribal Police officer, with an obvious suspect, marks the beginning of a complicated plot. In the end it involves a Vietnamese family whom the CIA resettled in the United States following the war and Leaphorn's new companion, Professor Louisa Bourebonette. Janet Pete, back from Washington, represents the presumed murderer and has a growing fondness for Chee, while the colorful trading post operator John "Shorty" McGinnis makes a return appearance.

Between moments of fast-paced action, Hillerman inserted a tender subplot of teenage love that leads to an important witness. The manner by which Leaphorn learns of this witness was unintentionally suggested by Hillerman's brother. A discussion around a kitchen table had prompted the idea that the two should join forces and produce a book about the landscape that played such an important role in Tony's mysteries. Barney would supply the photographs and Tony the text. For the first time since their days on the staff of *The Covered Wagon*, the University of Oklahoma's student humor magazine, they would work together.[24]

In the years since graduation, Tony had become a successful and nationally known author, but Barney's road had been challenging. After several years in the petroleum business, he chose to set aside his degree in geology and pursue his love of photography professionally. In 1953 Barney opened a studio in Oklahoma City that provided the work he wanted to do but generated little money. He and his wife, Irene, whom he married in 1962, scraped together enough to get their three adopted children through college. But they struggled financially and at one point could not afford to visit the child who attended Notre Dame in Illinois.[25]

With his cameras, Barney traveled about the Navajo Nation and the lands surrounding it. "I sent him lengthy listings of places he needed to photograph to go with my text," said Tony. "He'd send me great sheets of contact prints of totally different landscape—proving that I was still Little Brother and that photographers march to their own drums." When they found the time, the brothers traveled together.[26]

They chose not to photograph people, especially Indians. Tony, in particular, worried about the presence of cameras. He regularly refused to permit photographers to accompany him when he visited his Navajo acquaintances, viewing it as an intrusion on their private life. "The relationship is between me and Austin Sam and Austin Sam's mother," he said.[27]

Like Tony, who studied clouds and let his imagination roam, Barney looked for images in cliffs, rock formations, and canyons. On one occasion, Barney asked Tony if he saw the image of a pipe-smoking zebra in a rock formation. No, said Tony. They backed up until Tony was in the right spot to see the zebra. In the process of chasing images on rock, Barney instructed his brother in the optics of telescopic lenses and how they change what one sees. Tony seized on this information for *Coyote Waits*. Tony had the teenage boy inscribe a message of love in white paint on basalt rocks that the object of his passion could see only from the perspective of her hogan.

Coyote Waits came out in July and immediately made it onto the *New York Times* Best Sellers list, climbing to number three behind books by Scott Turow and Danielle Steele. "The fact that we are already at 235,000 in four printings (which is higher than we've ever gotten before) indicates that we have succeeded in taking your sales to yet another plateau," Shinker told Hillerman three weeks after the book's debut.[28]

The trade press loved the new book, and the *New York Times* reviewer said *Coyote Waits* was emblematic of Hillerman's great achievement. "In this book, the author continues to prove himself one of the nation's most convincing and authentic interpreters of Navajo culture, as well as one of our best and most innovative modern mystery writers," wrote Robert F. Gish. "An extra payoff of *Coyote Waits* is an ever so light-handed but utterly convincing advocacy of Native American culture and an enchanting depiction of the spirit of the Southwest."[29]

The success of *Coyote Waits* fueled sales of Hillerman's other books. The paperback edition of *A Thief of Time* had sold more than one million copies, and HarperCollins was rapidly reissuing paperback editions of all his books. "I can't recall working with a writer who has accomplished reaching a new plateau of sales and a larger readership with each book," Shinker said. With three successive best sellers, Hillerman had become a kind of literary tour guide to a domestic but foreign and exotic world at a moment when the public's interest in Native American art, fashion, and culture was rising. A few years earlier the New York literati had had no time for him. Now Hillerman found himself invited to share the stage of the 92nd Street Y, one of New York City's premier venues, with Tom Wolfe, Elmore Leonard, and Robert B. Parker at a benefit for AIDS research.[30]

"Mystery author Tony Hillerman has finally achieved literary stardom," wrote a Scripps Howard News Service reporter. "His books are bestsellers, he's been profiled in the *New York Times*, and Robert Redford is creating a movie from one of his novels."[31]

"Creating" may have been too positive a word. In the waning summer heat Robert Redford had a disaster on his hands in northern Arizona, where filming of *The Dark Wind* was underway. It began with his choice of a director. Whereas he had picked two producers who had already achieved moviemaking success, Redford named as director Errol Morris, who had never directed a feature film. Rather, the forty-year-old Morris's reputation rested on his documentary *The Thin Blue Line*. He immediately came into conflict with Sanford and Pillsbury. Redford replaced the women with his friend Patrick Markey, whose two credits were a science fiction film and a crime thriller.

The new team did not even have a chance to begin filming before a new set of problems emerged. Some Hopi leaders threatened to block entry to their lands because the script, which Hillerman did not write, depicted the members of their tribe as murderous drug users and included sacrilegious depictions of secret religious ceremonies. Meanwhile, Navajos called for protests because Redford had failed to hire Native Americans for the leading roles, despite promising to do so. "An ill wind continues to govern the direction of Robert Redford's 'The Dark Wind,'" reported syndicated columnist Marilyn Beck.[32]

Hillerman had warned Redford and his producers that the Hopi would not cooperate and had urged that Navajos be hired as actors. But they had not listened. In December the filmmakers returned to Hollywood to make sense of what they had filmed. "The Dark Wind has been howling relentlessly for three months, but it did not defeat us," the producer Patrick Markey wrote to Hillerman. "Now our worlds come back into balance."[33]

Redford sent Hillerman a rough cut of the movie. At the time Louis A. Hieb, who had just published an eighty-eight-page bibliography of Hillerman's work, was visiting with his son.

"As fans, my son and I enjoyed the movie, but Hillerman was troubled," Hieb said. "Although there were a number of visually interesting scenes, the plot was too convoluted for even Hillerman-the-author to follow, and he was concerned about the attribution of authorship."[34]

Redford let Hillerman know that he would be willing to take the author's name off the credits. The film would not be released in the United States. Instead it was only seen in theaters in England, France, Italy, Taiwan, and Switzerland. Hillerman agreed to waive the requirement that he be listed in the film's credits. Robert Redford pondered removing his name as well. But Tim Knowlton, Perry Knowlton's son, who handled a lot of the firm's film deals, urged that doing so could have a worse effect than leaving the credits in place. Journalists and critics might write about it, which would create further negative publicity. "Unsavory, sensational headlines like 'Redford Spurns Redskin Movie' come to mind a bit too easily," Knowlton said. Instead, he urged that Hillerman and Redford make it publicly clear they were disappointed in the movie and that Redford would direct the next one to avoid the problems that came up in *The Dark Wind*.[35]

"You must wonder at times if I'm related to the Scarlet Pimpernel," a contrite Redford later wrote Hillerman. "I was quite upset with the misstep on the first venture with Errol Morris."[36]

In the first visible indication of the money his books were generating, Tony and Marie moved out of the Texas Street house they had owned since moving to Albuquerque in 1963 when Tony began his studies at the University of New Mexico. In early 1991 they settled into a custom-built house in Village of Los Ranchos, a quiet subdivision close by the eastern banks of the Rio Grande, six miles north of Old Town. Marie bought new furnishings for the three-bedroom house, which featured high ceilings, built-in bookcases, and a pair of fireplaces. Tony, however, retained his favorite pigeonhole desk, which he got from an old hotel office.

"Albuquerque is too big for a bona fide country boy," Tony said in explaining their move from a city neighborhood to the more rural setting. Other places he considered did not offer, in his words, "the odd mixture of social, geographic, ecological, and historical delights I enjoy here." Among the delights for Hillerman was the patchwork of drains, canals, irrigation ditches, and levees. Less than two hundred yards from the front door lay the Griego y Gallegos acequia. "When [one needs] to flee from one's desk and its clutter of unanswered mail and undone work," Hillerman said, "that ditch offers a smooth path, lots of shade, endless rows of backyards to look down into if the yard dogs aren't barking at you."[37]

Beyond building a new house, the Hillermans made few alterations in their lifestyle. "I'm not going to change just because all of a sudden I got a lot of money,"

Hillerman said. "We still buy what we call 'used-bread,'" said Hillerman. "We always go by the day-old-bread store." But Hillerman admitted to a reporter that he had given thought to trading in his old car with its cracked windshield. He had been to a showroom to look at a Jaguar but the salesman, unaware of the identity of his rumpled visitor, ignored him. Buying a British luxury car was a big step for the frugal author. "All my life I've always admired the Jaguar, but I cannot bring myself to buy one, he told a Catholic magazine after moving into their new home. "It symbolizes conspicuous consumption, unfortunately." In the end he gave in, buying first a used Jaguar with a hundred thousand miles on it, then eventually a new one. "Marie has taken to referring to us as the Clampetts," said Tony. (The Clampett family was featured in the 1960s television series *The Beverly Hillbillies*.)[38]

After settling into their new house, Tony and Marie left in May for New York City, where he received the Mystery Writers of America Grand Master of Crime Fiction Award. "I think the reason I'm getting this award is that I'm sixty-five, I'm forty pounds overweight, and I have bags under my eyes," he told reporters. "I think they looked at me and said, 'We better get this guy now he's not taking good care of himself.'" From New York, Tony and Marie continued on to France for a short book tour and for him to receive the $1,625 Prix de l'Astrolabe at a literary festival in St. Malo for the French editions of his novels translated by Pierre Bondil. By this time, Hillerman mysteries were also published in translation in Israel, Germany, Italy, Brazil, Japan, Korea, and a half dozen other countries. "You're totally at the translator's mercy," he said. In one of the Japanese editions, a stop made by Leaphorn at the Ganado Conoco gas station was mistranslated as a police station. "He stopped to call a police station. It created a certain amount of confusion," Hillerman said.[39]

Back in Albuquerque, Hillerman resumed work on his next book. It would be called *The Clown* or *Koshare*, Hillerman told Eamon Dolan, who had taken over an increasing number of editorial duties from Larry Ashmead. The story would revolve around one of the six Tewa-speaking pueblos and it would involve Lincoln canes, prized possessions in almost all of the nineteen pueblos of New Mexico. In 1863, they were presented with ebony canes whose silver top was engraved "A. Lincoln" and the pueblo's name. The tribes viewed the gift from a head of state as a recognition of their sovereignty. "I do not have a good version of either plot or necessary subplots involving Chee-Leaphorn, Chee–Janet Pete, and Leaphorn-Professor worked out yet," Hillerman warned.[40]

After designer Peter Thorpe spoke to Hillerman, he worked up a prototype of the cover with the title "Mudhead Kiva." The title combined two Puebloan terms.

"Mudhead" is used in several pueblos to describe the clown who serves as disciplinarian, joker, and village crier in ceremonies, while "kiva" is an underground ceremonial and religious structure common to all the pueblos.

Ashmead sent Hillerman the Peter Thorpe design, featuring a Koshare—a Puebloan clown—with a skeleton head. Ashmead said the book would be listed in the next catalog. "I know—we know—this may be premature," Ashmead wrote. "We haven't done this to put any sort of pressure on you so don't feel any."[41]

Meanwhile, Hillerman had three nonfiction books coming out in rapid succession. The University of New Mexico Press published a slim paperback called *Talking Mysteries* that Ernie Bulow assembled with Hillerman. Bulow, who had worked around Navajos most of his life, had befriended Hillerman over the years and, in several instances, had provided research assistance. Meanwhile, HarperCollins published *The Best of the West: An Anthology of Classic Writing from the American West*, listing Hillerman as the editor. The more than five-hundred-page collection contained selections from memoirs, letters, diaries, novels, and short stories. Most of the contents were drawn from the nine-thousand-volume personal library of Hillerman's friend Jack Rittenhouse, the editor with whom he had published *The Spell of New Mexico* in 1976. "Why, then, isn't Jack Rittenhouse's name on the dust jacket?" Hillerman wrote in the introduction to the volume. "Because, odd as it seems, he didn't want it there." Rather, Rittenhouse was persuaded that the name of a well-known novelist would attract new readers. "A two-line mention would please me most," Rittenhouse told Hillerman, who instead wrote a twenty-two-line description of his friend.[42]

But the third book was the one in which Hillerman had the greatest emotional investment. Arriving in the mail was the coffee table book of photographs and text that Tony and Barney had worked on for years. Designed for HarperCollins by a San Francisco book packager and printed in Hong Kong, the oversized, lavishly illustrated 240-page tome called *Hillerman Country: A Journey through the Southwest with Tony Hillerman* was filled with dramatic photos of wide-open expanses, cliffs, and waterways, all under the cobalt blue southwestern sky dotted with white clouds. "I've lived under that sky for two-thirds of a longish life," Hillerman wrote in the introduction, "and it still has the power to stop me cold with its cloudscapes." Tony had assigned all the royalties from the book to his brother. Money was not something he needed any longer.[43]

Barney bought hearing aids in preparation for a book tour. Bitten by the publication bug, while waiting for the planned book events, he went to Duncan, Oklahoma, to start shooting photographs for the next book he had in mind.

While there he had a fatal heart attack. At age sixty-eight, he had never seen the interior of a hospital. He had signed only one copy of the book, for their sister Margaret Mary, to whom the two brothers had dedicated the book as the one "who taught us to keep the crayon between the lines." On the front door of his photography studio back in Oklahoma City, a sign was posted:

Bernard (Barney) Hillerman 1/27/23–10/7/91
Gone to photograph another area.
(Good shooting.)[44]

Despite having been separated from his brother by geography for most of his adult life, Tony had remained close to Barney. He felt the loss of his childhood playmate, whom he had followed to war, shared pranks with at the University of Oklahoma, and now collaborated on a book. A few months earlier Tony had attended the Catholic Press Association convention in Phoenix, sitting with the Oklahoma delegation during lunch. Barney was acknowledged for processing photograph film for the *Sooner Catholic* newspaper. Tony was not surprised. He regarded his older brother as the "most Christian person I've ever known." He was widely known for regularly posting bail for his employees who found themselves in the drunk tank, and credited his Good Samaritan behavior as having been learned from their father. "That's how our Dad did it."[45]

Tony's Navajo friend James Peshlakai, who greatly admired the book, wrote to him upon learning of Barney's death. Making reference to the Navajo practice of burying the dead with a small leather pouch containing yellow corn pollen, he told Tony, "Barney's work will live in the hearts of the Navajo people forever and someday we will follow his footsteps, but our pollen trails will also guide those who come after us, just as we see Barney's pollen footprints along the Blessing Way, maybe we see it more clearly now."[46]

CHAPTER 25

❖ Into a Heart of Darkness ❖

For Tony Hillerman, death made its presence felt in the fall of 1991. In addition to having lost his brother, Hillerman's longtime friend and sometime book partner Jack Rittenhouse died of cancer. A few weeks later, Hillerman learned that he too had the disease. Doctors discovered cancer in his prostate. This was his second encounter with an affliction of aging in as many years. In 1989, he had developed rheumatoid arthritis. He told a friend the ailment "gives me a choice of swollen wrists, hands and knuckles or taking heavy doses of stuff which causes one to feel lousy otherwise."[1]

Hillerman's cancer surgery was delayed so that the hospital could set aside a supply of his blood should a transfusion become necessary. During the delay the cancer spread to his bladder. In the end it took three operations to successfully remove all of it. The recovery was long and difficult, and the removal of a portion of his bladder left him with incontinence issues.[2]

Throughout his ordeal, the sixty-six-year-old Hillerman did not lose his well-known graciousness. Norman Boucher, a Boston writer arriving in Albuquerque to write a profile of the author, discovered that his subject was ill. "Although the cancer treatments were no doubt fatiguing him," said Boucher, "he gave me all the time I wanted that day, even though I was a complete unknown to him and his sickness had seriously delayed work on his new novel."[3]

When Hillerman recovered from his surgeries, he considered retiring. "I thought, 'Why not quit?' but then everywhere I go people ask when the next book is coming out," he said. "I feel guilty if I'm not satisfying that national need for a Navajo fix." The manuscript he had left in midstream on his computer when he became ill no longer appealed to him. Instead, he began again fresh, keeping a few aspects of the original plan and renaming the book. The promotional "Mudhead Kiva" cover, created the year before and sent to stores, soon became a collector's item.[4]

"It took a long time to get over" the cancer surgeries, Hillerman said. For months afterwards he struggled to get his energy back and return to work. His first step was doing some public events. In January 1992, Hillerman traveled to Tucson, where he and novelist Barbara Kingsolver headlined a writing conference. The local press, noting his recent illness, referred to his appearance as a "kind of triumphant coming-out party." He followed that event with a trip to speak to students at Texas Christian University in Fort Worth, and in May gave a lecture in Santa Fe sponsored by the School of American Research. He was slower in returning to his writing, though it was always on his mind. "I've got to get back to work," he told the Santa Fe newspaper reporter covering his talk. "I'm working on a long overdue mystery. It was advertised as a fall '91 book." At the same time, he harbored some doubts. "I hope I haven't lost my touch—I've been out of fiction writing for a year."[5]

By summer Hillerman was making progress on a replacement for his abandoned manuscript. He retained two major elements from his first try at the book. The novel would remain centered on a pueblo, in this case the fictional Tano Pueblo, and include the Lincoln canes.

Pueblos had long interested Hillerman. He had set *Dance Hall of the Dead* in and around Zuni Pueblo. In *The Dark Wind*, the Hopi villages played an important role. It was while learning about the Hopis for that book, as well as for an *Arizona Highways* magazine article, that Hillerman decided he wanted someday to return to a Pueblo setting. Once in the 1980s he spent the night in his truck near the Hopi village of Walpi. Waking early in the morning, he watched a Hopi man come out from a house and raise a bundled eight-day-old infant toward the sun. Hillerman learned that what he had witnessed was similar to a Christian baptism. The chant that had accompanied the act was a promise to raise the child according to the Creator's rule and an acknowledgment that the father and mother were only foster parents, as the infant was a child of God. The almost sacred status of Pueblo children fascinated Hillerman. He felt it explained why he had never seen a Pueblo child physically punished.

From Hillerman's point of view, the Puebloans had an admirable means of keeping social order. Setting his book in the fictional Tano Pueblo would, Hillerman hoped, give readers insights into a culture that maintained its morals and ethics for centuries without any kind of policing or repressive system. "The Hopi don't have internal police to impose tribal mores on everybody," he said. Instead, they developed clown fraternities that appeared at religious ceremonies, mocking and making fun of transgressive behavior. "We enforce our ethics and mores with gun and force," he said. "They enforce with laughter and mockery and scorn."[6]

In the book, Jim Chee now works directly for Leaphorn where, as Hillerman told Eamon Dolan, "he won't have so many chances to violate rules." And, Hillerman added, the moment might be a precursor to the day when Leaphorn would retire and Chee would replace him. When the book opens, Chee is watching the kachina dances at the Tano Pueblo in the company of Hopi policeman Cowboy Dashee and the lawyer and Chee's love interest, Janet Pete. As in *The Ghostway*, Chee is in pursuit of a runaway. This time, instead of a girl from St. Catherine's in Santa Fe, it is a boy from the St. Bonaventure Mission and School in Thoreau. Both were schools that Hillerman admired and supported financially.

A murder during the Tano ceremony, where the missing boy had been spotted, and another killing back at the school in Thoreau set the stage for the mystery. A third death, this one due to a hit-and-run collision, provided Hillerman with a chance to contrast Navajo beliefs of justice with those held by whites and offer perhaps his most passionate exposition on *hózhó*, or harmony.

Chee identifies the driver of the car in the fatal hit-and-run. He is Clement Hoski, who is raising Ernie, his mentally disabled grandson, a likely sufferer from fetal alcohol syndrome. In Navajo fashion, Hoski had apologized for his actions and begun making restitution payments to the victim's family. Chee and Pete, who are now on the verge of a romantic relationship, hold opposing views on the matter. Pete believes the man's transgression requires he be punished.

In one of the final scenes of *Sacred Clowns*, Pete and Chee sit in his car in front of the house where the child and grandfather live. "You have to believe in justice or you get out of the business," Pete tells Chee. "I don't disagree," replies Chee. "The question is *bilagáana* justice, or Navajo justice. Or maybe it's, Do you try for punishment or do you try for *hózhó*?"[7]

If Hoski is arrested, he won't be able to care for Ernie or support the victim's family. Chee could carry out his law enforcement duties and earn himself a promotion by apprehending Hoski. Instead, he gives Ernie a new bumper sticker to replace the "Ernie is the greatest" one on his grandfather's car that ties the vehicle to the deadly accident. The new sticker reads "I have the world champion grandson." Pete is impressed with Chee's compassionate approach.

Chee provides her with an explanation. *Hózhó*, the Beauty Way, is a way of adapting. In a drought Christians, Hopis, and Muslims all pray for rain. "The Navajo has the proper ceremony done to restore himself to harmony with the drought," Chee tells Pete. "The system is designed to recognize what is beyond human power to change, and then to change the human's attitude to be content with the inevitable." Hoski had confessed to his community on the radio and was making restitution payments. If Chee interfered, he would only disturb the balance that was being restored.

In this discussion, Hillerman offers Navajo beliefs that he has come to see as of enormous value. They are, to him, the Navajo equivalent of Christian theologian Reinhold Niebuhr's Serenity Prayer. Adjusting and adapting, says Chee, is "why we Navajos have endured. Survived with our culture alive. This philosophy of *hózhó* kept us alive."

The manuscript complete and his health on the mend, Hillerman let Ashmead know he could schedule this book, now titled *Sacred Clowns*, for publication with certainty. It would be the fifth novel in which Chee and Leaphorn appear together. "Whenever I finish a book, I finish it in a great cloud of disappointment because I didn't accomplish everything I set out to do." Hillerman said at the time. "But on this book, however, my editor, who is not fulsome in his praise, said it was by far the best thing I have done. So, I think it will be okay."[8]

Soon after Hillerman turned in his manuscript, he began to receive telephone calls from New York journalists. A form of the hantavirus previously unknown to epidemiologists had surfaced in the Four Corners region, and most of the dozen deaths were Navajo. The reporters were hunting for quotations from the now-famous writer that would illustrate the allegedly superstitious beliefs of Navajos. "For example," Hillerman told a friend, "one reporter asked if I could blame it on a Hopi curse." He responded as if he were back in his University of New Mexico journalism classroom. He lectured the distant reporters that evoking superstition would be offensive to Navajos. Furthermore, the media frenzy building around the hantavirus outbreak in the Navajo Nation was disrespectful. "The traditional Navajos don't like to talk about the dead, especially in the first four days, and here comes a reporter asking all sorts of questions." One reporter asked him if Navajos had an unusual fear of death. Hillerman replied that the Navajos he knew "live with death, and they're less likely to get panicky about it than someone in your average New York City newsroom."[9]

At the end of the summer, *Sacred Clowns* was published. Its launch was made hectic for HarperCollins when Hilleman insisted on changing the ending after the publisher had distributed advance reading copies to booksellers and reviewers at the American Booksellers Association May trade show. Larry Ashmead told the press that the Navajo concept of justice requires that the gods, not humans, punish the criminal. In the new ending, reported Charlotte Hays, the gossip columnist for the New York *Daily News*, Hillerman's detective makes it clear that the gods will do the punishing.[10]

The review copies with the original ending did not dismay the critics, however. "The byplay between prickly Leaphorn and spiritual Chee; Chee's sobering reflections on Navajo and white people's justice; problem-strewn new romantic intrigues for both heroes—all of these make this not only a masterful novel in its own right, but an object lesson in how to develop an outstanding series," said *Kirkus*. Similar praise came from *Publishers Weekly*.[11]

"How long can Tony Hillerman keep it up?" asked Dick Adler, a mystery reviewer for the *Chicago Tribune*. All the great writers write a book that signals the beginning of the end, explained Adler. "Well, it hasn't happened yet to Hillerman. *Sacred Clowns* is as good as any of his previous evocative and engaging books. "And best of all, it's a book as full of kindness, love and compassion as it is of murder, sadness and mystery.[12]

Yet other critics spotted flaws that were becoming apparent in Hillerman's novels, ones which his editors had passed over and would have done better by him to have marked for cutting. In particular, the *Washington Post* critic noticed long, slow passages with no connection to the plot nor any other purpose. "I would much prefer to be a Tony Hillerman fan," the critic wrote. "Obvious criticisms like these should have been his editor's job."[13]

Four weeks after it was published, *Sacred Clowns* became Hillerman's fourth book to make it onto the *New York Times* Best Sellers list, remaining there for eleven weeks. At one point it rose to number three, behind *The Bridges of Madison County* by Robert James Waller, then in its sixty-first week on the list, and Anne Rice's new book *Lasher*. HarperCollins had not made a mistake in printing 350,000 copies, more than twice the print run for *Coyote Waits*. When

Hillerman had a several-year gap between novels as a beginning writer it had created a marketing problem. Now the elapsed time fueled demand among his legion of fans. As one bookstore's advertisement read, "Finally, after three years of waiting, a new Joe Leaphorn and Jim Chee Murder Mystery!"[14]

One financial beneficiary of *Sacred Clowns*, aside from the publisher, stores, and author, was the St. Bonaventure Mission and School, in Thoreau, along the very road that had taken Hillerman to his first encounter with Navajos in 1945. Hillerman used it as the site of one of the murders, and in the front of the book he included a note about the work of the mission along with its mailing address. "It just makes you feel good to be around people like the gang at that school, who are dedicating a big chunk of their lives to helping other people," Hillerman said. Since the book's publication the three-hundred-student school had received a steady stream of contributions from readers.[15]

After eleven Navajo mysteries, Hillerman had a surprise in the works for his readers. His next book would make no mention of *hózhó* or *bilagáanas*. In fact, Leaphorn and Chee would be entirely absent. After years of telling his agent and editor he wanted to do a mainstream novel, Hillerman decided the time had come.

The idea for the novel had been gestating in Hillerman's mind since his time as an editor at the *Santa Fe New Mexican*. In his last three years at the paper, he had published a steady stream of wire service dispatches on the protracted and violent war that had erupted in the Republic of the Congo after the nation gained its independence from Belgium. Reflecting on his own wartime experiences, Hillerman got the notion of putting a protagonist into a scene of lawlessness like that emerging in the Congo. "I wanted to write about an average man in a place where civilization had ceased, to examine how surviving amid chaos changes him," he said.[16]

In 1985, he and Marie had watched a television documentary on Vietnam aired on the tenth anniversary of the fall of Saigon. "Scenes of civilians struggling at the gates of our embassy reminded me of the chaos I had intended to depict in Stanleyville," he said. "With the Congo bloodbath long forgotten by the world, I decided to move the story to Southeast Asia." But on the various times Hillerman brought up the idea of doing a standalone novel, both Perry Knowlton and his HarperCollins editor talked him out of it. "My own common sense told me they were right," he said. "It would be stupid to stop writing Navajo tribal police mysteries, sales of which were soaring, to turn out a book nobody wants."[17]

Hillerman talked the idea over with his wife. "Marie, as always, advised me to trust my own judgement. If I saw a good book, write it," he said. Three years earlier, HarperCollins's adult trade group publisher, William Shinker, had given in and promised his best-selling author that he could do a non-Navajo mystery, adding he would publish anything Hillerman wrote. In return for agreeing to publish this new novel set in Asia, Shinker got Hillerman's signature in the fall of 1993 on a $6 million contract for two books, the second one being a return to the Navajo Nation.

Eamon Dolan, who was now editing Hillerman's books, was called on to explain the company's view. "Tony felt—and we agree—that this would be a good time to put his Southwestern mysteries on hold temporarily and pursue this new direction," Dolan said, "and certainly, we're excited at the prospect of another book in the Leaphorn and Chee series, as the series' many thousands of fans will be."[18]

Hillerman ceased daydreaming and began to work in earnest on a plot. He shared his plans with Ollie Reed Jr., a friend and respected writer for the *Albuquerque Tribune*. "His footing seems less sure when he strays onto unfamiliar turf as he did when he sent Leaphorn off to Washington in 1989's *Talking God*," observed Reed in an article about Hillerman's *Sacred Clowns*. "So, you would not be surprised if he were a little nervous about the novel growing in his word processor now."[19]

The plot, as he had worked it out, centered on a rural newspaper editor who searches for his dead brother's daughter through the Philippines and then into Cambodia and Vietnam during the 1974 turmoil. Hillerman had the material for the setting. But Vietnam and Cambodia were not granting visas to Americans. Instead, Hillerman thought he might find what he needed in the Philippines and perhaps find a way across the South China Sea to Vietnam. The opportunity to see if he were right came when he received an offer to join a group of travel writers to visit the Philippines on an all-expenses-paid trip.

As the plane ferrying Hillerman and the travel writers approached the Philippines in February 1986, enormous changes were underway in the island nation. President Ferdinand Marcos and his wife had just gone into exile, and Corazon Aquino was assuming the presidency. She was the widow of Benigno Aquino Jr., the Marcos opponent who had been assassinated three years earlier at the Manila International Airport, where Hillerman's plane was setting down. The chaotic situation on the ground worked to Hillerman's advantage. He was traveling on an expired passport, having left his new one in his office, but the preoccupied customs agents didn't notice.

Once in Manila, however, Hillerman found that he was barred from his first destination. His plot required a prison break, and he had hoped to tour the infamous Bilibid prison. It had been behind those walls that President Marcos had locked up political prisoners. The facility was off-limits to visitors. Instead Hillerman obtained permission to visit a maximum-security prison on Palawan, an island in the western Philippines.

To reach it, Hillerman caught a flight on a cramped island-hopping plane. His seatmate was an exporter of items including bamboo blowguns. As the plane neared Palawan, Hillerman looked out his window. "What caught my eye," he said, "was a two-masted sailing ship, its fresh paint as white as snow, a pearl set in a field of barnacles. Even before our plane touched the weedy landing strip at Puerto Princesa, I had collected two characters—my seatmate and this dazzling vessel."[20]

An aging jeepney—apparently there were only six taxis in the city—took Hillerman out to the Palawan prison. He found the setting he needed for his jailbreak. The talkative driver ran Hillerman back to Puerto Princesa, where he spent the twilight hours prowling the wharves, taking note of the sounds and insects, and inspecting the ship he had seen from the plane. "Lovingly inscribed on the ship's bow was its name: *Glory of the Sea*. Any novelist could get a character across the South China Sea on that."[21]

The next day Hillerman and his jeepney driver ate grilled sea bass on the beach, looking out on the South China Sea. "It was 800 miles to Vietnam, but it no longer really mattered if I got there," said Hillerman. "I had converted the cabbie into the captain of *Glory of the Sea*, and the Palawan Island has provided me with the headful of images a writer needs to build his book."

Back in Manila, Hillerman continued his good fortune with taxi drivers and collected several more locations to use in the book. Then, on an evening walk, heavy rain drove Hillerman into Manila's cathedral. In the darkness, waiting for the squall to pass, the light from the candles and the smell of incense led him to divine a key scene of the novel. Sitting at his computer upon his return home, Hillerman switches places with his protagonist. The man, a lapsed Catholic also driven into the church by rain, meets a young priest with whom he engages in soul-searching conversations. It was, said Hillerman, "one of those rare and joyful moments when you know you're writing well." The writing, however, came to a sudden stop.[22]

Late in the day, on Sunday May 1, 1994, Tony complained of chest pains. The discomfort was ominous. A few years earlier, doctors had spotted some partially blocked arteries. Instead of calling for an ambulance, the always frugal Marie put her husband in the car and drove him the eight miles to Presbyterian Hospital, where their daughter Janet met them. "Never drive him, Mom," Janet told Marie. "Always call an ambulance. Because what if he has another one in the car?"[23]

Sixty-nine-year-old Tony was admitted. The family called Dr. Neal Shadoff, a cardiologist and neighbor. He found his patient unconcerned and claiming that Marie was overreacting. The following morning Shadoff inserted dye into Hillerman's bloodstream to make his blood vessels visible on an X-ray as family members watched on a screen. The procedure was followed by an angioplasty, in which a deflated sausage-shaped balloon was guided to the clogged coronary artery and inflated to widen the passage and increase blood flow. By Tuesday morning, Tony was ready to be released. His eldest daughter Anne told reporters she had heard that her father "was already telling the nurses what to do."[24]

Hillerman's heart attack, like his earlier bout with prostate cancer, had kept him away briefly from his weekly poker game, but little else was ever permitted to interfere with his attendance. The eight-man Tuesday-evening card game was as incommutable in Hillerman's schedule as Sunday mass. Once, a member of Robert Redford's staff called to see if Hillerman could meet the actor for dinner on Tuesday. "I said I was tied up Tuesday nights playing cards with old friends," Hillerman said. "How about Wednesday?" At the game that week, Hillerman told the men about turning down the dinner offer. "The old duffers understood perfectly (as did Mr. Redford) with no explanation needed that no decent person would break a social engagement to talk business," Hillerman said. "The younger players were amazed." Until the end of his public appearances, Hillerman was frequently asked to confirm the tale. "When I explain that Redford would not have expected me to forgo the poker game, they look at me as if I am either a liar or an idiot."[25]

Outside of his family, the fellow poker players were his best friends. Hillerman's enthusiasm for the game had begun in the army during the war. "In the Third General Hospital at Aix, the poker game was about as religious as things got," he recalled. His participation in the weekly game dated back two decades. Jess Price, the director of the University of New Mexico Public Information Office, had been chatting about poker with Jim Belshaw, a former Hillerman student and now a university writer. Price, who had been Hillerman's city editor at the *Santa Fe New Mexican*, confessed a devotion to the game. When he returned to his desk, he called Hillerman and asked his former boss if he wanted to be part of a new weekly game. Price recruited five more players. Several years into the games, the group spawned a Thursday-night game as well. It was larger and played the Texas hold 'em version of poker. "After a period of time," said Belshaw, "the games became almost institutionalized, became such a part of our lives."[26]

The men played for low stakes. Belshaw considered Hillerman the most optimistic player he had known. "I didn't think it was possible to have so much confidence in two mediocre pairs," he said, "but he never failed to ride them to the awful, inevitable end." Hillerman's storytelling made him a central figure of the gathering. Exhibiting his wry sense of humor, Hillerman would sometimes interrupt the banter at the table, asking "Did you birds come to talk or to play poker?" The players would teasingly grumble but grow quiet. "He was the only one who could get away with saying it," according to Belshaw. "And then half the time, Hillerman would begin telling a story of his own."[27]

At one game, John Whiteside, the university's financial aid director, announced he had read Hillerman's 1971 novel *The Fly on the Wall* and he had a question about the poker scene. "The hero is a reporter, which I guess is supposed to be you," said Whiteside. "I want to know who wrote that poker scene for you. You have this hero folding and folding and folding. You never folded a hand in your life. You couldn't have written that scene. So, who did?" Whiteside's ribbing was typical of the evening's merriment. Hillerman carried the fun into his books. When he wrote *The Fallen Man*, Hillerman placed Whiteside, Bill Buchanan, and Jim Stapp clinging perilously to the steep wall of Shiprock, a dramatic lava plug in New Mexico. They were ill-suited rock climbers, particularly Buchanan who weighed 325 pounds. The game itself made the pages of the book. "He played in a poker game in which Whiteside was called 'Two-Dollar John' because of his unshakable faith that the dealer would give him the fifth heart if he needed one." And as a final tribute to his friends, Hillerman dedicated *The Fallen Man* to the group, "which for the past quarter-century has gathered each Tuesday evening to test the laws of probability and sometimes, alas, the Chaos Theory."

Of the men at the table, Hillerman and Buchanan were the most accomplished book authors. The two men had become friends in 1975 after Buchanan contacted him for advice. The retired air force colonel had sold an article to *Reader's Digest* about twenty-six-year-old track star John Baker who, as he was dying of cancer, continued coaching elementary school students. Movie studios were interested in the story, and Buchanan called Hillerman for advice on finding an agent. Hillerman returned the call but reached Buchanan's son, who left a note for his father that a "Mr. Hilly Turner" had called. Two weeks passed until one night his son spotted Hillerman's name in the *New Mexico* magazine. "Hey," he said to his father. "That's who called."[28]

"So much for adolescent phonetics," Buchanan wrote Hillerman, explaining why he had not called back. "Your son," said Hillerman, "had the same problem many of my students experience—understanding my East-Okie accent." He suggested agent Ann Elmo who, despite his complaints, Hillerman conceded knew a lot about film options. "My problem is I'm often optioned but never produced," he said. When they finally connected, the two writers became fast friends. Buchanan's original *Reader's Digest* story grew into a book. *A Shining Season* sold more than 250,000 copies and became a film starring Timothy Bottoms. Hillerman penned introductions to several subsequent Buchanan books.[29]

The gatherings, which ran from seven to eleven at night, provided a place where Hillerman could be who he had been before *A Thief of Time* turned him into an instantly recognizable figure, particularly in Albuquerque. The game also offered something else to Hillerman. One night, Belshaw, a veteran of the Vietnam War, folded a hand early and looked around the table at the men. "It dawned on me that seven of the eight players were military veterans and among the seven were three wars: World War II, Korea, and Vietnam." After the game, he and Hillerman drove home. Since turning sixty-seven in 1992, Hillerman had for the most part given up night driving. "I became his de facto poker game driver," said Belshaw.

"You know what I really like about this poker game?" Hillerman asked as the two men through the city in the darkness.

"What?" said Belshaw.

"It kind of reminds me of being in the squad."

Belshaw thought about all the poker games he had played in the barracks during his tour of duty. "He was right, that's what it felt like."

Five decades after the war, the comradery Hillerman had found among the men with whom he had served remained one of the emotional touchstones of his life. Attending a Company C, 410th Infantry reunion in the 1950s, Hillerman spotted Robert Lewis, his mortar gun firing partner, getting out of a car. "He always had a funny way of walking, and I thought: *There goes Bob Lewis.* And I felt this wave of love and affection sweep over me."[30]

Hillerman's loyalty to his army brotherhood sent him to the Department of Veterans Affairs hospital in Albuquerque for medical care, despite the fact that he could afford to pay for care anywhere he chose. When he had been discharged from the military hospital in Texas after recuperating from his war wounds, there had been no talk of post-traumatic stress disorder (PTSD). The term entered the lexicon during the Vietnam era. "Many of them looked okay because they went to work, got married, they raised families—but that doesn't mean they didn't have PTSD," according to Paula Schnurr, executive director of the National Center for PTSD and a highly regarded expert on the syndrome.[31]

Schnurr's extensive studies of World War II veterans revealed that they tended to suffer privately, often choosing not to talk about the war at all, and the symptoms surfaced episodically. When Hillerman's daughter Janet Grado first learned about PTSD, she wondered if her father didn't suffer from it. "Because I always knew something was wrong but he wouldn't talk about it," she said. "He was just like a lot of people in his generation—he was getting on with his life."[32]

In fact, for many veterans of the war, according to Schnurr, work was a form of coping. "At the time he came out of the war," said Schnurr, "we didn't have any effective treatment for PTSD." In Hillerman's case it could be that the all-consuming nature of writing helped, but also his drive to capture for his readers the Navajo pursuit of *hózhó* provided him with his own sense of harmony. If so, Hillerman's path to coping was consistent with that of many of the veterans Schnurr studied.[33]

It was clear, even if he didn't visibly manifest it, that Hillerman's time in combat still haunted him these many years later. "Those who have endured combat tend to be drawn by bad dreams back into terrible, dark and violent memories of war," Hillerman wrote in an unfinished bit of writing in 1984. "In the years since the final winter of World War II, I have had my share of those."[34]

"Somehow, the noise of shells roaring over, the zipper sound of German machine guns, the cold, the fear, the feel of icy water draining off our helmets down the back of our necks, the flash of exploding 'potato masher' grenades in the dark alleys, those sights and sounds of war in its most dangerous moments just refuse to be forgotten. They intrude, unwelcome and uninvited in those drowsy moments when one is trying to sleep."[35]

One night, as Belshaw and Hillerman traveled back in the dark from the weekly poker game, Hillerman turned to his friend. "This doctor told me I had PTSD," Hillerman said.

"Oh yeah? What did you think about that?"

"She might be right."[36]

CHAPTER 26

❖ A Fallen Man ❖

Tony Hillerman took the draft pages of the novel he had always wanted to write to FedEx on the afternoon of May 12, 1995, and sent it off to Eamon Dolan at HarperCollins. *Finding Moon* still needed polishing, and that night he had invited Dr. Neal Shadoff over to help fix the early scenes with doctors. But on the whole, he had accomplished what he had longed to do since leaving the *Santa Fe New Mexican* in 1963—writing a standalone novel of character. Perhaps it was not the Great American Novel he had once dreamed of but it was going to be his one stab at one. "That book was special for me," Hillerman told Peter Thorpe, the designer of his book covers. "The best bona fide novel I ever did."[1]

When Dolan opened the FedEx box, he found the longest novel Hillerman had ever written. And it was certainly different. The protagonist Mathis Moon, who goes by "Moon," leaves his job as the editor of a Colorado newspaper when his aging mother falls ill while on her way to the Philippines. It turns out she has learned that her other son, who died in Vietnam, left behind an orphaned infant daughter—her only grandchild. Moon goes to the Philippines, and eventually Vietnam and Cambodia, in search of his niece. The novel brings together a cast of people all searching for something through the chaos during the fall of the Republic of Vietnam in 1975: Moon for his niece, a woman for her missing missionary brother, and a Chinese man for an urn containing ancestral bones. Moon accomplishes his goal of locating his baby niece but in doing so he is changed. He overcomes his self-loathing and guilt for a fatal youthful mistake and discovers strength he never knew he had. He finds himself.

Loyal readers may have been tempted to search for autobiographical elements in *Finding Moon*, especially in fathoming Hillerman's departure from his series. But the novel held none. The only portion of the book directly connected to Hillerman's life were the names he gave to many of his characters. He drew them from the roster of C Company, 410th Infantry, to whom he dedicated the work. Moon was an homage to Carl Edward Mathias, a staff sergeant in the infantry who earned a Purple Heart and Bronze Star. "A bona fide hero by my standards," Hillerman said.[2]

"I have borrowed only the names of these old friends and not their personalities," Hillerman wrote in an unusual note to readers titled "An Apology, Acknowledgments, Denial, and Dedication," a foreword he may have come to regret. "To my fellow desert rats," Hillerman wrote, "my apologies for wandering away from our beloved Navajo canyon country."[3]

Reviewers unhappy with the book, and there were many, seized on what Hillerman had written. For instance, the Associated Press reviewer wrote, "In an apologetic note, Hillerman promises to return to the reservation in his next book. It is fervently hoped he does so." *Finding Moon* made a short appearance of six weeks on the *New York Times* Best Sellers list, but never among the top ten books. *Finding Moon* was, Hillerman said, "closest to my heart, but not to those of editor, publisher, and many of my readers."[4]

HarperCollins wanted the book to succeed, but its paramount interest was to safeguard the Leaphorn/Chee brand. When Thorpe developed the cover for *Finding Moon*, he painted a moon rising above the mountains of Cambodia with the silhouette of a man outlined against it. Hillerman loved it but his affection was not shared in New York City. "The bean counters at HarperColllins decided it wasn't Navajo enough," Hillerman told Thorpe. The publisher instructed Thorpe to replace the image with an illustration of an Asian jar with a skull and bones scattered at its base, a design more in keeping with Hillerman's previous books. It was, said Hillerman, "the sort of development that reminds writers of their place in the publishing world."[5]

Hillerman's on-again, off-again relationship with Hollywood was suddenly on again. After the disaster with *The Dark Wind*, Hillerman doubted his work would ever come to the screen. But Robert Redford had not given up. In 1993, he and his son Jamie were on an Omaha-bound flight out of Denver. Since age fifteen, Jamie had suffered from ulcerative colitis. The painful condition had taken a potentially deadly turn six years earlier when he had been diagnosed with sclerosing cholangitis, a rare condition causing blockage of the liver's bile ducts. Father and son were now heading to the University of Nebraska Medical Center for a liver transplant.

Airborne, Robert bemoaned the failure of *The Dark Wind* and turned to Jamie with a proposal. Would he be willing to look at the remaining Hillerman novels, all of which were still under option? The question was genuine, not idle chitchat. Although raised mostly in New York City, Jamie shared his father's love of the Southwest from summers spent riding dirt bikes in southern Utah and exploring the Four Corners region. He had graduated from the University of Colorado, which his dad had attended briefly, with a double major in English and film, and had earned an MA in literature from Northwestern University. Now thirty-one years old, Jamie had been working as a writer and had done some screenwriting.

"Because you know this landscape and you have a feel for it and the people down there," Robert continued, "if we were to start this up again, where would you think would be an interesting place to break into these books, which book would be a good place to start?"[6]

"As far as I was concerned, it was just a fun favor," said Jamie. At this point, the only Hillerman book he had read was *A Thief of Time*. So Jamie read the other ten mysteries while waiting for his liver transplants—the first transplant didn't take—and during his convalescence.

In March 1994, Jamie Redford installed himself in a room at Rancho Encantado, an aging resort on the northern outskirts of Santa Fe. Taking out two pieces of the resort's stationery, he penned a deferential letter to Hillerman. "I'm writing to tell you that your worst Hollywood nightmare is about to come true," he began. He explained that he was Robert Redford's son and his dad had approached him about writing a screenplay for one of the Hillerman books under option. "Perhaps after 'Dark Wind,'" he said, "you've tried to desperately forget?" At length, Redford filled Hillerman in on his background, his love of the Southwest, and the kind of writing he had done. "In other words, I'm not an L.A. scriptwriter who would be compelled to turn *Skinwalkers* into "Terminator 3—Death in the Desert." He closed by asking to meet with Hillerman.[7]

The author agreed. Redford drove down to join Hillerman for breakfast at the Winrock Town Center mall in Albuquerque. Developed by Winthrop Rockefeller—hence the name—and the University of New Mexico, the shopping center was topped with a massive orange pyramid. Redford sat in the restaurant for a while but saw no sign of Hillerman. When he rose to use the restroom, he spotted a man sitting in the back. It was Hillerman, who had chosen the most inconspicuous spot to wait for Redford. Apologies made and accepted, the two men talked at length about making a film from Hillerman's work.

Redford was worried Hillerman would see him negatively. "It's not uncommon for novelists to really loathe screenwriters because in the transition to film so many things happen," said Redford. "You end up in development hell with twenty other people giving notes and you end up with something that's like, with too much paint on canvas, a big brown blob."

Hillerman sat back, pushed away his plate, now empty of bacon and eggs. "Hey, let me tell you about me and words," he said launching into stories about his first job as a writer doing radio advertisements for Ralston Purina Pig Chow. "So, you know that's my origin so your dear level of concern is unwarranted," Hillerman told the young writer. "We all do what we do." Redford was grateful.[8]

Now, a year later in the fall of 1995, Jamie Redford had completed a screenplay adaptation of *Skinwalkers*. "I have to thank you for creating the characters that I've since adopted as my own," he wrote Hillerman. "I spent a year with them, and I must say they are very good company." He sent the script to Rachel Pfeffer, who ran Robert Redford's Wildwood Enterprises. "She's very fired up about the script," Jamie told Hillerman, "and everyone, including my father, seems excited to get your books moving again."[9]

But as with the previous Hollywood flirtation, silence again descended. And Hillerman had a book to write. Now that *Finding Moon* was complete and published, Hillerman had a tight schedule to meet his contractual obligation to HarperCollins.

Hillerman had promised to deliver a new Leaphorn and Chee mystery in time for publication in 1996. In searching his files, he had come across an unabashed fan letter Bob Rosebrough had written to Hillerman in 1987. In it, the Gallup attorney described his passion for rock climbing and how he had scaled Shiprock twice in recent years. "It occurs to me that climbing on Shiprock might be something which might interest you for a future plot," Rosebrough wrote.[10]

The rock, known to Navajos as Tsé Bit'a'í or "winged rock," had become one of the coveted ascents among climbers. Rising 1,583 feet, the lava plug towered over the open landscape of northwestern New Mexico. Climbers continued to ascend the landmark despite a Navajo Nation ban on climbing the venerated monolith. Several died in their attempts to scale the face.

Now, eight years later, Hillerman wanted to meet with Rosebrough. In the midst of a separation and eventual divorce from his wife, Rosebrough was going through a dark time and was living in a rented house. "Hi, this is Tony Hillerman," said the voice on the telephone. "I'm looking for Bob Rosebrough. Do I have the right number?"[11]

He explained he was following up on Rosebrough's idea and had questions about rock climbing. On December 27, 1995, Rosebrough and his two oldest children, eager to meet a famous author, sat waiting in his law office on Second Street in Gallup. At 10 A.M. Tony and Marie Hillerman entered. The couple warmly greeted the children. Rosebrough provided a mini-course on the ins and outs of rock climbing. During the meeting Marie watched and listened attentively, seemingly absorbing everything. "I would have bet real money that Marie was a novelist," said Rosebrough. Tony, on the other hand, remained mostly quiet, in "a Columbo-esque interview style." But just as the lawyer began to think the writer had tuned out, Hillerman asked a probing question that revealed he too had been taking in everything.[12]

Rosebrough provided the setting for a plot Hillerman had devised over a period of months prior to meeting the lawyer. Joe Leaphorn is retired but takes up one of his unsolved cases when a body found on Shiprock turns out to be that of Hal Breedlove, who went missing eleven years earlier. Jim Chee, now a lieutenant, joins the pursuit and, making her maiden appearance, is Bernadette Manuelito, who proves her worth as a rookie by arresting a cattle thief in a concurrent subplot. By way of thanks, Hillerman cast Rosebrough in a dramatic role in which he descends a rope ladder from a helicopter to the top of Shiprock to retrieve important evidence.

In writing what would be his twelfth Navajo mystery, Hillerman resumed his much-loved evocations of southwestern landscape and Chee and Leaphorn's ruminations on Navajo culture. But he used the plot to expound on his beliefs about the materialism and obsession with making money in Anglo culture. "If this is a crime it's a white man's crime," Leaphorn says when he considers where the corpse was found. "No Navajo would kill anyone on that sacred mountain. I doubt if a Navajo would be disrespectful enough even to climb it. Among my people, murder tends to be motivated by whiskey or sexual jealousy. Among white people, I've noticed crime is more likely to be motivated by money."[13]

Despite now being wealthy, Hillerman retained the us-versus-them perspective he had acquired during high school in Konawa. Now older and wiser, Hillerman also found Genesis-like tragedy in those to whom all is given. The victim was wealthy and in line to inherit a ranch. His brother-in-law saw Chee carrying the folder on the case. "He had it labeled 'Fallen Man,'" Eldon Demott told Leaphorn. "I thought, Yes, that described Hal. The old man gave him paradise and it wasn't enough for him."[14]

In a clue that after a dozen detective novels, Hillerman was still struggling to create endings—the hardest part for many mystery writers—he recycled the extralegal fate accorded to the murderer in *Dance Hall of the Dead*. Here, his criminal is permitted to end his own life rather than be judged in a court.

Hillerman worked rapidly through the spring of 1996 and delivered *The Fallen Man* in time for publication by the end of the year. It immediately landed on the *New York Times* Best Sellers list, rising at one point to number three during its ten-week run. Marilyn Stasio at the *New York Times*, who knew Hillerman and was solidly in his camp, called it "another gripping chapter in the evocative series." *Kirkus* was more circumspect. "The autumnal 12th entry in this distinguished series is less complex and energetic than *Sacred Clowns* (1993), but Hillerman's legion of fans, impatient for a return to the reservation ever since the author's Vietnam novel, *Finding Moon* (1995), will likely find it irresistible." But the very thing that appealed to his huge following was also the dilemma that sequels of all sorts face; namely, the loss of novelty. "The trouble with series like Hillerman's is that with each succeeding book the fresh and unique qualities that made them so popular become ever more stale and tired," Wilda Williams wrote in *Library Journal*. "While Hillerman still evokes the exotic beauty of Navajo land and its traditions, his mystery is not very mysterious or interesting."[15]

In November, Hillerman was one of six prominent Oklahoma-born figures inducted into the state's hall of fame. Two thousand people turned out for the sixty-ninth annual induction ceremonies held in Oklahoma City's Civic Center Music Hall. When it was Hillerman's turn to come to the stage, his friend the historian Robert Allen Rutland introduced him. But Hillerman did not appear right away. When he did show, he began by paying tribute to his late parents and brother. "Barney, my older brother, once told me to try to find something you like to do that you can do all your life," Hillerman said, "That's good advice and that's what I've always tried to do." Afterward, when he joined his family,

Hillerman explained his delay in reaching the stage. He had ripped the front of his tuxedo pants when he stood up. The cameraman, noticing his dilemma, taped the pants shut with black tape and it looked to all the world like a cummerbund. "He thought it was hilarious and Mom was a wreck," said Janet.[16]

Back home Hillerman resumed work on a book he was calling *The First Eagle*. He was struggling with his plot, which by his own admission, "was even more convoluted than those I usually impose on readers." Hillerman turned to one of his favorite scary aspects of life in the Southwest: the occasional resurgence of the bubonic plague. Marie, who had been a microbiology major, lent her expertise. The retired Joe Leaphorn, referred to at least ten times as "the legendary lieutenant," is hired to track down a wealthy woman's niece who has gone missing while catching fleas to track the plague. Chee, pursuing a concurrent murder, once again teams with his former boss. The up-and-down soap opera romance between Chee and Janet Pete comes to an end, but Leaphorn's relationship with Louisa Bourebonette grows, even as it brings back bittersweet memories of his late wife, Emma.

One day Hillerman searched the AAA Indian Country Guide map he kept above his desk (as did Leaphorn). He wanted an out-of-the-way place for a climactic scene in *The First Eagle*. Hillerman had a fondness for unusual place-names such as Lower Greasewood, Burnt Water, and Rotten Bananas Butte. "I was looking for something new," he said. He spotted Goldtooth a couple dozen miles southeast of Tuba City. He used his many years of driving around that portion of the Navajo Nation to describe the spot without actually going there. "A lot of readers tell me they like my landscapes better than my stories, so my rule has been accuracy. The violation bothered me," said Hillerman. "So, Marie and I headed for Goldtooth."

Getting there turned out not to be so easy. Hours of driving were made longer by Tony and Marie's inability to resist stopping at intriguing spots and their failure to find the town. At the Tuba City trading post, the Navajo clerk provided vintage Navajo instructions. She told them to retrace their steps to a certain place, then lower the window and watch the edge of the pavement. "In just a mile or so you'll see where people have been turning off the highway and out into the sagebrush," she continued. "That's where you turn off. Then it's about fifteen miles to Goldtooth."[17]

Tony and Marie found the town and it seemed abandoned except for one hogan. Tony walked over to it, hoping to meet its occupant, perhaps Goldtooth's only resident. The place was empty save a dog lying in the shade. "He showed the courtesy so typical of the Diné, rising to his feet to smile at me as I approached," said Hillerman. "But he also did his guard dog duty, and the smile began showing teeth when I got too close to the door." On their way back to the highway, the Hillermans came across the man who lived in the hogan. "'How did my dog treat you?' he asked. "When I reported it had been dutiful but polite, he nodded, smiled, and said, 'A Navajo dog.'"

Hillerman delivered the manuscript in January 1998. "Your new novel is wonderful," wrote Larry Ashmead, now a company vice president and executive editor, in a handwritten note. *The First Eagle* was in stores at summer's end. Reviews were strongly positive. The book, said *Kirkus*, "reminds you, in case you've forgotten, that Hillerman's mysteries are in a class of their own." It became the second Hillerman book to reach the number two spot on the *New York Times* Best Sellers list, right behind Tom Clancy's new novel.[18]

Hillerman returned to the keyboard, but not to write another novel, although more were in the works. Rather, at age seventy-two the author began work on his life story. "Your 'memoir' would be a book I would want to read," Ashmead told Hillerman. "The question is not whether you will write it but when." It was decided that the next contract—worth $5.5 million—would include a memoir along with two more yet-to-be-titled Navajo mysteries. But before Hillerman could start work on the memoir he had another mystery to deliver, the second of two novels for which HarperCollins had already provided a $4 million advance.[19]

Material for his new book fell into Hillerman's lap in May 1998 when he read about a Colorado police officer who was shot to death after pulling over three men in a water truck that had been reported stolen. One of the men fired twenty-nine bullets, killing Officer Dale Claxton before he could undo his seat belt. Three other officers were wounded as they gave chase. Despite roadblocks, the criminals—dressed in camouflage and carrying automatic weapons—disappeared into the barren and uninhabited landscape of the Four Corners region that a century earlier had hidden Butch Cassidy and the Sundance Kid.

One of the men was soon found dead at a campsite. More than five hundred officers from federal, state, and tribal agencies scoured the canyons in vain for the other two suspects. "Searchers have used infrared cameras, night-vision scopes, motion detectors, radios with encrypted transmissions, smoke bombs, armored personnel carriers, four-wheel-drive vehicles, airplanes and helicopters," wrote James Brooke in the *New York Times*. "While today's wanted posters offering a

$327,000 bounty are broadcast on television, the searchers are finding themselves as empty handed as the Pinkertons in territorial days, when posters for the two outlaws and their Hole in the Wall gang were circulated by hand."[20]

Hillerman went out to Bluff, Utah, where Charlie DeLorme lived. DeLorme had guided him down the San Juan River to research *A Thief of Time*. He was surprised to learn what residents had to put up with. The bungled search, led by the FBI, seemed to Hillerman to offer a perfect plot. Instead of a stolen water truck, Hillerman makes a Ute casino the scene of a robbery and shooting. The book's fast-paced story of intrigue, treachery, and surprise revelation brings together the retired Joe Leaphorn, Jim Chee, Cowboy Dashee, Bernadette Manuelito, Captain Largo, Louisa Bourebonette, and Jay Kennedy, a retired FBI agent. In the end, Leaphorn and gang succeed where the FBI fails in their pursuit of the cop-killing robbers.

But Hillerman surprised his readers by ending the life of Hosteen Frank Sam Nakai. Jim Chee's uncle had first appeared in *People of Darkness* when Hillerman introduced his new police officer. The famous shaman had been Chee's teacher in all things from his pursuit of becoming a *hataalii* to reading tracks. Now Hillerman, who had survived cancer, portrays Nakai's last days with the disease, trapped in a white person's hospital.

With Chee by his side, Nakai removes his oxygen mask. "The *bilagáana* do not understand death," he said.

> It is the other end of the circle, not something that should be fought and struggled against. Have you noticed that people die just at the end of night, when the stars are still shining in the west and you can sense the brightness of Dawn Boy on the eastern mountains? That's so the Holy Wind within them can go to bless the new day. I always thought I would die like that. In the summer. At our camp in the Chuskas. With the stars above me.[21]

Chee and Manuelito decide to grant his final wish and bring him home, against the advice of the doctor. Back in his hogan, Nakai movingly provides Chee with his final lesson.

Hunting Badger reached stores in November 1999, one week after the body of the second cop killer was found. "Pretty good timing, wasn't it?" Hillerman asked a reporter. "My editor said, 'How'd you manage that?'" (The skeleton of the third criminal was not found until 2007.) The fastest-selling book of the series, *Hunting Badger* received some of the best reviews a Hillerman book had ever gotten, spending nine weeks on the *New York Times* Best Sellers list.

Hillerman fans were happy. In Tucson, 394 of them put their names on a four-month waiting list for one of the eighty-four copies in the library system. But the book had a visible detractor. In Cortez, Colorado, where the shooting of Officer Claxton had occurred, the police chief let it be known he was unhappy with the unflattering account of the search for the killers. "I'm not even going to read the book," he said.[22]

When *Hunting Badger* was published, Hillerman took a call from Jeff Guinn, a reporter for the *Fort Worth Star-Telegram* who would later become a best-selling author himself. Guinn was writing an article and wanted to know if Hillerman, now seventy-four, was burned out after more than a dozen books based on the same characters. "In a way, every book is harder," Hillerman told Guinn. "You don't want to repeat yourself. I think I'll reach the time when the quality is diminished. I'm concerned about that."[23]

"Readers do pay close attention. I get letters from ones who just read to find errors," he said. Errors have always been the bane of writers. As Hillerman's books grew in popularity, he began increasingly to hear from readers who spotted mistakes. Early on, a biologist complained that Hillerman's mention of a particular bush in *The Blessing Way* was inaccurate. "Creosote bush is an indicator of altitude between 2,500 and 4,000 feet in the general," the scientist wrote. "Most of the reservation is too high." This was a mistake Hillerman had repeated in four succeeding books, but he ceased after receiving the correction.[24]

Another member of the scientific community took issue with Hillerman's placement of the moon. "It is October and the text notes that there is a half-moon," wrote the director of a planetarium. "This would result in the Moon setting about four or five hours after sunset at the latitude involved. Yet the Moon is still up at about 3:00 A.M."[25]

"The best one I've ever had," Hillerman commented with regard to reader complaints, "was when I got a call at 10 P.M. one night. The fellow said, 'I used to have a lot of respect for you until I've just been reading *Dance Hall of the Dead*. Don't you know deer don't have gall bladders?'"[26]

Over the course of eighteen Navajo novels, Hillerman would err no more than most writers but his immense readership included many eagle-eyed fans. Janet Pete worked for the Federal Public Defender's office, not the Department of Justice. "We are proud to have her," said the federal public defender who pointed out the error. Anthropologists don't dig up objects, those are archaeologists, pointed out an anthropology professor who added, "I've never dug a hole in my career." Sometimes Hillerman triggered letters when for literary purposes he made slight geographical adjustments. In *The Dark Wind* he placed Wepo Wash a few miles to the west of its actual location. "I moved it because I liked the name, and I regret it," Hillerman said years later. "I still get letters."[27]

Hillerman began work on his memoir in the spring of 2000, when the lawn outside his study was filled with dandelions, and finished it when his lawn was covered with yellow cottonwood leaves. The pages that came off his computer, recounting his childhood, service in the war, years as a journalist, work at the University of New Mexico, and career as a writer, were charming, evocative, and immensely readable. The manuscript also provided Hillerman, at long last, with a means to unburden himself of his war memories, something about which he had remained tight-lipped since returning to civilian life in 1945. He wrote gripping accounts of the battlefields of Alsace, his encounter with death at the young age of nineteen, and his own near-death experience after stepping on a mine. Getting these memories down on paper was so important to him that he ended up devoting 35 percent of the book to the war.

Ashmead welcomed the book with effusive praise: "You have written a splendid memoir, an affectionate and unvarnished recollection of your life." He was correct; Hillerman's skill as a writer had not faded, though his memory had. "I have an unsatisfactory chronological memory, marked by great year-long gaps and vacancies," he confessed early in the memoir. But the book was filled with errors that should have been fact-checked. He recalled attending a Fats Domino concert prior to shipping out to war in 1944, when the performer's career was years from beginning; misspelled the name of his writing mentor Morris Freedman; misremembered the name of the man whose execution he witnessed; referred to using a Radio Shack computer seven years before it existed; and described writing the wrong book during the summer spent in Mexico. Most of the errors could have easily been caught by a copyeditor, but HarperCollins was not alone in lessening the emphasis on preventing mistakes. Ashmead had been diligent in line editing the book and providing substantial developmental guidance. But when it came to copyediting, the reserve of the publisher's back shop, the publisher failed.[28]

"It's an error-filled project, and I think HarperCollins was really, in a sense, dismissive to him," said Peter Thorpe. This kind of lack of attention was not limited to HarperCollins. Publishers, buffeted by Amazon's destruction of independent bookstores, the coming of e-books, and the emergence of self-publishing, were retreating from their commitment to copyediting.[29]

Nonetheless, *Seldom Disappointed*, the title chosen by Ashmead, struck an emotional chord with readers, although it was not a best seller. The *New York Times* did, however, offer its endorsement. "He belongs to a generation that is about to disappear over the edge of history," wrote reviewer Timothy Foote. "Laced with humor and worldly wisdom, *Seldom Disappointed* is a splendid and disarming remembrance of things past."[30]

CHAPTER 27

◈ The Farewell Quartet ◈

On February 2, 2002, hundreds of people crammed into the high school gymnasium in Jemez Springs, a small mountain town north of Albuquerque. They came from as far away as Seattle, New York City, and Detroit, arriving early in hopes of getting a good seat. Sharing a stage for the first time ever were Tony Hillerman; Rudolfo Anaya, widely considered the father of Chicano literature and the author of *Bless Me, Última*; and N. Scott Momaday, whose novel *House Made of Dawn* had won the Pulitzer Prize. The event had been organized as a fundraiser for the village's tiny library. It confirmed that the state, which had inspired such outsiders as Willa Cather, D. H. Lawrence, and Paul Horgan, had brought another writer into its fold. Oklahoma-born Tony Hillerman had become a New Mexico treasure.

State citizens' affection for the writer would be confirmed two years later when he was selected as the 2004 Notable New Mexican by the Albuquerque Museum Foundation. A portrait by Pulitzer-prize-winning photographer Don Bartletti was commissioned for the museum's permanent collection and a gala dinner was organized in his honor. Hillerman told the press he hoped it would not be a black-tie event. "One thing that makes New Mexico dear to my heart is that we have managed to resist this insidious and obnoxious policy of causing normal, intelligent human beings to dress up like penguins at public events," he said. Instead, the feted author wore a dark suit and tie to the dinner.[1]

Three months after visiting Jemez Springs, Tony, accompanied by Marie and their daughter Anne, traveled to Washington, DC, to receive a lifetime achievement award from the mystery writers' and publishers' organization

Malice Domestic. The award was added to his Grand Master and Edgar Allan Poe awards from the Mystery Writers of America, his Ambassador Award from the Center for the American Indian, and his Silver Spur Award from the Western Writers of America for best novel set in the West.

The author gave no hint of slowing down. He was under contract for two more Navajo mysteries over the next two years, for advances nearing $3 million a book. With nearly twenty million copies of his novels in print, Hillerman was among the nation's best-known mystery writers. "I'm in a position now, I guess I can say this, where lots of people would buy any book I write," he told reporter Jeff Guinn a few years earlier. Approaching his seventy-seventh birthday, Hillerman told an interviewer, "I've had a couple of heart attacks, I've had cancer and got rid of it, I think. I've got arthritis, etc., and I'm getting old, but I still like to write."[2]

On Memorial Day, May 27, 2002, a Tony Hillerman novel was back in stores with *The Wailing Wind*. In the eyes of critics, the author they loved had returned to his winning style. "The 15th Chee/Leaphorn mystery (after 1999's relatively weak *Hunting Badger*) finds MWA Grand Master Hillerman back at the top of his form as his two Navajo peace officers look into both a past and present mystery," reported *Publishers Weekly* in a starred review.[3]

Hillerman gave *The Wailing Wind* an Othello tinge, bringing up Shakespeare's work twice in a plot that centered on a wealthy man whose obsession with a lost mine causes him to unintentionally choose between it and his loving young wife. Sadly, he tells Leaphorn that when he obtained a copy of the play from the library, he learned that Othello "was just about as stupid as me. But with me, I didn't have someone egging me on. I did it to myself. Looking for a treasure when I already had one."[4]

Hillerman provided an engaging plot with rewarding moments of growth in Leaphorn, who was confronting life changes in retirement, and Jim Chee, who was growing interested in a Navajo woman after two failed romances. In fact, the object of his interest, Officer Bernadette Manuelito, dominates so much of the story that, at times, she seems to be the protagonist. Hillerman also brought back his witty "Cowboy" Dashee, who had first appeared in *The Dark Wind*, and Professor Louisa Bourebonette, who arrived in *Coyote Waits*, partially filling the emptiness left by Emma Leaphorn's death. For close readers, there was a wistful tone to *The Wailing Wind*. When Leaphorn makes his first appearance in the book, Hillerman writes, "Joe Leaphorn had been slow to learn how to cope with retirement, but he had learned."[5]

The novel also gave Hillerman a chance to provide a literary thank-you to James Peshlakai, one member of the author's circle of Navajo advisers who over the years had included Alex Etcitty, Austin Sam, and Kenneth Tsosie. "Better than almost anyone I know of his generation, he knows and understands the Navajo religion and its culture," Hillerman told a reporter doing an article on Peshlakai. Born in 1945, the same year Hillerman encountered his first Navajos, Peshlakai was a silversmith, musician, and medicine man. But he was best known for his effort to teach Diné culture to Navajo children and to *bilagáanas* such as Hillerman. "He was able to bridge the cultural gaps with his knowledge," said one who remembered watching Peshlakai teach young children, including herself, the Hoop and Eagle Dances.[6]

Peshlakai lent Hillerman a hand on several occasions. "We'd meet here and there and go out into the country and just talk about little things," Peshlakai recalled. Often, they would discuss plants and where they grew. Other times the topics turned to serious matters of Navajo culture. When Hillerman wanted Jim Chee to show Mary Landon a traditional Navajo wedding, Peshlakai sent a videotape of his daughter's wedding.[7]

With Peshlakai's permission, Hillerman made him a character in *The Wailing Wind* and used his namesake to poke fun at the FBI, a favorite target of Hillerman's scorn that he once referred to as the "Federal Bureau of Ineptitude." In the scene, Chee is with FBI agent Jerry Osborne, who is trying to extract information about a shooting from Peshlakai, who seems not to understand English. "Chee glanced at Peshlakai, who had looked faintly amused at Osborne's description," wrote Hillerman. "To Mr. Peshlakai Chee nodded again, and said in Navajo: 'He doesn't know you understand English.' Peshlakai erased the beginnings of a smile, looked very somber, and said in Navajo: 'It is true.'"[8]

Coming on the tails of *Seldom Disappointed*, along with a big marketing budget, *The Wailing Wind* should have "a healthy run on the bestseller lists," predicted *Publishers Weekly*. Within two weeks, the book landed on the *New York Times* Best Sellers list, coming in at number six on May 26. By July 7, it fell off the list. The same fate awaited the audio version, read by George Guidall. It started at number eleven, right above three Harry Potter Books, but did not sustain high sales in the coming weeks.[9]

With the advent and exponential growth of audio books, George Guidall recordings were how many fans *read* Tony Hillerman's books. The actor's honeyed delivery, his distinctive voicing of Leaphorn, Chee, and other characters, and his authentic pronunciation of Navajo words and place-names brought a new dimension to Hillerman's work. In fact, it wasn't until the two men met at a Michigan event that Hillerman came to understand what Guidall was doing with his work. When Hillerman heard a Guidall recording, he realized the actor was performing, not merely reading his work as he himself had done for Harper Audio. Hillerman was pleased but surprised. "He hadn't thought that what he wrote sounded like that," Guidall said.[10]

Guidall had begun narrating Hillerman books in 1990 with the author's first book, *The Blessing Way*. A Broadway actor, Guidall started recording books in his spare time in the 1980s. "Then my agent called me and said there's this company called Recorded Books and they are auditioning for a series by this western writer Tony Hillerman, whoever he is," he recalled. "That was the beginning of an amazing relationship with Recorded Books. I owe my career to those books." Guidall went on to record thousands of books and become the single most prolific and popular voice of audio books.

An unsolicited letter from Maryanne Noonan, a retired Los Angeles–area US Customs Service official, gave Hillerman the germ of an idea for his next book. Noonan told the author there was a unit of Native Americans called the Shadow Wolves operating along the border, looking for undocumented migrants and drug smugglers. The agents, some of them Navajos, used the tracking skills they acquired growing up to look for telltale markers such as bent twigs, snagged cloth fibers, or faint footprints to gauge whether the walker was carrying extra weight. "I'd heard about it, but I didn't realize how they were doing it," said Hillerman. Noonan suggested the job might be right for Bernadette Manuelito. Hillerman seized on the idea to force Jim Chee to act on his budding romance with the female officer.

The idea for the title and main object of the conspiracy came to Hillerman from an acquaintance in the US Department of the Treasury who told him government officials were worried about abandoned pipelines crossing the southern border, but no one had followed up on the concern. Lunch with Marie while in Washington, DC, cured Hillerman's traditional first chapter problem. They dined in a tiny restaurant near Union Station favored by the power elite on the Senate side of the Capitol. "You see people sitting there having these heavy conversations—as people do in Washington a lot—and I thought, 'I'm going to remember that and use it.'" He did, setting the opening of the book in Bistro Bis, and adding another biographical touch by referring to one of the men eating as a "doer of undignified deeds," the title he had given himself in his memoir to describe his work for University of New Mexico president Popejoy years earlier.[11]

The final touch to the novel came from Carolyn Marino, who had taken over editing Hillerman's books as Ashmead prepared for retirement. She recommended the book have an epilogue because readers would wonder what happened to several of the characters. "So, I change the voice to a detached voice in the epilogue," said Hillerman. The five-page wrap-up, which began with "And so it was," ended with a reward for Manuelito and Chee's patient fans. "I had fun writing it."[12]

While Hillerman had relented to the editorial team's previous insistence that he change the title of his manuscript "The Golden Calf" to *The Wailing Wind*, for this book he vetoed a similar request. "He stood his ground with *The Sinister Pig*, despite the reservations of the marketing folks about that title," said Marino.

Six months later, on a November Sunday evening, television viewers saw something they had never before seen before on PBS's long-running *Mystery!* series. Since its inception in 1980, the program, produced by WGBH in Boston, had shown only British-produced mysteries. On this night, however, small English villages gave way to the landscape of the Southwest, tea in cluttered parlors became Nescafé in hogans, and in place of detectives with British accents were a pair of Navajo cops. After fifteen years of travail, Robert Redford's screen incarnation of Tony Hillerman's work had finally become a reality. "I had such a struggle in the late '80s and through the '90s, and everybody said give up the ghost," said Redford. "I went to PBS as a last stance." More than twelve million Americans watched "Skinwalkers," making it the highest rated show on PBS that year. "PBS said the next morning—as soon as the ratings started to come in—*More*, which is the one word you want to hear," said Rebecca Easton, who served as executive producer along with Redford.[13]

Selecting Chris Eyre (Cheyenne-Arapaho) as director and actors Wes Studi (Cherokee) and Adam Beach (Saulteaux) to play the parts of Leaphorn and Chee buried the failure to cast Native Americans in *The Dark Wind* twelve years earlier. Studi, who grew up in Oklahoma 150 miles from Hillerman's birthplace, had been a fan of Hillerman mysteries since reading *Skinwalkers* in the late 1980s. "But I had this gnawing fear in the back of my mind that pretty soon some Lone Ranger type was going to show up and show them how to solve the mystery," Studi said. "But to Tony Hillerman's credit, that never happened."[14]

The script by Robert's son Jamie Redford, had been revised several times since his meeting with Hillerman over breakfast in Albuquerque six years earlier. It cut out much of the original story in the *Skinwalkers* novel to make the plot fit in a ninety-seven-minute film. But Jamie had retained Emma Leaphorn's battle with cancer, which other writers might have eliminated. Having been saved from death by an organ transplant, he was inspired by Emma's acceptance of her fate. "The idea you can come to harmony even if you're dying was really compelling to me personally," he said when discussing the film with Hillerman.[15]

Hillerman had not read the script. "If I were directing a movie," he said, "I would have an absolute prohibition that would keep an author like me from getting anywhere near where they were making the movie." But Hillerman was happy. After three decades of unsuccessful movie deals and one movie that had been relegated to overseas theaters, he had a well-done film version of his work.[16]

In the same month as *Skinwalkers* aired on PBS, *The Sinister Pig* was published. *New York Times* reviewer Marilyn Stasio, a reliable fan, said the book offered "an extraordinary display of sheer plotting craftsmanship." *Kirkus* complained it was "Hillerman Lite." Critic Clay Evans had his reservations. "Don't get me wrong," he wrote. "Even Hillerman's weakest is a joy to read. But this time, the Mystery Writers of American Grand Master seems to be going through the motions just a bit, not unlike some other writers in their twilight years." Despite its somewhat mixed critical reception, *The Sinister Pig* reached the number four position on the *New York Times* Best Sellers list. Yet it did not have lasting sales power in a summer when Dan Brown's *The Da Vinci Code* and thrillers by James Patterson, Clive Cussler, and John Grisham ruled.[17]

Hillerman, used to being buffeted by critics, moved on to his next book. At seventy-eight he had to wonder if he might be falling into a trap he himself had identified a decade earlier. "Now, I hate it when somebody with a big reputation writes a good book, then a bad one, then more books of varying quality. I dread the thought of writing a bad one. That would betray all the good folks who've bought my previous books and given me the life I've always wanted to lead."[18]

Hillerman's contract dictated he have a new book ready in January, but World War II was on his mind. He had returned home from Las Vegas, Nevada, where he attended a reunion of the 103rd Infantry Division. Sixty years after the war, the number of attendees was dwindling at each successive gathering. In the novel Hillerman was writing, retired lawman Joe Leaphorn visits his old friend Shorty McGinnis to ask about a missing diamond. "Too many old friends are dying. I didn't really think I could learn anything about that diamond out here. I just wanted to see if I could bring back some old memories about when I was really a policeman. Maybe it would help me get into harmony with living with so many of my friends gone."[19]

In Hillerman's case, memories of being a soldier were also coming to the fore because he had been recruited to work on what he considered a remarkable project. A collection of World War II photographs had been found in an Ohio attic, and Kent State University Press was planning on publishing them. The photographs were gripping and uncensored, unlike many photographs of the European battlefields. Joanna Hildebrand Craig, associate director and acquiring editor at the press, lined up a military historian to write captions and any needed text. But she wanted a well-known writer to pen a foreword for the book. Visiting her father, William Hildebrand, who was a Hillerman fan, she spotted a copy of *Seldom Disappointed*. "My dad really, really liked that book and he had it sitting on a counter," Craig said. "I picked it up and I read it and it was his tone. That's the foreword tone I would like."[20]

Eager to pursue Craig's plan, the press's director Will Underwood reached Hillerman through Luther Wilson, director of the University of New Mexico Press and a good friend of Hillerman's. At first, Hillerman was reluctant to accept the project. "When I said I was too busy with a manuscript for HarperCollins to do the job he sent me a sample of the photographs, guessing that if I saw them, I couldn't refuse the book," said Hillerman. "He was right."[21]

The historian who had agreed to provide the text for the book fell ill. What might be a disaster to another editor became an opportunity for Craig. She asked Hillerman if he would be willing to expand his short foreword into a substantially larger text that could be used throughout the photographic book. "Put the reader in the foxhole, on the rubble-strewn street, at the hedgerow and let them smell the cigarette smoke, body odor, and fear," Craig told Hillerman. The photographs would tell the story but a Hillerman text would provide meaning. He did not say no.[22]

"To get to the bottom line," Hillerman told Craig, "I have very little time with the manuscript of my next book due in New York 'this autumn' and only about a third written." Nevertheless, within a week the affable young editor had talked him into it. The press sent him a contract providing him with no advance and 6 percent of the net income, about a quarter of the royalties he would normally earn. The author, who now received $3 million advances, put his signature on the contract. Soon Hillerman and Craig were holding lengthy telephone conversations. "My original feeling that I'd enjoy working with you has now been confirmed," Hillerman told Craig after a few calls. But working by phone grew difficult. "Wish we could do this at a table with the pics spread out before us," he wrote to Craig.[23]

Craig got the hint, booked a flight to Albuquerque, and secured a motel room near the Hillerman home. Each morning she arrived at the house at 8:30 and had a bran muffin and coffee with Marie and Tony in the kitchen. Then the editor and author retreated to his office and went to work. Hillerman sat at his desk and Craig on the floor with a batch of photographs strewn in front of her. As she handed him a photograph, Hillerman would lean back in his desk chair and talk. "I would take notes," Craig said. "He did no writing. He would just talk and I'd take prolific notes on the back of photocopies of the photographs." He connected deeply with the images, particularly ones that showed a chaplain saying mass. "It was those human moments that really caught his attention, then he would tell stories about that."

At the end of one afternoon, the Hillermans took Craig to JB's, an old family-style restaurant on Fourth Street, where everyone knew Tony and Marie. They went during the time when the restaurant offered a reduced-price early-bird dinner, often with a coupon Marie had clipped from the newspaper. Frugality was ingrained in both the Hillermans. Tony insisted Kent State University Press pay for return postage.

Craig returned to Ohio and assembled a text out of Hillerman's remembrances using her notes. The two settled on the title for the book: *Kilroy Was There*, after the sketch of a man with a large nose looking over a wall with the caption "Kilroy was here" drawn by servicemen all over Europe. "This was important to

him," said Craig. "Not just on a personal level; he would talk about Kilroy as the infantryman and that emphasis on the infantrymen was very important to him."[24]

Fifty-eight years after Hillerman had spent nights in freezing, wet foxholes, fired mortars that killed unseen enemies, then was seriously wounded, working on *Kilroy Was There* provided an almost celebratory, maybe cathartic, moment. "We WWII Kilroys took home with us the sure knowledge that we could justly call our war 'the last good war,'" said Hillerman on the closing page of the book. "It was a war that had to be won. And the Kilroys won it."[25]

After the success of Robert Redford's first Hillerman film, which had been shot in southern Arizona, the state of New Mexico provided tax breaks and subsidies that lured the film company to the Land of Enchantment. Aside from the financial benefit, the location worked better. In Arizona the cameramen had to work hard to keep saguaro cactuses and palm trees out of their viewfinders.

Both *Coyote Waits* and *A Thief of Time* were filmed in a period of a few months in early 2003.

Hillerman broke his rule of remaining uninvolved. After reading the script for *A Thief of Time*, this time written by Alice Arlen, he offered suggestions. Most were minor but his biggest complaint was the screenplay's portrayal of anthropologist Maxie Davis. In the book, when Leaphorn first spies Davis in the distance he notices how striking she is: "It was not just the beauty of youth and health, it was something unique and remarkable. Leaphorn had seen such beauty in Emma, nineteen then, and walking across the campus at Arizona State University." In the script, Hillerman felt Davis came across as "a sort of sex-mad vamp" suitable for the Fox network or viewers of the Jerry Springer shows. "I believe many of your PBS viewers see women as much more than sex objects and would not find a serious scholar of anthropology creditable in the role of vamp," he wrote to producer Rebecca Easton. "It demeans women, and successful women in particular." The final version mostly retained the portrayal to which Hillerman objected. As he had said earlier when declining to read the *Skinwalkers* script, "It's not my art."[26]

The first of the two new Hillerman films, *Coyote Waits*, aired in November 2003 on PBS. Critics complained of a slow beginning and weak acting among the supporting cast. Yet its imagery and break from tradition were hailed. "The best element of both movies," said television columnist Vince Horiuchi, "is their portrayal of normal Navajo life. They give detail and a sense of place on the reservation that hasn't been seen in movies."[27]

In the end, however, the Hillerman series did not catch on with viewers. In contrast to the thirty-three-episode *Inspector Morse* series or the seventy-episode *Poirot* series, PBS aired only three Joe Leaphorn–Jim Chee films. Jamie Redford, who wrote the script for the first one, may have identified the problem. "Truth is, Mr. Hillerman, bringing what makes your work so special to the screen is, in some ways, futile," he told him. "It requires the abandonment of your descriptive language—a language as beautiful, spare and focused as the landscape it describes."[28]

New Mexico governor Bill Richardson, newly elected in 2002, saw Redford's films as a way to promote moviemaking in the state. He hosted a gala reception on November 6, 2003, at the Governor's Mansion in Santa Fe. Robert Redford did not attend but Jane Fonda, who had recently purchased a 2,300-acre ranch near Santa Fe, accepted an invitation. She had remained friends with Redford since 1967 when they co-starred in *Barefoot in the Park* and was a supporter of the governor's national political ambitions. Her star power lit up the room, and when a PBS photographer approached Hillerman, she draped her arm over the guest of honor's shoulders and clung to him while he looked sheepishly at the lens. Most of the time, however, Hillerman sat quietly by the fireplace. "He was very gracious when people came up to him," recalled Richardson. "I could sense he was not in the mood of mingling."[29]

For the next two years Hillerman worked at fulfilling his contract with Harper-Collins for two more books, for which they were providing a $6 million advance. It was not the money that kept Hillerman at the computer though. "My dad loved writing, loved telling stories. It was who he was," said Anne Hillerman. "He had no reason to give it up." However, becoming more infirm, particularly due to growing breathing difficulties, Hillerman increasingly traveled less, accepted fewer speaking engagements, and cut back on book signings. His world was contracting to his three passions: Marie, the weekly poker games, and fishing, which became harder with his growing loss of balance. "I claim to be a fisherman—a trout fisherman—but I'm not very good at it," he told *Publishers Weekly* that spring. "So, if I'm not writing, I don't know what to do with myself."[30]

After the governor's gala Hillerman resumed work on the first of the two mysteries promised to HarperCollins. He told Joanna Craig, who was still working with him to get *Kilroy Was There* ready for publication, "The novel is HARD, this one—Kilroy's war—is fun." Hillerman found a way to add some amusement to his work on the novel, which he titled *The Skeleton Man*. In January, Hillerman sent an e-mail to Craig: "Want to ask you what you think of me renaming a key character in *The Skeleton Man*, which is about eighty percent finished now, from Wanda Shaw to Joanna Craig. . . . She is an embittered woman whose dad died in that historic 1956 collision of two airlines over Grand Canyon, killing 172 folks and setting the record then for air crash deaths. (Her dad is fictional not the crash) and Shaw is determined to get even with the sleazy lawyer who cheated her now-deceased Mom out of a huge inheritance."[31]

Flattered, Craig consented and Hillerman included playful updates as the two finished work on *Kilroy Was There*. "I must report that your fictional version is about to be washed away in a flash flood sweeping down one of those hundreds of canyons which drain the mesas into the Grand Canyon," he wrote two weeks later. "I hope I can save her today." Later, he informed her of his success in getting her fictional persona cleared of attempted murder. In February Hillerman prepared to make the final corrections on the edited manuscript. "Your last chance to decide you don't want to be a vengeful fictional woman," Hillerman warned Craig.[32]

The camaraderie between Hillerman and his young editor also led to a confession about his work. In public Hillerman always spoke of the joy of writing. But when Craig complained about the final push to get their joint book completed, Hillerman shared his experience with the weariness attendant on book writing. "I never started work on a book yet that I wasn't sick and tired of before it was finished," he told her. "I usually start getting over it in about three years, having by then gotten over the pain of bum reveiws (reviews?)"[33]

In December *The Skeleton Man*, which Hillerman called "Joanna Craig's Grand Canyon adventure," was published. In it, a diamond that might be linked to a briefcase full of gems brings Leaphorn, Chee, and Manuelito together to aid Cowboy Dashee's cousin, who is wrongfully locked up in jail. The plot on the whole pleased reviewers, though they and readers spotted a considerable number of loose ends. One of his most loyal admirers was saddened by Hillerman's insistence on continuing to write books, comparing him to a boxer past his prime. Mick McAllister, who held a PhD in eighteenth-century English fiction and taught composition to North Dakota Indian students, had maintained a blog for years, chronicling and reviewing every Hillerman mystery. "The familiar elements of the Hillerman recipe are all here, but the result is about as interesting as an intact dead squirrel," he wrote. *The Skeleton Man* appeared briefly on the *New York Times* Best Sellers list over Christmastime.[34]

Unlike for the launches of his previous books, Hillerman undertook no book tour and did few interviews because of his weakened health, worse this winter, plus the need to work on his next novel. There would be no drives to the Navajo Nation for this book. Instead, Hillerman depended on the landscape of his mind to concoct his story of a valuable and historically important Navajo rug and the murder of a longtime friend connected to an old case Leaphorn had worked four decades earlier. Hillerman told the story by means of many flashbacks, a languishing style that slowed the pace in comparison to his previous works. Close to fifty times, Hillerman ruminated on Leaphorn's retirement and his inability to cease investigating cases. "I can't seem to let this thing go," Leaphorn tells a Flagstaff police sergeant, Kelly Garcia, who wants to know why he persists.[35]

"Somebody told me you were going to retire," Garcia continues. "I said, no way. Old Leaphorn ain't the kind of man you'll see out there chasing those golf balls around the grass. Just couldn't quite imagine that." The answer mirrors one Hillerman gave a reporter almost fifteen years earlier. "Writing, whether news stories or, later, books, is the thing I do naturally. That's my work and hobby," he told Jeff Guinn. "I can't imagine playing golf."[36]

And so Hillerman, like Leaphorn, carried on. He told Peter Thorpe, "I will be eighty in May, just surviving from a long bout with influenza (yes, I did take the flu shot) and am feeling about ninety today, but am still writing."[37]

CHAPTER 28

◈ The Blue Flint Girl ◈

On January 8, 2008, under gray skies rare for New Mexico, Johnny D. Boggs drove his 2006 Ford Mustang a little more than an hour down from his home in Eldorado, New Mexico, to Tony Hillerman's house. The prolific writer of Westerns had arranged to interview Hillerman, who had been selected for that year's Owen Wister Award, regarded as the highest honor given by the Western Writers of America.[1]

The day before Boggs's visit, the paperback edition of Hillerman's *The Shape Shifter*, number eighteen in his series of Navajo mysteries, made it onto *Publishers Weekly*'s paperback best-seller list at number seven, having sold 332,256 hardback copies since its publication thirteen months earlier. After having dedicated his books variously to his sister, his brother, his brother-in-law, fallen police officers, members of his infantry unit, poker friends, Navajo schools and their students, several Navajos, and Marie, Hillerman had dedicated his last book to his children. Naming them he wrote, "in order of the date they arrived to brighten our lives."

All ten of the Navajo novels he had written since *A Thief of Time* was published in 1988 had made it onto the *New York Times* Best Sellers list. The two fictional Navajo police officers Hillerman had made famous still had fans. In fact, clue number 45 down in an upcoming nationally syndicated crossword puzzle was "Tony Hillerman detective Jim."

Hillerman greeted Boggs dressed in a robe. Boggs put away the camera he had brought. "As soon as I saw him, I knew he wouldn't want those photos taken then," Boggs recalled. "He said maybe we could do it some other time. We never did." Hillerman reported he was working on an essay, planning a new novel, and reading *The Worst Hard Times*, Timothy Egan's book on the dust bowl. It stirred memories. "I remember looking out the kitchen window across a cotton yard in Sacred Heart, Oklahoma, to see if my dad was coming home," Hillerman told Boggs. "The cotton yard was maybe 60 yards wide, and it was noon and the dust was so thick you couldn't see across the cotton yard."[2]

Boggs found Hillerman his usual courteous self, funny and friendly, answering all the questions with typical detours down memory lane. "But his health was obviously failing," Boggs recalled, "he'd struggle sometimes to find the right words, but his memory seemed fine, and he still loved to tell stories."

Hillerman was suffering from interstitial lung disease. The ailment, also known as pulmonary fibrosis, is a scarring of the lungs that stiffens lung tissue and makes breathing effortful. Hillerman may have inherited the disease, as his father had similar symptoms before he died. It could also have been caused by Hillerman's rheumatoid arthritis or by something harmful he breathed. His cardiologist, Dr. Neal Shadoff, believed it began during the time the author spent in the Philippines in 1986 to research *Finding Moon*. No matter the cause, Hillerman was short of breath, made frequent use of an oxygen tank, couldn't tolerate any exertion, and was losing weight. In fact, he weighed 166 pounds, a drop of more than seventy pounds that almost returned him to his weight as a scrawny World War II army inductee. "He was miserable but retained an attitude of gratefulness that the worst day is nothing in comparison to the problems others faced," Shadoff recalled.[3]

In the years since his 1994 heart attack, Hillerman had made frequent use of Shadoff when he needed another kind of medical assistance. He would invite the doctor, who lived in the neighborhood, to come by the house and help him develop plausible medical situations as needed for his books. "He'd sit at the computer, as I was talking, he would just type it in," said Shadoff. Later Hillerman would send Shadoff the finished manuscript. "But few, if any, changes were made," Shadoff said. "He had the ability to create a scenario that would fit the book. He'd type it and that would be the final version."

In turn, Shadoff, who grew up in Massachusetts, found that his patient provided much-needed advice on practicing medicine in the Southwest. "He helped me a lot in understanding the culture of Native Americans, particularly Zuni and Navajo," Shadoff said. Once Shadoff was tending a dying patient from the Jemez Pueblo who did not want a heart transplant. Following advice from Hillerman, Shadoff permitted a Pueblo healer to come into the hospital, place corn pollen around the bed, and perform chants, easing the patient's end. "Tony helped me understand how to help these people," Shadoff said.

If Hillerman's health issues did not already cause him to greet 2008 with thoughts of death, a letter from the *New York Times* certainly did. Written with care and circumspection, the letter from video journalist Erik Olsen asked if Hillerman would consent to a lengthy interview for posthumous use on the newspaper's website. It took almost three weeks for Hillerman to reply. "My excuse," he said, "is being eighty-two years old and dealing with some of those ailments which Shakespeare has his King Lear tell us "all old men fall heir to." Nonetheless Hillerman said he would be happy to participate. "I think it's a good idea to give young folks who want to do difficult things a chance to hear those who managed to do it and let them know how it happened," Hillerman wrote Olsen. But Hillerman grew more infirm and the interview never took place.[4]

In May, Hillerman turned eighty-three. Newspapers listed him along with other celebrities born on May 27: Henry Kissinger and actors Lee Meriwether and Louis Gossett Jr. His books continued to sell steadily. The mass-market paperback of his last book, *The Shape Shifter*, was a best seller, and travelers were picking it up in airports. Hillerman had remained with HarperCollins since it had acquired his first book in 1969 as Harper & Row. That type of loyalty was becoming an anomaly in the world of publishing. More authors were following the path of Tom Wolfe who was leaving Farrar, Straus & Giroux after forty years in search of a $5 million advance.

Hillerman's body of work was so established that reviews of other books often compared them to Hillerman's writing in a manner that presumed a reader's familiarity. Editors and authors constantly solicited him for blurbs. He could never say no, describing himself as "a blurb slut." Even in ill health he offered "Unforgettable characters, twisty plot and strong sense of place" for the book jacket of *Missing Witness*, Gordon Campbell's debut novel.

Hillerman's daughter Anne and Jean Schaumberg had launched an annual writing conference in 2001 and, beginning in 2006, it awarded the Tony Hillerman Prize of $10,000 and a publishing contract for the best first mystery. Hillerman attended the conference in the fall of 2007. "He didn't feel well but did his best," recalled Schaumberg.[5]

Attending any event grew increasingly challenging. Hillerman gave up the First Friday Albuquerque authors' lunches and the Tuesday-night poker games—and more terrifying, he ceased writing. Fifteen years earlier, Hillerman tried to describe how important writing was to him: "There are people who say, 'I would like to write if I had the time.' To me, that's like saying I would breathe if I had the time." Now, however, breathing was hard and writing impossible. It would be up to another writer to make Leaphorn, Chee, and Manuelito pursue criminals again.[6]

His failing health also prevented him from traveling to Scottsdale, Arizona, in June to receive the Owen Wister Award for lifetime achievement as a writer of the American West. That prize would join his two Edgars and two teapot-shaped Agathas in his study. But the most prominent spot remained reserved for the wooden plaque naming him a "Special Friend to the Diné," given to him by the Navajo Nation in 1987. When it came to his writing, Hillerman said, "The thing that is of importance to me is how the Navajo react."[7]

For many years, Navajos in need of gas or food stopped in at the Navajo-owned Mora's Conoco and Grocery Store at the intersection of Routes 264 and 191 in Ganado, a settlement named after Ganado Mucho, an important nineteenth-century Navajo leader. One day, the customers there included a fictitious Navajo Tribal policeman. JoAnn, one of the Mora children, was amazed to read in a Hillerman novel that Joe Leaphorn stopped to gas up in Ganado. She came running to her sisters, exclaiming that the family's gas station was in the book. "After that we all started reading his books," said her sister Jeanna Dowes.[8]

About the same time as JoAnn made her discovery, Della Toadlena, who was born in Canyon del Muerto, a branch of Canyon de Chelly, and grew up around the Black Rock area in northeastern Arizona, was teaching composition at Navajo Community College (now Diné College) in Tsaile, Arizona. The Navajo professor had been astonished when she read her first Hillerman novel a few years earlier. "As a Navajo, I felt no white man could see and record my world. Yet here was a foreigner describing vividly and with near-accuracy the everyday life of my people," she wrote in a 1985 article. She did find mistakes in Hillerman's work and wondered briefly if some might have been made on purpose to protect the confidentiality of rituals, much as a medicine man sometimes distorts a story so as not to give away all that he knows. "My message to Tony Hillerman is: Keep those marvelous books coming because some Navajo children who would not ordinarily be interested in books are reading them."[9]

By 1988, Hillerman's work was widely known on the Navajo Nation. Peter Freese, a German scholar traveling in the Southwest, found "that even in the remotest trading posts, tucked away in almost inaccessible corners of the endless Navajo Reservation, there were shelves with assorted Hillerman pocketbooks."[10]

Schoolteachers on the Navajo Nation were early fans. They took to using Hillerman books in their classrooms. Three Anglo and Navajo teachers at the Pine Hill Middle and High Schools of the Ramah Navajo Community read aloud *Dance Hall of the Dead* as their students followed along in their own copies of the book. The students were enthusiastic, including a Zuni girl. An Anglo English teacher at the Laguna-Acoma High School, which had a small number of Navajo students in addition to students from the two pueblos, used Hillerman's early novels in her classes. "They have worked a few minor miracles in the lives of some previous non-book readers," Vicki Holmsten told Hillerman in 1981. In fact, Hillerman's books helped lessen tensions between the Puebloans and the few Navajo students, who were derogatorily called "mutton eaters." "His books are another way of bridging the gap of what's happening in today's world and the teaching of our culture," Jennie Joe, a Navajo anthropologist and an activist who ran a health clinic during the 1969 occupation of Alcatraz, told the *Los Angeles Times* in 1988.[11]

From his first book on, Hillerman's Navajo fan mail was extensive. Hardly a week went by in the 1980s and 1990s when he didn't receive a letter from a young Navajo. "I was really impressed to read about my people," wrote sixteen-year-old Deljean Carroll. Evelen Sombrero wrote, "I am very glad you have used your knowledge on Navajo culture in this manner." Devin Howard, a teenager who said he was of Zuni, Hopi, and Navajo ancestry, wrote, "When I started reading your books, I was amazed so I started reading more and more."[12]

The resonance of his works for Native American youth had not been on Hillerman's mind in the late 1960s when he worked on early drafts of his first novel, *The Blessing Way*. He had decided to set his story on the Navajo Nation and include a Navajo tribal police officer in hopes that if his plot failed to win readers, the exotic backdrop and unusual detective might. His approach led to an eighteen-book series over four decades, with sales approaching twenty million copies worldwide. "Tony doesn't get credit—being an Indian in 1968, when he was first writing, was not cool, not like it is nowadays," said Craig Johnson, who was inspired in part by Hillerman to write his best-selling Longmire books beginning in 2004.[13]

In the course of writing the sleuthing adventures of Joe Leaphorn, Jim Chee, and Bernadette Manuelito, Hillerman fell in love with Navajo culture. He was drawn in by its spirituality, reverence for nature, aversion to materialism, and belief in the importance of community welfare. In short, Hillerman believed

Navajo spiritual life mirrored a type of Christianity he wished Christians practiced. "When you are around Navajos and Hopis whose lives are very much
affected by a belief in God, a faith, then you can't help but be affected by that and
made a little bit better yourself," he told *St. Anthony Messenger* in 1991. Perhaps
most important, Hillerman saw in the Navajo determination to achieve *hózhó*
the kind of harmony he sought for his own life.[14]

In Hillerman's stories, it is the *bilagáana* and the outside world that bring evil
and disruption to Navajo life. Alcoholism and drug use on an epidemic scale,
abject poverty, illiteracy, and corruption—to name several of the disheartening
challenges endemic to the Navajo Nation—are absent from Hillerman's books.
"Sure, that's there," he said, acknowledging the social ills Navajos combat. "But if
you go out there and you're not careful that is all you see." In his work, Hillerman
said, "you see the kind of Navajos I see, not the kind of Navajos that lots of other
whites see." He viewed himself, as he told National Public Radio, as a kind of
"reverse missionary."[15]

Hillerman felt like the Navajo were his country cousins. "The reason I feel
comfortable with Navajos and am attracted to them is that, in many ways, they
are the same kind of people I am," Hillerman explained in a 1984 interview. Like
him, most Navajos are raised in rural poverty, undereducated, religious, and
friendly people who place a high value on telling stories. "I don't think blood
makes much of a difference," Hillerman told an audience in Key West, Florida,
several years later. "I think the Navajos are very much like I am." A Navajo woman
once challenged him about how he, as a white person, had the authority to write
about her people. "How can you do this?" she asked. "Well, are you arguing that
you guys are somehow genetically different from us—that racism is valid?" he
replied. Being raised poor in rural America, Hillerman saw commonalities
between his life and Navajos' lives. "I feel very much at home with the Navajo,"
he said. "I see my kinfolks, the kinds of people I grew up with."[16]

As a journalist turned fiction writer, Hillerman sought authenticity in telling
his stories. He wanted to get the facts correct to the extent compatible with his
story. He unquestionably succeeded when it came to police matters, although
he expanded the jurisdiction of the Navajo police. Murders were the province
of the FBI. "I'll admit the Navajo police as I present them are romanticized," he
told a Farmington, New Mexico, audience in 1984 before becoming a best-selling
writer. "But I am not in the business of writing exposés about law enforcement

or anything like that. I am in the business of writing entertainments and giving people a look at the Navajo culture."[17]

"The stories are accurate. It fits right in: the traditional cultures, the values," Navajo Police Lieutenant Ben Shirley told *Smithsonian Magazine* in 1989. His view was seconded by Navajo Tribal Police Chief Leonard Butler a decade later. "I appreciate what he has done and the fact that he has given name recognition to the Navajo Nation and the Navajo Police Department through his writing."[18]

Some Navajos became veritable apostles for Hillerman's works. James Peshlakai, the medicine man who had befriended Hillerman, found "the elders told him stories about things their own children never asked about." Peshlakai believed Navajos were pressured to assimilate and become like whites. "And then Tony Hillerman came along and started writing books about Navajos, and then our schools started using his books in literature classes, and the little kids started asking questions," Peshlakai said, "He brought the young people's interest back into their culture. Tony Hillerman woke us up to this."[19]

Navajo students validated the idea that Hillerman revived interest in their culture. For instance, St. Catherine's Indian School pupils were among his enthusiastic readers. "Young people learn a lot from his books," Marci Platero told a writer in 1991. An eighteen-year-old Navajo from Crownpoint who later became a nurse in the Indian Health Service, Platero explained that some parents had been "modernized" and didn't know Navajo ceremonies. "But Hillerman's books show us how to get back to the old way; they show us how to live." Her first cousin, four years younger, shared Platero's reverence for the books. "When you read his books," said Marie Delgarito, "you are proud to be a Navajo."[20]

The Navajos who provided information in the course of Hillerman's research sensed his genuine interest. He was never focused on book sales or fame. Rather his deference when researching and then his writing transcended cultural difference. Kenneth Tsosie, a Navajo from Crownpoint who helped Hillerman, found that reading scenes in the books brought back memories of spending time at trading posts in his youth. "I am amazed at how you write and the sequence of your work seems to fall into place so well," Tsosie told Hillerman. "You must be part Navajo somehow, if not physical, maybe spiritually."[21]

Hillerman extensively popularized the Beauty Way and the Navajo pursuit of *hózhó*. Readers around the world became intrigued with the beliefs and practices he described in his books. This interest cut both ways. To the consternation of Navajos, some Anglo-American women began adopting and transforming the Blessing Way into a new age baby shower. A Vermont family who lost their son,

Branden Scott Peters, when his motorcycle crashed into a truck exemplified a more respectful use of Navajo beliefs. For the open casket service, the parents placed in the casket two photographs of their son, one at age four and one with his Harley motorcycle at thirty. Between the two, they placed a copy of Hillerman's version of the "In the house made of dawn chant" taken from *The Blessing Way*, which ends with these words:

> with beauty all around him, he walks
> with beauty it is finished,
> with beauty it is finished.

"I don't know if I can tell you how much this has meant to his family but I would like to thank you for exposing me to this through your books," Scott's father wrote to Hillerman. "I would like you to know what you have done for a family you've never met."[22]

In the years since Hillerman wrote *The Blessing Way* there had been a sea change in attitudes regarding Native Americans' rights to mediate their own culture. "In the late 1980s, ownership of knowledge and artistic creations traceable to the world's indigenous societies emerged, seemingly out of nowhere, as a major social issue," noted Michael F. Brown, president of the School for Advanced Research in Santa Fe. "Before then, museum curators, archivists, and anthropologists had rarely worried about whether the information they collected and managed should be treated as someone else's property. Today the situation is radically different." Triggered by the Native American Graves Protection and Repatriation Act, museums had begun repatriating items to tribes, school and professional sports teams changed their names and mascots, corporations examined their use of Native American imagery, and fashion designers faced boycotts for using American Indian motifs. "Non-Indians have stolen everything we had—our land, our resources, and now the concept of Indian has become a marketable commodity, they want to steal that from us," said David Bradley, a Chippewa painter and activist.[23]

Luci Tapahonso, the first poet laureate of the Navajo Nation, said there were Navajos who believed Hillerman's books were transgressive. "There are things that he wrote about that are really dangerous, to even just verbalize," she said. "He wrote about things he didn't understand, couldn't have understood because you have to know Navajo to know about some of those rituals and ceremonies."

What he did speaks to the issue of privilege. In particular, Tapahonso cites the time Hillerman went through the wastebasket at KNDN radio to retrieve forms Navajos had completed in order to air announcements. "Even if it was in the trashcan," she said, "it was a personal matter not for the general public."[24]

Increasingly, Native Americans took action to protect their cultural and religious heritage. In 1995, for instance, representatives from nine Apache tribes, whose tribal name adorned helicopters and trucks, met in Albuquerque and signed a document pledging to work together on safeguarding Apache cultural property. "It has implications for historians, for people who might write stories about us," said Carey Vicenti, chief judge of the Jicarilla Apache tribal court. "If someone wants to take Tony Hillerman's place as a non-Indian writing about Apaches, he's going to have to do so with our permission because we claim complete control of our cultural heritage."[25]

Increasingly, Navajos complained about Hillerman's work. "Some people are a little resentful because they think he's getting rich off them," said Kathi Curley, the marketing coordinator for the Navajo Nation tourism office. But she added that in her position she credited an increase in tourism to Hillerman's books.[26]

"He's capitalizing on something that's not his," Tom Arviso told CNN in 2000. The Navajo publisher of the *Navajo Times*, the largest Native American–owned newspaper in the world, Arviso voiced a sentiment heard among his readers. "He's not Native American, he's not Navajo, and he's presenting something that doesn't belong to him. He's presenting something that he has no way he could possibly understand the significance of what it is he's writing about."[27]

"I don't think it's fair because I think I have given them something back," Hillerman replied on the CNN broadcast. "I think I've made a piece of the world, at least, aware of what a wonderful culture they have." As for the idea that only Navajos could write about Navajo culture, Hillerman had no patience with it. "If you want to write about the Amish, do you have to be an Amish? I think not."

The most scathing attack on Hillerman's work came in 1992. Ward Churchill, a professor at the University of Colorado, Boulder, took aim at the portrayal of Native Americans in popular culture in a compact book called *Fantasies of the Master Race*, published by a small publisher in Maine. Churchill, who was later fired for plagiarism and embroiled in a dispute over his claims of Native American descent, charged that Hillerman's books favorably portrayed those Navajos who had accepted white culture and diminished those who had not. "They are instead the very quintessence of modern colonialist fiction in the United States," Churchill wrote. These words became the most frequently cited criticism of Hillerman, followed by a similar attack from Larry Emerson, a Navajo professor: "Tony Hillerman privileged and authorized himself to write about Navajo and in doing so appropriated, re-imagined, and recreated 'Hillerman Navajos' at the expense of Diné realities. Hillerman created a new dominion of knowledge while cashing in at the same time."[28]

Hillerman acknowledged the complaints but understood that they were part of a larger shift regarding issues of racial and cultural identity. He did not go on the defense, believing to the end that the critics who mattered most were the Navajos to whom he had devoted his writing life over four decades. Repeatedly, when he was asked about the prizes and reviews he had received over the years, Hillerman returned to two points. One, he would remind critics that he was the only *bilagáana* honored as a "Special Friend to the Diné." Two, he would recount a conversation he had with a Navajo librarian. The two discussed the works of Leslie Marmon Silko (Laguna Pueblo), who had written *Ceremony*, a novel about a returning World War II veteran, and N. Scott Momaday, who won a Pulitzer Prize for his novel *House Made of Dawn*.[29]

"They are artists," Hillerman told the librarian. "I am a storyteller."

"Yes," replied the librarian. "We read them and their books are beautiful. We say, 'Yes, this is us. This is reality.'"

But, she continued, the works by Marmon and Momaday leave us sad. "We read of Jim Chee and Joe Leaphorn and old man Tso and Margaret Cigaret and the Tsosies and Begays and again we say, 'Yes this us. But now we win.' Like the stories our grandmothers used to tell us, they make us feel good about being Navajo."

Tempted as he might have been, Hillerman never challenged those who believed he profited from the Navajo Nation without sharing his wealth. "I felt this way for a time," said Tom Arviso Jr., publisher of the *Navajo Times*, who had criticized Hillerman on the CNN broadcast. "But I came to realize that he was giving it back in his own way and privately."[30]

Tony and Marie maintained privacy about their philanthropy. "The deal we always make is, it's strictly anonymous. We are believing Christians, and when the Good Lord asks if you want credit here on Earth, or if you want it credited to your account to make up for your sins later on, we choose the latter," Tony said.[31]

The St. Bonaventure Indian Mission and School received donations from the Hillermans totaling $500,000. They also enabled the purchase of water trucks that made daily deliveries of potable water to Navajos without wells. Tony is credited with purchasing a double-wide modular home to serve as a shelter for battered Navajo women and for paying for the lights that illuminate a Navajo high school athletic field. Almost all requests that came from charitable organizations serving the Navajos received a donation.

Their charity was not limited to the Navajo Nation. They paid, for instance, for the construction of two additional infirmary cells at the Christ in the Desert Monastery, and supplied the entire $50,000 the Good Shepherd Manor was trying to raise for repairs to its homeless shelter in Albuquerque. In a short space of time, the Franciscan Friars of Our Lady of Guadalupe Province and Catholic Social Services of New Mexico received $50,000, and the Barrett House homeless shelter received $200,000.

When Father Joel Garner of the Norbertine Santa Maria de la Vid Abbey in Albuquerque was raising funds for a church, he was advised to contact Tony Hillerman. He telephoned the author, knowing little about him. Hillerman declined a visit from the father and insisted he and Marie would come out to see the abbey instead. During their visit, Father Garner reviewed the plans for the church and explained they had raised $300,000 of the needed $500,000. He left for a few minutes to fetch a brochure and a donation envelope. When he returned Tony handed him a check for the entire $200,000 shortfall. He stipulated the donation was to remain secret. "Marie and I have a theory that there're no pockets in shrouds," Hillerman later told the *Denver Post*'s Jack Cox. "Our theory is to give it away as we get it."[32]

It is impossible to ascertain the extent of the Hillermans' philanthropy. Tony's archival papers are littered with fundraising letters on which he scribbled sums. Toward the end of his life he established charitable remainder trusts at the Catholic Foundation in Santa Fe valued in the millions of dollars. It is reasonable to conclude that the Hillermans donated several million dollars from his royalties after his books became bestsellers in the United States and abroad. Cox accepted Tony Hillerman's explanation for making anonymous donations. "But one suspects," he wrote, "there's a deeper reason for Hillerman's low-profile approach to philanthropy—one rooted in respect and admiration for the Navajo culture, including a tradition of never calling attention to oneself."

The Hillermans' eldest son remembered learning of his father's generosity. In the summertime, the Hillermans would pack all six children into the station wagon and make the long drive to Oklahoma. Usually, Tony would leave Marie and the children in Shawnee with her family, and he would double back and visit his mother and brother in Oklahoma City. The Unzners in Shawnee were more welcoming to a gaggle of children than Tony's mother, who had grown dour in her old age. Heading back to Albuquerque on one such trip, Tony pulled over on spotting a 1950s car, loaded like his with a family, on the side of the road with its hood up.[33]

Tony Jr. watched his father exit the car and walk over to the stranger looking at his overheated engine. The two men talked, but Tony Jr. could not hear what they said. "Then my dad reaches into his pocket and pulls out his wallet, takes out a wad of cash and gives it to this guy," recalled Tony Jr. "They shake hands and he leaves." Later on, when he had a turn in the front seat, Tony Jr. turned to his father. "Dad, why did you give that guy money?" he asked. "Because," replied his father, "he needed it worse than I did."

When Hillerman was in his mid-seventies, he discussed his faith and thoughts about death with Anne Simpkinson, who worked for a Christian spiritual website. "If all of a sudden I'm beset with an incurable disease, I'd be distraught at first, disappointed," Hillerman said. "Then it would dawn on me, 'I'm getting a chance to get my act together before I'm called before the great Judge.' I'd rather be run over by a train or something like that where it's quick and painless."[34]

That wish was not to be granted. By late the spring of 2008, Hillerman's breathing became ominously labored and he no longer had the strength to do ordinary tasks like hanging his robe on a hook. "I'm 84 now, feeling 104," he wrote to a fellow World War II veteran in July (actually Hillerman had just turned eighty-three). "But I have another book brewing in my mind." He shared his idea for a nineteenth Navajo mystery with Anne. It would involve the recent discovery of elevated concentrations of mercury in fish in Navajo waterways, which could pose a danger to people and bald eagles.

Father Joel Garner came to the house several times. He found Hillerman retained his spirits though his body was failing him. The two talked as Hillerman reminisced, then Father Garner led him through the Catholic sacrament of Anointing of the Sick, formerly known as Extreme Unction. In what would be their final conversation, Father Garner found his parishioner calm and strong in his faith.[35]

In October, Hillerman's daughter Janet came to see her dad. She and her husband, Rudy Grado, were going on a cruise, their first big vacation in their thirty years of marriage. "It was very hard to say goodbye to him because I knew how tentative his health was, and I knew he was failing," she said. Three days following their departure, Marie went to retrieve the mail while Tony was napping. When she returned to the house, she found her husband was not breathing. Tony was taken to Presbyterian Hospital and placed on a respirator.[36]

As the family gathered, Marie was insistent that Janet not be told so as not to ruin her vacation. For days the other children and Marie kept vigil. Anne brought her father coffee and turned his pillow so that his skin was against the cool side. Janet and Rudy rushed back on disembarking from the cruise ship when they learned what had happened. The entire family was present on Sunday, October 29, at 2:39 P.M., when Anthony Grove Hillerman took his last breath.

The following Friday flags flew at half-mast throughout New Mexico. Hillerman's body was brought to Our Lady of the Annunciation Church, a block from the Texas Street home where he had written his first novel. Looking over the flag-draped coffin and the hundreds of mourners who packed the church, Reverend Bennett Voohies said, "There were no airs, no pretensions. He was just Tony."[37]

At the end of the funeral service, a Native American approached the family and asked if he could perform a song in Navajo. "He sang 'Amazing Grace' his clear deep voice sounding throughout the church," recalled Anne.

T'óó ahayói atí'éł'į	Through many dangers, toils and snares
Bitahdéé' shééhozin	I have already come;
Bijooba'ii éí shilááh neel'á	'Tis grace hath brought me safe thus far
Éí bee baa nídeeshdááł	And grace will lead me home.

That afternoon, Hillerman was buried on the top of a hill overlooking Santa Fe in the National Cemetery with thousands of other veterans.

Of the fictional characters to which Hillerman had given life, it was Navajo Tribal Police Officer Joe Leaphorn who had been his most steadfast companion. "I've lived with Leaphorn now for about half my life," Hillerman told a reporter in 2003. "As he and I both grow older, he picks up my eccentricities, my prejudices." He gave Leaphorn his own love of Mount Taylor, right up to the last book. In *The Shape Shifter* the policeman sees the sunlight reflecting off the snowpack on Mount Taylor. So named, wrote Hillerman, "on *bilagáana* road maps, or Tsoodził to traditional Navajo shaman; it was Joe Leaphorn's favorite view." As it was for Hillerman. From seeing it each morning and evening as he was commuting to and from work at the University of New Mexico to watching it rise from the western horizon as he and Marie headed off on another exploration of Navajoland, Mount Taylor had become a talisman to Tony Hillerman. One of the four mountains marking the boundaries of Diné land, the mountain sat like a sentinel on the southeastern edge of the Navajo Nation. In particular, Hillerman loved to drive up Interstate 40 and turn on to back roads leading to La Mosca Lookout on the north side of the mountain. "I like to come on summer afternoons when the Turquoise Mountain is playing its role as mother of thunderstorms," he said.[38]

Once, years before, he had come to this spot and sat quietly on a log as the mist drifted in, obliterating the forest from view. The rumble of forming thunderstorms reminded him of the struggle between Walking Giant and Monster Slayer in Navajo stories. After decades of talking to Navajos, driving across their land, and writing about them, the Oklahoma-born author felt at home high above the New Mexico landscape. He found himself putting aside thoughts of the Hero Twins and instead recalling some Navajo poetry. "It teaches that to shelter Blue Flint Girl on this peak, First Man built a house made of morning mist, a house made of dawn. . . . On a day like that it was easy to believe that the holy girl still lives in such a house, just out of sight behind the firs, keeping her eternal promise to preserve harmony."

◈ Epilogue ◈

Marie Elizabeth Hillerman outlived Tony by nearly a decade, dying on February 12, 2015, at age eighty-seven. During the sixty years of their marriage, Marie had chosen to remain as much as she could in the background of her famous and instantly recognizable husband. But those who knew the couple recognized the important role she had played in Tony's success. She had given up the prospect of a professional career, possibly as a scientist, to accompany her husband to Borger, Texas; Lawton, Oklahoma; Oklahoma City; Santa Fe, New Mexico; and eventually Albuquerque. It had fallen primarily to her to raise their six children and keep the household together. She had unequivocally supported Tony's midlife decision to give up a newspaper career to pursue writing fiction. She had been his first editor when the pages came off the typewriter, and later, the printer. "My mom was such an avid reader that her passionate love for good writing really infused the whole family," Anne Hillerman said. "And people think of my dad as the literary one."[1]

Marie is buried alongside Tony at the Santa Fe National Cemetery. Their grown children—Anne, Janet, Tony Jr., Steve, Monica, and Daniel—were present for the interment, along with a collection of grandchildren and great-grandchildren. In 2017, Steve passed away from cancer.

Several years after her father's death in 2008, Anne assumed her father's mantle and began to write new Joe Leaphorn, Jim Chee, and Bernie Manuelito mysteries. An established journalist and writer of nonfiction, Anne frequently heard the same question when she spoke about her father. "People would say to me, 'Was there another novel in his computer or in a desk drawer?'" The question got her thinking. "I felt as though Chee and Leaphorn were my adopted uncles," she said. In 2013, overcoming her nervousness that fans of her father's work would disapprove, Anne published her first of several sequels. They were an immediate hit, landing as her father's books had, on the *New York Times* Best Sellers list.[2]

Other writers' children have become writers: John Cheever's daughter Susan Cheever; William F. Buckley's son Christopher Buckley; Stephen King's son, who uses the pen name Joe Hill; and Kingsley Amis's son Martin Amis, to name a few examples. Thriller writer Lee Child turned over his Jack Reacher series to his brother. But rare—if not unique—is the offspring who keeps alive the characters created by a deceased parent.

Anne's continuation of her father's literary work has provided her a precious opportunity to connect with him years after his passing. But she feels an acute loss at not being able to get his advice. "When I get to one of those stuck places," Anne said, "it would just be great to call him up and say, 'So, if this was your book, what would you do here?'"[3]

◈ Author's Note ◈

Tony Hillerman: A Life is an independently written biography, not an authorized or a commissioned work. It was written with the consent of Hillerman's literary executor, Anne Hillerman. Under the terms of the permission, Anne Hillerman read the work twice and corrected any factual mistakes, and I and the University of Oklahoma Press agreed to take seriously and in good faith her comments regarding other aspects of the work. In the end, she raised no objections to any portion of this account of her father's life and provided some useful corrections.

This book fulfills my idea dating back at least seven years that Tony Hillerman was overdue for a biography. His significance does not come solely from his writing of spellbinding mysteries and his influence on mystery writing. Rather it was his use of the popular genre to unlock the mysteries of Navajo culture for non–Native Americans. Just as Mary Renault did earlier with Ancient Greece, Hillerman's books introduced millions of readers to the Diné way of life in a respectful and compelling manner that remains a relevant model for cross-cultural communication.

I used many works to produce this biography, but I would like to draw attention to four books in particular that readers may find useful in learning more about Hillerman:

Martin H. Greenberg, ed., *The Tony Hillerman Companion: A Comprehensive Guide to His Life and Work* (New York: HarperCollins, 1994). Assiduously compiled, the book is like a concordance with details on all the fictional characters, an interview with Hillerman, and information on Navajo clans, among other content.

Laurance D. Linford, *Navajo Land: Hideouts, Haunts, and Havens in the Joe Leaphorn and Jim Chee Mysteries*, expanded 3rd ed. (Provo: University of Utah Press, 2011). This remarkable work is a must for anyone who is a Hillerman fan and doubly valuable should one visit the Navajo Nation.

Tony Hillerman and Ernie Bulow, *Talking Mysteries: A Conversation with Tony Hillerman* (Albuquerque: University of New Mexico Press, 2004). This charming, slim paperback was compiled by Ernie Bulow, a friend of Hillerman's and longtime Gallup resident.

John M. Reilly, *Tony Hillerman: A Critical Companion* (Westport, CT: Greenwood Press, 1996). This book offers thirteen essays on eleven titles in Hillerman's Navajo series and on his two stand-alone novels.

I would also invite readers to visit *e-Hillerman: Tony Hillerman Portal*. It is an interactive guide to his life and work and includes a complete bibliography of his books, access to many of his articles, photographs, and interesting material related to Hillerman's research. Sponsored by UNM University Libraries it may be found here: https://ehillerman.unm.eduhttps://ehillerman.unm.edu.

I am frequently asked which of Hillerman's eighteen Navajo novels is the best starting point for someone who has not read his work. My choice is *The Dance Hall of the Dead*, his third novel but the second in the series. The consensus as to Hillerman's best book of the series is undoubtedly *A Thief of Time*. But Hillerman's favorite book was not part of the work for which he became famous. Rather, it was the standalone novel *Finding Moon*. Readers should not overlook his short nonfiction tale "The Great Taos Bank Robbery." It is a delightful laugh-aloud story that Mark Twain would have been proud to have written.

Finally, careful readers will note that I worked hard not to include any plot spoilers in my discussions of Hillerman's novels. I decided that readers of this biography who have not enjoyed all the Hillerman mysteries would be grateful. Fans who forgot "who done it" will have another reason to take a Hillerman book down from the shelf.

◈ Acknowledgments ◈

From Navajos who welcomed me to a Blessing Way ceremony to Oklahoma monks with whom I broke bread, from archivists who opened their collections to me to river guides who showed me the splendor of the San Juan River, an inordinate number of people contributed to the making of this book. In providing thanks here, I know I will miss out on listing someone. I apologize and hope that any such oversight is not taken as a lack of appreciation.

Members of the Tony and Marie Hillerman family contributed greatly to his book. Janet Grado, Tony Hillerman Jr., Monica Atwell, and Daniel Hillerman sat down for interviews with me and graciously responded to my endless email questions. I interviewed Anne Hillerman, executor of Hillerman's estate, several times. She helped me obtain permission to view academic transcripts and read the manuscript. Sadly, I was unable to interview Stephen Hillerman, who passed away in 2017. Tony Hillerman's sister, Margaret Mary Chambers, granted several in-person and telephone interviews prior to her death in 2019. Marie Hillerman's sister, Teresa Sifford, provided immensely helpful information. Karl Hillerman, son of Tony's brother Barney Hillerman, also contributed to my research and provided some photographs.

On my travels to research this book, I obtained assistance from many people. I thank:

In Sacred Heart, Oklahoma: Father Adrian, Christian, and Ken Landry, at the Pottawatomie County Museum.
In Konawa, Oklahoma: Sean Walker, Sandra Johnson, and Don Gallagher.

In Gallup, New Mexico: Bob Rosebrough and Ernie Bulow.

In Borger, Texas: Janis Wiseman; Joetta Tadlock; Deputy Sheriff Ron Cromer; Constable Kendell McWilliams; Jack and Sharon Worsham; Debbie Cauthon, Ruth DeRossa, Erica Mann, Ashley Keeney, and Maylee Freeman at the Hutchinson County Library; Judge Leslie Ford, justice of the peace; Clay Renick, director, and Addison Killough, registrar, at the Hutchinson County Historical Museum; and Rick Nunez, general manager, *Borger News Herald*.

In Lawton, Oklahoma: Joanne Linville at Blessed Sacrament Church; Deborah Anna Baroff, senior curator at the Museum of the Great Plains; and Jacob Brower of *The Lawton Constitution*.

In Oklahoma City: AP Capitol Correspondent Sean Murphy; Michael McNutt, then communications director in the governor's office; and Mallory Covington, Manuscripts Department supervisor, Oklahoma Historical Society.

In Norman, Oklahoma, at the University of Oklahoma: Ed Kelley, dean of Gaylord College of Journalism and Mass Communication, and Jacquelyn Slater Reese, librarian, Western History Collections.

In Stillwater, Oklahoma: Sara Mayo, in the Office of the Registrar at Oklahoma State University.

In Shawnee, Oklahoma: Leon Bruno and Ruby Withrow.

In Bluff, Utah: Susan and Charlie DeLorme, who had rafted the San Juan River with Hillerman and with whom my wife and I stayed, and our river guides Kevin Christensen and Louis Williams.

On the Navajo Nation: Navajo Tribal Police Lieutenant Ophelia Begay, Navajo Nation Historic Preservation Department Director Richard M. Begay, David Bha, Jeanna and Jim Dowes, Daniel Draper, Justin Kaye, Henry Kinlicheene Jr. and Violet Kinlicheene, Joanna Mora, and Austin Sam.

In Zuni: Chris Carroll, Tom Kennedy, and Kenny Bowekaty.

In Albuquerque: Matt Alexander of Picture Perfect provided assistance with the older photographs used in this book.

Donn G. Duncan, MD, and Raphiel Benjamin, MD, helped me decipher Hillerman's health records; and Dr. Mahlon Soloway reviewed my description of how Hillerman's war injury to his eyes was treated.

The following people went out of their way to assist me in research for this book: Fred Bales; Linda Lyn Carfagno; Steve Carr; Frank Clifford; Sally Denton; Dennis Drabelle; Peter Freese; Tamar Ginossar; Paul Grasmehr, at the Pritzker Military Museum; Seth Givens; Christopher Halter, director, and the staff of the St. Bonaventure Indian Mission and School in Thoreau, New Mexico; Wendy Hopkins, Sundance Institute; Jennie Joe; Carol Joiner; Jerry Kammer; Carol Kreis; Robert K. Landers; Norma Libman; Robin McKinney Martin, publisher, *Santa Fe New Mexican*; Mick McAllister, whose remarkable reviews of Hillerman's works provided keen insights; Robert McPherson; Barb Messer, interlibrary loan librarian, Santa Fe Public Library; Sharon Niederman; Jeff Nilsson, archivist, *Saturday Evening Post*; Barbara J. Niss, director of the Arthur H. Aufses Jr., MD, Archives and Mount Sinai Records Management Program; Erik Olsen; Alison Owings; Barbara Peters of the Poisoned Pen Bookstore; Jennifer Reibenspies, Cushing Memorial Library and Archives, Texas A&M University; Sherry Robinson; Jean Schaumberg; Kathryn Seidel, manager, Special Collections Library, Albuquerque and Bernalillo County Public Libraries; Thomas Shakeshaft; Kenneth M. Swope, Department of History, University of Southern Mississippi; Carol and Don Tallman; Andrick and Lynette Tsabetsaye and their daughter Nicole; Marie-Line Weiss, mayor of Eschbach; and Carla Wright.

Beyond the Hillerman family, the following individuals granted me interviews: Fred Bales, Gabe Barillas, Joanna Craig, Paul B. Davis, Eamon Dolan, Mary Dudley, Tim Duggan, Vicki Holmsten, Father Joel Garner, Hoytt Gimlin, Lisa Marie Griffith (executive director of the Mercy Education System of the Americas) and other members of the Sisters of Mercy, Craig Johnson, George Johnson, Neal Isaacs, Bonni Lee, Michael McGarrity, Carolyn Marino, Robin McKinney Martin, Joe McKinney, Kathleen Murphy, Stephen Northup, Carmella Padilla, John Perovich, Dick Pfaff, Sarah Pillsbury, the late Jamie Redford, Robert Redford, Governor Bill Richardson, Sherry Robinson, Nancy Rutland, Karl Schwerin, Dr. Neal Shadoff, Luci Tapahonso, Peter Thorpe, Hugh Van Dusen, Susan Walton, and Alan Warhaftig.

Thanks to Kate Morris, Laura Hardin, Dave McGrath, and especially Ariel Rae Lilly, of Creative Production in New York City, for assistance in researching the style of Marie Unzner's wedding dress.

Jim Belshaw deserves special mention here. A longtime friend of Hillerman's, he not only granted me extensive interviews but never lost his enthusiasm in responding to my questions. Breakfast with Jim was one of the best parts of working on this book. At times I almost felt like Hillerman was a third member of our meals at Hannah and Nate's in Corrales.

New Mexico writers who lent a hand include the late Rudolfo Anaya, Johnny D. Boggs, Diana Gabaldon, the late Max Evans, George R. R. Martin, David Morrell, and John Nichols.

The custodians of the Tony Hillerman Papers contributed greatly to my work. I owe thanks to Director Tomas Jaehn, University Archivist Portia Vescio, Pictorial Archivist Cindy Abel Morris, and the entire staff of the Center for Southwest Research. In particular, Archivist Christopher Geherin was a constant help and provided terrific guidance to the collection.

As with most of my previous biographies, my membership in E/T&LDS was a sustaining element during my work on the book. In the midst of the pandemic I found I could always count on support from its director J. Revell Carr.

Linda DiPaolo Love worked assiduously on proofing various versions of the manuscript, hunting typos, incorrect usage, and my bad attachment to words better suited for the Dickensian period. Lucy Moore, author of the marvelous *Into the Canyon: Seven Years in Navajo Country*, saved me from many embarrassing mistakes and greatly improved the work with her close reading.

David O. Stewart, a distinguished lawyer, novelist, and historian, read a great portion of this book. As with previous works of mine, Stewart's suggestions were immensely helpful.

The Women of the Gym Lofts—the nickname for a long-existing biweekly writers' group based in Albuquerque, with members in Santa Fe, Detroit, and Dublin—read almost the entire manuscript as the pages came off my printer. The group's reading and the ensuing lengthy discussions strengthened the book. The members at the time of this work's composition were Ellen Dworsky (founder), Catherine Dowling, Lisa Knighton, Keena Neal, Debra Pappler, Alan Parker, Jennifer Ruden, and Neal Singer.

David Dunaway, who knew Hillerman and has done important work on preserving the voices of significant southwestern writers, read the manuscript and contributed many useful suggestions. The same is true for Michael Snyder and Richard Etulain, whose diligent review of the manuscript improved the work.

I am grateful that Charles E. "Chuck" Rankin, retired editor-in-chief at the University of Oklahoma Press, acquired the book. He shared my enthusiasm about the need for a Hillerman biography. A writer could not ask for a better team than the one who worked on the book when I returned with the completed manuscript. I am in debt to Alessandra Jacobi-Tamulevich, senior acquisition editor, Steven Baker, managing editor, Anna María Rodríguez, production coordinator, and Dale Bennie, director. A special thanks is also owed to Kirsteen E. Anderson for the excellent copyediting. Margaret Moore Booker produced a superb index that readers will appreciate. When I come to the end of writing a book, I always feel a sense of gratitude for my agent Alan Nevins. He has unfailingly represented me, even when my ideas seem a bit daft, and has become a good friend.

This book, which could possibly be my last biography, is dedicated to the person to whom I dedicated my first biography. In the forty years we've been together, Patty McGrath Morris has remained a steadfast supporter of my writing ambitions. We had great fun together with this book, especially on our trip down the San Juan River and our journey to Zuni, and her suggestions from two separate readings of the entire manuscript will make readers grateful I married her.

❖ Notes ❖

Abbreviations

AHP   Anne Hillerman Papers, privately held
DDSWR David Dunaway Writing the Southwest research and recordings, 1976–2005, Center for Southwest Research, Zimmerman Library, University of New Mexico
NARA   National Archives and Records Administration
PTP   Peter Thorpe Papers, privately held
RMMP   Robin McKinney Martin Papers, privately held
THP   Tony Hillerman Papers, the Center for Southwest Research, Zimmerman Library, University of New Mexico
THUP   Tony Hillerman Unprocessed Papers, the Center for Southwest Research, Zimmerman Library, University of New Mexico

When citing unpublished documents, I have, when possible, provided box and file numbers. However, in some cases this information may change over time. The numbered callout for each note appears at the point in the text where I begin using the source. So quotations in subsequent paragraphs stem from the same source unless otherwise noted.

Some readers may notice that some news accounts cited here come from newspapers, often smaller ones, geographically far from the event being described. The reason is that these newspapers made extensive use of wire services and syndicates and often ran the entire article, whereas the big-city newspapers ran shorter versions.

Prologue

1. Tony Hillerman, *Hillerman Country: A Journey through the Southwest with Tony Hillerman*, photos by Barney Hillerman (New York: HarperCollins, 1991), 41.

Chapter 1. Sacred Heart

1. Certificate of death for Henry Anthony Hillerman, 12/5/1872, Texas Death Certificates, 1903–1982, Texas Department of State Health Services. Baptism records, Census records, Sacred Heart Church, Sacred Heart, OK. Thirty-eight years earlier, another Basque member of the monastery had performed the same ritual with six-month-old Jim Thorpe, whose achievements as an Olympic gold medalist, as well as a professional football, baseball, and basketball player, were certainly known to the congregants.

His mother, Charlotte Vieux Thorpe, a member of the Sac and Fox Tribe, rested in the graveyard a few hundred feet from the church. Matt Mitchell, "Grace Thorpe Remembers Dad as an Athlete," *Allentown (PA) Morning Call*, 5/26/1988.

2. Joseph F. Murphy, *Tenacious Monks: The Oklahoma Benedictines, 1875–1975; Indian Missionaries, Catholic Founders, Educators, Agriculturists* (Shawnee, OK: Benedictine Color Press, 1974), 23; Richard V. Francavigli, *The Cast Iron Forest: A Natural and Cultural History of the North American Cross Timbers* (Austin: University of Texas Press, 2010).

3. "The forest was so impenetrable that we could not pass through on horseback without cutting down some trees with axes and knives," wrote Captain Don Domingo Ramón in 1716. "We lost two knives." Paul Joseph Foik, ed., *Captain Don Domingo Ramón's Diary of His Expedition into Texas in 1716* (Austin: St. Edward's University, 1933), 15.

4. "The Pottawatomie Indians, who came to the Indian Territory in the early seventies, were practically Catholic in religion teaching and sentiment," Father Bernard Murphy, unpublished one-page typescript, 1/28/1925, folder 7, Joseph Thoburn Collection, Oklahoma Historical Center.

5. John H. Pickering to *Educational Review*, 11/12/1874, quoted in Murphy, *Tenacious Monks*, 12; "Sacred Heart Parish: Birthplace of the Catholic Church in What Is Now the State of Oklahoma," published by Sacred Heart Church, n.d., author's files; Kenny Arthur Franks, *Oklahoma: The Land and Its People* (Norman: University of Oklahoma Press, 1997), 51; Rev. M. F. Moore, "How the Benedictine Monks Brought Their Religious Work into the Oklahoma Wilderness," *Daily Oklahoman*, 4/19/1908, 25; Marcella Phillips, "Remember Sacred Heart" (series of interviews with residents), *Shawnee News-Star*, 1953, folder 57, box 19, Tony Hillerman Unprocessed Papers, Center for Southwest Research, Zimmerman Library, University of New Mexico (hereafter THUP); *Sacred Heart Catholic Church: 125 Years of Catholic Tradition, 1877–2002* (Shawnee, OK: Gordon Cooper Technology Center, 2002); Blanche E. Little, "Education of the Indian," 6/24/1899, *The School Journal*, vol. 58 (Chicago: E. L. Kellogg & Co.), 1902, 732; Catherine Wright and Mary Ann Anders, "Sacred Heart Mission Site," National Register of Historic Places—Nomination Form, 1983; "Sacred Heart Mission: Home to the C. B. Potawatomi," *How-Ni-Kan* 9, no. 5 (May 1987).

6. Burnis Argo, "Sacred Heart 'Cradle of Catholicism,'" *The Oklahoman*, 4/22/1984; James D. White, "Catholic Church," in *The Encyclopedia of Oklahoma History and Culture*, https://www.okhistory.org/publications/enc/entry.php?entryname= CATHOLIC%20CHURCH; *The Indian Advocate* (Sacred Heart, OK), no. 14, Apr. 1901. "It was a heart-rendering feeling to watch all our labor, so cheerfully given, destroyed in so short a time," said John Bruno, a Potawatomi who had helped build the mission and who, after the conflagration, made bricks to rebuild the priory, https://www.okhistory.org/publications/encyclopediaonline; Dzurisin, "Sacred Heart Konawa to Celebrate 100th Anniversary," *Sooner Catholic*, 6/14/2015, 13.

7. Margaret Mary Chambers, interview with the author, 9/4/2017. Gus Hillerman described himself as short and stout on his draft registration card, US Selective

Service System, World War I Selective Service System Draft Registration Cards, 1917–1918," 9/12/1918, M1509, National Archives and Records Administration (hereafter NARA), Washington, DC; Tony Hillerman, *Seldom Disappointed: A Memoir* (New York: HarperCollins, 2001), 11; Hillerman, "You Can't Find Yesterday," p. 3, 1963, folder 4, box 8, THUP.

8. Census records, family documents, and marriage certificate; Sacred Heart Catholic Church cemetery records; Hillerman, *Seldom Disappointed*, 6. The Hillerman name likely derives from Hillern near Soltau, Germany; Patrick Hanks, ed., *Dictionary of American Family Names* (Oxford: Oxford University Press, 2013).

9. Chambers, interview, 9/4/2017; Sacred Heart Catholic Church cemetery records. Mary Celesta appears in one census record as Celestia and Gertrude as Getrud.

10. Family records, Anne Hillerman Papers (hereafter AHP), privately held; Hillerman to Barney Hillerman's children, 12/22/1995, AHP; Chambers, interview, 9/4/2017.

11. Marcella Phillips, "Remember Sacred Heart," *Shawnee (OK) News-Star*, [May (?)] 1953, folder 57, box 19, THUP.

12. Hillerman *Seldom Disappointed*, 47–49.

13. Chambers, interview, 9/4/2017; Oklahoma City Directory; *The Acorn* (Oklahoma City, OK: St. Anthony School of Nursing, 1941), 60; marriage license, Oklahoma County Marriage Records 1889–1951, book 38, p. 89.

14. Chambers, interview, 8/17/2017; Hillerman, *Seldom Disappointed*, 19.

15. T. Hillerman to Barney Hillerman's children; Hillerman, *Seldom Disappointed*, 21.

16. Hillerman, *Seldom Disappointed*, 19; Chambers, interview, 9/4/2017.

17. Chambers, interview, 8/17/2017.

18. Chambers, interview, 9/4/2017.

19. Chambers, interview, 8/17/2017.

20. Hillerman, *Seldom Disappointed*, 10.

21. Hillerman, *Seldom Disappointed*, 46, 49.

22. Ruby E. Withrow and Leon Bruno, interview with the author, 7/12/2018; information on the fourth vow from Lisa Griffith, executive director of Mercy Education System of the Americas, interview with the author, 9/6/18.

23. "Q&A with Bob Levey," *Washington Post*, 5/6/2003, http://www.washingtonpost .com/wp-srv/liveonline/03/regular/metro/levey/r_metro_levey050603.htm.

24. Chambers, interview, 9/4/2017.

25. Chambers, interview, 9/4/2017; Hillerman, *Seldom Disappointed*, 19.

26. Hillerman, *Seldom Disappointed*, 30. Church records list the dates of Hillerman's Confirmation and First Communion. The change in order may have been necessitated by the fact that the archbishop rarely came to the rural town.

27. Hillerman, *Seldom Disappointed*, 30; *The Gregorian* (Shawnee, OK), Mar. 1938, p. 1; Oct. 1939, p. 4; Murphy, *Tenacious Monks*, 418–19.

28. Hillerman, *Seldom Disappointed*, 30–31; Hillerman, "The Aztec Temple of Death," *Los Angeles Times Book Reviews*, 3/20/1998, 1. Jude P. Dougherty, who was once dean of the School of Philosophy at the Catholic University of America, used Hillerman's discovery and book catalog for an article on the kind of reading necessary

in preparation for the priesthood. "When Hillerman enlisted in the U.S. Army and found his way into the world beyond his native Oklahoma," Dougherty concluded, "he had already met in his literary world characters he was to meet in the flesh." "Tony Hillerman's Benedictine Library," *Homiletic & Pastoral Review*, July 2003.

29. Tom Noland, "Hillerman Country," *Mystery Scene* 87 (2004): 15; Hillerman to Barney Hillerman's children.

30. Linda D. Wilson, "Public Libraries," in *Encyclopedia of Oklahoma History and Culture*, https://www.okhistory.org/publications/enc/entry.php?entry=PU008.

31. Hillerman, *Seldom Disappointed*, 31. Hillerman told versions of this story on many occasions. When he referred to the Pollyanna books he was undoubtedly thinking of Eleanor Emily Hodgman's series, but there is none by that title; *Oklahoma Libraries, 1900–1937: A History and Handbook* (Oklahoma City: Oklahoma Library Commission, 1937), 223.

32. Chambers, interview, 9/4/2017; Hillerman, "You Can't Find Yesterday," 5–6, folder 4, box 8, THUP.

33. Hillerman to Barney Hillerman's children; Chambers, interview, 9/4/2017. The incident was long remembered. In 1988, Kathleen DeLonais Lowery wrote to Tony, "One story my husband and I were told was about three mischievous boys shooting matches out of their B-B guns in the old cotton gin and started a fire, do you remember that story? Ha!"

34. Hillerman, *Seldom Disappointed*, 9.

35. Hillerman, *Seldom Disappointed*, 9; Anne Hillerman, interview with the author 8/11/2018; Gus hardly noticed his children's birthdays. Several times Gus and Tony would be out together doing a chore and he would say, "Hey, this is your birthday, isn't it?" "Yeah," replied his son. "Happy birthday," replied Gus.

36. Hillerman, *Seldom Disappointed*, 16–17; Chambers, interview, 9/4/2017; Hillerman TH to Barney Hillerman's children; *Seldom Disappointed*, 19.

37. Hillerman, *Seldom Disappointed*, 29.

Chapter 2. The World Beyond

1. Hillerman, *Seldom Disappointed*, 28.

2. Hillerman, *Seldom Disappointed*, 26–27; Hillerman, "You Can't Find Yesterday," 7, folder 7, box 8, THUP. Author's notes and photographs from visits to the ruins of the house in 2017 and 2018.

3. Hillerman, *Seldom Disappointed*, 29.

4. Arthur Ward Kennedy, *They Came from Everywhere and Settled Here*, vol. 5 (Konawa, OK: Kennedy Memorial Library of Konawa, 1995), 1378. Kennedy was a dedicated local historian.

5. Hillerman, "Mystery, Country Boys, and the Big Reservation," in Tony Hillerman and Ernie Bulow, *Talking Mysteries: A Conversation with Tony Hillerman* (Albuquerque: University of New Mexico Press, 2004), 24. "Sacred Heart was small enough so we were considered country kids, as opposed to town kids who lived in Konawa," said Hillerman (*Seldom Disappointed*, 10–11).

6. Konawa High School academic records, Konawa, OK; *Ada Evening News*, 4/13/1941, 9; Hillerman, *Seldom Disappointed*, 35.

7. Hillerman, *Seldom Disappointed*, 185. Hillerman said the coach was reprimanded for using such language in the presence of mothers.

8. Konawa High School academic records.

9. Anne Hillerman, interview with the author, 7/27/2018; Hillerman, *Seldom Disappointed*, 46.

10. *Ada Evening News*, 2/1/1942, 9; Hillerman, *Seldom Disappointed*, 27.

11. Chambers, interview, 9/4/2017.

12. Graduation program reprinted in Kennedy, *They Came from Everywhere*, 1379.

13. His incongruous photo may have been the result of having missed picture day at school, but his choice of a photo with such obvious merriment indicates anticipation for what might come next.

14. *My High School Days* (1942 Konawa High School yearbook), Tony Hillerman Papers, Center for Southwest Research, Zimmerman Library, University of New Mexico (hereafter THP).

15. Hillerman, *Seldom Disappointed*, 24–25.

16. Hillerman, *Seldom Disappointed*, 34.

17. Hillerman, *Seldom Disappointed*, 36.

18. Oklahoma A&M College (now Oklahoma State University) transcript; Hillerman recalls receiving better grades of A in English, D in chemistry, C in trigonometry and "a W in Intermediate Algebra (saved from an F by being kicked out of class for sleeping.)" *Seldom Disappointed*, 46.

19. Hillerman, *Seldom Disappointed*, 41.

20. Hillerman, *Seldom Disappointed*, 38. Hillerman recalled the student's name as Sam Singletery Elliot, but no one by that name was enrolled in the college then, nor could I find any census records by this name.

21. Hillerman, *Seldom Disappointed*, 40–41.

22. Hillerman, *Seldom Disappointed*, 43.

23. "Beneficiary Identification Records Locator Subsystem (BIRLS) Death File," US Department of Veterans Affairs, Washington, DC; Hillerman, *Seldom Disappointed*, 43.

24. Hillerman, *Seldom Disappointed*, 43–44.

Chapter 3. Inductee

1. *Miami Daily News-Record*, 8/17/1943, 1; J. L. Baldwin, *The Weather of 1943 in the United States* (Washington, DC: War Department, Office of the Chief Signal Office, 1943), 198.

2. Tony Hillerman's draft card, US World War II Draft Registration Cards, Record Group (hereafter RG) 147, NARA. "As the last available son of a widowed farm woman, I was exempt from military service," according to Hillerman (*Seldom Disappointed*, 50). In his comment, Hillerman was interpreting the three draft classifications, III-B, III-C, and III-D that provided exemptions for men whose parents or farm depended

on them. Tony's brother, Barney, was an inch shorter and weighed the same. Average weight and height cited in Harold P. Godwin, "Tailor to Millions," *Quartermaster Review*, May–June 1945.

3. *Time*, 8/16/1943, 23.

4. Hillerman, *Seldom Disappointed*, 50, 53; Robert M. Huckins's draft card, US World War II Draft Registration Cards, RG 147, NARA.

5. John E. Walters, *Military Career of Private John E. Walters* (privately printed), folder 45, box 19, THUP; Tony Hillerman, interview with Daniel Hillerman, 2006, DVD, box 16, THUP.

6. Hillerman to Don F. Hadwiger, 3/22/1993, folder 45, box 19, THP; Hillerman, *Seldom Disappointed*, 55–57. Hillerman completed one semester (three months) of study of basic engineering. Separation Qualification Records, courtesy of Anne Hillerman, author's collection.

7. Robert R. Palmer, Bell I. Wiley, and William R. Keast, *The Army Ground Forces: The Procurement and Training of Ground Combat Troops* (Washington, DC: Department of the Army, 1948), 28–39.

8. Booklet about Camp Howze published by Southwestern Bell Telephone Co., reproduced in Robert D. Quinn, ed., *Company I, 410th Infantry Regt. 103rd Infantry Division, 1944–1945* (Westlake, OH: Hedgewood Press, 2008).

9. Hillerman, *Seldom Disappointed*, 85–86.

10. Hillerman, *Seldom Disappointed*, 87.

11. Hillerman, *Seldom Disappointed*, 90–91.

12. Hillerman, *Seldom Disappointed*, 66, 69. As he did with many older recollections in his memoir, Hillerman confused the dates and details of his furlough. US Army Morning Reports listed the furloughs he was granted. WW II Operations Reports, Historical Records Section, Department of the Army, RG 407, NARA.

13. Pierce Evans, *Papa's War* (privately published), ii, 8; Hillerman, *Seldom Disappointed*, 91.

14. H. K. Brown, *H. K. Brown's WWII 1944–1945 Diary*, pt.1; David Levine, "Remembering Camp Shanks," *Hudson Valley Magazine*, Sept. 2010.

15. Ralph Mueller and Jerry Turk, *Report after Action: The Story of the 103rd Infantry Division* (Innsbruck: Headquarters, 103rd , Infantry Division, US Army, 1945), 11; Hillerman, *Seldom Disappointed*, 69–70; Hillerman, interview with Dan Hillerman.

16. Evans, *Papa's War*, 14, 15.

17. Hillerman, *Seldom Disappointed*, 71; NavSource Online: Service Ship Photo Archive, USS *General J. R. Brooke* (AP-132), http://www.navsource.org/archives/09/22/22132 .htm.

18. Evans, *Papa's War*, 14, 15; Walters, *Military Career of Private John E. Walters*.

19. Erwin E. King, *Combat Diary: A Personal Look at Combat* (privately published), Dale Center for the Study of War and Society, University of Southern Mississippi, Hattiesburg; Frank L. Romano, taped interview, Nashville Reunion 2009, 103d Division World War II Collection, Special Collections, McCain Library, University of Southern

Mississippi, Hattiesburg; Walters, *Military Career of Private John E. Walters*, 5; Brown, *H. K. Brown's WWII Diary*, pt. 1; Hillerman, *Seldom Disappointed*, 71.

20. Quinn, *Company I*; Gustav Enyedy Jr., *Combat Diary* (privately published, 2006), 1.

21. Hillerman, *Seldom Disappointed*, 72.

22. Specifically, they were ordered to relieve a company from the 30th Infantry Division, then one of the most storied units among the forces that had landed in Normandy six months earlier. Mueller and Turk, *Report after Action*, 23; Rick Atkinson, *The Guns of Last Light: The War in Western Europe, 1944–1945* (New York: Henry Holt, 2013), 312.

23. Date from 103d Infantry Division World War II Association, "The 103d Infantry Division History: World War II," http://103divwwii.usm.edu/assets/103d-history .html; Hillerman, *Seldom Disappointed*, 73.

Chapter 4. War

1. King, *Combat Diary*, sec. II, 2.

2. Atkinson, *Guns of Last Light*, 313; Paul Shelton, ed., *No Use Both of Us Getting Killed . . . You Go! A Quarter Century of Life, Love, and War* (Bloomington, IN: AuthorHouse, 2011), 296.

3. Dwight D. Eisenhower, *Crusade in Europe* (New York: Doubleday, 1948), 322.

4. Hillerman, *Kilroy Was There: A GI's War in Photographs* (Kent, OH: Kent State University, 2004), 39; Keith Bonn, *When the Odds Were Even: The Vosges Mountains Campaign, October 1944–January 1945* (New York: Random House, 2007).

5. "November 1944, Narrative Operations in France—410 Inf Reg," WW II Operations Reports, Historical Records Section, Department of the Army, The Adjutant General's Office, Departmental Records Branch, AGO., WWII Operations Reports, Historical Records Section, RG 407, NARA; Hillerman, *Seldom Disappointed*, 76.

6. Hillerman, *Seldom Disappointed*, 77, 77–78; Hickman Powell, "America's Vest-Pocket Cannon Is a Machine-Gun Destroyer," *Popular Science*, Oct. 1942, 56–60; "November 1944, Narrative Operations in France," 78, NARA.

7. Mueller and Turk, *Report after Action*, 43; Brown, WW II 1944–1945 Diary; Hillerman, *Seldom Disappointed*, 81.

8. Hillerman, *Seldom Disappointed*, 84.

9. Hillerman, *Seldom Disappointed*, 80.

10. Hillerman, "A Strange Encounter with the Enemy," *Reader's Digest*, May 1986, 56.

11. Hillerman, *Seldom Disappointed*, 87.

12. "Morning report, November 1944, 410 Inf Reg," WW II Operations Reports, Historical Records Section, Department of the Army, RG 407, NARA; Hillerman *Seldom Disappointed*, 87. Lucchesi is buried in the Epinal Cemetery in France.

13. Hillerman, "Conjuring up Itterswiller: Memories of an Alsatian Vineyard," *Appellation*, May 1998, 33.

14. Hillerman, *Kilroy Was There*, xiii, 49; Mueller and Turk, *Report after Action*, 33; Atkinson, *Guns of Last Light*, 408.

15. Hillerman, *Seldom Disappointed*, 101. Hillerman claims to have been an eyewitness to this event, and also that the men were court-martialed. Many cases similar to the one Hillerman recounts have been documented, so there is no particular reason to doubt his recollection. I have been unable to locate the court-martial records however.

16. Charles B. MacDonald, *United States Army in WWII—Europe—The Lorraine Campaign* (Florence, AL: Whitman, 2012); Robert Ross Smith and Jeffrey J. Clarke, *Riviera to the Rhine: United States Army in WWII, The European Theater of Operations* (Washington, DC: US Army Center of Military History, 1993), vol. 3, pt. 8, 212; Atkinson, *Guns of Last Light*, 418, 338–40; Mueller and Turk, *Report after Action*, 41, 44.

17. Hillerman, *Kilroy Was There*, 40.

18. Hillerman, *Kilroy Was There*, 28–29.

19. Hillerman, *Kilroy Was There*, 102, 27–28.

20. Hillerman, *Seldom Disappointed*, 87–88.

Chapter 5. Battle

1. Hillerman to Lucy Hillerman, quoted in Beatrice Stahl, "He Stood Fearlessly," *Daily Oklahoman*, 4/29/1945, 12C. World War II correspondence between Tony and his family was not preserved. However, portions of three letters were quoted in this article. In his memoir, Hillerman said he spent the night in Walbourg, but a chronology put together by veterans of the company, which usually matches military records, places the men in Wissembourg on December 18, 1944.

2. Hillerman, *Seldom Disappointed*, 111–12. Hillerman identifies the town as Eschbach, but there is no building there like the one he described. In a letter to me Eschbach mayor Marie-Line Weiss suggests that the town was more likely Walbourg, which Hillerman had earlier confused with Wissembourg.

3. Seth A. Givens, "Bringing Back Memories: GIs, Souvenir Hunting, and Looting in Germany, 1945" (MA thesis, College of Arts and Sciences, Ohio University, 2010), 51.

4. In an account provided to his son Daniel in 2006, Tony said the men blew open the safe with a bazooka, not a grenade. However, because of the danger of ricochet, it seems unlikely they would have used a firearm. T. Hillerman, interview with Daniel Hillerman, 2006, box 16, THUP; Hillerman, *Seldom Disappointed*, 111.

5. Givens, *Bringing Back Memories*, 61, 21; Atkinson, *Guns of Last Light*, 545; Janet Grado, interview with the author, 1/30/20.

6. Thomas Morick, "Schillersdorf," unpublished typescript and handwritten text, folder 38, box 19, THUP.

7. King, *Combat Diary*, sec. II, 2, 8.

8. Hillerman, *Seldom Disappointed*, 115.

9. Stahl, "He Stood Fearlessly"; King, *Combat Diary*, sec. II, 2, 8. Letters from GIs took between one and four weeks to reach home, except for V-Mail. In this popular service, developed during the war, letters were photographed and the microfilm was sent back to the United States for printing and mailing.

10. Mueller and Turk, *Report after Action*, 55.

11. Hillerman, *Seldom Disappointed*, 72.
12. Hillerman, *Seldom Disappointed*, 118–19.
13. Hillerman, *Seldom Disappointed*, 122; General Orders No. 55, 2/8/1945, Headquarters, Office of the Commanding General, 103rd Infantry Division, AHP.
14. Shakeshaft recorded his war memories when he toured the battlefields in 1994. An excerpt appears in a letter from Jerry's son Thomas Shakeshaft to friends, 10/27/2008, Condolence Letters, box 16, THUP.
15. In his memoir, Hillerman wrote that several weeks earlier a member of the platoon had thrown a grenade that bounced back, giving the soldiers several seconds of terror until someone noticed the pin had not been pulled. Thereafter soldier was greeted with "pull the pin" (*Seldom Disappointed*, 124).
16. Hillerman, *Seldom Disappointed*, 123.
17. Hillerman, *Seldom Disappointed*, 122.
18. Public Relations Office Press Release, William Beaumont General Hospital, El Paso, TX, 7/7/1945, box 11, THUP.
19. Hillerman, *Seldom Disappointed*, 131.
20. Atkinson, *Guns of Last Light*, 339–40.
21. Martin Gilbert, *The Second World War: A Complete History* (New York: Henry Holt, 1989), 599.
22. Hillerman, *Seldom Disappointed*, 132; US Army Morning Reports.
23. Photograph provided by Anne Hillerman.
24. General Orders No. 55, 2/8/1945, AHP.
25. Hillerman, *Seldom Disappointed*, 134.
26. Hillerman, *Seldom Disappointed*, 90.
27. Hillerman, interview with Daniel Hillerman, 2006, THUP.
28. Morick, "Schillersdorf," unpublished typescript, THUP.
29. Hillerman, *Seldom Disappointed*, 136.
30. Hillerman, interview with Daniel Hillerman, 2006, THUP; Hillerman, *Seldom Disappointed*, 137.

Chapter 6. Wounded

1. Hillerman, *Seldom Disappointed*, 137–38. Hillerman recalls being tended to by a Lieutenant Weeks. I could not locate this nurse's name on the roster of the hospital staff. Interestingly, the nurses were given the rank of lieutenant so that their instructions to patients could be interpreted as orders, according to Barbara Niss, director, Arthur H. Aufses Jr., MD, Archives & Mount Sinai Records Management Program, New York, NY. Christopherson was buried in the Epinal American Cemetery in Dinozé, France.
2. Descriptions of the hospital and its operation drawn from Ralph Moloshok, "History 3rd General Hospital," Aufses Archives. This facility was the best the medical staff had worked in during its eighteen-month tour of duty, which had taken them to Tunisia and Italy before they came to France.
3. Disposition Board Proceeding, Transfer of Patient to Zone of Interior, 5/8/1945, Headquarters, 3rd General Hospital, AHP; Hillerman, *Seldom Disappointed*, 138.

4. Hillerman, *Seldom Disappointed*, 138.
5. Richard Conniff, "Penicillin: Wonder Drug of World War II," *Military History*, July 2013, 28–43. As many as eighty soldiers a day received doses for venereal disease from the Army 3rd General Hospital's ample supply, according to Dr. Ralph Moloshok, a forty-two-year-old pediatrician who had volunteered with others from Mount Sinai Hospital.
6. Hillerman, *Seldom Disappointed*, 140.
7. Moloshok, "History of 3rd General Hospital."
8. Disposition Board Proceeding, Transfer of Patient to Zone of Interior, AHP.
9. Hillerman, *Seldom Disappointed*, 140–41; Moloshok, "History 3rd General Hospital," 224.
10. Hillerman, "Confessions of an Ink-Stained Wretch," unpublished manuscript, box 12, THUP.
11. Hillerman, "The Replacement," *New Mexico Quarterly* 27, no. 3 (Autumn 1967): 276–80.
12. Hillerman, *Seldom Disappointed*, 142. A photograph also shows Hillerman in a blue bathrobe.
13. Moloshok, "History of 3rd General Hospital," 223; Hillerman, *Seldom Disappointed*, 147.
14. Hillerman, *Seldom Disappointed*, 21, 112. Oddly, although John P. Arras's name shows up on Company C's morning reports, it cannot be found on casualty reports. Hillerman reports that a member of the company visited Arras after the war and found him playing with toys in the care of his mother (*Seldom Disappointed*, 112).
15. Hillerman, *Seldom Disappointed*, 146.
16. Hillerman, *Seldom Disappointed*, 148.
17. Moloshok, "History of 3rd General Hospital," 225.
18. Disposition Board Proceedings, Transfer of Patient to Zone of the Interior, AHP.
19. Barney Hillerman to Tony Hillerman, May 27, 1949 [incorrectly dated], folder 57, box 19, THUP.
20. Enlisted Records and Report of Separation, undated, AHP; Hillerman, *Seldom Disappointed*, 150–51.
21. Michael T. Fleming, "United States Army Hospital Trains: A Brief History of American Rail Casualty Transportation," *The Timetable*, the newsletter of the Piedmont Division, n.d.; Hillerman, *Seldom Disappointed*, 151–52; Certificate of Disability for Discharge, AHP.
22. Hillerman, "You Can't Find Yesterday," THUP. Hillerman offers a different recollection in his memoir. I selected the 1963 version because forty years later his memory had become less reliable.

Chapter 7. Enemy Way

1. Hillerman, *Seldom Disappointed*, 154; *Daily Oklahoman*, 8/14/1945, 1.
2. Stahl, "He Stood Fearlessly." Stahl was born in Washington, DC. I determined her work history using 1930 and 1940 census records.

3. Hillerman, *Seldom Disappointed*, 155.

4. Christopher Grove to Herbert Grove, 8/13/1945, folder 57, box 19, THUP.

5. Hillerman, *Seldom Disappointed*, 160; "It's Over," *Smithsonian Magazine*, Aug. 2005.

6. Hillerman, *Seldom Disappointed*, 156–58.

7. Hillerman, *Hillerman Country*, 34

8. See Jeré Franco, "Loyal and Heroic Service: The Navajos and World War II," *Journal of Arizona History* 27, no. 4 (Winter 1986), 391–406.

9. Rachel Dickinson, "The Navajo Way," *Arizona Daily Star*, 5/28/2006, E10.

10. Hillerman, *Hillerman Country*, 34.

11. Hillerman, *Seldom Disappointed*, 162.

12. Hillerman, *Seldom Disappointed*, 161. The house is situated at 801 N. University Blvd., and was still standing in 2018.

Chapter 8. University of Oklahoma

1. *Sooner*, Dec. 1947, 19; *Sooner Magazine*, Winter 1990, 4; George Lynn Cross, *The University of Oklahoma and World War II* (Norman: University of Oklahoma Press, 1980), 173–74. There was such a housing shortage that a leader of the veterans threatened to erect a tent city if the university didn't find lodging for the new students. Five hundred prefabricated one- and two-bedroom houses were procured and placed end-to-end on open land.

2. Cross, *University of Oklahoma and World War II*, 203, 205.

3. *Daily Oklahoman*, 3/4/1946, 50; Cross, *University of Oklahoma and World War II*, 130, 202.

4. OU transcript, copy in author's files.

5. John McPartland, "Intercollegiate Bull Session," *Life*, 3/28/1949, 113.

6. *Sooner Magazine*, Feb. 1948, 10; Hillerman, *Seldom Disappointed*, 172.

7. Students presented Ray with a bouquet of flowers at the end of the 1947 semester in thanks for her assistance in placing articles they had written while taking her class (*Sooner*, June 1947, 4); Hillerman, *Seldom Disappointed*, 171; Eve Sandstrom, "Making Crime Pay," *Sooner Magazine*, Winter 1990, 4.

8. *Covered Wagon*, Mar. 1947, 13. The covers, artwork, and articles made it "the most collegiate magazine," according to the editors of *Old Line*, the University of Maryland magazine (*Daily Oklahoman*, 8/18/1947, 11).

9. Hillerman, "The Secret Life of Walter Wenchless," *Covered Wagon*, Jan. 1947, 5.

10. Hillerman, "First Epistle to the Freshmen," *Covered Wagon*, Feb. 1947.

11. *The Sooner Yearbook*, 1947, 212; Hillerman, "The Fifth Wheel," *Covered Wagon*, Oct. 1947, 18.

12. Hillerman, "The Fifth Wheel," *Covered Wagon*, Dec. 1947, 5. Hillerman got the number of reindeer wrong. It was then eight and grew to nine in 1949 after Rudolph was added.

13. Hillerman, *Seldom Disappointed*, 174. Hillerman dates his feelings of loneliness to May 1947. *Sooner Magazine*, Dec. 1947, 19; Teresa Sifford, interview with the author, 8/21/2019.

14. *Sooner Yearbook*, 1948, 394.

15. Hillerman, *Seldom Disappointed*, 39, 177–78.

16. Teresa Sifford, interview with the author, 8/21/19.

17. Hillerman, *Seldom Disappointed*, 178; Sifford, interview, 8/21/2019.

18. Sifford, interview, 3/8/2018.

19. Sifford, interview, 8/21/2019. Anne Hillerman recounted a similar story in a 9/3/2019 interview.

20. Hillerman, "History Major Is Soaring Success," *Oklahoma Daily*, 12/17/1947, 1. Souter did not become a commercial pilot but continued to fly small planes as a member of the Parakeet Flying Club in Guthrie, OK.

21. *Daily Oklahoman*, 1/13/1948, 12.

22. *Sooner Magazine*, Dec. 1947, 19; *Sooner*, Fall 2002, 20–21; *OU Today Radio Show*, likely aired in January 1993, program no. 9206, Western History Collection, University of Oklahoma. Both Hillerman's name and Larry Grove's appear on the masthead of the Nov. and Dec. 1947 issues of the *Oklahoma Daily*.

23. *Oklahoma Daily*, 01/04/1948, 11, and 02/08/1948, D11.

24. Hillerman, "A Wagon Educational Feature: Culture Comes to Indian Country," *Covered Wagon*, Feb. 1948, 6–7.

25. *Oklahoma Daily*, 2/18/1948, 1.

26. *Miami (OK) Daily News-Record*, 2/18/1948, 1; *Daily Oklahoman*, 2/19/1948, 9.

27. Editor's Note, "From the Horse's Mouth," *Covered Wagon*, Mar. 1948, 3.

28. Editor's Note, 3–4. In the midst of the brouhaha over *The Covered Wagon*, Hillerman wrote a supportive letter to Joan Forsyth, editor of the *Purple Parrot*, the humor magazine at Northwestern University, who had been ousted over complaints of excessive material about sex and liquor. In 1998, when Hillerman had become well known, Forsythe wrote to him. Looking through her 1948 college scrapbook in preparation for her fiftieth Northwestern University class reunion, she had come across Hillerman's letter. "That letter got me through a lot of bad days," she told him. "You are allowed one nostalgic chuckle and a remembrance of doing one very uplifting thing for a downtrodden soul back on February 18, 1948" (box 12, THUP).

29. *Daily Oklahoman*, 6/1/1948, 2.

30. *Sooner Magazine*, May 1951, 5.

31. Hillerman, *Seldom Disappointed*, 178.

Chapter 9. Borger

1. At the time the black clouds above Borger were visible from twenty to thirty miles away, according to Andries Voet, *Chemical & Engineering News*, 1/16/1964, 5; H. Allen Anderson, "Carbon Black Industry," in *Handbook of Texas Online*, www.tshaonline .org/index.php/handbook/entries/carbon-black-industry; Glenn Baxter, *Good Kind Things for Others: A True Story of Corruption in the Texas Panhandle* (n.p.: Xlibris, 2006), 12–13. "For years as you drove along Highway 66 you could look across the border and see this smudge on the horizon and that was Borger," said Hillerman

(*Publishers Weekly*, 10/24/1980, 7). In *Seldom Disappointed*, Hillerman recalled arriving on a Monday in late May. Evidence suggests he more likely arrived on the first or second of June.

2. The cost of the groceries cited here comes from Hillerman's article, "Money Was Scarce, But Good Old Days Were Cheap Anyway," *Borger News-Herald*, 8/6/1948, 1. Similar figures are found in Bureau of Labor Statistics, *Retail Prices of Food, 1948*, Bulletin no. 965 (Washington, DC: Department of Labor, 1949), and Thomas A. Stapleford, *The Cost of Living in America: A Political History of Economic Statistics, 1880–2000* (Cambridge: Cambridge University Press, 2009).

3. Hillerman, *Seldom Disappointed*, 178.

4. The series by Hoover ran in the paper in June and July 1948. Typical of the local coverage related to communism was a report on July 23, 1948 about an anti-communist league being formed. In *Seldom Disappointed*, Hillerman recounts a story that J. C. Phillips sought to plant accusatory questions at a rally for a congressional candidate who was a University of Texas law school graduate Phillips considered soft on communism. However, there was no candidate fitting that description in that year's election, and both the Republican and Democrat were very conservative.

5. Hutchinson County Historical Commission, *History of Hutchinson County, Texas: 104 Years, 1876–1980* (Dallas, TX: Taylor, 1980); H. Allen Anderson, "Borger, TX," in *Handbook of Texas Online*, http://www.tshaonline.org/handbook/online/articles/heb10; *City Directory of Borger, Texas: 1948–1949* (Amarillo, TX: W. J. Winter, 1948).

6. Hillerman, *Seldom Disappointed*, 181–82.

7. "Two Killed in Alamo Explosion," *Borger News-Herald*, 6/3/1945, 1 (if not written by Hillerman, it certainly includes his reporting); Hillerman, *Seldom Disappointed*, 181.

8. Mary Jo Nelson, "Borger: The Town That 'Okies' Built," *Daily Oklahoman*, 11/11/1982, 1B; Hillerman, *Seldom Disappointed*, 180.

9. Borger residents who knew Anderson, interviews with the author, Apr. 2018.

10. Hillerman, "Trio Has Respect for Tough Texas Officers," *Borger News-Herald*, 6/4/1948, 1.

11. Hillerman, *Seldom Disappointed*, 184.

12. Janis Wiseman, longtime employee in the sheriff's office, interview with the author, 4/22/2018.

13. Hillerman, *Seldom Disappointed*, 183.

14. Hillerman, "Borger Girl Leaves for 50-Day Trip to Europe," *Borger News-Herald*, 6/13/1948, 9; and "Layne Chased by Gassers; Hubbers Win," *Borger News-Herald*, 6/28/1948, 4.

15. Hillerman, "Watch Your Step or Old Laws Can Put You Behind Bars," *Borger News-Herald*, 7/15/1948, 1; Hillerman, *Seldom Disappointed*, 186.

16. Hillerman, *Seldom Disappointed*, 186.

17. Hillerman, *Seldom Disappointed*, 185.

18. Hillerman, *Seldom Disappointed*, 189–92.

19. Teresa Sifford, interview with the author, 3/8/2018.
20. Sifford, interviews, 3/8/2018 and 5/2/2018.
21. Sharon and Jack Vorsham, interview with the author, 4/22/2018. The Vorshams lived in the same converted garage when they moved to Borger in 1950.
22. Sifford, interviews, 3/8/2018 and 5/2/2018.
23. Hillerman, *Seldom Disappointed*, 192–93; *City Directory of Borger, Texas*, 1948–1949, 5; Jose Ricardo Zanettim, *Saint John the Evangelist Roman Catholic Parish, 90th Anniversary 1926–2016, Celebrating Ninety Years of Catholic Presence in Borger, Texas* (Amarillo, TX: Roman Catholic Diocese, 2016), 19–20.

Chapter 10. Feeding the Wire

1. Hillerman, *Seldom Disappointed*, 203. Hillerman misspelled Sullivant's last name as Sullivan. "Longtime Political Writer, 72, Dead," *Oklahoman*, 12/10/1974, 1.
2. "Otis Sullivant Is a Professional," *Sooner*, Jan. 1967.
3. Hillerman, *Seldom Disappointed*, 203.
4. Hillerman, *Seldom Disappointed*, 197.
5. Hillerman, *Seldom Disappointed*, 198; "Off to War Again: The Pre-War Boom," *Lawton Constitution*, 8/5/1976, 6F–12F.
6. Hillerman, *Seldom Disappointed*, 198.
7. "Merger of Press and Constitution Scheduled Sunday," *Lawton Morning Press*, 5/14/1949, 1; Hillerman, *Seldom Disappointed*, 198.
8. *Santa Fe New Mexican*, 7/21/49, 3; Hillerman, *Indian Country: America's Sacred Land* (Flagstaff, AZ: Northland Press, 1987), [21].
9. Hillerman, "The Old Lady of Marcy Street," *Santa Fe New Mexican*, 7/11/1949, 45; Anne Hillerman, notes of interview with her father, 2003, AHP. Tony told his daughter Lacy's house was on Camino Sin Nombre but the city directory has Lacy living on Acequia Madre at the time.
10. Hillerman, "Mountain Park Has Its 'Miracle Baby,'" *Daily Oklahoman*, 8/28/1949, 1; Hillerman, *Seldom Disappointed*, 199.
11. Hillerman, *Seldom Disappointed*, 201.
12. Hillerman, *Seldom Disappointed*, 199.
13. Hillerman, *Seldom Disappointed*, 213.
14. Catherine Breslin, "Tony Hillerman," *Publishers Weekly*, 6/10/1988, 58.
15. "Former Newspaper Editor Dies," *Daily Oklahoman*, 12/13/1997, 10, and 1/15/1952, 22; J. E. McReynolds, "Keyboard Cowboys Ride Herd at State Capitol" *Daily Oklahoman*, 10/24/1993, 24; Hillerman, *Seldom Disappointed*, 202.
16. Hillerman, "Lowered Probe Boom Has State Capitol Departments in Zither," *Guymon Daily Herald*, 8/22/1951, 5.
17. Hillerman, "Cat Food for Relief? That Is on Books," *Guymon Daily Herald*, 8/29/1951, 1.
18. Hillerman, "Sooners Lead in Big Seven, Down Colorado," *Guymon Daily Herald*, 10/28/1951.
19. A draft of the short story can be found in folder 2, box 8, THUP.

Chapter 11. Santa Fe

1. *Santa Fe New Mexican*, 7/21/1949, 3. It is likely that Hillerman stopped in at the *New Mexican* office because the paper published an item about them being in town. Hillerman, *Seldom Disappointed*, 204–5; *Santa Fe New Mexican*, 9/29/1952, 15. Anne Hillerman, interview with the author, 2/21/2019. Anne said her father could not leave work to meet the train and instead sent his one bureau staff member to do the job. "I don't think my mom ever quite forgave him for that."

2. Thomas W. Pew Jr., "Route 66: Ghost Road of Okies," *American Heritage* 28, no. 5 (Aug. 1977); John Steinbeck, *The Grapes of Wrath* (New York: Penguin Books, 2006), 118.

3. John Pen La Farge, *Turn Left at the Sleeping Dog: Scripting the Santa Fe Legend, 1920–1955* (Albuquerque: University of New Mexico Press, 2001), 369.

4. Hillerman, *Seldom Disappointed*, 207.

5. Hillerman, *Seldom Disappointed*, 206, 208.

6. Hillerman, *Seldom Disappointed*, 212–13.

7. Hillerman, *Seldom Disappointed*, 214.

8. *Las Cruces Sun*, 3/7/1954, 1.

9. *Santa Fe New Mexican*, 2/3/1951, 1.

10. *Santa Fe New Mexican*, 2/5/1951, 16.

11. *Albuquerque Journal*, 7/21/54, 12; Stephen Northup, interview with the author, 12/3/2018.

12. Hillerman, "The Great Taos Bank Robbery and Other Recollections" (master's thesis, University of New Mexico, Albuquerque, 1966), 85. The essay from which this comment was taken appears in a slightly different form in various editions of *The Great Taos Bank Robbery*, first published in 1973 by University of New Mexico Press.

13. Tony Hillerman, preface to Robert M. McKinney, *The Toad and the Water Witch* (Santa Fe: Press of the New Mexican, 1997), vii; McKinney, *Hymn to Wreckage* (New York: Henry Holt, 1947. The *New York Times* (6/26/2001, C15) named it as one of the ten best books of poetry published in 1947.

14. *New York Times*, 6/28/2001, B8; Anne Hillerman, interview, 2/21/2019; Robin McKinney Martin, interview with the author, 2/22/2019.

15. See *Santa Fe New Mexican*, 10/10/1954, 1; 8/22/1954, 7; 9/17/54, 3; and 12/10/1954, 12.

16. *Albuquerque Journal*, 1/4/1957, 1; and 1/22/1957, 1.

17. *Albuquerque Journal*, 1/27/57, 1; *Santa Fe New Mexican*, 1/28/1957, 1; 1/29/1957, 1; and 11/20/1957, 16.

18. *Santa Fe New Mexican*, 1/29/1957, 1.

19. *Santa Fe New Mexican*, 1/30/1957, 1; and 1/31/1957, 1.

20. *Albuquerque Journal*, 1/12/1958, 24.

21. *Santa Fe New Mexican*, 1/21/1962, 1; and 12/7/1961, 6.

22. *Santa Fe New Mexican*, 3/26/1954, 4.

23. The paper was filled with society notices and gossip. The fact that no mention was ever made of Mrs. H. Pincus or her daughter, Lulu Maude Pincus, increases the

likelihood that they were fictional. Hillerman may have been comfortable with a spoof on the editorial page but making up a news item would have been a line he would have been unwilling to cross.

24. *Santa Fe New Mexican*, 7/15/1957, 18.

25. *Santa Fe New Mexican*, 7/17/1957, 20.

26. *Santa Fe New Mexican*, 11/4/1957, 4.

27. *Pasatiempo*, 11/21–27/2008, 37–38. Thompson claimed it was Hillerman's idea to create Mrs. Pincus. However, the first letter appeared before Hillerman came to work at the paper.

28. *Santa Fe New Mexican*, 7/18/1961, 9.

29. *Santa Fe New Mexican*, 10/11/1961, 11.

30. Stephen Northup, interview with the author, 12/3/2018.

31. Earl English to Hillerman, 5/18/1959, box 11, THUP.

32. *Santa Fe New Mexican*, 1/8/1960, 1, 5.

33. Hillerman, "Roman Holiday Crowd Watches Execution," *Santa Fe New Mexican*, 10/29/1954, 1; Jim Belshaw, "Killing and the Killers," *Albuquerque Journal*, 1/29/1999, B1.

34. Hillerman, "First Lead Gasser," *Ellery Queen*, Apr. 1993, 13.

35. *Albuquerque Tribune*, 3/13/1970. "Burned out" are Hillerman's words. *Arizona Republic*, 3/26/85, C1.

36. Hillerman to Robert McKinney, 11/24/1962, Robin McKinney Martin Papers, privately held (hereafter RMMP).

Chapter 12. Back to School

1. Hillerman, *Seldom Disappointed*, 236; *Time*, 9/8/1961.

2. Hillerman, *Seldom Disappointed*, 260; Anne Hillerman, interview, 2/21/2019. Marie did work as a substitute teacher when the family moved to Albuquerque.

3. Sifford, interview, 1/27/2020; Anne Hillerman, interview, 2/21/2019; Hillerman, *Seldom Disappointed*, 221.

4. Janet Grado to the author, 3/18/2019; Anne Hillerman, interview 8/11/2017; *Santa Fe New Mexican*, 2/15/1954.

5. Monica Atwell, interview with the author, 7/22/2019; Hillerman, *Seldom Disappointed*, 223.

6. Hillerman, *Seldom Disappointed*, 223; Janet Grado, interview, 1/30/2020.

7. *Santa Fe New Mexican*, 7/18/1962, 18.

8. Copy of résumé in Tony Hillerman, box 13, Faculty File Collection, University of New Mexico Archives.

9. Hillerman, *Seldom Disappointed*, 237; John Perovich, former UNM comptroller attended the meeting but recalled few of its particulars (Perovich, interview with the author, 12/4/2018).

10. UNM News Bureau press release, Dec. 1962; salary in *Albuquerque Journal*, 12/2/1962, 2; *Current Population Reports*, Consumer Income, Series P-60, no. 40, 6/26/1963; *Santa Fe New Mexican*, 4/13/1962, 28 Today, the chain is branded as Blake's

Lotaburger; *Albuquerque Journal*, 11/22/63, 73; and 11/10/1962, 13; Hillerman, *Seldom Disappointed*, 237.

11. Hillerman to Robert McKinney, 11/24/1962, RMMP.

12. *Santa Fe New Mexican*, 12/7/1962, 1; *Albuquerque Journal*, 12/8/1962, 2.

13. *Albuquerque Journal*, 1/3/1963, 7; Hillerman, *Seldom Disappointed*, 238; Debra Levy Martinelli, "Seldom Disappointed," *Sooner Magazine*, Fall 2002.

14. "Hillerman to Aid U," undated clipping, likely from *The Lobo*, in Hillerman, Faculty File Collection, box 13, University of New Mexico Archives; *Las Vegas Optic*, 2/12/1963, 5; Perovich, interview, 12/4/2018.

15. Hillerman, *Seldom Disappointed*, 238. Story from Dora Wang, *The Daily Practice of Compassion: A History of the University of New Mexico School of Medicine, Its People, and Its Mission, 1964–2014* (Albuquerque: UNM School of Medicine, 2014), 37–39. Hillerman also repeated the tale in a 1993 interview with the UNM student newspaper. Former UNM comptroller John Perovich confirmed that Hillerman obtained the mattresses for the jail and that the donation helped win a committee vote (Perovich, interview, 12/4/2018). But as with many other instances, Hillerman's recollections in his memoir appear inaccurate.

16. Hillerman, introduction to Tom Miller, *The Panama Hat Trail* (Washington, DC: National Geographic, 2001), galleys in folder 17, box 19, THUP; Hillerman, *Seldom Disappointed*, 240. I could find no mention of the incident in the press, nor could I locate any university records or retired administrators to confirm the episode. However, Anne Hillerman recalled her parents traveling to Quito and Marie, who read Tony's memoir, would have objected to the account if it had not happened. The year is likely to have been 1964.

17. Paul B. Davis, interview with the author, 4/12/2019; Hillerman, *Seldom Disappointed*; UNM Catalog 1962–63, 20. The poet Robert Creeley was among the first to obtain a master's in this manner at UNM.

18. Hillerman, UNM course transcript, in possession of the author.

19. *Washington Post*, 4/28/2015.

20. Morris Freedman, *Confessions of a Conformist* (New York: Norton, 1961), 32; *Chicago Tribune Magazine of Books*, 3/19/1961, 4; *Albuquerque Journal*, 6/28/1963, C12.

21. Hillerman, interview with Don Swaim, 7/14/1988, cassette 208, box 7, Don Swaim Collection, Ohio University Library, Athens; Hillerman, *Seldom Disappointed*, 233.

22. Hillerman, "You Can't Find Yesterday," folder 4, box 8, THUP. This is the first paper he wrote when he entered the UNM graduate writing program in 1963. Hillerman retained most of the papers he wrote as a UNM student. They reveal how carefully they were read by Freedman as well as his devotion to his student.

23. Hillerman, *Seldom Disappointed*, 234; Freedman, *Confessions*, 16, 29, 101.

24. Hillerman, "Hunt Pressed in Taos for 'Intended Robbers,'" *Santa Fe New Mexican*, 11/14/1957, 1.

25. *Santa Fe New Mexican*, 11/13/1957, 4.

26. Hillerman, "The Great Taos Bank Robbery and Other Recollections" (master's thesis, UNM, Albuquerque, 1966), 11.

27. Rebecca West, *The Meaning of Treason* (New York: Viking Press, 1947), 5, 67; Hillerman, "Great Taos Bank Robbery" (master's thesis), 25.

Chapter 13. No More Excuses

1. *Taos News*, 6/4/1964, 8; *Albuquerque Journal*, 5/6/1964, 13; Anne Hillerman, conversation with the author.
2. "It was a personal business. It seemed very small and personal, everybody knew everyone else," recalled Hugh Van Dusen, who worked for sixty years at HarperCollins (interview with the author, 10/12/2018). Hillerman, *Seldom Disappointed*, 234–35. In the early 1980s, Ann Elmo was my agent. Hillerman's account of his brief meeting with her was identical to my experience.
3. Hillerman, *Seldom Disappointed*, 235.
4. Richard Combs, "Pleasing the Man with a Magazine," *American Libraries* 3, no. 9 (1972), 1004; Dick Adler to Hillerman, 7/22/1964 and 8/6/1964, folder 1, box 7, THUP. The editors made the same request to Hillerman's agent. "They would like you to pursue the matter in a detective-mystery manner," Elmo wrote (Ann Elmo to Hillerman, 7/22/1964, folder 3, box 6, THP). The current name of the plague bacterium is *Yersinia pestis*.
5. Hillerman, "Black Death in the Southwest," *True*, Jan. 1966, 66.
6. Hillerman, "Black Death," 70.
7. Hillerman, "Black Death," 72.
8. Hillerman, "Black Death," 72.
9. Howard Cohn notes, date unclear [August or early September 1964?], and Elmo to Hillerman, 10/13/1964, both in folder 1, box 7, THP.
10. Earlier in the year he had published two articles in the *New Mexico* magazine, both regarding UNM's seventy-fifth anniversary, and he had extensively spruced up the president's annual report to gain notice from the press. "The new report is a marked departure from previous reports, which followed a more scholarly format," said the *Albuquerque Journal*, 3/22/1964, 25.
11. Elmo to Hillerman, 4/6/1965, folder 1, box 7, THP.
12. Robert Shea to Hillerman, 5/3/1965, folder 4, box 6, THP; Douglas Preston, "The Mystery of Sandia Cave," *New Yorker*, 6/12/1995. Shea later went on to co-author *Iluminatus*, a science fiction fantasy trilogy that became a cult classic.
13. Shea to Hillerman, 6/14/1965, folder 2, box 8, THUP.
14. Anne Hillerman, "Father's Day—A Time for Cookies and Family," *Santa Fe New Mexican*, 6/20/2015; Hillerman to Shea, 6/21/1964, folder 2, box 8, THUP.
15. Andrew Mills to Hillerman, 12/22/1965, folder 2, box 8, THUP.
16. Hillerman to Mills, 1/20/1966, folder 2, box 8, THUP; Hillerman, "A Long Search for the First Americans," *True*, June 1967, 56.
17. Shea to Hillerman, 6/14/1965, folder 2, box 8, THUP; Hillerman, "Long Search."
18. *Santa Fe New Mexican*, 2/10/1966, A7.
19. Hillerman, *Seldom Disappointed*, 224–25; Daniel Hillerman, interview with the author, 2/12/2020; *Albuquerque Journal*, 11/5/1967, A3.

20. Daniel Hillerman, interview, 2/12/2020.

21. Hillerman and Bulow, *Talking Mysteries*, 29; Hillerman to Ann Elmo, 3/7/1966, folder, 1, box 7, THP.

22. Hillerman and Bulow, *Talking Mysteries*, 28.

23. Hillerman and Bulow, *Talking Mysteries*, 29; Lynn Simross, "Master of Mystery—Sans Reservation," *Los Angeles Times*, 3/20/1988, G1.

24. John Carr, "Evil and a Good Ol' Boy: Tony Hillerman," *Albuquerque Journal Magazine*, 2/5/1985. Quotations are drawn from p. 13 of a longer, unedited draft of the article, in folder 2, box 10, THP. Alan Warhaftig, "Going in Beauty: An Interview with Tony Hillerman," folder 5, box 8, THUP.

25. Hillerman and Bulow, *Talking Mysteries*, 27.

26. Hillerman, "Mystery, Country Boys, and The Big Reservation," in Hillerman and Bulow, *Talking Mysteries*, 30.

27. Joan Kahn, "Editing the Mystery and Suspense Novel," *The Writer*, July 1966, 18–19. Several years later, Hillerman told Kahn that the article had inspired him to write *Blessing Way*. In fact, the article certainly encouraged him, but he had already started on the novel.

28. Hillerman and Bulow, *Talking Mysteries*, 47.

29. Hillerman and Bulow, *Talking Mysteries*, 29.

Chapter 14. The Birth of Leaphorn

1. Hillerman and Bulow, *Talking Mysteries*, 32.

2. Tony Hillerman, *The Blessing Way* (New York: HarperCollins Paperback, 2009), 17; "Blessing Way," draft manuscript, folder 4, box 1, THP.

3. Hillerman and Bulow, *Talking Mysteries*, 30; Mario Materassi, "The Case of Tony Hillerman: An Interview," *Journal of the Southwest* 50, no. 4 (Winter 2008), 449.

4. Materassi, "Case of Tony Hillerman"; Cynthia Gorney, "Hillerman & His Navajo Mysteries," *Washington Post*, 1/29/1987, C1; Hillerman, *Seldom Disappointed*, 269; Tony Hillerman, interview with David Dunaway, Writing the Southwest research and recordings, 1976–2005, Center for Southwest Research, Zimmerman Library, UNM (hereafter DDSWR).

5. The connection between Hillerman and Upfield is confusing in great part because Hillerman mistakenly remembered having read Upfield stories when he was young. In interviews, Hillerman began mentioning Upfield after reviewers pointed out the similarity, beginning with a *New York Times* review of his first book. "I went to the library and checked that out," Hillerman said. He was amazed to recall that he had read Upfield's works serialized in magazines as a boy in Sacred Heart, Oklahoma. "I used to sell the *Saturday Evening Post*.... I remembered his vivid descriptions of the Australian Outback." (Mary Campbell, "Mystery Writer Illuminates Native American Life." AP article printed in Jacksonville, FL, *Journal Courier*, 11/3/1991, 28.) In the article he mentions a "Boston reviewer" but the first connection made between Hillerman and Upfield was in the 1970 *New York Times* review. Two other authors who were somewhat similar to Upfield were Robert Hans van Gulik, a Dutch

diplomat who wrote a series featuring an eighteenth-century Chinese detective, and Henry R. F. Keating, an English crime fiction writer who wrote a series featuring Inspector Ghote of Bombay.

6. See *Fifth Annual Report of the Bureau of Ethnology, 1883–1884* (Washington, DC: GPO, 1884). In Father Berard Haile's article he found a deeply detailed account of the Enemy Way and pages of translations of Navajo chants and songs. Haile, who grew up in a Catholic orphanage in Ohio, became priest in 1898. He came to the Navajo Nation as a missionary, an *ednishodi* (long-robed one) as the Diné called him. He learned the Navajo language, earned a master's degree at Catholic University, and helped devise a written Navajo alphabet.

7. Hillerman, *Blessing Way*, 1.

8. Even though Canyon de Chelly did not appear in his manuscript, Hillerman used the place to collect sensory impressions. Walking its sandy floor, he noted the way the wind sounded, the booming of thunder echoing off the high canyon walls, and the smell of sage and wet sand after a rain.

9. Three years later when a copyeditor asked Hillerman to identify the source, he could no longer find it.

10. Hillerman, "Places for Spirits, Places for Ghosts," in *New Mexico, Rio Grande, and Other Essays* (Portland, OR: Graphic Arts Center, 1992), 106. Again, it was a visit to Canyon de Chelly, where Hillerman studied the ancestral cliff houses, that provided the idea for how his protagonist, an archaeologist, would use his knowledge of the ancient dwelling to engineer his final escape.

11. Hillerman and Bulow, *Talking Mysteries*, 31.

12. *Santa Fe New Mexican*, 5/9/1961, 1. *The Sun* (Flagstaff, AZ), 9/6/1981, A7; Hillerman, interview, Don Swaim Collection, cassette 208, box 7, Ohio University, Athens.

13. Dale H. Ross and Charles L. P. Silet, "Interview with Tony Hillerman," *Clues* 10, no. 2 (Fall/Winter 1989), 120.

14. Hillerman, interview, Don Swaim Collection; quotation from John Carr, "Evil and a Good Ol' Boy," 14, draft manuscript, folder 2, box 10, THP.

15. Hillerman to Ann Elmo, 3/7/1966, and Elmo to Hillerman, 9/9/1966, folder 1, box 7, THP.

16. "A Day in the Life of Chapter Two," in *The Tony Hillerman Companion*, ed. Martin Greenberg (New York: HarperCollins, 1994), 316; Hillerman, interview, Don Swaim Collection; Hillerman, *Seldom Disappointed*, 233. Tony Hillerman Jr., interview with the author, 7/21/2019.

17. Tony Hillerman Jr., interview, 7/21/2019.

18. Marie Hillerman notebooks, AHP.

19. Ross and Silet, "Interview with Tony Hillerman," 134–35.

20. Monica Atwell, interview, 7/22/2019; Tony Hillerman Jr., interview, 7/21/2019; Dawn Wink, "Anne Hillerman on Writing and Her Dad, Tony Hillerman," https://dawnwink.wordpress.com/2013/04/29/anne-hillerman-on-writing-and-her-dad-tony-hillerman/; Hillerman and Bulow, *Talking Mysteries*, 36.

21. Mary Dudley, interview with the author, 11/09/2018. This version of the manuscript is among Hillerman's papers in THP.

22. Hillerman, *Seldom Disappointed*, 270.

23. Grace M. Prather, "Mystery Editor Vacations in State," *Albuquerque Journal*, 7/28/1971, A-10; Sheila Rule, "Joan Kahn, 80, Respected Editor of Mysteries, Dies," *New York Times*, 11/13/1994, 43; Hugh Van Dusen, interview with the author, 10/12/2018.

24. Hillerman to Joan Kahn, 4/2/1969, folder 8, box 1, THP.

25. Hillerman to Kahn, 5/9/1969 and 4/10/1969, Kahn to Hillerman, 4/17/1969, all folder 3, box 7, THP.

26. Joan Kahn, "From Puzzles to People," *The Writer*, Feb. 1969, 20.

27. *Journalism Education*, June 1, 1969, 445; Hillerman, *Seldom Disappointed*, 272.

28. Hillerman, *Seldom Disappointed*, 272.

29. Anne Hillerman, interview, 9/3/2019.

30. *Publishers Weekly*, 12/29/1969, 22; Hillerman, *Seldom Disappointed*, 272; Kahn to Hillerman, 5/6/1969, folder 3, box 7, THP.

31. Elmo to Hillerman, 5/15/1969, folder 1, box 7, THP; Hillerman and Bulow, *Talking Mysteries*, 33. A copy of the 5/26/1969, contract is in box 24, THUP.

32. Hillerman, interview, DDSWR.

33. Kahn to Hillerman, 5/6/1969, folder 3, box 7, THP.

34. Hillerman, "Blessing Way," edited manuscript, 51, folder 7, box 1, THP.

35. Hillerman, "Blessing Way," edited manuscript.

36. Kahn to Hillerman, 5/14/1969, folder 3, box 7, THP.

37. Hillerman to Mary McGuinn, 8/1/1969, folder 9, box 1, THP.

38. *Albuquerque Journal*, 6/4/1969, 36; Hillerman, *Seldom Disappointed*, 51.

39. Hillerman, *Seldom Disappointed*, 45.

40. Hillerman to Carl Skiff, 3/11/1970, folder 14, box 7, THP.

Chapter 15. Professor Hillerman

1. Hillerman, "The Mountain on the Guardrail at Exit 164B," in *The Great Taos Bank Robbery and Other True Stories* (Albuquerque: University of New Mexico Press, 2012), 2; Hillerman, "Places for Spirits, Places for Ghosts," 102. Thanks to Tony Hillerman Jr. for help identifying his father's car.

2. Hillerman, "Places for Spirits, Places for Ghosts," 26.

3. A fact noted by a visitor. "Probably when Marron Hall was a women's dormitory," he said, "the room was a parlor, the parlor of the house mother's suite, perhaps. Now, it is aging, a little shabby, and very comfortable (Paul Sweitzer, "The Storyteller," *Arizona Daily Sun*, 9/6/1981, 7). Dick Pfaff, interview with the author, 2/12/2020.

4. Mary Dudley, interview with the author, 11/09/2018; Hillerman, "Landscape of the Sky," *New Mexico*, Aug. 1985, 49; Hillerman, "My Rationale for Watching Clouds," box 11, THUP.

5. *Albuquerque Journal*, 1/11/1970, C2.

6. Sharon Niederman to the author, 12/21/2019; Hillerman, *Seldom Disappointed*, 262; George Johnson remembrance, author's files.

7. Judy Redman to the author, 10/18/2018; *Santa Fe New Mexican*, 12/22/1961, 1; Hillerman, *Seldom Disappointed*, 172. Hillerman recounted how, in 1961, he had published a front-page story revealing that half a million cigarette revenue stamps had gone missing. Two days after the story appeared, Hillerman's phone rang. "Merry Christmas, you just cost me my job," said the voice on the line. "His boss," explained Hillerman, "had seen his name in the paper, told him the auditing firm couldn't stand even a hint of suspicion, told him to find another job. Not easy, my victim said, when you've been fired under a cloud of suspicion." The person's name actually was not published in the paper.

8. Hillerman, lecture notes, folder 11, box 8, THP.

9. Hillerman, rules and lecture notes on style, folder 13, box 8, THP.

10. Mexico Summer Notebook, folder 1, box 2, THP; lecture notes, folder 10, box 8, THP.

11. Hillerman, *Seldom Disappointed*, 267; Susan Walton, interview with the author, 1/31/20.

12. Hillerman to Carl Skiff, n.d. [Feb. 1970], folder 14, box 7, THP.

13. George Johnson, interview with the author, 1/31/2019.

14. Hillerman to "Laura" and Hillerman to "Felipe," folder 12, box 9, THP.

15. Hillerman, *Seldom Disappointed*, 268.

16. Mexico Summer Notebook, folder 1, box 2, THP.

17. Hillerman, *Seldom Disappointed*, 233–34.

18. Jim Belshaw, "Hillerman Leaves Last Mystery," *Albuquerque Journal*, 10/28/2008, 3.

19. Hillerman to Jim Belshaw, 4/1/1979, box 7, THP.

20. Judy Redman to the author, 10/28/2018.

21. Carmella Padilla, interview with the author, 9/11/2019.

22. Anne Hillerman, interview, 8/11/2017.

Chapter 16. The Great American Novel

1. Hillerman, *Seldom Disappointed*, 274.

2. Hillerman to Khan, 5/9/1969, folder 3, box 7, THP; Hillerman, "Mystery, Country Boys, and the Big Reservation," in Hillerman and Bulow, *Talking Mysteries*, 34.

3. Betty Parker and Riley Parker, "Hillerman Country," *The Armchair Detective* 20, no. 1 (1987), 8.

4. Hillerman and Bulow, *Talking Mysteries*, 35.

5. Hillerman, "Cash Flows in SF's Ballot Market," *Santa Fe New Mexican*, 5/9/1962, 1. Hoyt Gimlin, a UP reporter who worked alongside Hillerman, said the extent and visibility of corruption often caused him and Hillerman to wonder what they might be missing (Swaim Collection, cassette 208; box 7; Hillerman to Ray Newton, 9/2/1971, folder 15, box 7, THP; Hoyt Gimlin, interview with the author, 2/23/2018. "I run into reporters all over who say, 'I know which State Capitol you are using. You use Jefferson City, Missouri or . . . ,'" said Hillerman. "You know they tend to be alike. It was actually based on the Capitol at Oklahoma City, where I had worked" (Parker and Parker, "Hillerman Country," 8). I was one of those reporters. I asked Hillerman that very question when I wrote him a fan letter while working as a state

capital correspondent in Jefferson City, MO. My letter is among Tony Hillerman's papers.

6. Hillerman, *Hillerman Country*, 171. In the novel, Cotton and his romantic interest also argue over a newspaper story exposing the possible theft of state tobacco tax stamps, which caused a state employee to wrongly lose his job, based on the case he used frequently in his journalism classes (see chap. 15, n. 7).

7. Daniel Hillerman, interview, 2/15/2020.

8. Dick Pfaff, interview, 2/12/2020; Janet Grado, interview, 1/31/2020.

9. *Albuquerque Journal*, 1/11/1970, C2.

10. Hillerman, *The Fly on the Wall* (New York: HarperCollins Paperback, 2011), 30.

11. Hillerman, *Seldom Disappointed*, 273; "Artist, 43, Leaps to His Death," *Pittsburgh Courier*, 12/20/1969, 1.

12. *New York Times Book Reviews*, 4/19/1970, 334; *Publishers Weekly*, 12/19/1969; *Kirkus*, 3/1/1970; *Saturday Review*, 3/28/1970; *Los Angeles Times*, 4/16/1970, 44.

13. Kahn to Hillerman, 3/31/1970, folder 3, box 7; Hillerman to Morris Freedman, 4/7/1970, folder 4, box 7; Kahn to Hillerman, 4/27/1970, folder 3, box 7; Elmo to Hillerman, 5/4/1970, folder 1, box 7, all in THP.

14. Kahn to Hillerman, 6/9/1970 , folder 1, box 7, THP; *Publishers Weekly*, 12/29/1969, 22.

15. Kahn to Hillerman, 2/2/1970, folder 3, box 7, THP; Hillerman to Elmo, n.d., folder 1, box 7, THP.

16. Elmo to Hillerman, 5/4/1970, folder 1, box 7, THP.

17. Elmo to Hillerman, 9/9/1970, folder 1, box 7, THP.

18. Kahn to Hillerman, 9/3/1970, folder 3, box 7, THP.

19. Kahn to Hillerman, 9/11/1970, folder 3, box 7, THP; Elmo to Hillerman, 12/23/1970, folder 1, box 7, THP.

20. Elmo to Hillerman, 5/26/1970, folder 1, box 7, THP; Kahn to Hillerman, 6/9/1970, folder 3, box 7, THP. A description of Hillerman's potential nonfiction work on the search for early Americans is contained in box 25, THUP.

21. Ross and Silet, "Interview with Tony Hillerman," 122.

22. Hillerman to Tom Pace, n.d. [Apr. 1970], folder 14, box 7, THP; Alan Warhaftig, "Going in Beauty: An Interview with Tony Hillerman," *Los Angeles Review of Books*, 12/6/2017; Hillerman and Bulow, *Talking Mysteries*, 34–35; Malcom Jones, "A Mosaic of the Southwest," *St. Petersburg Times*, 10/30/1988, D1.

Chapter 17. Leaphorn Returns

1. Hillerman, *The Great Taos Bank Robbery and Other True Stories* (Albuquerque: University of New Mexico Press, 1973), 26.

2. Hillerman to Leland C. Wyman, 7/8/1971, folder 15, box 1, THP; Hillerman to Tom Pace, [Apr. 1970], folder 14, box 7, THP; Warhaftig, "Going in Beauty."

3. Maggie Wilson, "Zuni Shalako Ritual Called 'Mystical,'" *Arizona Republic*, 12/12/1970, M3.

4. Hillerman, "The Messenger Birds," in *The Great Taos Bank Robbery*, 1973 ed., 42–43.

5. Hillerman, *Seldom Disappointed*, 283–84.

6. Sue Bernell and Michaela Karni, conversation with Tony Hillerman, folder 3, box 10, THP.

7. Ross and Silert, "Interview with Tony Hillerman," 129.

8. *Kirkus*, 9/1/1971; *Publishers Weekly*, 7/26/1971, 45; *New York Times Book Reviews*, 11/7/1971, 26; *Chicago Tribune*, 11/11/1971, B13.

9. Hillerman to Richard Nokes, 7/23/1974, folder 18, box 7, THP.

10. Hillerman to Evelyn Ely, 2/17/1972, folder 16, box 7, THP; Hillerman to Kahn, 4/5/1972, folder 3, box 7, THP.

11. Janet Grado, interview, 1/30/2020; Hillerman to Kahn, 4/5/1972, folder 3, box 7, THP.

12. Barney Hillerman recounted Gus's attitude on lateness in Robert C. Mercer, "The Brothers Hillerman: Barney and Tony Together," *Oklahoma Today*, Jan.–Feb. 1992, 41.

13. Edmund J. Robins to Hillerman, 2/14/1972, and Hillerman to Robins, n.d., folder 16, box 7, THP; Hillerman, *Seldom Disappointed*, 277; Hillerman to Thomas Scott, 3/10/1972, folder 16, box 7, THP.

14. Tony Hillerman Jr. to the author, 1/20/2020; Hillerman to Wesley Lau, 6/6/1973, folder 16, box 7, THP; Tom Scott to Hillerman, 4/30/1972, folder 16, box 7, THP; Janet Grado, interview, 1/30/2020; Daniel Hillerman, interview, 2/12/2020.

15. Janet Grado, interview, 1/30/2020.

16. Hillerman, *Seldom Disappointed*, 280.

17. Hillerman, *Dance Hall of the Dead* (New York: HarperCollins Paperback, 2009) 5.

18. Hillerman, *Dance Hall of the Dead*, 75; Hillerman, *Blessing Way*, 90.

19. Hillerman, "Leaphorn, Chee, and the Navajo Way," e-book extra to *Listening Woman* (New York: HarperCollins, 2002).

20. Hillerman, "Long Search," 68; Hillerman, *Dance Hall of the Dead*, 30.

21. Hillerman, lecture notes, folder 10, box 8, THP; and teaching notes, folder 11, box 8, THP; Hillerman, "The Reader As Partner," *The Writer*, Oct. 1987, 16.

22. Hillerman, "Building without Blueprints," *The Writer*, May 2007. This article is a modified republication of "Building without Blueprints," *The Writer*, Feb. 1986, 8.

23. Kahn to Hillerman, 3/1/1973, folder 3, box 7, THP.

Chapter 18. The Edgar

1. Hillerman to Carl Brandt, 4/19/1973, folder 17, box 7, THP.

2. Kahn to Hillerman, 3/1/1973, folder 3, box 7, THP.

3. Hillerman to Kahn, 6/4/1973, folder 3, box 7, THP; Hillerman, *Seldom Disappointed*, 295; Hillerman to Keen Rafferty, 2/19/1974, folder 18, box 7, THP.

4. David Muench and Tony Hillerman. *New Mexico: Photography* (Portland, OR: C. H. Belding, 1974); Hillerman to Charles H. Belding, 2/3/1975, folder 8, box 7, THP.

5. *The Great Taos Bank Robbery* appeared with several different subtitles in the years after. In 1976 drugstore's name was changed to Lobo Campus Pharmacy. It remained Lobo Campus Pharmacy until 1998, when it became the Saint Joseph's Square Professional Pharmacy.

6. Hillerman to Keen Rafferty, 2/27/1974, folder 18, box 7, THP.

7. *Kirkus*, 10/1/1973; *New York Times*, 11/25/1973, 49; *Chicago Tribune Book World*, 10/28/1973, 6; Kahn to Hillerman, 10/18/1973, folder 3, box 7, THP.

8. Hillerman to Kahn, 6/4/1973, and n.d. [late spring 1973], folder 3, box 7, THP.

9. Don Schellie, "Tony's Edgar," *Tucson Daily Citizen*, 5/10/1974, 21.

10. *Chicago Tribune Book World*, 4/28/1974, 7.

11. Calla Hay, "Hillerman Finalist for Award," *Santa Fe New Mexican*, 3/17/1974, C5.

12. Carol Potenza, "A Look at the 1974 Edgar Award Finalists: Tony Hillerman, P. D. James, and More," 5/24/2019, https://www.criminalelement.com/1974-edgar-awards, The hotel had been much in the news that spring. It was where disgraced Attorney General John Mitchell, on trial for his role in Watergate, had taken up residence after he and his wife separated.

13. Hillerman, "Tony Hillerman Talks about His Favorites," *Rio Grande Sun*, 6/17/1975, 15.

14. Hillerman to Keen Rafferty, 2/27/1974, folder 18, box 7, THP.

15. John Fischer to Hillerman, 8/1/1975, and Hillerman to Lewis Lapham, 7/28/1975, both in folder 19, box 7, THP.

16. Nick Allison to Hillerman, 2/22/1989, folder 27, box 13, THLP; Larry Ashmead to Hillerman, 10/8/1987, box 5, folder 16, THP; David King Dunaway and Sara L. Spurgeon, eds, *Writing the Southwest* (Albuquerque: University of New Mexico Press, 2003), xlii.

17. Hillerman, "They Sang It Like it Was," *Fodor's Old West* (New York: David McKay Co, 1976), 93; Hillerman to Gregory McNamee, n.d. [1983?], folder 28, box 7, THP.

18. Hillerman to Elmo, 8/16/1971, folder 1, box 7, THP; Frank Hamilton Cushing, "The Origin of the Dragonfly and of the Corn Priests, or Guardians of the Seed," *The Millstone*, Mar. 1884, 38; Tony Hillerman, *The Boy Who Made Dragonfly* (Albuquerque: University of New Mexico Press, 1986), 73–74; Lucille Schultz to Hillerman, 9/9/1971, folder 1, box 7, THP. Schultz also told Hillerman Harper Junior Books would publish the book with black-and-white illustrations and asked if he knew "any good Indian artists." Letters were sent to two Pueblo artists. It's not known if they replied, and in the end Harper selected a white artist.

19. Kahn to Hillerman, 3/8/1971, folder 3, box 7, THP; Hillerman to Charlotte Zolotow, 4/25/1971, folder 1, box 7, THP. In 1998, the Charlotte Zolotow Award was created as an annual prize for outstanding writing in a picture book.

20. Harold Cruse, *Rebellion or Revolution?* (New York: Morrow, 1968), 122.

21. Hillerman, graduation speech, May 23, 1976, folder 6, box 10, THP.

22. Norman Boucher, "West Seller," *Boston Globe Magazine*, 12/8/1991.

23. Hillerman, *Seldom Disappointed*, 285.

24. *Albuquerque Journal*, 8/19/1976, C9; Janet Grado, interview, 1/30/2020.

25. Monica Atwell to the author, 4/16/2020.

26. Janet Grado, interview, 1/30/2020.

27. Hillerman, *Seldom Disappointed*, 277.

28. Dick Pfaff, interview with the author, 2/12/2020

29. Anne Hillerman, "Adopted Family Very Real," *Albuquerque Journal*, 12/17/2000, E10.

Chapter 19. Trouble with Leaphorn

1. Hillerman, *Seldom Disappointed*, 252. Fascinatingly, Hillerman identifies Etcitty's matrilineal clan as Taadii Dine'e, or Slow-Talking People, a fictitious clan invented for Leaphorn and used for Chee as well.

2. Hillerman, "Dinétah, If I Forget You . . ." *Arizona Highways*, Aug. 1979, 4.

3. Hillerman, "Dinétah, If I Forget You . . ." 9.

4. Hillerman, foreword to Leroy DeJolie, *Navajoland: A Native Son Shares His Legacy* (Phoenix: Arizona Highways, 2005), 13. Hillerman told this story so frequently that on some occasions he misattributed the conversation to Austin Sam, another Navajo acquaintance.

5. Hillerman, "Building without Blueprints," *The Writer*, Feb. 1986, 8; Hillerman to Jan Broberg, 2/13/1974, folder 18, box 7, THP.

6. Hillerman, "Building without Blueprints," 8.

7. Hillerman, "Building without Blueprints," 9.

8. Hillerman, "A Day in the Life of Chapter Two," in Greenberg, *Tony Hillerman Companion*, 316–17.

9. Hillerman, "Building without Blueprints," 8-9.

10. Hillerman, "Building without Blueprints," 9; Deborah Uroda, "Mystery Writer Draws Material for Books from Navajo Culture," *Durango (CO) Herald*, 1984, copy in author's files.

11. Hillerman and Bulow, *Talking Mysteries*, 48.

12. Hillerman, "Building without Blueprints," 9.

13. Alex Ward, "Navajo Cops on the Case," *New York Times Magazine*, 5/14/1989, 39; also see Greenberg, *Tony Hillerman Companion*, 18–19.

14. Hillerman, *Listening Woman* (New York: HarperCollins, 2010), 64-65.

15. Kahn to Hillerman, 12/9/1976, folder 16, box 2, THP.

16. Kahn to Hillerman, 3/7/1977, and Hillerman to Kahn, 9/20/1977, folder 16, box 2, THP.

17. Elmo to Hillerman, 9/25/1975, and Tom Egan to Elmo, 9/20/1977, folder 1, box 7, THP.

18. Hillerman to Elmo, 9/7/1977, folder 1, box 7, THP.

19. Alan Nevins to the author, 4/14/2020.

20. Hillerman to Kahn, 9/20/1977, folder 16, box 2, THP.

Chapter 20. The Invention of Chee

1. Hillerman to Claire M. Smith, 3/18/1976, folder 20, box 7, THP.

2. *Santa Cruz Sentinel*, 8/24/1977, 22; guestbook posting in *New York Times*, 11/6/2007.

3. John Nichols to Hillerman, 1/11/1975, folder 19, box 7, THP. The strikingly handsome Knowlton was said to have been one of the original Marlboro men in cigarette advertisements. I could not confirm this family tale.

4. Hillerman, *Seldom Disappointed*, 295–96; guestbook posting in *New York Times*, 11/6/2007.

5. Hillerman, *Seldom Disappointed*, 297, 253.

6. Jon L. Breen, "Interview with Tony Hillerman," in Greenberg, *Hillerman Companion*, 58.

7. *Albuquerque Journal*, 11/12/1963, A5; *Albuquerque Journal*, 6/24/1938, 11.

8. *Daily News-Sun*, Hobbs, NM, 5/25/1978, 14; Hillerman to Kahn, 9/20/1977, folder 16, box 2, THP.

9. Jack Janowski, "Tony Hillerman: Rare, Radiant Author," *Albuquerque Journal*, 4/16/1978, D4.

10. Hillerman, "Building without Blueprints," *The Writer*, May 2007, 25.

11. Hillerman to Cathy and Charly Bullock, 4/13/1988, "Letters from the Famous," box 12, THUP. The Bullocks bought and restored the Anne Baxter house, which was likely designed by the architect's grandson Erick Lloyd Wright.

12. Materassi, "Case of Tony Hillerman," 451.

13. Bernell and Karni, "Conversation with Tony Hillerman," folder 3, box 10, THP; "Interview with Tony Hillerman," 5, DDSWR; Warhaftig, "Going in Beauty"; Ross and Silet, "Interview with Tony Hillerman," 134–35; Hillerman to Ellen Strenski and Robley Evans, 12/1/1981, folder 25, box 7, THP.

14. Douglas Preston, *Talking to the Ground* (New York: Simon & Schuster, 2019) 276.

15. Michael Haederle, "'All Navajo, All the Time': With a Homely Mix of Music, News and Gossip, KNDN Binds a Far-Flung Indian Community," *Los Angeles Times*, 8/3/1992.

16. Greenberg, *Tony Hillerman Companion*, 64.

17. Hillerman, *People of Darkness* (New York: HarperCollins Paperback, 2009), 6, 7.

18. Ruth Lopez, "Book Notes," *Santa Fe New Mexican*, 8/23/1998, F2.

19. Hillerman, *People of Darkness*, 137; Parker and Parker, "Hillerman Country," 11; David Stephens to Hillerman, 7/13/1989, folder 25, box 12, THP.

20. Hillerman, *Seldom Disappointed*, 57, 60.

21. *Publishers Weekly*, 3/13/1978, 107; *Kirkus*, 4/1/78; *New York Times Book Reviews*, 5/7/1978, 7.

22. *Albuquerque Journal*, 3/30/1979, E1.

23. Hillerman, *Seldom Disappointed*, 248.

24. *Santa Fe New Mexican*, 5/13/1979, D3.

25. Kahn to Hillerman, 10/16/1979, folder 10, box 3, THP.

26. Hillerman, *People of Darkness*, 112.

27. *New York Daily News*, 10/22/1980, J7.

28. Tim Duggan, interview with the author, 11/6/2017.

29. *Kirkus*, 10/1/1980; Patricia Holt, "Tony Hillerman," *Publisher's Weekly*, 10/24/1980, 6.

Chapter 21. Two Stories, Two Novels

1. Anna Poole, "Tony Hillerman and the Spell of New Mexico," *New Mexico*, June 1982, 29; Larry Ashmead to Hillerman, 10/27/1980, and 11/20/1980, folder 10, box 3, THP.

2. Perry Knowlton to Hillerman, 6/25/1980, "Chee's Witch" folder, box 11, THUP; D. H. Lynn, "Editor's Notes," *Kenyon Review*, n.s., 18, no. 3–4 (Summer–Autumn, 1996), 1.

3. Hillerman and Bulow, *Talking Mysteries*, 80.

4. Hillerman to Susan Caldrella, 12/10/1979, box 10, THUP.

5. Alice K. Turner to Hillerman, 7/24/1980, "Chee's Witch" folder, box 11, THUP.

6. Turner to Hillerman, 10/3/1980, Chee's Witch" folder, box 11, THUP.

7. Ross and Silet, "Interview with Tony Hillerman," 135.

8. *Salt Lake Tribune*, 6/10/1984, 8E; Hillerman and Bulow, *Talking Mysteries*, 50.

9. *Albuquerque Journal*, 6/11/1989, G1.

10. Hillerman and Bulow, *Talking Mysteries*, 51. Hillerman actually says Leaphorn rather than Chee in this interview. It was not the only time he confused his characters when later telling stories about his books.

11. Michael Parfit, "Weaving Mysteries That Tell of Life among the Navajos," *Smithsonian* 21, no. 9 (1990), 98.

12. Hillerman, "Indian Holy Wars: Of Shrines and Eagles' Nests," *Los Angeles Times*, 8/16/1981, pt. 5, 3.

13. *Kirkus*, 4/1/1982; *Berkeley Gazette*, 4/4/1982, 11; *Chicago Tribune*, 6/27/1982, sec. 7, 4; *Philadelphia Inquirer*, 5/23/1982, 7.

14. *Baltimore Sun*, 11/4/1983, B2; Lee Goerner to Ashmead, 1983, folder 27, box 7, THP.

15. Cam Rossie, "Writers Hope to Debunk Myths about West," *Albuquerque Journal*, 6/27/1982, E5; Lewis Preston, "Shootout at the P.C. Corral: WNA's 1982 Santa Fe Convention," *Roundup*, Oct. 2020, 20.

16. Anna Dooling, "Realists Call for Showdown with the Cowboy Fantasy," *Albuquerque Journal*, 7/4/1982, D1.

17. Hillerman to "Doug," n.d. [1980], folder 24, box 7, THP; Beth Ann Krier, "He Walks in Indian's Moccasins," *Los Angeles Times*, 5/27/1982, V17.

18. Hillerman to Ellen Strenski and Robley Evans, 12/1/1981, folder 25, box 7, THP.

19. Hillerman to Diana Stein, 6/17/1983, folder 28, box 7, THP; Hillerman, *Seldom Disappointed*, 324; Meg Scherch, "No Simple Solution," *Taos (NM) News*, 7/10/1984, C3.

20. Hillerman, *Ghost Way* (New York: HarperCollins Paperback, 2010), 52.

21. Parker and Parker, "Hillerman Country," 8–9; *Salt Lake Tribune*, 6/10/1984, 8E.

22. Hillerman to Rick Layman, 2/18/1986, folder 7, box 7, THP; Hillerman and Bulow, *Talking Mysteries*, 38–39; Hillerman, *Ghost Way*, 4.

23. Hillerman, *Seldom Disappointed*, 299–300; Frederick Turner to Hillerman, 1/7/1979, folder 23, box 7, THP.

24. *Kansas City Times*, 8/16/1983, A4; *Salt Lake Tribune*, 6/10/1984, 8E; Joe Blades to Hillerman, 6/12/1984, folder 4, box 7, THP; Ashmead to Hillerman, 7/26/1982, folder 3, box 7, THP.

Chapter 22. Character Identity Crisis

1. John Carr, "Evil and a Good Ol' Boy," draft manuscript, folder 2, box 10, THP.

2. Carr, manuscript of "Evil and a Good Ol' Boy," 7–8.

3. Hillerman, *Blessing Way*, 93–94.

4. Hillerman, *The Shape Shifter* (New York: HarperCollins Paperback, 2006), 14.

5. Typed notes for article, Cat Project folder, box 11, THUP.

6. *Publishers Weekly*, 4/13/1990, 26; and 10/11/1993, 61; Ashmead to Hillerman, 2/4/1985 and 3/18/1985, both in folder 3, box 7, THP.

7. *New York Times Book Review*, 6/2/1985, 38; Hillerman, *Seldom Disappointed*, 263.

8. "Tony Hillerman's New Mexico," KNMW Notable New Mexicans, aired 5/11/2004; Sherry Robinson, interview with the author, 3/7/2020; *New Mexico Daily Lobo*, 5/6/1985, 1.

9. Steve Hillerman, KOB Newscast, 8/16/2006.

10. *Philadelphia Daily News*, 3/12/1986, 43; *St. Petersburg (FL) Times*, 3/24/1987, 70; Hillerman, *Seldom Disappointed*, 298–99.

11. Brad Crawford, "7 Questions with Tony Hillerman, *Writer's Digest*, Jan. 2000; Hillerman, *Skinwalkers* (New York: HarperCollins Paperback, 2011), 69–70.

12. Hillerman, "Making Mysteries with Navajo Materials," in *Literature and Anthropology*, ed. Philip A. Dennis and Wendell Aycock (Lubbock: Texas Tech University Press, 1989), 7.

13. Hillerman, interview, in Craig McNeil, James Redford, Chris Eyre, Robert Redford, and Wes Studi, *Skinwalkers*, DVD (Burbank, CA: Warner Home Video, 2002).

14. Hillerman, *Dance Hall of the Dead*, 140.

15. Hillerman and Bulow, *Talking Mysteries*, 83.

16. Hillerman, "Navajos Call Them Skinwalkers, *New Mexico Magazine*, July 1992, 66.

17. Materassi, "Case of Tony Hillerman," 450.

18. Hillerman, *Skinwalkers*, 79–80.

19. *Contact*, 3/31/1986, folder 16, box 10, THP; Ursula Le Guin to Hillerman, 9/20/1986, and Dennis Zook to William Shinker, 10/8/1986, both in folder 3, box 7, THP.

20. Knowlton to Hillerman, 9/8/1986, folder 2, box 7, THP; Ani Chamichian to Hillerman, n.d. [fall 1986], folder 1, box 8, THP; Ashmead to Hillerman, 5/22/1987, folder 10, box 5, THP.

21. *Santa Fe New Mexican*, 2/3/1986, E1.

22. *Santa Fe New Mexican*, 6/6/1986, B4.

23. Elmo to Hillerman, 8/27/1985, folder 1, box 7, THP.

24. Janet Grado, interview, 1/30/2020; Elizabeth Hadas to Hillerman, 8/11/1992, folder 1, box 16, THP. Previous editions had listed Hillerman as the author on the cover and only included "retold by" on the title page. The copyright of the text in both editions remained with Hillerman.

25. *Kirkus*, 1/1/1987.

26. Martin Cruz Smith, "When the Owl Became a Wolf," *San Francisco Chronicle Review*, 12/21/1986, 1. Smith had New Mexico connections, one of which was that as a child his dad played sax at Casa Manana, a nightspot he used in his most recent thriller. Dennis Drabelle to the author, 6/12/2020.

27. Peter Thorpe, interview with the author, 3/17/2020.

28. Hillerman, *Ghostway*, 50.

29. Lewis MacAdams, "Navajo Gumshoe," *LA Weekly*, 3/5/1987, 59.

30. Hillerman to William Tydeman, 10/2/1986, Accessions folder, THP; Paul Craig, "Mysteries Master Navajo Setting," *Sacramento Bee*, 2/1/1987, 30; William Shinker to Hillerman and others, 1/23/1987, folder 10, box 15, THP.

31. Robert Redford, interview with the author, 7/2/2019.

32. *Santa Fe Reporter*, 3/14/1990, 11.

33. Hillerman, interview, p. 6, DDSWR.

34. Hillerman, interview with David Dunaway, p. 8, box 3, THUP; Hillerman, *Seldom Disappointed*, 294.

35. Donna Schober to Hillerman, 6/23/1989, folder 24, box 12, THP.

Chapter 23. Breakout

1. *San Juan Record*, 7/29/1981, 5. Unless indicated otherwise, the description of Hillerman's San Juan River journey and his comments are drawn from his article, "A Canyon, An Egret . . . And a Mystery," *Audubon*, July 1989, 30–36, as well as my own trip in 2019 retracing Hillerman's float.

2. Nancy Dahl to the author, 7/3/2019; Dan Murphy obituary, https://www.stlouiscremation.com/obituary/dan-murphy.

3. Hillerman, "Places for Spirits, Places for Ghosts," in *New Mexico*, 107.

4. On a 2019 visit I found the spot unchanged. Even the moss and ivy still grew.

5. Hillerman, *Skinwalkers*, 135.

6. Hillerman, *A Thief of Time* (New York: HarperCollins Paperback, 2009), 187–88.

7. Hillerman, *Thief of Time*, 314.

8. *Arizona Daily Sun*, Flagstaff, 9/4/1986, A6; Rachel Dickinson, "Land of Mysteries," *Arizona Highways*, June 2006, 14.

9. Patricia O'Connor, "Chief of Detectives," *Southwest Airlines Spirit*, May 1992, 31–33, 44–49; Catherine Walsh, "Tony Hillerman," *St. Anthony Messenger* 99, no. 1 (June 1991), 28.

10. Ashmead to Hillerman, 10/8/1987; John Mitchell to Hillerman, 10/22/1987; William M. Shinker to Hillerman, 10/27/1987, all in folder 16, box 5, THP.

11. *New York Times*, 3/31/1987, 1; Knowlton to Hillerman, 11/6/1987, folder 2, box 7, THP; Knowlton to Hillerman, 12/22/1987, folder 14, box 10, THP.

12. Joseph Montebello to Hillerman, 11/20/1987, folder 3, box 7, THP.

13. Peter Thorpe, interview with the author, 3/17/2020.

14. Thorpe, interview, 3/17/2020.

15. Chauncey Mabe, "Literary Circles," *Fort Lauderdale News*, 1/16/1988, 17.

16. Chauncey Mabe, "Crime Novel a Fertile Field for an Author," *Fort Lauderdale News*, 1/10/1988, F1; Marilyn Stasio, "Remembering Tony Hillerman," 10/30/2008, https://artsbeat.blogs.nytimes.com/2008/10/30/remembering-tony-hillerman.

17. Review of *A Thief of Time*, *Publisher's Weekly*, 06/03/1988; Steve Paul, "Probing Mysteries in the Southwest," *Kansas City Star*, 6/26/1988, C1; *New York Times*, 8/16/1988, C15.

18. Gabe Barillas, interview with the author, 3/16/2020.

19. Hillerman, interview, Don Swaim Collection.

20. Ashmead to Hillerman, 8/10/1988, folder 3, box 7, THP; Sue Grafton to Hillerman, 9/7/1988, folder 28, box 7, THP.

Chapter 24. Leaphorn and Chee Go to Hollywood

1. "Movie of Hillerman Novel Possible for NM," *Carlsbad Current-Argus*, 3/19/1989, 4.
2. Scott D. Pierce, "Redford on Hillerman," *Deseret News*, 8/11/2002; Robert Redford, interview with the author 7/2/2019; Susan King, "The Bestseller They Couldn't Sell," *Los Angeles Times*, 11/17/2002.
3. Aljean Harmetz, "2 Women Succeed as Producers, but Easy Street Is Down the Road," *New York Times*, 9/14/1988, C19.
4. Bonni Lee, interview with the author, 7/24/2019; Tony Hillerman Jr., interview, 7/21/2019; *Library Journal*, 5/15/1989, 108; *Santa Fe Reporter*, 3/14/1990, 11.
5. Hillerman, "The Good and the Ugly," box 11, THUP; *Santa Fe Reporter*, 3/14/1990, 11.
6. Jim Arnholz, interview with Hillerman, *Albuquerque Journal*, 6/11/1989, G1. Arnholz would later change his name to Belshaw.
7. Patrick O'Driscoll, "Still the Guy Down the Block," Contemporary, *Sunday Denver Post*, 9/24/1989, 9.
8. Jim Barlow, "Tony Hillerman," *Houston Chronicle Magazine*, 4/22/1990, 6; O'Driscoll, "Still the Guy Down the Block," 9.
9. Hillerman to John Michel, 1/24/1989, folder 2, box 6, THP; Ross and Silet, "Interview with Tony Hillerman," 126.
10. Bernard St. Germain, a conductor on the Santa Fe Railway for almost forty years, helped Hillerman with the scenes around the railroad tracks and later with *Finding Moon*.
11. Hillerman, *Seldom Disappointed*, 326; Hillerman loved his dig at the Smithsonian. In particular, Hillerman's enmity was directed at Aleš Hrdlička, an early anthropologist who used his pulpit at the world-famous museum to advance his theory there was no "Early Man" in the Americas because the remains did not possess Neanderthal characteristics. While prowling the Smithsonian National Museum of Natural History in the course of researching *Talking God*, Hillerman came across a bust of Hrdlička. "The legend at its base didn't mention that his major contribution to science was to demonstrate that 'Invincible Ignorance' is indeed possible if endorsed by the Smithsonian Institut[ion]." Hillerman, foreword to *A Thief of Time*, written in May 1999, box 11, THUP.
12. Alex Ward, "Navajo Cops on the Case," *New York Times Magazine*, 5/14/1989, 39.
13. Hillerman, *Talking God* (New York: Harper Paperback Edition, 2010), 47.
14. John Michel to Hillerman, 6/24/1989, folder 14, box 12, THP.
15. Catherine Healy to Hillerman, 10/13/1989, folder 28, and Vivian Howes to Hillerman, 6/22/1989, folder 24, both in box 12, THP.
16. Ashmead to Hillerman, 7/29/1989, folder 8, box 15, THP.
17. Kathleen Ferris to Hillerman, 5/31/1989, and William Tydeman, notes, 10/2/1986, in Manuscripts Accession folder, THP. At the time, Hillerman was "not 100 percent

sure" about signing documents legally committing his papers to the university because he had named his daughter Anne as the literary executor of his estate.

18. O'Driscoll, "Still the Guy Down the Block," 11.

19. Edward J. Sparks to Hillerman, 8/16/1989, folder 26, box 12, THP.

20. Shinker to Hillerman, 3/6/1989, folder 8, box 15, THP.

21. O'Driscoll, "Still the Guy Down the Block," 9; Ross and Silet, "Interview with Tony Hillerman," 153.

22. Shinker to Hillerman, 8/24/1989 and 9/7/1989, folder 8, box 15, THP.

23. John Michel to Hillerman, 3/9/1990, and Shinker to Hillerman, 3/20/1990, folder 8, box 15, THP.

24. Robert R. Mercer, "The Brothers Hillerman," *Oklahoma Today*, Jan.–Feb. 1992, 42.

25. Mercer, "Brothers Hillerman," 41.

26. Hillerman, *Seldom Disappointed*, 327.

27. Mercer, "Brothers Hillerman," 44.

28. Shinker to Hillerman, 7/23/1990, folder 8, box 15, THP.

29. Robert F. Gish, "Officer Chee Has Something to Prove, *New York Times*, 6/24/1990, sec. 7, 12.

30. Shinker to Hillerman, 7/23/1990, folder 8, box 15, THP.

31. *Star-Gazette*, Elmira, NY, 6/20/1989, 4.

32. *Deseret News*, 12/30/1992, B5.

33. Patrick Markey to Hillerman, postcard, n.d. [Dec. 1990], box 12, THUP.

34. Louis A. Hieb, "In Memoriam: Tony Hillerman, 1925–2008," *New Mexico Historical Review* 84, no. 1 (Winter 2009): 124.

35. Tim Knowlton to Hillerman, 1/1/1991, box 18, THUP; Knowlton to Bonni Lee, 8/9/1991, box 10, THUP.

36. Robert Redford to Hillerman, 12/22/1992, box 12, THUP.

37. Hillerman, "Why Los Ranchos," box 11, THUP.

38. O'Driscoll, "Still the Guy Down the Block," 13; Catherine Walsh, "Tony Hillerman," *St. Anthony Messenger*, June 1991, 34; Jim Barlow, "Tony Hillerman," *Houston Chronicle Magazine*, 4/22/1990, 7.

39. *Santa Fe Reporter*, 5/8/1991, 12; *Headlight*, Deming, NM, 4/26/1991, 2; Mary Campbell, "Navajos and Hillerman Remain Friends," Cedar Rapids, IA, *Gazette*, 11/3/1991, 2F.

40. Hillerman to Eamon Dolan, 3/28/1991, Peter Thorpe Papers, privately held (hereafter PTP).

41. Ashmead to Hillerman, 6/18/1991, "Mudhead Kiva" folder, box 10, THUP.

42. Hillerman, ed., *The Best of the West: An Anthology of Classic Writing from the American West* (New York: HarperCollins, 1991), xiv.

43. Hillerman, *Hillerman Country: A Journey through the Southwest with Tony Hillerman*, photographs by Barney Hillerman (New York: HarperCollins, 1991), 18.

44. Robert R. Mercer, "Barney and Tony Together," *Oklahoma Today*, Feb. 1992, 44.

45. David Monahan, "For the Time Being," *Sooner Catholic*, 6/9/1991, 9; Mercer, "Barney and Tony Together," 42.

46. James Peshlakai to Hillerman, 2/17/1982, folder 6, box 15, THUP.

Chapter 25. Into a Heart of Darkness

1. Hillerman to Martin Greenberg, 4/14/1989, folder 22, box 12, THP.

2. Ollie Reed Jr., "Here's to Your Health, Tony," *Albuquerque Tribune*, 9/7/1993; Janet Grado to author, 7/14/2020.

3. Stasio, "Remembering Tony Hillerman," https://artsbeat.blogs.nytimes.com/2008 /10/30/remembering-tony-hillerman.

4. Jeff Guinn, "Taking the Long Way Home to Success," *Fort Worth Star-Telegram*, 4/6/1992, 2. One can still find copies of "Mudhead Kiva" book jackets for sale.

5. John Robinson, "Tony Hillerman: A Mystery Writer Who Regularly Turns out Best Sellers," *Greensboro News & Record*, 11/1/1992; J. C. Martin, "Kingsolver and Hillerman to Headline 20th Annual Writers' Conference," *Arizona Daily Star*, 12/14/1992, B3; Pasatiempo, *Santa Fe New Mexican*, 5/15/1992, 13; Guinn, "Taking the Long Way Home," 2.

6. Mary Campbell, "Navajos and Hillerman Remain Friend.," *The Gazette*, Cedar Rapids, IA, 11/3/1991, 2F.

7. Hillerman, *Sacred Clowns* (New York: HarperCollins Paperbacks, 2009). 316–18.

8. Reed, "Here's to Your Health."

9. Larry Calloway, "The Curse of the N.Y. Journalist," *Albuquerque Journal*, 6/6/1993, C1.

10. New York *Daily News*, 6/16/1992, 12.

11. *Kirkus*, 8/1/1993.

12. Dick Adler, "Two Linked Murders Bemuse Tony Hillerman's Navajo Cops," *Chicago Tribune*, 9/26/1993.

13. Donald Craig, "Death of a Shaman," *Washington Post*, 9/5/1993.

14. *Reno Gazetteer Journal*, 9/19/1993, C8.

15. Richard Benke, "School Turning Dreams into Reality," *Albuquerque Journal*, 1/2/1994, C3.

16. Hillerman, "Palawan," *Islands*, Sept.–Oct., 1998, 70.

17. Hillerman, *Seldom Disappointed*, 311–12.

18. HarperCollins press release, 11/16/1993, folder 2, box 18, THP.

19. Ollie Reed Jr., "Hillerman's Back," *Honolulu Star Bulletin*, 9/11/1993, B2.

20. Hillerman, "Palawan," 72.

21. Hillerman, "Palawan," 73.

22. Hillerman, *Seldom Disappointed*, 316.

23. Janet Grado, interview, 1/30/2020.

24. Dr. Neal Shadoff, interview with the author, 2/17/2020; *Albuquerque Journal*, 5/4/1994, C1.

25. Hillerman, *Seldom Disappointed*, 291; *Santa Fe Reporter*, 3/28/1990, 5. There are various versions of this tale. His 1990 account, closer to the date of the proposed dinner, is likely to be the most accurate.

26. Jim Belshaw, interview with the author, 3/7/2020; Dick Pfaff, interview with the author, 2/12/2020.

27. Jim Belshaw, "Hillerman Leaves Last Mystery," *Albuquerque Journal*, 10/28/2008, A3.

28. Jim Belshaw, "Laughter Is the Best Obituary," *Albuquerque Journal*, 3/20/2005, B1. Belshaw used the same headline eleven years earlier for a remembrance of Jesse Price, another member of the poker group; William J. Buchanan to Hillerman, 8/16/1975, folder 14, box 7, THP.

29. Hillerman to William J. Buchanan, 8/20/1975, folder 14, box 7, THP.

30. Jim Belshaw, "In War There Is Love," *Albuquerque Journal*, 5/24/2005, B4.

31. Tim Madigan, "Their War Ended 70 Years Ago. Their Trauma Didn't, *Washington Post,* 9/11/2015.

32. Janet Grado, interview, 1/30/2020.

33. Paula Schnurr, interview with the author, 6/17/2020.

34. Hillerman, scrap of writing from 1984, box 2, THUP.

35. Hillerman, scrap of writing, box 12, THUP.

36. Belshaw, interview with the author, 3/7/2020.

Chapter 26. A Fallen Man

1. Hillerman to Peter Thorpe, Mar. 2005, PTP.

2. Hillerman to Thorpe, Mar. 2005, PTP.

3. Hillerman, "An Apology, Acknowledgments, Denial, and Dedication," foreword to *Finding Moon* (New York: HarperCollins Paperback, 2011).

4. *La Crosse Tribune*, 11/9/1995, D13.

5. Hillerman to Thorpe, Mar. 2005, PTP; Hillerman, *Seldom Disappointed*, 328.

6. Jamie Redford, interview with the author, 7/10/2019.

7. Jamie Redford to Hillerman, n.d. [Mar. 1994], box 12, THUP.

8. Jamie Redford, interview with the author, 7/10/2019.

9. Jamie Redford to Hillerman, n.d. [fall 1995], box 12, THUP.

10. Bob Rosebrough to Hillerman, 7/29/1987, box 12, THUP; Rosebrough, interview with the author, 1/21/2020.

11. Bob Rosebrough, *The Talus Slope* (privately published, 2002), 30.

12. Rosebrough, *Talus Slope*, 32; Rosebrough, interview with the author, 1/21/2020. Rosebrough is referring to the long-running TV crime drama series *Columbo*.

13. Hillerman, *The Fallen Man* (New York: HarperCollins Paperback, 2010), 108.

14. Hillerman, *Fallen Man*, 201.

15. Marilyn Stasio, review of *The Fallen Man*, *New York Times*, 12/8/1996; *Kirkus*, 10/1/1996; Wilda Williams, review of *The Fallen Man*, *Library Journal*, 10/15/1996. 90.

16. *Daily Oklahoman*, 11/21/1997, 40; Janet Grado, interview, 6/12/2020.

17. Hillerman, "Getting to Goldtooth," *Arizona Highways*, Dec. 2005, 13–14.

18. Ashmead to Hillerman, 2/10/1998, box 10, THUP.

19. It's not clear whose idea it was to write a memoir. The correspondence indicates that it was Hillerman's but Anne Hillerman recalls her father saying it had been his editor's idea.

20. James Brooke, "Like Butch and Sundance, Fugitives Elude Police in Desert," *New York Times*, 8/3/1998, 10.

21. Hillerman, *Hunting Badger* (New York: HarperCollins Paperbacks, 2010), 101.

22. *Arizona Daily Star*, 2/14/2000, A8; *Deseret News*, 11/14/1999.

23. Jeff Guinn, "Hillerman's Navajo Heroes Live On—For Now, at Least," *Fort Worth Star-Telegram*, 1/19/2000, F1, https://www.chicagotribune.com/news/ct-xpm-2000 -02-09-0002090040-story.html.

24. Lora Shields to Diana Stein, 1/2/1984, folder 29, box 7, THP. The letter was passed on to Hillerman.

25. Von Del Chamberlain to Hillerman, 7/20/1988, folder 7, box 8, THP.

26. Steve Paul, "Native Thriller Stumbles in 'Strange Landscape,'" *Gazette*, Montreal, 7/22/1989, K11.

27. Tova Indritz to Hillerman, 8/27/1990, and Claire R. Farrer to Hillerman, 9/26/1988, folder 6, box 15, THP; Michael Parfit, "Weaving Mysteries That Tell of Life among the Navajos," *Smithsonian* 21, no. 9 (1990), 98.

28. Hillerman, *Seldom Disappointed*, 67.

29. Peter Thorpe, interview with the author, 3/17/2020.

30. Timothy Foote, "Where Leaphorn Leapt From," *New York Times*, 10/28/2001, sec. 7, 34.

Chapter 27. The Farewell Quartet

1. *Albuquerque Journal*, 1/11/2004, F6; Janet Grado to the author, 7/28/2020. Hillerman's aversion to tuxedos was not, however, absolute. In 1976, for instance, he made an exception for his daughter Janet, wearing one to her wedding.

2. Jeff Guinn, "Taking the Long Way Home," *Fort Worth Star-Telegram*, 4/6/1992, 2; *Baltimore Sun*, 5/2/2002, 3E.

3. *Publishers Weekly*, 4/15/2002, 46.

4. Hillerman, *The Wailing Wind* (New York: HarperCollins Paperbacks, 2010).

5. Hillerman, *Wailing Wind*, 9.

6. "Peshlakai Proud to Offer Visitors a True Native American Show," *Williams–Grand Canyon News*, July 27, 2000, williamsnews.com/news/2000/jul/27/peshlakai-proud -to-offer-visitorsbra-true-native-; Erin Ford, "Walking in Beauty: Navajo Educator, Dancer, Musician and Medicine Man James Peshlakai Passes at 71," *Navajo-Hopi Observer*, 3/21/2017.

7. Hillerman, *Seldom Disappointed*; "Peshlakai Proud to Offer Visitors."

8. Hillerman, *Wailing Wind*, 131.

9. *Publishers Weekly*, 4/15/2002, 44.

10. George Guidall, interview with the author, 6/17/2020.

11. "Leaphorn and Chee books Were Based on Real-Life Experiences," *This Week Community News*, 11/6/2008, https://www.thisweeknews.com/article/20081106/NEWS /311069558.

12. Carolyn Marino, interview with the author, 6/17/2020.

13. Jacqueline Cutler, "PBS Will Air Tony Hillerman Novel–Based 'Coyote Waits,'" *Post-Star*, Glen Falls, NY, E1; Deborah Baker, "After One Success, Two More Tony Hillerman Mysteries," *New York Times*, 5/4/2003, C3.

14. Richard Benke, "'Joe Leaphorn' Is Different for TV, but Author Tony Hillerman Is Happy," *Leaf-Chronicle*, Clarksville, TN, 11/24/2002.

15. Interviews with Hillerman and Robert Redford, in Craig McNeil, James Redford, Chris Eyre, Robert Redford, and Wes Studi, *Skinwalkers*," DVD (Burbank, CA: Warner Home Video, 2002).

16. *Albuquerque Journal*, 8/18/2002, F3.

17. *New York Times*, 5/4/2003, sec. 7, 19; *Kirkus*, 4/1/2003; Clay Evans, "Sweet Sixteen," *Fresno (CA) Bee*, 6/8/2003, J3.

18. Guinn, "Taking the Long Way Home," 2.

19. Hillerman, *Skeleton Man* (New York: HarperCollins Paperbacks, 2010), 55–56.

20. Joanna Craig, interview with the author, 7/10/2020.

21. Hillerman to Carol Cartwright, 7/18/2004, box 19, THUP.

22. Joanna Craig to Hillerman, 8/26/2003, box 3, THUP.

23. Hillerman to Joanna Craig, 8/23/2004, 9/26/2003, and 9/16/2003, Joanna Craig Papers, privately held.

24. On James Kilroy, who created the saying and drawing, see Kate Kelly, "Kilroy Was Here—A Story from World War II," https://americacomesalive.com/kilroy-story -world-war-ii .

25. Hillerman, *Kilroy Was There: A GI's War in Photographs*, photos from the collection of Frank Kessler (Kent, OH: Kent State University Press, 2004), 74.

26. *A Thief of Time*, 24-25; Hillerman to Easton, 8/28/2002, and Hillerman to Jamie Redford, 8/19/1998, both in box 7, THUP.

27. Vince Horiuchi, "Tedious First Half Muzzles Hillerman's 'Coyote Waits' on PBS," *Salt Lake Tribune*, 11/14/2003, D15.

28. Jamie Redford to Hillerman, n.d., folder 2, box 10, THUP.

29. Bill Richardson, interview with the author, 4/13/2020.

30. Anne Hillerman to the author, 7/28/2020; *Publishers Weekly*, 4/14/2003.

31. Hillerman to Joanna Craig, 1/14/2004, Craig Papers.

32. Hillerman to Craig, 1/22/2004, 1/31/2004, and 2/9/2004, Craig Papers.

33. Hillerman to Craig, 2/20/2004, Craig Papers.

34. "Tony Hillerman's Jim Chee and Joe Leaphorn Mysteries," http://www.dancingbadger .com/tony_hillerman.htm.

35. Hillerman, *Shape Shifter*, 145.

36. Hillerman, *Shape Shifter*, 52; Guinn, "Hillerman's Navajo Heroes."

37. Hillerman to Peter Thorpe, Mar. 2005, Peter Thorpe Papers.

Chapter 28. The Blue Flint Girl

1. Johnny Boggs to the author, 7/3/2020. Earlier, after Boggs sent Hillerman a formal letter about the prize committee's unanimous decision, Hillerman left a message on Boggs's answering machine. "He was just bubbling with excitement in that Oklahoma accent, wanted to know if there was a certificate or something like that," said Boggs, "I called back and said there was a big bronze award that came with that."

2. Johnny D. Boggs, "Interview with Tony Hillerman," *Wild West*, June 2008.

14. Richard Benke, "'Joe Leaphorn' Is Different for TV, but Author Tony Hillerman Is Happy," *Leaf-Chronicle*, Clarksville, TN, 11/24/2002.
15. Interviews with Hillerman and Robert Redford, in Craig McNeil, James Redford, Chris Eyre, Robert Redford, and Wes Studi, *Skinwalkers*," DVD (Burbank, CA: Warner Home Video, 2002).
16. *Albuquerque Journal*, 8/18/2002, F3.
17. *New York Times*, 5/4/2003, sec. 7, 19; *Kirkus*, 4/1/2003; Clay Evans, "Sweet Sixteen," *Fresno (CA) Bee*, 6/8/2003, J3.
18. Guinn, "Taking the Long Way Home," 2.
19. Hillerman, *Skeleton Man* (New York: HarperCollins Paperbacks, 2010), 55–56.
20. Joanna Craig, interview with the author, 7/10/2020.
21. Hillerman to Carol Cartwright, 7/18/2004, box 19, THUP.
22. Joanna Craig to Hillerman, 8/26/2003, box 3, THUP.
23. Hillerman to Joanna Craig, 8/23/2004, 9/26/2003, and 9/16/2003, Joanna Craig Papers, privately held.
24. On James Kilroy, who created the saying and drawing, see Kate Kelly, "Kilroy Was Here—A Story from World War II," https://americacomesalive.com/kilroy-story-world-war-ii .
25. Hillerman, *Kilroy Was There: A GI's War in Photographs*, photos from the collection of Frank Kessler (Kent, OH: Kent State University Press, 2004), 74.
26. *A Thief of Time*, 24-25; Hillerman to Easton, 8/28/2002, and Hillerman to Jamie Redford, 8/19/1998, both in box 7, THUP.
27. Vince Horiuchi, "Tedious First Half Muzzles Hillerman's 'Coyote Waits' on PBS," *Salt Lake Tribune*, 11/14/2003, D15.
28. Jamie Redford to Hillerman, n.d., folder 2, box 10, THUP.
29. Bill Richardson, interview with the author, 4/13/2020.
30. Anne Hillerman to the author, 7/28/2020; *Publishers Weekly*, 4/14/2003.
31. Hillerman to Joanna Craig, 1/14/2004, Craig Papers.
32. Hillerman to Craig, 1/22/2004, 1/31/2004, and 2/9/2004, Craig Papers.
33. Hillerman to Craig, 2/20/2004, Craig Papers.
34. "Tony Hillerman's Jim Chee and Joe Leaphorn Mysteries," http://www.dancingbadger.com/tony_hillerman.htm.
35. Hillerman, *Shape Shifter*, 145.
36. Hillerman, *Shape Shifter*, 52; Guinn, "Hillerman's Navajo Heroes."
37. Hillerman to Peter Thorpe, Mar. 2005, Peter Thorpe Papers.

Chapter 28. The Blue Flint Girl

1. Johnny Boggs to the author, 7/3/2020. Earlier, after Boggs sent Hillerman a formal letter about the prize committee's unanimous decision, Hillerman left a message on Boggs's answering machine. "He was just bubbling with excitement in that Oklahoma accent, wanted to know if there was a certificate or something like that," said Boggs, "I called back and said there was a big bronze award that came with that."
2. Johnny D. Boggs, "Interview with Tony Hillerman," *Wild West*, June 2008.

Chapter 25. Into a Heart of Darkness

1. Hillerman to Martin Greenberg, 4/14/1989, folder 22, box 12, THP.
2. Ollie Reed Jr., "Here's to Your Health, Tony," *Albuquerque Tribune*, 9/7/1993; Janet Grado to author, 7/14/2020.
3. Stasio, "Remembering Tony Hillerman," https://artsbeat.blogs.nytimes.com/2008/10/30/remembering-tony-hillerman.
4. Jeff Guinn, "Taking the Long Way Home to Success," *Fort Worth Star-Telegram*, 4/6/1992, 2. One can still find copies of "Mudhead Kiva" book jackets for sale.
5. John Robinson, "Tony Hillerman: A Mystery Writer Who Regularly Turns out Best Sellers," *Greensboro News & Record*, 11/1/1992; J. C. Martin, "Kingsolver and Hillerman to Headline 20th Annual Writers' Conference," *Arizona Daily Star*, 12/14/1992, B3; Pasatiempo, *Santa Fe New Mexican*, 5/15/1992, 13; Guinn, "Taking the Long Way Home," 2.
6. Mary Campbell, "Navajos and Hillerman Remain Friend.," *The Gazette*, Cedar Rapids, IA, 11/3/1991, 2F.
7. Hillerman, *Sacred Clowns* (New York: HarperCollins Paperbacks, 2009). 316–18.
8. Reed, "Here's to Your Health."
9. Larry Calloway, "The Curse of the N.Y. Journalist," *Albuquerque Journal*, 6/6/1993, C1.
10. New York *Daily News*, 6/16/1992, 12.
11. *Kirkus*, 8/1/1993.
12. Dick Adler, "Two Linked Murders Bemuse Tony Hillerman's Navajo Cops," *Chicago Tribune*, 9/26/1993.
13. Donald Craig, "Death of a Shaman," *Washington Post*, 9/5/1993.
14. *Reno Gazetteer Journal*, 9/19/1993, C8.
15. Richard Benke, "School Turning Dreams into Reality," *Albuquerque Journal*, 1/2/1994, C3.
16. Hillerman, "Palawan," *Islands*, Sept.–Oct., 1998, 70.
17. Hillerman, *Seldom Disappointed*, 311–12.
18. HarperCollins press release, 11/16/1993, folder 2, box 18, THP.
19. Ollie Reed Jr., "Hillerman's Back," *Honolulu Star Bulletin*, 9/11/1993, B2.
20. Hillerman, "Palawan," 72.
21. Hillerman, "Palawan," 73.
22. Hillerman, *Seldom Disappointed*, 316.
23. Janet Grado, interview, 1/30/2020.
24. Dr. Neal Shadoff, interview with the author, 2/17/2020; *Albuquerque Journal*, 5/4/1994, C1.
25. Hillerman, *Seldom Disappointed*, 291; *Santa Fe Reporter*, 3/28/1990, 5. There are various versions of this tale. His 1990 account, closer to the date of the proposed dinner, is likely to be the most accurate.
26. Jim Belshaw, interview with the author, 3/7/2020; Dick Pfaff, interview with the author, 2/12/2020.
27. Jim Belshaw, "Hillerman Leaves Last Mystery," *Albuquerque Journal*, 10/28/2008, A3.

28. Jim Belshaw, "Laughter Is the Best Obituary," *Albuquerque Journal*, 3/20/2005, B1. Belshaw used the same headline eleven years earlier for a remembrance of Jesse Price, another member of the poker group; William J. Buchanan to Hillerman, 8/16/1975, folder 14, box 7, THP.

29. Hillerman to William J. Buchanan, 8/20/1975, folder 14, box 7, THP.

30. Jim Belshaw, "In War There Is Love," *Albuquerque Journal*, 5/24/2005, B4.

31. Tim Madigan, "Their War Ended 70 Years Ago. Their Trauma Didn't, *Washington Post*, 9/11/2015.

32. Janet Grado, interview, 1/30/2020.

33. Paula Schnurr, interview with the author, 6/17/2020.

34. Hillerman, scrap of writing from 1984, box 2, THUP.

35. Hillerman, scrap of writing, box 12, THUP.

36. Belshaw, interview with the author, 3/7/2020.

Chapter 26. A Fallen Man

1. Hillerman to Peter Thorpe, Mar. 2005, PTP.

2. Hillerman to Thorpe, Mar. 2005, PTP.

3. Hillerman, "An Apology, Acknowledgments, Denial, and Dedication," foreword to *Finding Moon* (New York: HarperCollins Paperback, 2011).

4. *La Crosse Tribune*, 11/9/1995, D13.

5. Hillerman to Thorpe, Mar. 2005, PTP; Hillerman, *Seldom Disappointed*, 328.

6. Jamie Redford, interview with the author, 7/10/2019.

7. Jamie Redford to Hillerman, n.d. [Mar. 1994], box 12, THUP.

8. Jamie Redford, interview with the author, 7/10/2019.

9. Jamie Redford to Hillerman, n.d. [fall 1995], box 12, THUP.

10. Bob Rosebrough to Hillerman, 7/29/1987, box 12, THUP; Rosebrough, interview with the author, 1/21/2020.

11. Bob Rosebrough, *The Talus Slope* (privately published, 2002), 30.

12. Rosebrough, *Talus Slope*, 32; Rosebrough, interview with the author, 1/21/2020. Rosebrough is referring to the long-running TV crime drama series *Columbo*.

13. Hillerman, *The Fallen Man* (New York: HarperCollins Paperback, 2010), 108.

14. Hillerman, *Fallen Man*, 201.

15. Marilyn Stasio, review of *The Fallen Man*, *New York Times*, 12/8/1996; *Kirkus*, 10/1/1996; Wilda Williams, review of *The Fallen Man*, *Library Journal*, 10/15/1996. 90.

16. *Daily Oklahoman*, 11/21/1997, 40; Janet Grado, interview, 6/12/2020.

17. Hillerman, "Getting to Goldtooth," *Arizona Highways*, Dec. 2005, 13–14.

18. Ashmead to Hillerman, 2/10/1998, box 10, THUP.

19. It's not clear whose idea it was to write a memoir. The correspondence indicates that it was Hillerman's but Anne Hillerman recalls her father saying it had been his editor's idea.

20. James Brooke, "Like Butch and Sundance, Fugitives Elude Police in Desert," *New York Times*, 8/3/1998, 10.

21. Hillerman, *Hunting Badger* (New York: HarperCollins Paperbacks, 2010

22. *Arizona Daily Star*, 2/14/2000, A8; *Deseret News*, 11/14/1999.

23. Jeff Guinn, "Hillerman's Navajo Heroes Live On—For Now, at Least," *Star-Telegram*, 1/19/2000, F1, https://www.chicagotribune.com/news/ct-02-09-0002090040-story.html.

24. Lora Shields to Diana Stein, 1/2/1984, folder 29, box 7, THP. The letter on to Hillerman.

25. Von Del Chamberlain to Hillerman, 7/20/1988, folder 7, box 8, THP.

26. Steve Paul, "Native Thriller Stumbles in 'Strange Landscape,'" *Gazett* 7/22/1989, K11.

27. Tova Indritz to Hillerman, 8/27/1990, and Claire R. Farrer to Hillerma folder 6, box 15, THP; Michael Parfit, "Weaving Mysteries That Tell o the Navajos," *Smithsonian* 21, no. 9 (1990), 98.

28. Hillerman, *Seldom Disappointed*, 67.

29. Peter Thorpe, interview with the author, 3/17/2020.

30. Timothy Foote, "Where Leaphorn Leapt From," *New York Time* sec. 7, 34.

Chapter 27. The Farewell Quartet

1. *Albuquerque Journal*, 1/11/2004, F6; Janet Grado to the author, 7/28/20 aversion to tuxedos was not, however, absolute. In 1976, for instan exception for his daughter Janet, wearing one to her wedding.

2. Jeff Guinn, "Taking the Long Way Home," *Fort Worth Star-Telegr Baltimore Sun*, 5/2/2002, 3E.

3. *Publishers Weekly*, 4/15/2002, 46.

4. Hillerman, *The Wailing Wind* (New York: HarperCollins Paperba

5. Hillerman, *Wailing Wind*, 9.

6. "Peshlakai Proud to Offer Visitors a True Native American Show," *Canyon News*, July 27, 2000, williamsnews.com/news/2000/jul/27 -to-offer-visitorsbra-true-native-; Erin Ford, "Walking in Beauty: Dancer, Musician and Medicine Man James Peshlakai Passes at *Observer*, 3/21/2017.

7. Hillerman, *Seldom Disappointed*; "Peshlakai Proud to Offer Vis

8. Hillerman, *Wailing Wind*, 131.

9. *Publishers Weekly*, 4/15/2002, 44.

10. George Guidall, interview with the author, 6/17/2020.

11. "Leaphorn and Chee books Were Based on Real-Life Experience *munity News*, 11/6/2008, https://www.thisweeknews.com/artic /311069558.

12. Carolyn Marino, interview with the author, 6/17/2020.

13. Jacqueline Cutler, "PBS Will Air Tony Hillerman Novel–Ba *Post-Star*, Glen Falls, NY, E1; Deborah Baker, "After One Suc Hillerman Mysteries," *New York Times*, 5/4/2003, C3.

3. Neil Shadoff, interview with the author, 2/17/2020.

4. Erik Olsen to Hillerman, 1/10/2008, folder 20, box 24, THP; Hillerman to Olsen, email, 1/20/2008, in possession of Olsen. Hillerman's incorrect attribution to King Lear of the remark about ailments may have reflected his cognitive decline. He had begun making the Shakespearean reference in his letters when he approached his seventies. At first, he attributed it correctly to Hamlet's famous "To be, or not to be" soliloquy:

> To die—to sleep,
> No more; and by a sleep to say we end
> The heart-ache and the thousand natural shocks
> That flesh is heir to: 'tis a consummation
> Devoutly to be wish'd.

Hillerman's study of Shakespeare at the University of New Mexico in the early 1960s had remained with him. In *The Wailing Wind* he made effective use of Othello in foretelling the tragic death of the woman the murderer loved. Now, however, his recall was no longer sharp. He was likely thinking of the broken, eighty-year-old King Lear incapacitated and bedridden:

> Pray, do not mock me.
> I am a very foolish fond old man,
> Fourscore and upward, not an hour more nor less.
> And to deal plainly
> I fear I am not in my perfect mind.

"He quoted Hamlet but had Lear firmly in mind," opined Shakespeare scholar Michael Olmert. "Tony had learned from Shakespeare that life and stupidity and accidents get in the way of plans. But as an older man he knew it was only a matter of time until he would let everybody down. And himself as well. Like all of us, he wished to be pardoned in advance" (Olmert, interview with the author, 7/9/2020).

5. Jean Schaumberg to the author, 07/26/2020.

6. Richard Kelleher, "Here's Hoping Hillerman Writes Another Book," *Northeast Republic*, 6/11/2008, 26.

7. Jim Barlow, "Tony Hillerman," *Texas*, 4/22/1990, 8.

8. JoAnn Mora and Jeanna Dowes, interview and personal communication with the author.

9. Della Toadlena, "And Now a Few Words from the Other Side . . . ," Impact, *Albuquerque Journal Magazine*, 2/5/1985.

10. Peter Freese, "The Ethnic Detective," *Verlag Die Blaue Eule*, 1992, 7.

11. Albert Chee, Sena Fitzpatrick, and Elsie Wilson to Hillerman, 4/18/1983, and Vicki Holmsten to Hillerman, 4/7/1982, both in folder 28, box 7, THP; Lynn Simross, "Master of Mystery—Sans Reservation," *Los Angeles Times*, 3/20/1988, VI20.

12. Deljean Carroll, Evelen Sombrero, and Devin Howard to Hillerman, folders 24 and 25, box 15, THP.

13. Charles C. Poling, "Tony Hillerman: An Open Book," *New Mexico Magazine*, https://www.newmexico.org/nmmagazine/articles/post/tony-hillerman-an-open-book-93374.

14. Catherine Walsh, "Tony Hillerman," *St. Anthony Messenger*, June 1991.

15. O'Driscoll, "Still the Guy Down the Block," 12.

16. Authors notes from "Mysteries: Literature as a Mirror of American Subcultures," paper presented at the Key West Literary Seminar, 1/16/1988; Warhaftig, "Going in Beauty; Cynthia Gorney, "Hillerman & His Navajo Mysteries," *Washington Post*, 1/29/1987, C2; O'Driscoll, "Still the Guy Down the Block," 12.

17. Hillerman, talk presented at Farmington Public Library, 3/15/1984, audio cassette recording, folder 3, box 17, THP.

18. CNN, "Hillerman Country," aired 1/16/2000, http://www.cnn.com/TRANSCRIPTS/0001/16/impc.00.html.

19. Felicia Fonseca, "Hillerman, Gave, Received from Navajo Nation," *Albuquerque Journal*, 10/27/2008, 1; Poling, "Tony Hillerman: An Open Book," *New Mexico Magazine*.

20. "A Special Friend of Native American Youth," *St. Anthony Messenger*, June 1991, 32–33.

21. Kenneth Tsosie to Hillerman, n.d. [1993?], folder 31, box 7, THP.

22. Dennis Peters to Hillerman, n.d. [1993], folder 1, box 15, THP.

23. Michael F. Brown, *Who Owns Native Culture?* (Boston, MA: Harvard University Press, 2003), iii; *Santa Fe New Mexican*, 5/16/1993, D2.

24. Luci Tapahonso, interview with the author, 8/18/2020.

25. Phill Casaus, "Tribes Vow to Reclaim Apache Heritage," *Albuquerque Journal*, 11/5/1195, A3.

26. Jack Cox, "Mr. Congeniality: Mystery Writer Tony Hillerman Drops Hints about His Life, Legacy, and New Book," *Denver Post*, 2/17/2003, L1.

27. CNN, "Hillerman Country," 1/16/2000.

28. Ward Churchill, *Fantasies of the Master Race: Literature, Cinema and the Colonization of American Indians* (Monroe, ME: Common Courage Press, 1992), 89; "American Indians in Children's Literature," https://americanindiansinchildrensliterature.blogspot.com/2010/02/tony-hillerman.html.

29. Vikki Stea, "Novel Writer," *America West Airlines Magazine*, July 1987, Hillerman wrote an account of this conversation in Hillerman and Bulow, *Talking Mysteries*, and repeated it in many interviews.

30. Bill Donovan, "Hillerman, Creator of Leaphorn-Chee Mysteries, Dies," *Navajo Times*, 10/30/2008.

31. Cox, "Mr. Congeniality."

32. Father Joel Garner, interview with the author, 7/7/2020; Cox, "Mr. Congeniality."

33. Tony Hillerman Jr., interview, 7/21/2019.

34. Anne Simpkinson, "Talking God with Tony Hillerman," beliefnet.com/wellness/2002/01/talking-god-with-tony-hillerman.aspx.

35. Father Joel Garner, interview, 7/15/2020.

36. Janet Grado, interview, 1/30/2020.

37. Deborah Baker, "At Funeral, Writer Honored As 'Class Act,'" *Santa Fe New Mexican*, 11/1/2008, 1.

38. "Leaphorn and Chee Books Were Based on Real-Life Experiences, 11/6/2008, https://www.thisweeknews.com/article/20081106/NEWS/311069558; Hillerman, "Places for Spirits, Places for Ghosts," 103.

Epilogue

1. *Santa Fe New Mexican*, 2/21/15, A8.

2. Kathleen Roberts, "Leaphorn & Chee Together Again, *Albuquerque Journal*, 12/9/2012, 1; Bob Hahn, "The Return of Leaphorn and Chee: PW Talks with Anne Hillerman," *Publishers Weekly*, 8/5/2013.

3. Katie Chicklinski-Cahill, "Anne Hillerman Continues Mystery Series with New Book "The Tale Teller,'" *Durango (CO) Herald*, 3/7/2019.

◈ Index ◈